THE SEASONS OF GRACE

The Seasons of Grace

The Unauthorized Back Story of
PEYTON PLACE
Dave O. Dodge

The Seasons of Grace is a work of fiction. Parts of this novel are based on real life events and characters and it is not a biography. Space and time have been rearranged to suit the convenience of the book, and for story telling purposes. With the exception of public figures, any resemblance to persons living or dead is coincidental. The likeness of historical or famous figures have been used fictitiously; the author does not speak for or represent these people. All opinions expressed in this book are the author's, or fictional.

Copyright © 2021 by Dave O. Dodge

All rights reserved. No parts of the publication may be reproduced, disputed, or transmitted in any form or by means, including photo copying, recording or other electronic or mechanical methods, without prior written permission of the author, except in the case of a brief quotation embodied in critical reviews and certain other noncommercial uses permitted by copyright law.

ISBN: 978-1-7379423-0-6

Published by IDEATION NATION LLC

PO Box 22028, Phoenix, Arizona 85028

www.daveododge.com
dave@ideationnation.us

First Edition - Paperback September 2021

PREFACE:

For years I lived in the shadow of where I thought *Peyton Place* was located. I grew up in a small New Hampshire town and was raised not far from where Grace Metalious lived and wrote her once scandalous novels.

As a child, I remember Sunday afternoon drives with my parents through the nearby picturesque countryside searching for evidence of the author's tales of life nearby. It wasn't until many years later, when I actually read the book, that I realized there was not an actual town. *Peyton Place* didn't represent a physical place or even a physical location. Her book created a new word for our vocabulary meaning nothing more than: *an attitude of small-town life.*

Grace Metalious had pure genius. As a young writer she used what she knew best: the changing seasons, the surrounding landscape and the many stories she had heard. She had fashioned them all together into a record-breaking anthology of small-town New England life.

Every good book has its roots from a good story, something with an element of truth to it, and, along with the own author's twist, another story is created. *The Seasons of Grace* is the unauthorized back story on how a young housewife and mother of three created a scandalous sensation for her small town and the world during the 1950's.

Creating the back story of *Peyton Place* had taken countless hours of research and writing to create a historical novel that honors the life of the author, Grace Metalious. It follows her from childhood in New Hampshire to her journey to international literary success while paralleling the quintessential life in Northern New England that she loved so dearly.
With the same determination that Grace had to complete her book, I too finally found my voice to tell her story. I do hope you find *The Seasons of Grace* an honest and entertaining read.

Anybody who says he doesn't write about his own life is just a liar."

> Grace Metalious
> Gilmanton NH
> 1956

In the beginning…

William stood there, no longer crying, no longer shaking. What he had done had been unspeakable, and it was a statement to his freedom and a testimony to self-preservation, a final stand against the evil in their world. The bullet logged directly into his chest; no doubt had hit something of importance within that poisoned body of his father. Sylvester fell over onto the floor still grasping at the knife stuck into the side of his neck. Trying to pull it out was useless. The sliminess of the blood only allowed his now non-functioning fingers to grasp the handle of the knife. He was dying and both his children knew it.

CHAPTER 1

Winter comes to New England every year, sometimes like an old friend, but more often like an unwelcome relative, arriving early and staying too late. Old man winter is an unforgiving force that at times might send a warning sign, usually not in a form of a letter but with an unexpected ice storm. Rolling in at dusk and coating everything in its path with a crystal-clear coating of frozen rain as if in an attempt to protect it from things to come.

Mostly, winter is a transition from life to death, Mother Nature's way of reminding us that all things have a finale. Autumn, in the north country, is a time when leaves display their last attempt at life, boasting colors of red, yellow, and often purple, this is their last holdout, they silently scream, "Over here, don't forget me." Each leaf struggling against the odds of nature as they become dull, dry, brittle, and then fall to the earth crumbling onto the ground. The snow will soon arrive and press these last remnants of life into the soil, dissolving them, creating the much-needed nutrients to start fresh again in the spring.

Life can be measured in seasons, from birth to death. Everything has a spring, filled with hope and possibilities, followed by summer with its warm sunny days making everything grow stronger and taller, preparing us for our

Autumn, which is the last attempt of growth before the darkened winter of a frozen tundra.

Sometimes nature throws us a curveball with a glorious Indian Summer arriving after the first frost. This extra season is a fool's gold of sorts as it does its best to stave off a season of cold, misery and death which always comes with winter.

Evil is lurking about, disguised as a snow drift, or in a winter breeze, but mostly with the sun as it slowly descends below the horizon behind the foothills of the White Mountains. It is at dusk when the sun is all but gone in the December sky. The hills, back lit from the setting sun, create darkened monsters off in the distance, looking down onto the tiny village as if searching for more of their own.

December can be the beginning of transition, and that night was no exception. The evening air was cold and crisp with only a slight hint of a breeze. The storm clouds slowly converged over the town green blocking out the last remains of the day before the first snowflakes began to fall. It would be days before life returned to normal again.

The headlights off in the distance are from an approaching highway truck, as it neared the village green, illuminating its way and slowly spreading salt and gravel onto the narrow street. Another attempt at protection against the impending season. The driver hardly realized that this futile attempt had no power against what was to come. Road crews in New Hampshire are a hardy bunch. They work for hours with no breaks in sight, no reprieve from the falling snow and temperatures that drop as fast as the sand hitting the road surface.

Tonight, there was not a soul about. The village green, which is the center of life on warmer days, is deserted and dark. The single lamp above the row of park benches glowed, casting light on what could be a typical Currier and Ives scene. But not here, not that night, not in 1941. For one family, snow was a reminder of the changing seasons and the return to the old ways, the ways of their lives that have been almost forgotten during warmer times.

Leaving the village green with a fresh coat of salt, the truck turned down Maple Street, and with that, an eerie emptiness in the dark descended. Clouds have gathered overhead, and as if on cue the snow began to fall, gently at first; what seemed to be a breeze soon became a wind, and the falling snow would become a blizzard.

The village green, which to the outsider looks picture perfect, a setting of quintessential New England life, close to perfect one might think. Flatlanders would make the drive north from Massachusetts to admire its white picket fences, pillared front porches, rows of maple trees and perfectly manicured gardens in the summer. Around the green there are a few businesses and town offices. The old schoolhouse and a white clapboard building with an iron fire escape that served as the Town Hall, both having seen better days, were in need of repair.

New Englanders make do with what they have and learn how to get by. The depression hit hard in New Hampshire, and the village of Gilmanton was no exception. It was slow to recover and it never forgot the tough days of the past.

The real center of life here in the village was at a small shop. The Gilmanton Corner Store, as it was appropriately named, was the unofficial meeting place of town elders over coffee, mothers in need of tinned vegetables and local children with a few cents to spend on penny candy. The Store, as most referred to it, was always open. There was always a need for a newspaper or pint of Kruger Ale, but on this snowy night it was dark and closed. The sign flipped earlier as soon as the official word from the Boston weather station was announced. News of the day would have to wait until morning, provided the roads were clear.

Gilmanton residents were all tucked in for the night. Having finished their supper, they were now nestled around the radio next to the warmth of the wood stove. Nights like these throughout the country were a time to reflect on the day, listen to the news of the war, and hold your children a little closer. The war abroad seemed so far away from their tiny little town. For many, Poland was nothing more than a page in the encyclopedia, or an obscure entry in the family Bible that was never shared with their neighbors.

Snow continued to fall to near like blizzard conditions, quickly accumulating on any frozen surface. Drifts were beginning to form against the park benches and fences that neatly outlined the green. Off in the distance, the sound of a motor engine downshifting as it neared. Sounds at night, despite the storm, carry for miles. The air was dry and clear, with the falling snow acting like tiny amplifiers in the darkness.

A set of single headlights approached. The vehicle slowly made its way up the grade, downshifting the gears to slow down, never touching the brakes for fear of skidding off the narrow street into a snow drift. The bus from Concord was late. Most days you could set a watch to the daily arrival from the city south of Gilmanton. At almost six o'clock, despite the storm, it's only twenty minutes late. The bus slows to a stop, never sliding, as is creates the sound of salt being crush under its wheels. The Concord Trailways bus served as a reassuring reminder to the residents that life does exist outside of their town, and its routine a sublime message of things appearing to be normal.

The lever that opens the door of the coach made a gentle swoosh sound causing a burst of warm air out into the frigid night. The drifting snowbank is parted creating a small path to exit. Under the glow of the one streetlamp a single figure descends from the bus. A man, dressed in a short wool coat, a knitted hat and carrying a canvas duffle bag over his shoulder, carefully moved away from the bus. The driver closed the door and stepped on the accelerator slowly trying not to spin the tires as the bus pulled away from the lone man and the village green.

The center of the village is quiet again and empty, only the man standing under the dim light. He set down his bag in the snow drift and adjusted his coat, buttoning it as tight as possible under his chin and tugging his hat further down onto his head, trying to protect his ears. Looking up, he watches the snow fall and shakes his head in a form of disgust. It was a long ride from Boston. Changing buses three times and watching the approaching storm only caused him worry that he would never make it to his destination. The small bottle of whiskey in his coat pocket helped ease the ride, but it was nearly finished. Looking at the darkened windows of the store, he could see there was no way to buy another that night.

Evil arrived again on this dark night. The traveler would alter the course of life here for so many and for years to come. Embodied in him was a dark force, an appetite that had not been quenched for many months. Tonight, things would be as they once were for him.

Nearly six feet tall and almost two hundred pounds he was not a small man, yet one to be feared when his temper flared, something that he hated about himself. He bent over to retrieve his worn canvas duffle bag from the snowbank, and with one quick movement it was over his shoulder. He crossed the street in the direction of the store. On the corner next to the dimly lit shop there was a lone public phone. It was mounted to the side of the building, protected by a small wooden enclosure with the familiar metal sign verifying it was officially part of the Bell System. Being the only public phone for miles it could become busy at times. That night there was no one waiting patiently on the bench to use it.

Reaching for the handset, he stood for a second trying to adjust his eyes in the dim light. The enclosure helped block the snow and the wind, but caused the dial to be in the shadow of the street lamp. Squinting, he looked for the small sign that was attached to the wall that would have a familiar number on it.

"There it is." He whispered aloud, his voice angry and annoyed with a slight hint of a drunkard. Letting his duffle bag slip off his shoulder onto the wooden stoop, he grabbed the bottle in his pocket and with one quick slug, finished it and threw it into the snow with disgust. A nickel is produced from his pants front pocket; he lifts the handset and slides it into the slot. The coin clangs and clinks as it drops into the bottom of the phone.

"Operator," a voice calls out into the night air. "How can I help?" She continues, never an annoyance in her voice, just a genuine sense of helpfulness.

"ALPHA 439," he practically screamed into the phone, without a hint of civility.

"Oh, you are looking for Bud, I'm not sure he is working tonight," she says.

"Can you just ring him?" The man blurts back.

Bud was known to everyone in town. Bud Shepard's Taxi Service was one car strong with a 1939 black Buick sedan. No sign was needed as everyone knew the car and knew Bud. Like his father, Bud continued the taxi service because for so many it was the only transportation they had in Gilmanton. It was a lifeline of sorts.

There was a distant ringing in the receiver, as the operator connected the call.

"Yea, Bud here." the voice answered.

"Go ahead sir." The operator added. "Hey Bud, it's Sylvester. I need a ride up the hill. This fucking snow is pissing me off."

He was angry, Bud could tell and so could the operator who was listening. She always listened.

"I'm in front of the store." He added.

"Okay, give me ten minutes. The plow just went by, and I might have to shovel the car out."

Bud was slightly annoyed; he thought he was in for the night. Thinking to himself, what was Sylvester doing home from

Boston? Christmas was a few weeks away. Had something gone wrong. He knew Sylvester from days before, when they would sit in the only booth at the store and drink coffee and tell tales of hunting trips. Sylvester always tagged the biggest deer, at least that was his story.

Hanging up the phone, Sylvester moved under the overhang at the store. Trying to stay out of the snow, he leaned up against the door. His mood was still angry. He needed another drink soon. There was a crumpled pack of Chesterfields in his other coat pocket. A cigarette would taste good right about now, and it may help him ease his mood. The match lit on the first strike, and he raised it to light the cigarette that was in his mouth. The glow from the flame created a dramatic and frightening image of Sylvester and it was reflected in the store front window.

Sylvester Roberts was a man of few words, a typical New Englander, with a tough exterior and a solid build. He had a deep-rooted sense of pride, which was nothing more than a misplaced form of insecurity that only drinking would help. Like so many men of his time, he was forced to leave town in search of work elsewhere, joining the Merchant Marines after the death of his wife. A widower and father of two, this was his way to keep the home fires burning, sending money to his eldest daughter without having the burden of actually having to raise them.

Life was not perfect, but neither was he. Deep inside Sylvester lurked pure evil, not unlike the surrounding dark hills that loomed over the town at dusk. Sylvester's evil was less obvious, but so unspeakable that only a few knew it existed. His wife, who had passed away, had known about his inner demons, and his children knew and secretly wished he would one day fall overboard from one of his ships as he sailed far away from Gilmanton.

"Up on the hill" as everyone in town referred to it, was the Roberts' house, a modest midcentury wooden farmhouse with no farmland. There was enough space for a small garden and barn. With only two bedrooms, a center room that served as a living room, and a kitchen that was the center of life for the small family, it served its purpose. The Roberts children made it their own during the absence of their father. There was an outhouse down behind the house next to the barn, and a small enclosure attached to the barn that served as a pen for the one pig and four sheep. They were lucky enough to have running water in the sink in the house, cold only. On winter nights like this it was running with a slow trickle, keeping it moving, preventing it from freezing.

The Roberts were not a prominent family in Gilmanton. They were not founding members of the village, and there was no pretense to their way of life. They existed the best they could just like everyone else at that time. The house had been given to Sylvester on the death of his father, who also succumbed to the disease of the bottle. Ironically it was five years after that on the very same day that his wife died after a short battle with the dreaded cancer. No one knew what to do, and they slowly watched her waste away in the same bed as her father-in-law had laid. That day something died in Sylvester as well, and a form of evil was reborn from this tragedy.

The wood cookstove in the kitchen area was in full blaze, stoked as much as it could be, the heat rising and drifting out into the main living area. Next to the front door was a brown enameled metal parlor stove equally fired up omitting waves of warmth into the tiny farmhouse. Kerosene and wood were the choice of fuel the Roberts' used to the best of their abilities. Central heat was only for the wealthy, only for the big homes down the hill on the town green. Home to the wealthy and the judgmental. The Roberts' house, that night, was warm and cozy. Looking at it from the outside, it appeared safe and sound, a perfect setting, on such a stormy night.

From the back bedroom, a young woman emerged from behind the open drape that served as a door. It was Barbara, the eldest of the children. She had just turned nineteen, a pretty girl, a nice girl, older and wiser for her age after being forced to be the matriarch of the family at a young age. Her eyes were that of a Gypsy, dark and sultry, with long black hair. Her figure, early to develop, had been noticed by everyone in town. A senior in high school and an honor student, she had done a wonderful job holding it all together despite the internal turmoil she endured each day. Like the picture-perfect town green, no one knows what really goes on behind the façade of what appears to be normalcy.

She was proud of what she had done to keep her family together, small as it was. The house had never looked better. It was tidy, organized, and functional. She had made a home for William, her younger brother, and she hoped he would not let the darkness of the past cloud his future.

She placed two tin pie plates into the warming oven of the Glenwood wood stove. She sat down at the wooden kitchen table, listened to the wind outside the back door, rattling it slightly as it was trying to come in from the cold. With a deep sigh, she reflected briefly on her situation. No sense worrying about what she cannot change, but only be thankful for what she does have. This is what she believed was her only choice.

The fires were raging in full force, warming the house. The animals out back were tucked into the barn for another night. William worked quietly in his room, no doubt doing his homework. The meal would be ready soon, after which a little radio before turning in. December evenings were always short. Daylight was a rare commodity on nights like these.

Thinking about Christmas preoccupied her mind. Since the death of her mother and the absence of her father, Barbara held down the fort as best she could. Every day thinking of her mother and how things would have been different, but it wasn't meant to be. The upside was the departure of Sylvester, her father. He was the source of all the turmoil and evilness in their lives. Sylvester would send money orders from time to time to keep them afloat. The tin under the sink that hid their tiny fortune was getting low. If something didn't arrive in the mail soon, she wasn't sure how they could make ends meet. Another sheep to the slaughterhouse was the only thing she could think of, but it would have to be the last resort.

A gust of wind shook the house to its foundation, rattling the windows and causing a slight breath of frigid air to pass through the smallest of cracks in the tiny house. Barbara could smell the cold air, a mixture of burning wood and oil as it drifted by her. Awakened from her thoughts, Barbara got up to retrieve the warmed dinner from the oven; it was time to eat. They both were unaware that evil was returning to the Roberts' household.

"William, come on, suppa is ready," Barbara called out into the direction of the second bedroom. Walking into the tiny kitchen area, she took two plates from the warming oven. Using a kitchen towel, she moved them to the wooden table where they would eat their warmed leftovers from Sunday's main meal the day before.

"William." One word was all that was needed for him to come from his bedroom with a book in hand.

"No reading, isn't your homework finished?" she asks. Barbara, like her father, was a woman of few words, deeply conflicted and guarded with everything she said and did.

They sat at either end of the small table and quietly ate their warmed meals, not speaking, not looking at each other. A sense of brokenness in this house appeared from time to time. Not anger, not loneliness, just a quiet resolve, each planning an escape route from the drudgery of their lives. Barbara's plan was to wait until William finished school, and then she would walk down that hill and get on that bus, never looking back as she made it all the way to the ocean, getting off only when she smelled the sea air.

William was having his own thoughts of college and maybe even stardom. After all he was a handsome lad with almost girlish features in a frame of a football player, tall and athletic. He knew his good grades would get him into a scholarship program at the University of New Hampshire. His aspirations were grand, but they had always been grand.

The wind outside the tiny house howled around the eaves. They knew that by morning school would be cancelled, and they would spend the day shoveling out the snow drifts that always accumulated in front of the house. Both of the Roberts children knew their limitations, their roles. Though they resented them, it was their lot in life and no one could change that. Like all New Englanders, they made do, because complaining never helped.

Across from each other at the kitchen table, they ate their meal in silence. Heads down, wishing the chicken had not been as over cooked. Barbara looked up slowly, almost gently. Seeing her younger brother's face, studying it, she pondered what would become of him. A tiny tear had formed in the corner of her eye as she chewed the dry stringy meat that had tasted so good the day before.

The taxi slowly trudged up the hill, the tires slightly spinning as it turned the corner onto Gilman Street where the Roberts' house was located. Muted headlights were the only evidence that there was a car on the street; the storm had picked up so quickly that even the tracks in the road were covered instantly as the taxi passed.

From where she sat in the kitchen, Barbara noticed a flash of light as the taxi pulled up in front of the house. Instantly the hairs on the back of her neck stood up straight. A chill in the air struck her that not even the heat of the wood stove could take away. She sat up straighter in her chair. Without realizing it, she took the knife lying next to her plate and grasped it in her fist like a vice and looked directly at William. Her eyes searched his, questioning who would be out on a night like this. Not a word was spoken between them.

A car door slammed shut somewhere out there in the darkness. Silence followed. It was only a few seconds, but it seemed like an hour. Evil arriving made no noise as it approached the house in the freshly fallen snow.

Barbara grasped the knife until it began to hurt. She sat there watching the front door as the doorknob slowly began to turn.

CHAPTER 2

Grace, what are you doing?" The voice called up the stairs. "Grace!" A second call and still no answer. Turning from the long-carpeted staircase, the woman walked down the hall towards the kitchen that was in the back of the house. There was no use yelling any more, she knew there would be no answer.

Grace was lost in her own thoughts, totally absorbed by her very own world that filled her mind. This was her way of escaping, her way of altering the present and projecting a future that was more to her liking. Grace was writing.

"It was a huge bathtub" Grace had thought to herself; it was one of her favorite places to be. There was always lots of hot water and with no one to bother her, there she could be more creative, more honest, with no one looking over her shoulder. Even at that young age of sixteen, Grace knew she would be a writer.

"My aunt has a big house in the north end" Grace would tell her friends from school. Boasting about that house was one of her favorite things to do; it made her feel slightly better about herself knowing she had a place that was so grand, so fine. "Aunties," as she called it, was a far cry from the rows of triple decker tenement houses that lined the streets near the big woolen mill in Manchester, New Hampshire. Aunt Georgie's place was big and beautifully decorated with new furniture, not leftover from previous tenants, or bargains from the tag sale at the church. Auntie's was perfect, and here Grace felt alive and creative, but mostly she felt better than her peers; she felt rich.

Manchester was the largest city in New Hampshire and had seen better days than it was having now. From the Civil War and through the thirties, the town was the center of textile production, beating like a healthy heart pumping out wool and cotton into the world. Fueled by the mighty Merrimack River that bisected the city and employing cheap French speaking labor from Quebec, the city was once alive and vibrant. Grace's city now was struggling, and in 1941 there was a secret desire to go to war, helping those in Europe against Nazi oppression, but mostly to get the mills working three shifts again.

After school, Grace would race up Elm Street from downtown, always getting off the streetcar a few blocks away. She loved strolling up the sidewalk past the large brick and wooden houses, each one bigger than the last. These were testaments to a prosperous society, built on the backs of foreigners and on display for the world to see, the American dream at work. Grace loved the way she felt as she walked up the sidewalk, happy and free.

When the afternoon arrived, Grace had been a bit anxious and watched the clock in her junior grade classroom, waiting for the bell to ring at three o'clock. That was all she had thought about. Escaping to Aunt Georgie's was one of her rituals, leaving her life on the west side of town to head up the street to the east side of the river, leaving behind all things she hated.

Grace lived on the second floor of a three-story walk up, along with her mother, sister and grandmother. They were sandwiched between a very loud Italian family below and above them a couple from Greece. Her neighbors spoke very little English and always smelled of garlic. She had known that both families were from different countries, but she also had observed how very similar they were to each other. Grace loved watching people, making notes in her mind to use later, perhaps in one of her stories.

Grace's mother, Laurette, was born in America to "Frenchies" from Canada. Mill workers that emigrated with the help of the CNR, Canadian National Railway, at the turn of the century. Laborers were needed to help keep the mills operating after the depletion of men during the Civil War. Grace's grandfather was one of those laborers, and after thirty-seven years in the woolen mill, a fall in the factory took his life. It was then that Laurette decided to move back into the apartment to raise her two daughters and to look after her grandmother. That was eleven years ago, and the youngest sibling, Bunny, had adjusted to life in a tenement quite naturally, but Grace had an acute affliction of cabin fever if there ever was one.

The walk to Auntie's had to be quick; a winter storm was rolling in, and she had forgotten her mittens that morning before school. Grace was almost to the corner of Spruce and Elm, and she could see the white curved columns that held up the second-floor balcony forming a large elliptical porch in the front. Grace wondered if the White House in Washington was like this; after all they did seem to look alike.

Climbing the steps, Grace paused and turned to sit on the cold granite steps in front. She wanted to wait for the streetcar as it passed, in case someone she knew was on it, one of those other kids that actually did live in this part of town. She wanted to be noticed, to be seen, her desire to escape the west side was all she talked about these days.

"I want to be just like Auntie Georgie, when I'm older," she told her mother at breakfast earlier that morning, speaking only English so her grandmother would not be able to understand it all. "Oh, you will be your own person, my Grace, just be careful not to climb too high for you may fall." Laurette answered her daughter with only the slightest of a Quebecois accent, something she has worked on removing for years.

Grace sometimes didn't understand what she meant. In fact, at times it seemed to offend her young way of thinking. The older De 'Repentigny women were not overly aggressive. They thought a roof over their head and a meal on the table were good enough, but good enough was never what Grace signed on for. It was 1941 and she could do anything; she would be a senior next year and graduate before her eighteenth birthday, something that she planned long ago, achieving the extra credits needed to do it. Her plan was to take the world by storm; her plan was to write.

Grace waited patiently for the streetcar to pass, just a little disappointed that no one was on it that she recognized. She noticed the clouds above had now blocked the sun; she knew the storm would start soon, and a warm bath would feel great. Taking a bath was such a simple luxury for most, and yet for others it was a chore, something that had to be planned where she had lived. The only water heater in their flat had been a small gas heater, and it did not work very well. It was nothing like the old boiler in the cellar at Auntie's.

Her mother, Laurette, never understood Grace, and for years to come the division between them would be as cavernous as the Merrimack River is wide. Laurette claimed to have a true bloodline of sorts from an aristocratic society back in France. Her ancestors used Canada as a jumping off point to get to the United States, she would say. When, in actuality, she was from a long line of Canuks. Most of her people were from New Brunswick, having moved west to Montreal to seek a better life. Like in America, migration from the farm to the city occurred everywhere. It wasn't until after her grandparents arrived in Manchester did they realize the challenges ahead for them. The discrimination and the hardships they endured would harden even the softest of souls.

French Canadians, African Americans, and American Indians were often thought about in that pecking order. Laurette would have no part of that; her distortion of the reality was her form of escape. Creating elaborate tales of her family's heritage was just a start to her concealment of the truth. She would shop at thrift stores and church sales finding trinkets that would make their way home to be proudly displayed as family heirlooms from her made-up past. Elevating her family status was the paramount reasoning behind her mother. Grace wanted to rise above it all, but in her own way, on her own terms and if she fell, she would climb back up.

The sky now had grown darker, more foreboding, a contrast to the voice coming from behind where she sat. It was warm, soft and reassuring, like the comfort of being wrapped in a fine wool blanket sitting next to a roaring fire. "Are you coming in? It's freezing out there." Grace suddenly was brought back to reality; the all too familiar voice called from behind her. She would have to wait another day to show off to the next street car; gathering up her things she got up and ran into the house as fast as she could, doing her best not to let more heat escape into the cold afternoon.

It was a cast iron tub, giant in size Grace had thought and with huge claw feet supporting it in the center of the bathroom. Upstairs and down the hall was the most magnificent bathroom one could have, black and white tiles, porcelain sinks and beautiful crystal lights that illuminated the room; just like a spa in a fancy hotel, she imagined. Having never seen one but only in a photo in a magazine, she thought it must have looked that way. Auntie Georgie had class, and Grace could use it anytime she felt like it.

It was a ritual of sorts for Grace; filling the tub half-way up with water so hot she could barely stand it, then using a few drops of bath oil from her aunt's collection, trying never to use the same one twice in a row, all while hoping Auntie hadn't noticed. But she had noticed, and she did not mind. Grace was her godchild, and would nurture her the best way she could, like providing the simple luxury of a bath. Soaking in the lavender water and using the dressing stool as a table in the center of the tub, it made for a perfect writing platform.

There, time stood still; there, she could channel her inner self, retelling stories that she heard, never making them up in their entirety, only embellishing as any good writer would do. No one, not even Grace would imagine that her words that would begin so innocently could cause such a stir in the world, turning heads and unleashing a series of events exposing evil as well as good in their purest form.

That Monday was special to Grace; it was the start of a new beginning, and she wanted to be prepared for it; a hot bath and some writing in her journal were just what she needed to relax before her debut as a playwright later that evening. She could hardly wait for later, when her friends would gather in the basement of the old church to witness her genius. *The Murder At The Summer Barn Playhouse* was the title of her masterpiece, a one act play. Set somewhere in the backwoods of New England, a family secret, an escape and true freedom. Not unlike Agatha Christie's *A Doll's House* which she had read the summer before for extra credit. Her mind drifted; her writing was abruptly stopped when a gentle but firm knock was heard on the bathroom door.

"Grace dear, it's almost five o'clock, you better hurry" This time she heard Auntie's call from outside the closed door. She was right, and Grace needed to get dressed. It was now almost dark, and the walk to the church would be cold. The knock at the bathroom door was followed by it slowly opening with her aunt holding a chenille robe wide open. Grace cautiously climbed out of the tub, trying hard not to knock her journal into the water. She almost managed the maneuver, but her foot caught the leg of the stool and her prized newfangled ball point pen rolled off and into the now lukewarm water. "Shit, my pen." Grace muttered. A look from her aunt with no words caused Grace to mentally retract her words, swearing was what she did well, but never in front of her Auntie.

Her aunt reached into the tub and grabbed the pen which had been a gift to Grace from Auntie that past summer. "What was today's story?" She asked her niece. Grace, now drying herself and looking into the full-length mirror, casually answered. "Oh, it's about my brother; he is so interesting." She said beaming, looking at her aunt in the reflection of the mirror. Grace always beamed after writing; it was a high she always got after completing a story and having someone ask about it was the icing on the cake.

"You don't have a brother, Grace." Her Aunt reminded her. "I know; that's what makes him so interesting," With a slight chuckle she grabbed her clothes, and let the robe fall to the floor, and she began to dress. Her aunt smiled as well, taking the robe and hanging it on the hook next to the sink. "I'll be down in a minute, thank you, Auntie" She turns to give her a kiss on the cheek, knowing there will be a sandwich on the kitchen counter for her to eat on her walk to the church.

With the sandwich in one hand, she turned to wave one last time with the other. From the sidewalk she signaled a heartfelt thank you and a good bye to her aunt, who had been watching from the warmth of the foyer like a concerned parent. Grace made her way to the street and out into the cold evening.

The basement of the Unitarian Church was more like a recreational center for the neighborhood than a cellar of a place of worship. It had a full kitchen, along with a small stage with a working curtain and the old pews from upstairs that had been replaced years ago. They had created a small intimate theater that was used by children and adults during Christmas. The choir would not only practice but also perform here to smaller audiences, not only to members of the congregation; after all, Grace thought, you don't have to believe in god to appreciate music. It was the perfect setting for her play, she thought, and that night would be the first time for many to hear a story by Grace.

Sitting backstage, she felt a bit nervous; some of the voices in front of the drawn curtain were familiar. She knew her best friends would be there; Mark and John were two of the closest friends she had, and the three of them had been inseparable throughout school. Everyone knew their story, but no one would say it out loud, and if they did, Grace would help ease the situation that might arise with her candor, vulgarity and her loyalty. Mark and John were ahead of their time with each other's affections, and Grace protected it with all her soul.

She wanted so badly to peek out from behind the curtain but knowing how amateur it would be, she just sat and hoped that George was out there. George had been around for many years; they met so long ago in grammar school. A little younger than she by a couple of years, he was a Greek boy and nephew to the couple upstairs. Their friendship blossomed over time, usually only on Sundays when the family came to visit her upstairs neighbors. Grace and George would sit on the back wooden staircase and talk, they just talked. No one knew Grace better than George outside of her best boys, Mark and John, which seemed to be an adolescent ménage à trois of sorts.

Grace had a pet name for George. He would always be known to Grace and her inner circle as "Gee-Gee." "Why don't you find a nice boy to go out with. Those two are a disgrace, and that George smells of garlic and old cheese." That was the assessment from her mother, and another condemnation of her good will which had only caused her and her mother to drift further apart. "Why not a nice guy from the north end? George is Greek and beneath your place, you can do better." Her mother would go on and on, and Grace would hum to herself as she left her standing there, spewing evilness from her lips.

Grace could not believe some of the things that came out of Laurette's mouth; it was pure rubbish, and her reference to the niggers, the Jews and even the Irish was unrelenting at times. Manchester, like any other city, was divided into neighborhoods of poverty and ignorance. Prosperity and unity would be the only thing to save the city. Everyone needed more work and a sense of self-worth, this is what Grace believed. Her mother had been wrong; she thought, and Grace knew her Gee-Gee was the one, and no one would change her mind.

Looking down at her watch, she saw it was nearly seven, and the curtain would be going up shortly. In just a few minutes the writer, the director and the producer of this one act play would have to be on her toes. The thought of anyone from her family being in the audience would cause more disappointment and anger. Little did they realize, but Grace's ability in story telling would raise them all up from the drudgery of their lives forever. That night was the start of it all.

Holding the program of her play, she read the title and her name. An inner sense of satisfaction overcame her because it was the first time she had seen it in actual print, albeit being a mimeograph copy from the school office. Nevertheless, it was official, and that night of December 7th would be the first day on her journey, one she had worked so hard for.

The curtain slowly opened on the tiny stage. The lights dimmed over the audience. The play was about to begin. Success or flop, Grace had no idea what the outcome would be, but in the morning her world would awaken to a new outlook on life and things to come.

CHAPTER 3

 The taxi took longer than ten minutes to arrive and that had only angered Sylvester more. Standing under the overhang of the store he smoked another Chesterfield, watching the exhaled smoke drift off into the darkness as the wind took it and swirled with the snow like an eggbeater. Sylvester thought that Bud had better show up soon because the drifts were getting deeper and that climb up the hill would be a fucking mess.
 Something caught Sylvester's eye in the reflection of the store window. A bit startled at first, he turned from the window and saw a car approaching the front of the store, driving very slowly, almost silently in the fresh snow. The headlights were almost useless on a night like this. It was Bud. The Buick was completely covered in snow with only the two wipers visible, working as fast as they could, trying to keep the windshield clear.
 "Hey, Sylvester." Bud yells as he rolls down the driver's side window trying to keep the snow from falling into the front seat. Sylvester threw the lit cigarette into the snow drift and picked up his duffle bag. Stepping off the stoop and onto the curb found him landing in six inches of snow, something he was not dressed for. The freezing cold reached the top of his socks.
 "Fuck" was all he muttered as he opened the back door of the taxi and threw his bag into the back behind Bud. He slid

into the back seat and slammed the door. The smell of tobacco and hard cider was almost overwhelming. Instantly he knew that some of the guys had called Bud for a ride earlier in the evening. The smells of New England are never soon forgotten no matter how far you travel away from it.

"Where are you coming from this time? New Orleans? New York?" asked Bud as he pressed down hard on the gas pedal, the old Buick never spinning, grabbing the salt and gravel mixture for traction like a pro. "Yeah" Sylvester grunted, never liking to tell anyone too much. "I was down in Baltimore." And with that answer he just wanted to be up that hill and in his home, the anger still lingering from the day of annoyances and no drink in hand.

The night was so dark that the driver of the old Buick had to move slowly as he maneuvered it through the streets. The snow drifts on the road ahead were now deeper, and the chill in the cab felt as if there was a window open. Sitting there in silence was what Sylvester liked, especially in Bud's cab. Bud, like the operator on the other end of the telephone handset, was a bit of a busy body and a gossip. In a town like this the last thing he needed was his shit spread about like manure to sprout more stories.

Looking over his shoulder with one eye on the road, Bud glanced at Sylvester. He couldn't help himself; he had to pry a tiny bit more. "Saw Barb the other day near the Town Hall, she didn't mention you were coming home?" He paused and searched the rear-view mirror waiting for an answer. Nothing. "You home for a while?" Again nothing. Bud knew Sylvester was a hard man, a private kind of guy, but he did not take him for rude. He turned back to drive, keeping both eyes peeled as the Buick slowly and cautiously made its way through the town, not unlike a funeral procession on the way to Smith Hill cemetery, a route Bud knew all too well.

The Roberts' house would be warm and toasty, Sylvester thought, and seeing his daughter Barbara would do the trick on a cold night like this. An unconscious sneer appeared across his face; it went unnoticed by the driver and chilled even Sylvester to his core.

"Are you here through Christmas?" Bud asked from the front seat, never turning around. He tried his best to engage his passenger in some sort of conversation; it was not working, and at that moment he thought something was wrong with him. Driving was all he could do, so Bud started up the knoll, shifting it into second gear, a trick his father had taught him, and it always worked when climbing a hill in winter conditions. Up the road, a distant light could be seen at the end of the stone wall which was now covered in snow, the Roberts' house, dead ahead.

There was so much snow on the road at that point that the taxi seemed to silently float along Bean Hill coming to a stop just past the driveway. Sylvester stepped out of the car, grabbed his bag, and slammed the door. This was the only sound that was heard inside the tiny house.

Like a small boat adrift, the black Buick floated down its stream and into the night. Reaching for his lighter Sylvester lit the last of the cigarettes which had been hanging out of the corner of his mouth for the past few minutes. Looking up at the house, the house where he was raised, the house where his family was living, he stood emotionless, and all his thoughts were not for the joyous reunion of his loved ones, but to the hidden bottle of cheap Canadian whiskey he had stashed under the sink.

The headlights were the only evidence that there was a car on the street; the storm had picked up so quickly that even the tracks in the road were covered almost instantly as the taxi continued on its journey into the night.

From where she sat in the kitchen, Barbara had noticed a flash of light in front windows of the house. Instantly, the hairs on the back of her neck stood up straight, and there seemed to be a chill in the air that not even the heat of the wood stove could take away. She sat up straighter in her chair and, without realizing, she took the knife next to her plate, grasped it in her fist like a vice, and looked directly at William. Her eyes searching his, questioning who would be out on a night like this. Not a word was spoken between them.

That must have been the sound of a car door, she thought. It slammed shut somewhere out there in the darkness, but silence had followed. It was only a few seconds, but it seemed like an hour. Silence had been the sound of evil arriving. It made no noise as it approached the house in the fresh fallen snow.

Barbara grasped the knife until it began to hurt. She sat there watching the front door trying not to show the fear she felt to her younger brother who had now stopped eating and was staring at the front door.

Reaching the front porch, Sylvester had the duffle bag over his shoulder; snow was up over his ankles, and he stamped his feet to knock the frozen snow and ice off. The stomps could be heard throughout the house, echoing from the wooden porch floor, not unlike the big bad wolf huffing and puffing before blowing the tiny house over. Sylvester was the big bad wolf, and the poor piggies had no idea what would be next for them.

Barbara sat clutching the knife until it began to cut into her hand; she sat there and watched the front door as the doorknob slowly began to turn. She knew it was her father. It had to be Sylvester. The pit of her stomach ached with dread, like a tumor that needed to be removed.

"William, just sit there." She told her younger brother as he was about to get up in an attempt to ward off the evil that was coming through the front door. The door flew open, and like a scene out of a B horror movie, the snow blew in on a cold gust of wind and a silhouette of a man with his face in shadows. The Roberts children were convinced it was the devil.

"What, no hello?" He bellowed. He was mad, angry as a wet cat and vengeful like a cornered raccoon. Walking into the front room, slamming the door behind him, he flung his duffle bag and hat into the corner next to the parlor stove. Before either of the children could answer, he demanded, "Why was there no one to meet me at the bus stop?" This time Barbara knew he had been drinking, and his temper was flaring.

"Dad, we didn't ...." The sentence was not even out of her mouth before he retorted. "Fuck, I sent a card two weeks ago from the purser's office in Baltimore." The children had not seen it, never gotten it, and all the explaining in the world would not alleviate the situation.

"But Dad, we never got it." William tried to explain, getting up from the table and crossing over to his father. Without a word, only a look, Sylvester glared at his son in disgust and annoyance; he nodded his head and looked at the duffle bag next to the stove. "Pick it up, and put it in my bedroom." He told his son. "But, that's Barb's room now." Before the words came out of his mouth, he knew it was the wrong thing to say. "Oh, is it? We will see about that. Do it!", he barked. Seeing a look that could kill on Sylvester's face, William sheepishly grabbed the duffle bag and retreated into the other bedroom.

"So, you moved in with daddy, did you, Missy?" Sylvester glared directly at Barbara as she remained seated at the kitchen table, still holding the knife as if it were a lifeline against this sinking ship. The moment the words came out of his mouth, Barbara knew all too well what would happen. Her stomach started to churn, she felt light-headed as sweat began to form on her brow. The sense of hopelessness came over her, something she had tried to forget but could never get it completely out of her mind. The scene was playing. The same scene, over, and over, and she knew the cycle had to be broken.

Like a duel in a western motion picture, she slowly got up from the table and backed slightly away from the outlaw standing in front of her. They both stood staring at each other, waiting for the other to make a move. Her father, with a glare in his eyes, dripping wet from the melting snow on his clothes, and she, concealing the knife against her side, stood still. It seemed like an eternity before Sylvester stepped closer to her. She backed away slowly and inadvertently pinned herself against the sink, nowhere to go, nowhere to run. "How could this be happening again?" She screamed inside her head. Things were better. He had left. "This house is ours now," she had pleaded to herself. Then she spoke aloud. "Get Out, Get Out, Get Out!" Over and over the words she screamed fell on his deaf ears. Sylvester's eyes were glazed over, like a drug addict who needed a fix, and she knew she was his drug.

Sylvester lunged at her with both hands, just as Barbara shoved the wooden kitchen table between them. "Oh, a little feisty are you tonight? Come on girl I got what you want." He grabbed his crotch as if to intimidate her with his genitals. The sexual compulsion that was deeply seated in his soul was pure evilness rearing its horned head. Tears were forming in her eyes, and soon she would not be able to see. What would follow would be more of the same, she had thought. She also knew instantly if the fight was too much for him, she would find herself in the dirt cellar chained to that old metal cot, left in the cold and dark, until she would succumb to his demands. The dreaded feeling of what was ahead overcame her in a wave of terror and disgust.

Maybe she could reason with him, she thought. Barbara offered the only thing he would want second to his evil lustfulness. "Dad, how about a drink?" She pleaded with him. Without thinking it through, she dropped the knife and turned to retrieve the bottle of whiskey that was stashed under the sink, knowing at that very instant it had been the wrong move.

Like a mountain lion stalking his prey somewhere out there in the darkness, Sylvester lunged for his daughter grabbing her around the waist. A scream escaped her lips, loud and desperate, not unlike the blatting of a deer when it finally realizes the end has arrived. On that night the scream cannot be heard over the howling wind outside the tiny house; there was not a soul out there in the darkness.

She struggled against her father's assault, he grabbed and prodded her in places no decent person would dream about. His calloused hands reached for her blouse and ripped it open, buttons were no match for the strength of this merchant marine, her breasts were now exposed, covered only with a thin layer of cotton and elastic that was her bra.

This was happening so fast there was no time to think, no time to reason with this monster. Evil oozed out of his pores like a snake spewing out its venom inside its capture. "Stop it!" She screamed. That was all she managed, and with that he turned her around and struck her across the face, sending her flying to the floor, landing between the sink and the table. Barbara lay sobbing, grabbing at her torn blouse, trying to use it as a form of protection, but there was nothing she could do. It was just like all the other times. Her father was possessed by an evil force, a desire like a fire that only she could extinguish. Sensing he was moving in again, Barbra opened her eyes long enough to see the knife on the floor; it had fallen to her feet and was within reach. She had to get it, she had to do the unthinkable, the unimaginable.

"Come on, girl, show your old dad how much you love him, it's been a long time." Sylvester softened his tone long enough to send the wooden table over on its side as he pounced on top of Barbara, straddling her, trying to grab her hands as she screamed, trying her best to wiggle out from under him. The weight of his body was more than she could handle. The tears in her eyes were now blurring her vision, where was that knife? She screamed, but no one heard it; the sound never escaping her mind or mouth. Sylvester managed to grab her left hand, and with his right hand the fondling began. Not any of Barbara's struggling could stop him from his quest.

"Where's your cunt, girl, it needs its daddy" This time he whispered his evilness into her ear as she felt his right hand slowly make its way down her young body. The tears almost completely cut her vision, and like a blinded person she used her free hand to feel for the knife that lay only a few inches from her hand. Her father, the monster, had begun to grab at her vagina with such force, giving him a feeling of entitlement. That alone, Barbara had thought, was more painful and as unbearable as the act.

" Stop it!" A voice behind Sylvester demanded. "Get off her!" This time the demand was more of a command than a yell. Sylvester turned long enough to see his son, standing there near the overturned table, crying and doing his best to look as menacing as his father. William was holding a handgun, a .22 revolver that had been in the house for years, almost forgotten by everyone that lived there. William, using both hands, standing as tall as he could, pointed the gun directly at his father.

Almost snickering with a hint of amusement in his voice, he asked, "Now, where did you find that?" "Let her go, get off her." William wasn't crying; he was reaching deep down into his very being to muster as much manhood as was available. This time it would be different. The ending would be the beginning, he thought; this monster needed to leave.

"Listen, boy, don't worry. You'll get yours, just like all the other times. Daddy needs his boy, and you're looking mighty fine." Still with the tone of the devil, he let go of Barbara's private area and stretched his hand out. "Now, give me the gun." This time it was a demand.

In an instant, Barbara's moment of clarity came to light. Not only was the torment being inflicted on her, but he had been doing the same to her brother. Sweet, innocent William, now scared for his life. Dark secrets and memories to haunt him forever. She had to be quick. Wiping her eyes with her free hand, she could see again. In one last attempt to extend her arm further, a scream comes out of her. A guttural, almost primeval, scream escapes from her lungs that cannot bear the weight of the monster any longer. This time it would be heard throughout the house, and Sylvester was distracted long enough that his grip loosened so she could close in on the location of the knife just a few inches away.

"You are a monster, a pervert," screamed William, crying and shaking. The barrel of the gun now vibrated with the movements of his breathing, trying to steady his hand was more difficult than he thought. "Fuck you," was all Sylvester could say as time froze on that icy night.

Somewhere behind him, Sylvester felt a sudden pain, a sharp intrusion into the side of his neck. Instantly releasing Barbara's hand, he touched his neck, and the warmth of his blood was now spurting out of his body like a burst water pipe in the night. A sense of shock came over him as he grabbed at the wound and the knife still stuck in his neck. "You fucking little ….." And with those words the sound of the gun was heard in the tiny house, a deafening and defiant statement to the finale of this moment.

William stood there, no longer crying, no longer shaking. He had done the unspeakable, but it was a statement of freedom and a testimony to self-preservation. It was a final stand against the evil in their world. The bullet logged directly into his chest; no doubt it had hit something of importance within that poisoned body. Sylvester fell over, still grasping at the knife stuck in the side of his neck. Trying to pull it out was useless; the sliminess of the blood only caused his now non-functioning fingers to grasp at the handle. He was dying, and both of his children knew it.

CHAPTER 4

It was the sound of the applause that stirred Grace from her concentration backstage; the loud clapping and the general sounds from the small but mighty audience were something unlike she had ever heard. Grace felt that until that very moment she had been deaf, dulled for the sounds of the ordinary life she had lived and for the first time had been awakened to a new and glorious feeling. The sounds of approval and support were her new drug of choice, and it was giving her a high she had longed for her entire life.

There was just a thin layer of fabric separating backstage from the admiring public that sat anxiously waiting in the church basement for the author, director and producer to be introduced. *The Murder At The Summer Barn Playhouse* had been a success, so it seemed, and Grace's mind was spinning. Thoughts of what to do or what to say were rushing in. Her senses dulled, and her wit weakened. Standing up from the metal chair, clipboard still in hand, she started to retreat deeper backstage, almost hiding from the sound of the audience.

"Come on, Grace, take a bow." Mark rushed in from stage right, grabbing her arm as she was about to disappear into the night. "We were good, but they want to see you, the writer, the director." Mark added. He was not only one of the actors but the second bestie in their friendship trio. John pulled the curtain further apart and gently took the clipboard from Grace's hand. He tossed it onto the metal chair where the director had been sitting; the best friend duo turned Grace around and pushed her towards the curtain. "Go, Go!" John said. "Hold your fucking horses." Grace retorted. Her choice of words would become legendary as she matured, never mincing words in any situation. The fact was, she was scared, not for who was in the audience, but for who wasn't. Her Gee-Gee just had to still be out in the audience front and center, and if he wasn't, she would just judge the evening as a marginal success, something she would not stand for.

Taking a deep breath, she retorted, "Ok, let's do this." She looked directly at John, as he pulled the curtain to one side, and Mark nudged her a step forward. The boys dissolved backstage out of sight. This was Grace's moment; for better or worse it was her time. The audience, small and fierce, rose to their feet clapping faster and louder, the lights from above somewhat blinding her vision as she scanned the crowd for her Gee-Gee.

Grace was not prepared for this; feelings of embarrassment and shyness were overwhelming her. These emotions that were cutting her were like a double edge sword. On one hand, she loved it; it was all too exciting, but on the other hand, hating it for it was her worst nightmare, becoming a success. These emotions were not part of her makeup or her happiness. True happiness was something she thought would elude her now and perhaps for years to come.

The small row of overhead lights was more than adequate for the make-shift stage and almost blinded her as she continued to scan the audience. There he was. Her Gee-Gee. Right in the center of the back row, clapping and waving, and beaming as bright as the lights shining down upon her. Grace felt a huge sigh of relief, and in that instant, she became the proud recipient of all the accolades. Waving like a star, she took a bow and returned backstage. Her number one fans, Mark and John, were waiting with an ice-cold cup of real hard cider; it had been fermenting for months before they took it out of the cellar earlier that evening. "Here ya go, Gracie." Mark handed her a ceramic coffee mug filled with the fermented elixir. With an awkward gesture the three mugs make a clunking sound before the three downed the contents. Hard cider is somewhat an acquired taste, but the results are the same when real alcohol is not available.

"You did it, Gracie, they loved it!" Peter said. "Thanks, guys," she replied. She was still high on the audience rush, and the cider was giving her a little extra bump. "This is good," she said, holding out her mug in their direction. This had been Grace's first taste for "the drink" and without realizing it, not to be her last. It would be her downfall. Mark poured her another, and the three of them were gleefully happy.

Without Grace's first noticing, George appeared from behind them and cautiously walked toward Grace. His desire to surprise her was averted by Mark's expressive eyes as they widened. Seeing her friend's expression, she turned around to find the cause for his look. "Gee-Gee!" She exclaimed, and with that he leaned into her with a hug, a hug like no other. George was holding her for dear life, a real, god forsaken hug, one only a boy can give a girl early on in a relationship. This hug meant something more than just buddies. Grace was filled with emotion and a little bit light-headed from the hard cider, which left her body weakened for the first time. She knew George could be her strength and wanted it to be there for years to come; for the first time she felt that. She liked the way she felt. He held her tight, protecting her from anything evil that a sixteen-year-old girl might encounter.

"Let's go to The Puritan," he yelled, "We can celebrate with malts and fries." Looking at Grace patiently, he waited for her answer. She was so happy; the play, the crowd, the cider and now her Gee-Gee: it was all coming together. "Oh George, I would love too, but we promised to clean this place up." The area of the backstage where the performance had taken place, was littered with props, scenery and discarded cue cards. "Come on, I'll help you tomorrow. Besides, it's really snowing out there, and everyone is heading home," George added.

"You two go ahead, we will entertain ourselves after turning off the lights." Peter said to the pair. "Sure, I bet." Grace thought to herself that they would indeed. Maybe doing the deed finally and moving things along. Mark and John were not good at hiding their feelings, and Grace knew they were queer. She had known it from the start of their friendship, probably before they knew. But she loved them. Friends can be queers too, despite the general notion that they couldn't. A slight chuckle escaped her thoughts, and with that she had hoped they would finally do it, because it wouldn't be fair if she and George did it on their first date.

"So, are we going? George asked. "Yeah, for sure, hold your horses." That was her only attempt at taking her mother's advice on playing hard to get. Grace went to the coat rack to retrieve her wool coat and scarf. Casually presenting George with it, as if saying "Here you go, dear." Happily, he took her coat and helped her put it on, wrapping the scarf around her neck; Grace realized she could get used to this treatment. "Don't be loose with the boys." A voice was heard only in her head; it was Laurette, her mother. "You'll get a reputation." She closed her eyes for a brief second to wash that thought out of her head. "Like she has something to brag about, look at her life." Grace thought to herself. Eyes wide open, she grabbed her Gee-Gee's hand and headed for the front door.

They were both surprised with the amount of snow that had fallen while the play was on. The streets were now covered and there were no footprints on the sidewalks as they walked to the car. They held each other's hands ever so slightly, afraid of being too bold with each other. It had been the first time they had really embraced. Now they were touching, what in God's name would be next. Getting into the car, Grace could feel her mother's glare from the back seat, and she had to check to be sure she wasn't, in fact, there.

George was glad that The Puritan Ice Cream Shoppe was just up the street; it was the place to hang out, especially if you were dating and wanting everyone to know. The infamous drive-in was an icon among the young for a romantic and somewhat of an "in-your-face" night out in Manchester. The ride from the church was a quiet one. Grace was a little nervous, and so was George, but for different reasons. He had his father's car, and it was snowing. The roads were not very clear, but if that reason was not enough to put him in a slight panic, Grace had slid across the front seat next to him. He tried not to look at her and gripped the wheel with both hands. Grace could not only talk her way out of any situation, but she also had the knack of making it go her way. George's only thought was to stay on the street and not skid off into the gutter.

The silent drive to the north end of of town seemed to take forever, each deep in their own thoughts, Grace on a high and George trying to work one up. But even the falling snow could not diminish the bright lights from the giant sign that shouted, "The Puritan." It was open, and all was good in the world for another night. Pulling into the lot, he maneuvered the car into a freshly cleared spot, dark and in the shadow of the big Elm that lined the street.

Shutting off the car, George turned to Grace. "Your play tonight was terrific, you are terrific." And with that he leaned into her and kissed her on the lips. Feeling a little apprehensive and stunned, she kissed him back squarely on his mouth. She couldn't remember ever kissing anyone on the mouth before; her French-Canadian upbringing was always a couple of pecks on the cheek. The mouth was reserved for only the movies, so she thought. Then without any warning, George kissed back forcing his tongue into her mouth. Feeling like a mother guarding her infant, she did her best not to allow it, but in a moment of weakness, his tongue invaded her mouth, and she melted. She received it like the gift it was intended as.

With the slightest of persuasion, George gently pushed Grace down onto the front seat, and he laid on top of her, never breaking from the kiss that she now welcomed. The engine is off, and the wipers lay in silence as the snow now covered the windows; there is no need for a heater, and the windows were collecting steam. The young pair were completely lost in each other and securely parked in the shadows away from the entrance.

George reached for her breasts, he loved her breasts, they were larger than most girls her age, and they were firm, round, and longed to be touched. Gently he placed both hands on her two breasts, with the slightest of movements he began to caress them through her wool coat. Not exactly what he had in mind at the time, but he was trying to make the best of the situation; who knew it was going to be a nor'easter.

"George, don't" Grace squeaked out as she broke free of his grip. It sounded more like a suggestion than a command. "Why Gracie, you're my girl." With that he tried to kiss her again. "I am?" She managed to ask as his tongue was so deep in her mouth she could barely breath. "Gee-Gee, please!" She is now gasping.

"Don't worry Grace, I have done this before, I know what I am doing." Actually, he thought he had, but in fact he had not. Reading about it in a Dime-Store Pocket Book he had found at his uncle's was nothing like the real thing. George pushed on, and Grace yielded to him, giving up on her inner voice that was her mother's. Gently and with some awkwardness her coat was removed, her sweater unbuttoned, and her breasts bared to the steamy air inside his father's car. There was no looking back for this couple, each with desires of their own, each searching and finding it, if only for the moment.

The two were destined for each other. After that first brief meeting as kids on the back stairway of Grace's triple decker to the chance meeting at The Puritan, it was kismet from the start. Laying there as George cupped her breasts, his small hands trying desperately to cover them, claiming them as his own, she casually reached down to his crotch and touched his hardness. Almost pulling her hand away with a sense of fear, she defined the moment and grabbed it with confidence.

"Oh George, Oh Gee-Gee. Do it. Please do it!" She whispered into his ear. Without hesitation or a thought of Catholic guilt, he had to do it. He was so hard, so ready, he thought it would burst if he didn't do it. Taking his hands away from her breasts, he tries to undo his belt and zipper, his hands shaking so much it was nearly an impossible task in the position they were in. "Here, let me." Words were never spoken with more sincere admiration between two young lovers. Grace slipped both hands down, and with the movement of a synchronized swimmer, the belt, the zipper and the boxers were down, his manhood ready.

Grace had to now remove her pants. This would be easy, but she was very self-conscious of her butt. She never liked her ass, always too big, always too round. Like her breasts, it was bigger than most, but that is what George loved about it. The way it was going to feel in his hands; he had dreamed of this moment, and now it was happening. With their pants out of the way, Grace guided George's stiffness into her. She gasped, not out of pain, but out of being denied this pleasure for so long. Silently, in her mind, she cursed her mother for not telling her the whole truth.

George's hand returned to her breasts, and they moved in a sort of romantic harmony only broken when Grace demanded. "George kiss me, harder!" And with that it was over almost as fast as it started. He was so pleased with himself that he did not realize that their young love was now measured with what was spilled on the front seat. He was in ecstasy, and she was wet; what started out so good, ended so wrong. He had no idea that his task was not finished, and Grace was not as pleased as she could have been, but she knew she had to use caution when expressing her thoughts.

The sound of the wind outside the car had broken the silence, and the snow that piled on the windows all but blocked the light. The air inside the vehicle was damp and cooling off fast; it had been time to "Fish or cut bait." More pearls of wisdom from Grace's mother.

"Thanks George, that was great!" She meant it. She hoped to do it again soon; she hoped it would be different. All she wanted now was to go back to her aunt's around the corner and take a bath. A long and hot soak in her very own tub.

"Are you okay Gracie?" George asked. She nodded and explained it was time to go back; her aunt would worry because of the snow, and her mother, no doubt at the Franco-American club having a drink, would have no clue.

They both sat up and adjusted their clothes, all the while smiling and trying their best not to feel awkward. She did not pull away and even placed her hand on his right leg, assuring him all was good. George started the car, and the wipers started with such force; the snow, light and fluffy, easily blew off the windows. Backing out of the space, George felt a sense of foreboding but could not put his finger on it.

The ride over to Spruce Street was a short and quiet one. Neither of them knew what to say, but both knew it would be better in the daylight. Reaching the front of the house, George stopped in the center of the street; the snow kept him away from the curb. Grace leaned over and kissed him on the cheek, then she jumped out and waded through the snow up the steps; Auntie had left the light on. That made her happy. Looking back at George, she waved as if to give him permission to drive away. He did slowly, and Grace quickly went into the house. The light went off, and it was dark as the snow continued to come down. The snow had covered the ground, and it would be spring before the evidence of tonight's adventure would be felt.

The light of the day was still shining bright far away in Hawaii. Tomorrow in New Hampshire was still today in Asia. The young lovers would not have to wait until spring for their next chapter, for tonight a different sort of adventure was brewing in the South Pacific off the coast of Honolulu. The Japanese had other ideas for that snowy December night.

CHAPTER 5

William stood over the body of his father. He was shaking and trying his best to hold back tears. His father, the devil, now lay lifeless at his feet. Blood slowly dripped from the gash in his neck. Only a tiny spot of red on his plaid shirt in the center of his chest was visible. William's mind was spinning. Everything had happened so fast; it was all too confusing for him.

Moments before he was in Barbara's bedroom and heard the table crashing to the floor, followed by the crack of a slap against his poor sister's face. It was in that second, that he remembered the handgun so neatly hidden in the bottom of the chest of draws, wrapped in an old towel, never having seen the light of day for many years. "I'll scare him away," he thought to himself, retrieving the gun and quickly unwrapping it; an old .22 revolver that he wasn't even sure was loaded. Holding the gun with both hands, he emerged through the makeshift bedroom door made of fabric. At first, he went unnoticed by the devil that was attacking his prey in the middle of the kitchen floor.

William will never forget the look in in father's eyes; piercing and haunting as if cutting his son's soul in two when he realized he was not unlike a villain with a laser beam from one of his comic books. The shot was a deafening sound; it happened in an instant, and Sylvester was dead.

William was physically upset, and Barbara was scrambling to her feet in search of any dignity that had been taken by her father minutes earlier. The wind continued to howl around the eaves of the tiny house. The air was now cold and still inside, almost frozen. The dead of winter came early that night, and spring would be so far away.

Standing up and doing her best to button her torn sweater, Barbara tried to cover her exposed breasts, any vanity she had was now spilled on the kitchen floor in blood. She was embarrassed. Feelings of dread overwhelmed her, and she vomited. The contents of her stomach flew from her mouth landing directly on the body. A hint of steam rose from the acidic liquid. It was warmer than the surrounding air.

"I'm sorry, Barbara." The words weak and soft from William.

"Help me!" Barbara blurted out, cutting off his apology without acknowledging it. She rushed into the front room, wiping her mouth with the sleeve of her torn sweater. Frantically she looked for something, anything, to wrap the body in.

"Here, take this," she said, throwing the old wool army blanket from the back of the sofa into William's arms. He caught the blanket and looked down at the floor. There was more liquid there; he had not noticed before. He had had an accident as well. The Roberts family, together, without realizing what they had done, defaced the devil with their body excrement in a befitting manner deserved by their father.

"Don't worry about that now. Look in his pockets," she said as she raced to the floor on her knees trying not to get any more blood on herself. "William, we will both clean up and forget this ever happened." Words were never spoken with more authority from his big sister.

Together, like grave robbers, they emptied the contents of his pockets; they tossed their finds onto the floor out of the reach of the oozing blood that was now becoming thicker and darker with the cold night air. They found a pocket knife, some change, and a cigarette lighter, a small ring of keys, his leather wallet, and a crumpled bus ticket.

Barbara paused for a second, holding the wrinkled Trailways ticket. A feeling of dread washed over her. She knew she would be sick, but there was nothing left in her stomach. Only a slight dry heave followed along with a little discomfort, and then she continued with her mission. "Give me the blanket." She stretched out her hands, ready to catch the blanket from William. She spread the blanket on the clean side of the floor next to the body, aligning it with the head and the feet of the monster. "Grab his ankles!" She demanded. William, now down on his knees, placed his hands on his father's ankles. He looked up at his sister, and she grimaced as she placed her hands on his shoulders. Touching her rapist again was as repulsive to her as it had ever been. Together they rolled the body onto the blanket, twice over to completely cover it in army wool, scratchy and rough. "Perfect," she thought.

Quickly and almost systemically, she stood up and went to the drawers next to the kitchen sink. Like grabbing the brass ring on the carousel, she felt triumphant as they found a length of clothesline. The two of them, not speaking, not thinking, did what had to be done. They tied the white cotton rope around the feet and rolled the body over and over until the rope had securely encased the monster in a cocoon of wool and memories. Feeling like this task was only the beginning, they needed to finish the job before the blood would soak through the blanket.

"Open the door, now!" A slight sense of panic was starting to set in. Barbara would lose her nerve soon if they didn't do it fast. William stood there like he had before, in a trance, in shock. "Snap out of it, help me." That was all he needed. Helping his older sister was all he wanted to do. The mess they caused needed to be cleaned up.

They both grabbed the end of the tied blanket and dragged it towards the open back door. Snow that built up against it was being blown into the kitchen as the remaining heat escaped into the night air. The body was heavy, but together they mustered the strength to drag him out the back door, down the snowy steps as they made their way to the barn. There, they would have to decide soon what to do with the body.

"Kathunk, Kathunk," was the only noise heard through the dense wool blanket as his head slammed against the frozen steps. Under the fresh snow on his way out and down the path and into the darkness, being dragged by his children.

The further from the house the better, both children had thought. Slowly they dragged the body down the embankment, the snow and wind never let up, their fingers starting to feel the cold.

As they approached the barn, the animals in the pen, especially the sheep, seemed restless, frightened. They started to make noise, as they did when they sensed fear was near. Animals have a far-reaching sense of foreboding, even in the darkness. The blanket-wrapped monster on the ground next to the pen perhaps caused pain in their lives as well. Not satisfied with the carnal pleasure of his children, Sylvester might have looked to the flock for relief, a possibility too ugly to imagine or even to speak about.

"William, go get the lantern… Hurry!" The only thing Barbara had said throughout their entire ordeal. William ran up the path to the house, and even in the darkness he could see blood in the snow where the corpse was dragged. Barbara turned and opened the gate to let the animals out into the run. The snow was deep, and the gate did not swing freely, but she managed to open it enough to climb in and shoo the sheep out. They made noises of confusion and annoyance as the wooly animals were forced into the snowy night. The ground inside the pen was free of snow. The hay and dung that covered the ground kept it from freezing. This was Barbara's second moment of clarity that night, and she knew what to do.

William arrived back with the lit kerosene lantern. The opaque chimney of the lantern cast an eerie but sufficient light into the barnyard.

"Grab that shovel," Barbara commanded her brother. She pointed in the direction of the barn door; a long spade was resting against the door jam. Instinctively, William knew exactly what to do as he grabbed the shovel and joined her in the pen. No one spoke. William, like a professional grave digger, started to dig. He had finally mustered the confidence to focus, and his adrenaline kept him warm.

Barbara took a moment to step back, reflecting only slightly on what had happened. She wanted to cry, she wanted to scream, but she knew no one would understand. No one could ever know what her father had done to their family. She stood there holding the lantern for her younger brother, they did not speak of their ordeal, He dug, she watched, and the body started to stiffen in the cold snowbank.

The digging seemed to take forever. William never rested, and he sweated despite the freezing night. Snow continued to fall all around them outside of the enclosure where the sheep were kept. Putting his back into each shovel full, he was surprised how easy the earth could be removed; hardly any stones he thought. His mind drifted to summer when he replaced the fence posts around the pen; the rocks and granite ledges made it near impossible to dig. He was thankful that that wasn't the case that night.

"Good. I think it's deep enough," Barbara told William. "Let's get him." Barbara placed the lantern on the pile of dirt next to the four-foot-deep hole and went back out the gate to where the body was lying. William followed and together they brushed off the freshly fallen snow that was covering their monster. Grabbing the bundle by his ankles, they dragged him through the gate and into the shallow grave. In only a matter of minutes the body is covered with soil and hay, the dung kicked back over it in an attempt to cover their tracks, each trying to put it out of their mind.

"Let them back in, it's cold out there tonight." Barbara instructed William. He waded through the snow to the sheep that had been huddled together through this entire event. Relieved to be getting out of the storm, the sheep scurry through the snow, following William's tracks back into the pen.

Barbara secured the gate closed. The two walked in silence with the glow of the kerosene lamp lighting their way back up the path to the tiny house. The traces of their monster now completely covered with dirt and sheep excrement.

"If only it could be that easy." Barbara thought. As she reached the door and grabbed William's hand, they entered the ice-cold kitchen, the warmth of the night all but gone.

The winter of 1941 had been a harsh one for many reasons. With record snow falls in New Hampshire and the attack on Pearl Harbor, everyone was in survival mode. Staying warm and optimistic was the priority during this bleak time. War would arrive once again into their lives. WWII had been raging in Europe; if ever there was a time for spring it would be now.

CHAPTER 6

It should have been a time like no other. Spring arrived, and black fly season passed as fast as it came. The apple trees were about to lose their blossoms, and the salmon were returning to the river after spending the winter downstream. A New England spring, as only Mother Nature could present it, was as stimulating as the smell of freshly laundered sheets hanging in the sun to dry.

But, that spring of 1942 had a certain energy in the air that could not really be described. Some called it fear, but others would say it was a time of uncertainty. Things were changing. It had been a few months since the nation had entered the war. The mills in town were once again working three shifts. The looms were producing fabric that would not only clothe our fighting men but keep them warm at night as well. Things were happening fast. Life was evolving, and everyone was trying to catch up.

This would be the first war for many, but others remembered the last war and knew things could get difficult. There was talk of rationing the basics, and everywhere men of every age were making hard decisions.

Central High School, like every other school in the country, produced a fresh crop of graduates ready to make their mark in the world. The students were all eager to help their country in a time of need. Mothers would join the workforce, taking jobs their husbands had done. Daughters would learn, earlier than expected, how to care for the home, everything from cooking to tending to their younger siblings, while all the men in their lives seemed to slowly disappear. Gardening was no longer a hobby but a necessity. The world was engulfed in a showdown of good versus bad.

Manchester had a fair number of volunteers signing on for duty as soon as President Roosevelt declared war. The city was heavily populated by a mixture of immigrants and hard-core Wasps, all wanting to do their part against the Nazis or the Japs. It did not make a difference to the men; an enemy to America knew no race. WWII was raging in all corners of the globe, and the United States was in the thick of it.

Normally graduation was a time of celebration and reflection for most students. Each year classes around the country were excited to be taking the next step into their lives, at the same time, looking back on their childhood as a sort of proving ground for that moment of freedom. For most the feeling of holding the diploma was like a golden ticket to adulthood. Whatever came into their lives from that moment on would be on their terms. Graduating from high school was the first time many experienced the feeling of liberation and accomplishment all rolled into one. Emotions ran high for both parents and graduates; the proud parents knowing the graduates were not children anymore and the graduates ready to take on the world without knowing what might lay ahead.

Grace was like every other kid in her class, excited and ready to take on the world, but only after having her cake. Her celebration into adulthood was small and very quiet. Grace's party consisted of all the women in her life, her grandmother, Laurette, Auntie Georgie and her younger sister, Bunny. Everyone gathered in the dining room of their apartment around a yellow cake that her grandmother had made. The chocolate icing spread perfectly, frosted by a steady hand with years of experience.

The party was held a week after graduation on a Sunday, Laurette's free day. She had taken a job in the office at the Amoskeag Woolen Mills, something she despised, but the thought of factory work was far more distasteful. Auntie still maintained the house in the north end, and Grace's grandmother held down the apartment with her younger sister; the family matriarch was doing everything for her granddaughters.

Everyone was smiling and happy. Grace was trying her best not to share her secret desire to rush out and see her Gee-Gee, wherever he was. Her mother could tell what was going on in her daughter's head just by the look in her eyes, and she did not like it.

"Why date a Greek when there are so many nice boys from the north end out there?" Laurette carried on relentlessly, trying to change Grace's way of thinking. Her mother did not really dislike the boy; she had never taken the time to know him. What she disliked was all he stood for. A poor descendant of a family from another part of the world trying to make better lives for themselves in New Hampshire. His story was just a little too close to home for Laurette's liking; her daughter could do better. She had always thought that.

Grace did her best to ignore her mother when it came to George, but on that day she was too happy to be bothered. With her diploma neatly displayed on her dresser in her room and a sense of satisfaction, Laurette was not going to bother her. For that day she was free, free from school, free to sleep late and most importantly free to write anytime she wanted to. Her mind was bursting with thoughts. Everywhere she looked there was something to write about, a tragedy or a comedy, a world of stories to be told.

"Mémère', merci pour le gâteau!" Grace leaned over and whispered into her grandmother's ear and kissed her lightly on the cheek. Her grandmother, speaking only a little English, had loved it when Grace spoke French. Her true language which she hoped Grace would not forget. "I'm going for a walk," she announced to the room. Her walks were her time to think, her time to organize her thoughts, rehearsing her lines in her mind before she wrote them down.

Getting up from the table, Grace took her plate to the sink. Only a few crumbs remained and a hint of chocolate from the icing lay on the plate. The chocolate did not last long as Grace swiped it with her index finger and tasted the sweetness that her grandmother had made. The plate landed squarely in the sink. The thought of washing it never crossed her mind. Dishes and housework were up to someone else. Grabbing her sweater from the back of the dining room chair, she ran out of the side door and down the back stairs of their triple decker, carefully skipping a few steps and quickly finding herself on the landing. As if on a mission into her newfound freedom, she headed for the path along the river.

It was a beautiful late spring; the leaves of the maple trees were bright green. Grass along the river was tall, swaying in the wind, in need of a good cutting. As she walked, the sun hit her face, warming it, causing it to glow ever so slightly. That day she knew the glow was from within, and she was very happy about that. The sun's effects would be a great disguise as she walked along the river, reflecting and projecting her future like a play in her mind. Her thoughts were carefully staging one act to the next.

It had been a whirlwind the last few months. From the war, and her play, to her first orgasm, things were happening fast, but it was mainly because the world knew she and George were going steady. That is what she liked the most. Her Gee-Gee had made the right decision; going to college was what he wanted to do, and avoiding the draft was just the lucky outcome of it. She could not bear the thought of him in harm's way somewhere across the ocean. It was difficult enough having him over an hour away in Durham at the University.

She was deep in thought as she strolled along the path, recalling the day she heard the news. "I'm going early," George told her on the day of graduation. "I got a work study job at the cow barns all summer," he explained to her why he wasn't waiting until September to go to school. She understood but did not like it. She should have told him her secret then but did not want him to change his plans. She paused for a moment to look at the rapids in the river. The water was high from the melting snows far north in the White Mountains.

"Gracie," she did not hear the first call. "Grace, over here!" She turned from the river, looked across the way, and saw her friends Mark and John. The two of them waved and ran across the street without looking where she was standing.

"What are you doing?" John asked with a devilish grin on his face. "Are you okay?" She smiled but did not answer; sometimes the things not said are the best things said between friends.

"Want to go to the Mayflower with us?" John asked her. The Mayflower Coffee Shop was just up on Elm Street, and it was a perfect place to catch up with her friends. After all, it had been a whole week since they said their good byes after graduation. "We want you to be the first to know," added Mark. "News, we got news."

They all scurried across the Granite Street Bridge hoping it would not fall into the mighty Merrimack River. "Come on, Grace," Mark said, pulling her arm. "This old thing is ready to collapse." They all chuckled at the urban myth as they rounded the corner onto Elm Street.

The interior of the coffee shop had dark wooden walls, aged with time and a long white Formica counter along the far wall with several black and chrome stools all standing at attention, each one of them beckoning to the customers when they came through the revolving door into the diner. The smell of cigarettes and cigars lingered in the air only to be outdone by the smell of burnt coffee and fried bacon from earlier in the day.

The milk glass ceiling lights above the counter cast a clear light onto the room, making it appear clean with an almost antiseptic appeal that pleased most who ate there. That day the diner was almost empty. Only one lone customer sat at the counter with his mug of coffee in front of him holding the daily newspaper. *The Manchester Union Leader*, with an unyielding onslaught of conservation and biased writing, was their only source of news in town. "Perfect for this mill town," Grace had expressed her thoughts more than once; she hated the paper and the daily ranting of its publisher, some old guy named Loeb. Getting out of New Hampshire would be the topic at the diner that day. She knew it and escape could not come soon enough.

"Here, let's sit in a booth," Mark said, grabbing her arm again and trying to push her into the corner.

"Hey, slow down, what's the rush?" She blurted out as she sat on the black and white leather seats. John slid into the booth and sat to her left, with Mark to her right. Grace knew something was up, and there would be no escaping the conversation as they had her pinned in.

"Okay, spill it." She looked directly at Mark.

"Let's order first." He said, trying to contain his excitement.

Coffee arrived in ceramic white mugs. It was black and strong, just the way they all liked it. Milk and sugar were reserved for tea. Good character is determined by how you drink coffee, they thought.

"Well?" Grace leaned back in the booth, crossed her arms, and looked side to side at each of them. John spoke. "We are moving to New York City." Without a second to reply, Mark added with real enthusiasm, "Yes. we are! There is a place called Greenwich Village, It's a real village, in a real city. We read all about it and we are leaving next weekend." Mark reached over and grabbed John's hand, and in that moment of solidarity, they both smiled at each other. Grace casually grabbed their wrists and slowly brought them back to the moment at hand. "Well, you are not there yet," she exclaimed. "Settle down, it's still Manchester, in Cow Hampshire, not New York City." They all laughed. Pleased with the news and the progress of their relationship, Grace couldn't help but feel a bit saddened by her own relationship and what was happening with her Gee-Gee.

"What's wrong?" Mark asked.

"Nothing, I just miss my Gee-Gee." Almost in tears, she confides to her best friends everything she has been holding in for months. Professing her love for George, what happened in the parking lot that night at the Puritan after the play, and how she and he had experimented with sex until they finally got it right. Going on, she told them how she felt after she finally was liberated as a woman, experiencing the pleasure a man felt each time he fucked. She liked it; she like it a lot. But, sitting there with her boys, she craved the feeling of having George between her thighs once again. She could not wait another month before he returned from school.

"Go see him," John said. "Yeah, just go." added Mark.

"How the fuck will I get there? Hitchhike? The bus, I'm sure, left hours ago." Grace assumed with a sense of disgust. "Taxi!" exclaimed the boys in unison. "Take a taxi." She had a slight look of puzzlement on her face as she shook her head just before the corners of her mouth turned upward.

CHAPTER 7

    Sitting in the back seat of the taxi, Grace could smell the hint of stale cigarettes. She was thankful it was a nice spring day, and with the windows down the air was continually being refreshed. Leaning back in the seat, she stretched out a little; she wanted to sleep, but her mind wouldn't allow it. "How crazy is this?" She had thought. The taxi was easy enough to find on Elm Street. The driver knew exactly where to go but warned her it would take at least an hour and a half. She didn't care. She had to see George, her Gee-Gee, and she had to tell him first, he had to know.
    The road to the University of New Hampshire was picture perfect, she had thought. Looking out the window she tried to imagine the lives of the people in the homes she saw along the way. Country roads were mostly all the same once you left the city, windy and hilly as they made their way across the state nearer to the ocean. Made of centuries old granite, long elaborate stone walls lined the roads and enclosed huge tracts of field and farm as if they were a layer of protection against the outside world. The occasional white clapboard house, sitting high on the knoll next to the old barn overlooking a spread, was quintessentially a sign you were in New England. The small villages the driver had to maneuver through were the direct opposite of where she lived. There were no large brick mills, no

rows of shops and uninteresting buildings aged with soot from the factories, just beautiful homes, white picket fences, and in the distance, a white wooden spire of a church, a beacon of normalcy in this crazy new world.

As the taxi got closer to its destination, the scenery remained the same, always pretty, always charming. "How can that be?" She questioned, knowing all too well the hardships she had faced during her few short years on earth. The harrowing stories her mother would tell of the trek of her Grandparent's south from Canada to Manchester. Life in New England is not this picturesque. "What were they hiding?" That was her other question for that day.

The ride was closer to two hours, but the time seemed to fly by, as the scenes she created were like a movie in her head. She invented a cast of characters. They lurked behind trees or slept one off after a long night in the hay loft. There was even a lonely wife standing at the wood stove slowly cooking a meal for one, not knowing if her husband was on a ship in the Pacific or the Atlantic. They were all people Grace could see in her mind, could feel with her soul; her imagination was on fire, thoughts exploded with every turn in the lane, every dip in the road. She was worried that these images would be lost, that she would not remember them, because in her haste to find a taxi, she had forgotten to bring a notepad. She felt inspired, almost rejuvenated just by watching the rolling countryside. She had hoped it could have gone on forever, but as fast as it started, it abruptly came to an end.

"Thompson Hall, here we are." The taxi driver announced without looking at his passenger. Grace was forced back to reality, regretting she had left Manchester without something to write with. She hoped her thoughts would not be fleeting.

"That's fifteen dollars, Miss," the driver spoke again. Another feeling of regret came over her. She reached into the pocket of her cotton pants and pulled out three crumpled dollars. What had she been thinking? Grace had to think fast.

"I'll be right back." She leaped out of the car and without shutting the door started for the front door of the Hall. She had to find her Gee-Gee. He would fix this.

Having never been to the university before, let alone this far outside of the city, she was slightly intimidated by all the surroundings. Running up the stone steps, she paused and looked back at the taxi. The driver was now out of the car and leaned patiently against the passenger side with his arms folded in a disapproving manner. She could feel his glare and needed to quickly resolve this situation. The giant door swung open with the slightest of ease. The room was magnificent. Entering it she stood for a moment to take it all in, high ceilings, a grand staircase, hundreds of books on shelves and lots of overstuffed furniture in a beautifully decorated room that screamed masculinity, perfect for a men's fraternity house.

Rushing up to the first person she saw, she asked, "Gee-Gee, do you know where I can find him?" she asks.

"Who? No Gee-Gee here." The student explained. Feeling a bit embarrassed, she could hardly get the words out fast enough. "George; George Metalious. He lives here." Her words were barely out of her mouth when she heard her name. She turned and rushed up the grand staircase to the landing where he was standing. George held her tightly as if they had not seen each other for years. In reality, it had been only a week. They embraced passionately, and Grace broke down explaining to him what had happened.

"I don't have that kind of money," he told her.

"But, Gee-Gee, what am I to do?" She could really turn on the helpless victim persona when she wanted. He clearly saw through this, but he loved her unconditionally and secretly was glad she had come to visit him, even if it was a crazy idea.

They both went out to the street, cautiously trying to come up with a plausible story for Grace. They discovered that the taxi was no longer there and nowhere in sight. They looked at each other as if to say, "we dodged that bullet." Turning to go back into the hall, they were greeted by the house mother. Her look of disappointment was only the beginning. The driver had been so angry he drove directly to the University President's office to inform him of the young lady's bad intentions. Feeling himself responsible for his students, he paid the fare and sent the driver on his way. Immediately, he called the hall and instructed the house mother to gather George and Grace to his office. He had to get to the bottom of this story.

It was late when they walked back from the President's office. The sun was setting behind the hills that surrounded the school. The light-show it created made everything seem less dramatic, creating an almost serene quality.

"Things will be better in the morning," she said. The house mother made up a couch for Grace to sleep on, which was totally against the rules, but deep inside, she too longed to find such young love, something that had eluded her. She admired this young woman's devotion; no matter how nuts it had seemed.

The night was not as uneventful as the house mother thought. George snuck down to the main room. Quietly he woke Grace, and together they crept out the back door to where George's car was parked in the shadows. Crawling into the back seat, they snuggled and sipped some Canadian Whiskey from a flask he had stashed under the front seat. In low tones they talked about the previous week and her graduation gathering. In her mind, without him it was all boring and uneventful. George was her life, and she needed him to know that. When the glow returned to their faces from the effects of the whiskey, they became warm and had to roll the windows down slightly. It was hot in the car, and their clothes slowly came off.

That night in the backseat was a drastic contrast when compared to their adolescent lovemaking not so long ago on a wintery night. They had achieved a sort of fucking unison that only young love can produce. Each reaching fulfillment before stopping. He now waited until she was satisfied first. Never making that mistake again was his goal. She showed him her appreciation in many ways that night..

"Why didn't you let me pull out?" George asked as he zipped up his trousers. "You don't want to get pregnant, do you?"

Not wanting to answer him, she breathed a deep sigh. "I'm sorry, George, I have to tell you." Her hands clutched both his wrists and she looked him squarely in the face. Even in the darkened backseat with little to no moonlight she could see his expression. Like a mind reader from the carnival, he knew.

"Pulling out would not have made any difference," she whispered. Her eyes slightly cast downwards, almost ashamed, but secretly not. George's eyes grew large in a mixture of shock and elation; a baby was not in the plan. He knew instinctively what had to be done; morning would not come soon enough.

Their ride back to Manchester the next day was a quiet one. They left shortly after breakfast. Grace had insisted she was not hungry, but George was worried about the baby and walked across to the mess hall to bring back a banana and toast.

"You need to eat something." As he handed her the food, she looked up, saying thank you with her eyes. She wanted to stay with her Gee-Gee at the university. Going back to the city was the last thing she wanted.

From the front seat the scenery was not so pleasant, not so idyllic for her return trip. The sky was overcast, not quite a storm sky, just grey, dull and gloomy. Grace watched the same views as she had the day before; the granite stone walls seemed darker and menacing, no protection there. They looked more like a fortress, not unlike a prison to keep everyone trapped. The white spire of the churches were no longer beacons of faith but seemed to act as billboards to hypocrisy and false faith. She noticed the people in the towns they passed through. Studying their faces, she sensed they were hiding something, something dark. For example, the mother on the porch overlooking the field where the workers were. She knew one of them would be her lover before the day was over, and the absence of her husband faraway at war was just a distant memory. Everything in Grace's view was clouded in judgement and secrecy. Her own feelings began to surface as they silently returned to their world, knowing all too well it was time to reveal her secret. She hoped her family would not be as judgmental as she was being.

They were married in the rectory of Saint Joseph's Catholic Church. It was an impressive structure of red brick and stained glass perched on a slight rise where the entire city could look north and see the spire. It had been a typical February day, a bit dull from the overcast. Not cold enough to snow, not warm enough to be enjoyed.

It had been just a couple of months after Grace's confession to George in the back seat of his car, the same car where it all started that they now drove quietly from the church to the North End.

The house on Spruce Street seemed even more grand and whiter, bolder, enhanced by the gray sky. Auntie's house was the perfect location to host the reception after the wedding. Grace and George invited a few of their friends and family to celebrate the young lover's unity for the whole world to see

She had been upset at first, when the priest would not allow them to be married at the main altar, but her condition was now showing. The large men's shirts that she wore most days had become her trademark attire, and they would not hide her swelling stomach any longer. Her choice for the wedding had been a simple A-Line dress, loose fitting with long sleeves. The wool coat that her grandmother had made was a life saver in her efforts of concealment.

The Church and Laurette would not be embarrassed by what had happened. The wedding ceremony was held in the rectory; the foyer to the Priest's quarter would have to do, and with its side entrance next to the parking lot, it was very convenient.

"I now pronounce you man and wife," Father LaRouche said with all the authority he could muster. He wanted to really say. "And now go." Priests always had a habit of biting their tongues when they needed to.

Auntie Georgie was not at the service. She was back at Spruce Street tending to all the festivities for her favorite niece, wanting everything to be perfect. She had set up two long wooden banquet tables and covered them with her finest white linen. Fresh flowers were a rarity during winter months; Grace had been happy that carnations were found in time, as they were her favorite. The stark white flowers were neatly assembled in vases in the center of the tables. The food was laid out with thought. Auntie loved to entertain but did not do it often enough to feel comfortable. Her sister-in-law Laurette brought the finger sandwiches and deviled eggs earlier in the day on large porcelain platters that she had borrowed. They were beautiful if not pretentious for an event of this nature. "Georgette, no one will remember the food, but they will remember how it looked," she announced as she dropped them off.

The reception lasted only a couple of hours. Everyone who had gone to the service made their way back to Auntie's for food and good cheer. The guests seemed to enjoy themselves and were well-behaved, the Frenchies in one room and the Greeks in another, sharing a casual glance and smile between them at appropriate moments. Most in the room knew of Grace's condition, and her choice of attire could not conceal it. The ones who knew paid it no mention, and those who questioned it watched her every move to confirm the rumors that she was knocked up, but never uttering a word.

The young couple did their best to include their families in a conversation of sorts, spending time in each of the rooms, being aware not to allot more time to one than the other. When guests started to leave, it seemed others followed like sheep. At the end of the celebration only the new groom with his bride, her mother and grandmother remained. Auntie Georgie was somewhere out of sight in the kitchen, no doubt scrubbing dishes.

Grace and George were exhausted; they sat in the corner of the parlor next to the remnants of their small cake and a table of handwritten note cards and envelopes. She desperately wanted to open them but knew it would be in poor taste.

"*Venez Maman, aidez-nous a'nettoyer cela,*" Laurette barked to her mother that it was time to clean up. Grace's grandmother headed to the kitchen while the three older women returned the house to its normalcy. Grace watched as they cleared dishes, picked up napkins, and returned uneaten food to the kitchen. They did not need to speak; they knew what to do and did it.

George studied his young bride and tried his best to sort out what she was thinking. He could not. In her mind, as she watched them work, she realized that she was not prepared for being his wife or a mother to his child that she was carrying. Everything had always been done for her, and she was incapable of doing it on her own.

Her grandmother had managed their lives for as far back as she could remember. Her sister Bunny, and she, never made their beds, never did laundry, and never even boiled an egg. It was a life that most only heard about in their station, but her mother's warped sense of entitlement kept basic chores away from them, choosing to have their grandmother do it all. Grace was afraid, seriously afraid, for the first time in her life. Trying to conceal her inner feelings, she rose, and in a futile attempt she started to pick up the glassware. Deciding that the others could do it, she sat back down.

George crossed the room to where his new bride was in deep thought. He placed his hand on her shoulder and caressed it lightly. She looked up at him with a tear in her eye, feeling guilty that this should be the happiest day of her life, but feared it was not. They looked into each other's eyes, and soon they seemed to read each other's mind. "It will be ok. It has to be okay," they silently prayed.

CHAPTER 8

It was the end of summer when days were long and gracefully met the evening like an old friend. The sunlight at dusk lingered high in the sky, fading into nightfall slowly, almost cautiously. Each morning, the sun would rise a little later making the dew on the fields reflect the best light that Mother Nature had to offer. Daybreak in the north was always welcomed, like a hug, a sort of reassurance that the day ahead would be a good one.

A new day had begun with bright blue skies, not a cloud in sight and the air dry and crisp like cotton sheets fresh off the clothesline. The sun warmed the cool early morning air fast and furiously as its rays rose over the nearby mountains. The entire town seemed to be awake at that early morning hour. After all it was the unofficial end of summer and soon the start to a new school year.

Barbara, like her neighbors, was up. She had just finished her last load of laundry and hung it out on the front porch to dry. The tiny house on Gilman Street, perched high on the hill overlooking her village, had always captured the best breezes off the front of the house. She paid no mind that her laundry was there for the world to see; she had nothing to hide. That is exactly what she secretly wanted to convince herself and her neighbors.

Pausing ever so slightly, she turned away from the porch and looked down past the tall pine trees and through the clearing next to the white birches. A smile came across her face as it filled with a sort of self-satisfaction that the spire had not magically disappeared during the night. The slender white steeple of the Congregational Christian Church gleamed in the morning. The light, as the suns rays rose over the nearby hills, caught it ever so gently causing the structure to glow.

Barbara sat on the porch at daybreak waiting patiently as she had done every work day. This time of day allowed her to reflect on her life. Today she was grateful that the Laconia Shoe Shop was closed, and there would be no work.

The first Monday of September was traditionally a time for a celebration. The Labor Day holiday had been official for a few years. Gilmanton, like every other town in the state, would mark the special occasion with a small parade and a picnic. The mills and most stores were closed for a long weekend, giving local residents a much-needed reprieve from their daily tasks. It also served as a gentle reminder that autumn would arrive soon, and winter, once again, would revisit their tiny hamlet.

Barbara contemplated the quietness of the morning, there on the front porch; she sat with her thoughts. She and her brother had been managing just fine since that cold and deadly night so long ago; they took one day at a time. Their monster, now rested in the back sheep pen, concealed and almost forgotten. They did their best to move on by not thinking about what happened and always trying to keep up appearances. Normalcy can be an easy distraction if no one looks too closely.

After the horrors of that December, Barbara and William found a solidarity between them that many siblings go an entire lifetime without experiencing. In the months that followed, the Roberts' House found little to smile about or to celebrate. By the time the following June rolled around, they had mustered enough grit to sit around their small kitchen table which had been the scene of such ugliness. They ate cake and ice cream, a real treat for them.

William graduated from eighth grade, and Barbara finally said good bye to high school. She was now free to start her life but knowing all too well the cloud lingering over them would be her albatross and keep her close to home. She was like a mourning dove protecting her newly born chick. She watched over her little brother for any signs that might be cause for alarm with his behavior or a crack in his resolve.

The war had escalated to world status, and by the end of spring there was a need for workers in the shoe shop. Not ideal for Barbara, but it was miles from her surroundings, and it had placed more distance between her and her memories. It could only help.

It's amazing the difference only fourteen miles could make, going from the village green to a real town. Laconia, complete with a train station, supermarket and even a street car. It sat on the southern edge of Lake Winnipesaukee and was considered the gateway to the Lakes Region. That change of location was the distraction she needed to cope with her past troubles and to personally grow, all while trying to forget that snowy night.

"William, are you awake?" She yelled through the screen door toward the back of the house. Her brother wasn't like herself; mornings were always hard for him. "William, it's your last day before school starts. Let's have some fun for a change."

A slight groan or murmur could be heard from the back of the tiny house. That was all she needed to know he was awake. Sitting down on the floor of the front porch with her feet firmly planted on the old granite steps, her face deeply lined for such a young age, her mind continued drifting, and her thoughts returned to that night.

Sylvester was gone, never to return, never going to harm her or William ever again. That night was a blur, but the outcome of the event gave her clarity. Her father had taken something precious from both her and her brother, something neither one of them could ever regain. So, it was only fitting that they took something from him: his life and the contents of his pockets. That snowy night his wallet, an uncashed check from his employer, and the bloody braided rug that her mother had made were all burned with the rest of the week's garbage in the old oil drum. Barbara remembered the fire as it smoked, the distinct smell of evilness as it drifted past them into the night air. Despite the drifting snow, they never shivered, standing and watching the last remains of the devil go up in smoke.

It took several attempts to get all the blood out of the pine floor boards. Endless scrubbing on her knees with a mixture of bleach and vinegar, the dark stains of his dark life all but scrubbed out. She burned the dress she was wearing that night as well. The blood stains would not come out, and keeping it would have been another constant reminder.

William cleaned the gun, wrapped it in an old cloth as if it had never been fired, and returned it to the dresser drawer, this time just a little deeper under an assortment of never worn old clothes. His father and the gun would not be found, because no one was looking for either.

They had gotten through the months using the cash that was stuffed in Sylvester's wallet, almost two hundred dollars. It was a life saver for them over those bleak times. Barbara did her best to stretch it out until the first tomatoes were picked from their garden. They had always had a patch out back, and selling the bounty it yielded provided more than enough.

"It'll do William," Barbara would say before offering him a toasted tomato sandwich again. "I know. It'll do." He would say before gobbling down his sparse dinner. They were going to be just fine, she thought. She continued to stare out into the morning sunshine.

"I'm up. What's for breakfast?" Barbara could hear him from the front room. She got up from the steps and opened the screen door heading to the kitchen. William stood next to the sink and was dressed, shorts, a camp shirt and his summer shoes, ready for the day.

"How about pancakes? Those blueberries you picked will be perfect." She tells him.

"Thanks, Sis." he smiled and pulled out the wooden chair to sit down at the kitchen table.

She went into the kitchen and grabbed an old pickle jar she used as a flour canister. It was half full of flour. Looking down at the silver lid, she unscrewed it and like opening a can of worms, her mind went to the store owner who gave her the empty jar a few months prior.

"Still no word from your father?" Ned, the store owner and principal guardian of all things Gilmanton, asked. Not waiting for a response, he noticed the color in Barbara's face, as white as the flour she was buying.

"Any man who up and leaves his family should be shot. You two all alone up on that hill, I tell ya!" It didn't take Ned much to get going on any subject. His business or not, it made no difference. His opinion was like a wild brush fire in summer; one spark, and the town would be ablaze.

"Mr. Martin, we are fine, really." Barbara tried her best to simmer him down before another customer was in ear shot. "It's okay, Paw goes where the work is; he is gone for long stretches." She paused, then added, "Is that pickle jar finally empty? May I have it?" She added, trying her best to change the subject. It worked. He went off to the back room to retrieve it. She hated to lie; she hated to have to be constantly aware of what she said, and how she said it. Appearances, to most in the town, were like a billboard to your soul; if one good wind came along, it could cause a tear, and the entire sign could be ripped off exposing a completely different image. She had to keep hers and her brother's intact.

The pancakes were perfect, and the wild blueberries added just a hint of sweetness to them. They both enjoyed a liberal amount of homemade maple syrup to sweeten their breakfast even more. Finishing their pancakes, both pushed their last bite around their plate to collect as much of the amber sugar as they could. "So good!" Confirmed by William's smile.

"Are we ready to go see the parade?" Barbara asked. She placed their plates in the sink. Clean up would have to wait. "Let me get my sweater."

Standing on the front porch, she closed the screen door. Locking it was never a thought. No one locked their doors in town. The general consensus seemed to be that no one would enter a house where they did not belong. Small town life had a few small advantages, and this was one of them.

"Who's that?" William questioned, pointing to a black sedan turning into their driveway.

"No idea, keep quiet, okay!" She whispered to him. Stepping down off the porch they both walked in unison towards the car. Two men got out and stood next to the driver's side, both wearing what appeared to be a tan uniform and white caps on their heads. The gold emblem on the front visor caught the sunlight and reflected it, creating a tiny flash as the men turned to the Roberts children. They were not police. She was sure of that." But who were they?"

"Miss Roberts? Are you Barbara Roberts?" The taller of the two asked. He turned and took a step forward in their direction.

Panic, it was panic that she was feeling. It started in her stomach, and like a wave of discomfort it racked her entire body in less than a second. William sensed something was wrong, grabbed his sister's hand, and squeezed it tightly. That one action of sibling support grounded her in that instant. The uniformed men did not notice the beads of sweat that formed on her brow or the color in her face as it drained.

Clearing her throat slightly concealed her discomfort, "Yes, I'm Barbara Roberts," she replied. "Why do you ask?"

"Your father is Sylvester Roberts?"

She nodded yes and looked at William with a fake look of puzzlement.

"We have some questions for you. May we come in?" He asked.

"Well, we are on our way to the parade. What is this all about?" Standing her ground, she was protecting herself and her younger brother.

"It will only take a minute," the other man added.

"Well, you can ask me right here. We know nothing about our father. It's been over a year since we have seen him." Her lies were very convincing, so good she had started to believe them herself.

"Yeah, he is gone, just left!" William blurted out. It was Barbara's turn to squeeze his hand in a silent gesture for him to shut his mouth. They both stood there, waiting for some form of explanation for this visit.

The men explained that they were from the office of the US Navy. It seemed that their father, a member of the Merchant Marines, had wandered into the Shreveport, Louisiana recruiting office to volunteer for active duty last fall, well over a year ago. He had been accepted on a delayed enlistment program and was to begin basic training in January. He never reported to the Great Lakes Training center. They went on to tell the Roberts children, that with the outbreak of war and the flood of new recruits, the office got back logged, and his file was pushed to the bottom of the basket.

"And we are looking for him…" The man's voice was only an echo in her mind, bouncing around like shouts in an empty quarry. Her mind drifted in and out of what was happening, trying to focus on his words, and not letting it go there, to the bloody path in the snow that night.

William, biting his lower lip, just had to say something, holding back was too difficult. "He is gone, he left us. We told you that already," yelling at the men.

Barbara cut him off, "Like my brother says, he left us high and dry after our mother died. It's been months since last we heard anything. He said he was going out to sea." She was back in the moment and anger overtook her fear. "We got a card from Texas. Galveston, I think." That was true, the last card came in an envelope with some cash just before he wrote that he was shoving off.

The men looked at each other, not surprised with the story. It seemed to fit a pattern they had seen in the past. Men wanting to do the right thing but never able to get out of their own way to do it. Sylvester Roberts seemed to fall into that category, certainly not the family man one would think of from this perfect little town. Both men appeared to be satisfied with the questioning. The taller officer reached into his shirt pocket to retrieve a card.

"Here, this is my card." He tells Barbara. She sees the card he is holding and looks down at it. She had never seen a business card before, let alone having one offered to her. Like the forbidden fruit, she slowly and cautiously reached for it.

"If you hear from him, please call us, collect. Someone will accept the charges," he added. "Or, if you want, the Sheriff is aware that we are looking for your father, contact him in Laconia. He can always find me."

With that, the men removed their hats, neatly tucked them under their left arms, and made their way back to the black sedan parked in front of the tiny house on Gilman Street. The officers were not completely in the car when a passing motorist slowed down to watch the scene unfold.

The Roberts children turned towards the street and observed another black sedan as it passed from the other direction. The car moved ever so slowly with the driver peering through the passenger side window watching. Barbara knew instantly it was Bud's taxi. He, like Ned from the Store, was another gossip and an all-time meddler in affairs that were not his own.

The children watched the taxi, as did the uniformed men, with questions as to the behavior of the driver. Barbara's eyes locked on Bud's for a brief second. An icy chill ran through her soul and was gone in an instant. The men turned, got into their car, and slowly backed out of the driveway. The driver paused when he was directly in front of the children.

"Thank you for your time. We think it's another case of desertion." The driver tells her through the open window, while nodding his head. "We will be in town the rest of the day, Miss Roberts," he added. The children still stood in silence, in solidarity as the car went out of sight.

Like that night so long ago, a small trickle of a tear formed in the corner of Barbara's eye. She wiped it on the sleeve of her sweater. She looked at her brother as they walked back up the front porch steps and into the house. They both knew intuitively: there would be no celebrating that day. Locking the door behind them was the right thing to do.

CHAPTER 9

Grace looked across the sea grass, and with a slight nod of approval, admired the beautiful sky.

"Look, Marsha!" she exclaimed. "Those big ones are Canadian. They have floated all the way down from Canada." She told her daughter as she knelt down next to her, pointing up to an abundance of big, white and fluffy clouds dotting the horizon. Off the New England coast, the clouds floated ever-so graciously, changing shapes and merging together. They drifted by in harmony, not unlike a choreographed dance.

Grace laid back down on the plaid wool blanket and pulled her daughter a little closer. Her arms wrapped tightly around her shoulders, holding her, keeping her from floating away.

"Mommy, you're squeezing me so hard, I can't float," her daughter pleads.

"Silly me. I thought you might float away, and I couldn't bear it." Grace, let up a little, but never let go completely. Marsha was almost seven years old. Her darling daughter was her pride, and Grace never regretted having her at such a young age.

The entire world was now at Grace's fingertips. She was ready to grasp the brass ring and start fresh again. The war had come and gone; George would finish college soon and had been offered a teaching job in a small town north of the university where they had been living in a Quonset hut provided for students on the GI Bill.

She looked out in the direction of the beach over the sand dunes. Her Gee-Gee was in sight at the water's edge, both of his hands tightly gripping the wrists of two small children. Grinning ear-to-ear Grace turned toward Marsha and kissed her oldest on her head. Grace was happy, very happy for the first time in a very long time, and her mind was clear. The sea breeze was cleaning out the cobwebs that formed over the past few years.

"Mommy, why are you smiling?" Marsha asked.

"Because we are going on an adventure. Soon we will be moving to our own little house in the country," she explained. "Won't that be exciting?"

Grace closed her eyes, and Marsha laid her head on her mother's stomach. Both of them listened to the crashing surf. Sea breezes whistled around their ears as they drifted off, each into their own little world.

Shortly after his first daughter's birth, George had been recruited into the army. He was lucky enough to stay close to home at Fort Devens, just south of the border in Massachusetts. He would come home most weekends to their one bedroom, third floor apartment on the west side of Manchester. It was not a perfect situation for his young family, but it had been a fruitful one. Grace, without regrets, had two more children while living in their tiny apartment. The third-floor walkup was located in Frenchie town, a section where Grace had grown up and disliked immensely. The one advantage was that her grandmother lived close by and helped the young couple whenever she could.

The end of the war could not come fast enough for the new family, and by 1949, Marsha, the oldest, was in grammar school and the youngest still in diapers. Mike, a son, came the year after Marsha, almost to the day. By D-Day, Cindy, the youngest and most precocious, was born. Grace loved her little family and devoted her time to them. Still a child herself, she connected with them at a level she and her mother never did.

"Grace, set an example. You can't always say yes," Laurette would tell her. "Put your foot down."

She ignored her mother just as she had when she was growing up. Grace hoped her kids would actually like her as they grew up. George was the apple in all his kids eyes. His periods of absence during the early years only caused them to be a tighter-knit unit, and this was something Grace appreciated. Family was everything to her, and after a miscarriage that past winter, she realized that number four was not in the cards for them. The doctors warned her not to try again for fear it could do more harm to her than to the baby. Shortly after, her tubes were tied at the local hospital on the French side of town. That night, all alone, Grace sobbed, wishing she had something to ease her pain.

Her pain was for the loss and the chance to have another child. All the strife she managed during those early years was difficult. She never imagined how strenuous it would be to raise children on an Army salary. George's weekend visits were a huge blessing. He did most of the chores that her grandmother had not finished during the week. Grace was not the perfect homemaker, but she was determined to be the perfect friend to all her children.

Nights, when the three children were snuggled sound asleep in the bed they had shared, she would sit at the kitchen table all alone, somewhat lonely and reminiscent of the ways things could have been. She felt just a little sorry for herself with her Gee-Gee away in the army and her boys off in New York living their lives. The fellas hardly ever wrote anymore, and her few friends from school that she managed to keep in touch with, all seemed to be in parts unknown. Grace was grateful for receiving what she had been looking for, a family. One that was all hers. But, still, there was something missing. Something she always thought about but seldom did. It was her writing.

She never let her mood take her too low on those lonely nights. She would take out an old dog eared notebook and open it to a blank page. She sat in silence, listening to the city outside. The occasional horn of a car, the distant shift whistle from the woolen mill or the random dog barking in the alley behind her apartment would fade. She took comfort in her own words. Writing, she had decided, would be her fourth child. The one she could never have. She wrote as a form of nourishment for her soul. The occasional glass of Canadian whiskey helped the loneliness, giving her just a tad more inspiration.

"Gracie, Gracie!" A faint yell came from below interrupting her reminiscing. Tails of blustery wind caught her hair, causing the ponytail to come undone. Her long brown hair now covered her eyes. Quickly, standing up to see over the dune, she gently placed Marsha to one side as she slept soundly. Looking towards the beach, she searched for the origin of the yelling.

Like every mother, she feared the worst. Had something happened to the kids? Was George calling for help? Her mind raced and created imagines of such ugliness that no one should be able to think of them that fast. Had the kids been washed out with the tide? Had George fallen and hurt himself or was it that stranger they saw earlier on the beach? Had he abducted little Cindy?

"Ma, look!" Mike was there at the water's edge holding what looked like a perfect shell of a horseshoe crab. Her son was proud of the discovery and wanted to share it with the world. She could only imagine how it smelled or how many other creatures were living in it.

"Yuck!" She yelled from below and waved. "Come on up, it's time for lunch."

Mike dropped the carcass of the crab back along the tide's edge, leaving the treasure for another person to find. George bent down to pick up little Cindy. Resting her on his hip, they started in the direction of the dune and to Grace.

The coastline of New Hampshire is rather small, only twenty-one miles of beaches, harbors, and the occasional relics of forts built during previous wars. Odiorne Point was a favorite of Grace's for a secluded day with nature and her family. She had packed a small picnic lunch, with cucumber sandwiches, cookies, and a jug of lemonade. Her favorite spot was near the bunkers that were built during the last war. High off the rise behind them, sat gray cement all but hidden in the shifting sands and tall grass that grew like weeds. There in the symbolic shadow of the military's might of the United States, Grace felt a little more protected against the world that was changing fast around her.

The entire family sat in a tight circle on the blanket she spread out earlier. They ate lunch, trying not to let the wax paper that protected their sandwiches act like a kite when the wind grabbed it. Cindy was not paying attention, and, in an instant, the waxed wrapping was airborne, floating out to sea, never touching the ground, floating like a seagull, no doubt making its journey all the way across the pond.

Wax paper, military bunkers, and a mother's watchful eye, were all part of Grace's world now. These multiple layers of protection made Grace who she was. The children enjoyed their cookies that she made, and no one even noticed the bottoms were burnt, almost black. She left them too long on the baking tray, causing them to cook longer. Grace didn't care, and neither did her family. She smiled.

"Marsha, take your brother and sister for a walk over there," pointing to a small area of grass and a couple of benches along the path. "I want to tell your father something," With the kids safely finishing their dessert on the wooden bench across the way, Grace laid down with her head now in George's lap. "I have news." He looks down at his wife, smiles and brushes the hair from her face. "Well?" he asks. "George," she pauses, "I'm gonna have a baby, another baby," gleefully she tells him.

"That's not possible Grace," shaking his head slightly, not even realizing he is doing it.

Grace, now giddy and laughing, rolled over onto her elbows and stared out to the sea grass. George loved it when she was this excited, this joyful. This was the Grace he married, the Grace he loved. That day next to the sea, there was not a glimmer of the loneliness or the dark side he found in her during the war and when he returned home. They were all but forgotten that sunny afternoon by the sea.

"I'm not having a baby, I'm creating one," Grace said laughing. He was a little confused. "I've decided to write a book, a real book! It's gonna be a smash, you wait and see!" She stood up with her arms and hands moving about, talking as fast as she could, and using them to make a point as all French Canadians seem to do.

George stretched out and leaned back, crossing his arms behind his head, to watch her in action. He knew instinctively, when she got this way, it was better to sit tight and hold on. She explained that deep inside her soul there was a book, a real, honest to God book about all the things she knew. She couldn't write about made up things, things she would have to research. She wanted her book to be about New England.

"There was so much to write about," she said. She continued to tell him more about her thoughts. The changing seasons, the people she knew, the mills, or about New England traditions. She went on and on. George listened very attentively. Her love of the life that surrounded her and telling stories about it was the fuel that fed the flame that would nurture her literary baby.

"Are you listening to me?" she asked him. His eyes were closed trying to keep the blowing sands from getting into them.

"I heard every word," he assured her, smiling, never opening his eyes. "It all sounds like a great plan."

Looking down at him, she frowns slightly; she knows he heard her. "What should I call it?" She asked her husband.

"What, the baby?" He chuckled.

"No, the Book!" Stern and not smiling, she nudges him sharply with her bare foot into his ass. "I want this book to be memorable, something to be talked about for years to come," she added.

Grace had always been a writer in her heart, and a real reader in her early life. Reading was how she escaped from her west side upbringing. Her trips to the library were legendary all through school; she often checked out three books a week during the winter months. If she was not writing in her notebook, she was reading under the bedspread with the flashlight from the kitchen. She read everything but loved the classics. F. Scott Fitzgerald and Somerset Maugham were her all-time favorites. Stories of true love, gritty quarrels, and real-life issues were things she wanted to write about. It had been her secret desire to write a true masterpiece, a classic of her own. She wanted to show them, her classmates, and assorted relatives that frowned on her choices in life and mocked her when she mentioned writing. This was what she was going to do.

"So what do I call it?" again she asked. Never looking down at him only out toward the horizon, the clouds moving faster with the wind. Grace hoped the howl would be like a whisper to her, gently mentioning the title.

Looking past the children in the direction of the bunker, was a lone crab apple tree, planted a century ago when this was all farmland. The tree was now full of pink and white blossoms, the heaviness causing the limbs of the old tree to swag and sway with the wind. Blossoms blew off their branches and created a snowstorm of color in the air.

"Come on, George, let's dance in the snow!" Not waiting for an answer, she bent over and grabbed his hand and pulled him to his feet. She was practically dragging him off the dune towards the tree up the hill.

"The kids." he said and pointed toward them. It was too late; they had already seen their parents trudging up the hill and were running as fast as they could in their direction.

They all reached the base of the tree, breathing so hard and trying to catch their breath. The family laid down under the colorful display of the crab apple tree, with its hues of pink and white, some almost red as they were all popping on that spring day. The wind rustled the fluffy blossoms and caused them to come loose from their precious stems. It created a magical display. Thousands of flowers filled the space below the tree, making a blanket of life that only Mother Nature could deliver.

Grace stood up, and with her arms outstretched, started to twirl under the tree. She turned faster and faster, letting the blossoms caress her face as they gently floated to the ground. She was inspired at that moment. Her inspiration came from the wind, the clouds, the sun, and this perfect display of renewal. Each blossom, in the proper order of events, would create a new life, a new baby.

"I've got it!' she screamed, so happy, and thrilled that now she could move forward. Grace fell to the ground next to her husband, rolled over in the grass onto her elbows, looked directly into his eyes and announced the title.

"*The Tree and the Blossom.*" She paused waiting for his reaction. He looked down to her and smiled.
"That's it, that's the title!" She felt good; he felt good. They were glad it was spring, her favorite season.

CHAPTER 10

The village square in Gilmanton was alive with spring-time color. Tulips had popped from their wintery slumber, and the grass would soon be ready for its first mowing of the season. Life in the town could be measured with the passing seasons. Each winter got a little colder than the previous making each spring just a little more magical. Spring came not too soon and was welcomed as a fresh start, not unlike a great big do-over for its residents.

It seemed everyone was outdoors, breathing the crisp cool air, with not a hint of the previous stale winter that arrived too early and stayed too late. Fishermen cast their lines into the rushing brooks for the first time that spring with hopes of catching their limit of the elusive brown trout. Hardy gardeners took up their spades and overturned the soil in their victory gardens. Small patches of cultivation, a remnant of the war, which became a welcomed staple to small town life. Most windows in town were open, with white cape cod curtains, blowing in the wind and trying to escape into the bright blue sky. Mother Nature was breathing in a fresh outlook for everyone, letting the wind take their woes into the stratosphere.

It was a perfect day to begin anew, to be free, to start again. The day had come for Barbara Roberts to put the past behind her and look to the future, something she never thought possible. She would no longer live in fear of shame; the truth literally set her free.

"Yep, today is the day. She is going home." Ned said as a blanket statement into the air at his general store, without a care of where his words would land. They landed that morning on Rita Rowell, the town's librarian, as a tease to incite a reaction. Rita was looking over the potatoes in the bin and doing her best to ignore the shop keeper's attempt to capture her into a conversation. She was never a gossip, and she refused to become one then.

Judging the town's residents was a full-time job for some, but she had a real job. Her judgments were reflected in the assortment of books in the town library. She took great pride in selecting the right books that she felt the people of Gilmanton should read. The one hundred dollar a year budget had to be spent wisely by carefully choosing what was good for her card holders and what was proper.

"I'm just saying, we can all move past what happened." Ned continued. Rita, still not biting, approached the counter with her few items and placed them carefully on the glass top.

"Ned, can I get two cans of Boston Baked Beans?" She said and pointed to the top shelf behind him. The cans were out of reach, so Ned retrieved the gizmo he made from wood and metal that hung on a hook next to the counter. It acted just like an extension to his arm. With a vice like grip, he grabbed the cans and added them to her assorted purchases.

Using his pad and the stubby yellow pencil from behind his ear, he tabulated her total and put her items in a brown paper bag. Ned pulled the lever on the side of the cash register, and a faint ding from a bell from deep inside sounded as the drawer opened. He was busy making change from her five-dollar bill when she finally retorted to his statements.

"Ned, the town has been through a lot these past few months. It was an ordeal for everyone," she said. Not waiting for his reply, she continued, "Can't we all just pretend it didn't happen."

Handing her the change, he paused ever so slightly and looked directly into her eyes. "If you ask me, there is more to the story than we know." He still wanted to lure her into his version of common gossip and judgement of his neighbors. Rita held steadfast. With one swift motion she stuffed her change into her coin purse, snapped it closed, and grabbed her groceries. "Well, we may never know," She said, pausing to compose herself as the large screen door slammed behind her. She hoped her words were not overheard, hoping the spring breeze caught them and sent them sailing across the green.

She was not a happy woman and never pretended to be. At forty-three she had learned to deal with her heart ache, tragically losing her one-and-only true love in the battle of D-Day. She knew she would never recover.

After living six years in this tiny hamlet, Rita was still considered a new resident in town. She was unmarried, plain, and to most thought of as a spinster. Being the town librarian, she was entitled to be on the school board. She took both roles very seriously. Moving to Gilmanton was her fresh start, a place she thought of as innocent and safe, far from dirty old Boston where she started life.

Crossing the town green, Rita walked into the sunlight towards the direction of Webster Street where she lived. Her thoughts were scattered, first to Ned and his blatant baiting and then to the real tragedy. It was a chapter that everyone in the town needed to put behind them. But she thought, "How could they?"

Turning the corner onto Main Street she passed the bus stop, the very place where evil returned to the town so long ago and set the tragic events into motion. "If ever there was a murder that was justified, it was that of Sylvester Roberts, the filthy scum of the Earth," she thought. "Incest, his own daughter," She whispered the words to herself, shaking her head as she walked, all without realizing it. She would never speak of it to anyone for fear it would start a conversation, one she could not bear. Incest and murder embarrassed the town name and its residents. It was a black cloud of an impending storm that lingered over them that might start at any moment. Everyone, always looking up, waited for the first strike of lightning.

She walked past the library which closed at 4:00 pm and picked up the Laconia Evening Citizen newspaper thrown onto the walk. One of the perks as librarian was that she could read it into the library the next morning.

The headline was not a pleasant one, but hopefully it was the beginning of the end. "Sheep Pen Killer Released, Murder Charges Dropped" was printed in bold typeface across the front page.

She tucked the paper under her arm and started to cross the street. She waited and watched a lone car as it passed by. Nodding his head to acknowledge Rita, Bud and his black taxi drove ever so slowly. It was his gentle reminder to her that someone was always watching.

Things happen, worlds collide, paths are crossed, coincidences happen, and no one knows the real outcome of events for years. Bud just happened to get the call on that snowy night so long ago, the night of the Pearl Harbor attack. It had been Sylvester asking for a ride up the hill. Bud also happened to be driving by the Roberts house months later as the two Naval Officers were talking to Barbara and her brother in the front door yard, never paying it mind. These random events all collided for him at the corner store one day, the center of all life in Gilmanton.

A couple of years after those seemingly unrelated encounters, Bud was on a beer run for old lady Templeton, a town elder with a fondness for the drink. The local taxi served as her own personal runner because she was too old and usually too drunk to drive. Bud was bent over with his head in the beer case reaching for the fourth pint of Kruger Ale and did not notice the sheriff and a uniformed man enter the store. As he approached Ned at the counter to have Ned put the beer on her tab, Bud heard their conversation. Standing just out of sight behind a cigarette rack, he waited and listened. He eavesdropped on the men as they spoke in hushed tones. The uniformed men were asking Ned questions about Sylvester Roberts.

Bud couldn't stand it. Why had no one asked him? He was aching to speak. Unable to hold back any longer, he jumped in with both feet, like the true busy body that he was. His reputation held true.

"I saw him. I gave Sylvester a ride to his house the night those fucking Japs bombed Pearl Harbor. Why are you asking?"

And there it was, the smoking gun in the search for an AWOL scumbag. Bud sang like a canary, and poor old lady Templeton never did get her Kruger Ale.

It took a few months, but the story came out in pieces. The rape, the wintery murder in self-defense, the burial in the sheep pen, followed by long faces of judgment from the town's residents. Each one of them asking, how something this inconceivably horrible could be happening in their town. Those hideous crimes remained a dark chapter in Gilmanton, and no one would dare speak about it.

Rita caught herself rolling her eyes as she watched Bud drive by. It had been a nasty habit of hers, a visual sign of her own judgement which she hated. The taxi squealed as it turned around the corner in the direction of the store. Bud was on his way to another encounter, no doubt. She thought his innocent observations had proved a blessing for the defense team. No one really knew what happened up on the hill at the Roberts house. The only people that did were Barbara and William, and they were not talking. People in town speculated what happened right under their noses. They judged and gossiped, speaking in low voices on park benches, in living rooms, and across the clothes lines. The Sheep Pen Murder was news, and it also just happened to be one of their own.

Barbara Roberts would be released from the state penitentiary in Concord that afternoon, a homecoming that, by all rights, should be private and sedate. Prying eyes of the town would look in the other direction. After all, they never saw the tragedy as it was happening, so why should they take notice now?

Rita reached her modest house on the corner of Main and Webster. A traditional Cape cod style with a steep roof to keep the snow off, white clapboards, dark green shutters and a white picket fence. It was a storybook home perfect for a single librarian. She had fallen in love with the house from an advertisement in The *Boston Traveller*. One of the many daily papers from her past. One phone call and she bought it sight unseen. It was her ticket to a new life. She reached for the gate and released the latch. The big black spring caused it to swing open with ease, like arms stretched wide welcoming her home.

Turning back to latch the gate, she looked down the street; it was quiet. The gentle spring breeze caused the branches of the maple trees to sway. They bent in the wind, creating a dazzling display of fresh bright green leaves, shiny and new. They seemed to glow in the afternoon light with a sense of clarity. Rita, at that moment, hoped Barbara would enjoy them as well and that they might give her that same sense of renewal.

CHAPTER 11

    The heat of August can be as unbearable as the cold in January: unforgiving, relentless and at times unimaginable. There could be no reprieve. Along with it comes the summertime humidity acting like an unwelcome relative dropping in on a Sunday afternoon, causing tensions to rise and overstaying their welcome. The heat and the humidity turned the smells of everyday life into a stink.
    Gilmanton's heat wave was into its second week with no end in sight. Days started early with temperatures barely changing during the night. The red mercury in the giant thermometer attached to the side of the corner store displayed the evidence in plain sight for all the town to see. There was no escaping. It acted like an amusement park ride, once you were strapped in all you could do was hold on. But the incessant heat was not amusing to anyone that summer.
    Grace and George had made their migration north to settle close by in the tiny town of Belmont, three miles from Gilmanton. Belmont was barely a mark on the road map they had gotten from the Sinclair gas station weeks before as they planned their migration north to their fresh start and new life.
    The young couple, with their brood of children, had carefully planned their trek up the state highway a few months before. They had bought the old Packard from a friend in

Portsmouth, the seller throwing in a small wooden trailer that sealed the deal had worked perfectly. Every square inch of the car and trailer was packed tightly with precision, causing a puzzle-like display of all their worldly belongings.

"George, don't forget this!" Grace yelled as she carefully made her way down the front steps, carrying in her arms her most prized possession. She held it with both arms like a baby; her heavy cast metal Remington typewriter was the last thing, after the children, to be packed into the car.

"Don't worry Gracie. It will sit on the floor of the back seat." With that, George took it from her and gently placed it between Mike and Marsha, covering it with a blanket, not unlike the actions of a concerned father.

The drive across the state and then north was scenic. The entire clan was almost speechless during the ride, excitement building up in their minds for the adventure that soon lay ahead for them.

The house that George found in the classifieds was barely even a house; it turned out to be a shack. A small, wooden, two-story structure tucked into the woods down a long dirt road. It was secluded and not visible from the road. The grass was overgrown, and the lilacs were in need of a good trimming. The outhouse in the back had been a surprise to George. It was something that he never even thought about checking on but at that point, there was no looking back.

It reminded Grace of the apartment in Manchester during the war. Small enough to work, not large enough to get out of your own way. There were two small bedrooms, a kitchen and a large front room. The outhouse was not unlike the toilet down the hall they had shared in their apartment. The best feature it had was a back porch, screened in and overlooked the Tioga River. A small stream of sorts meandering east-west through the back woods behind the house.

Standing on the front steps with both hands on her hips, Grace made an announcement to George and the kids as they began to unload the stuff. *"It'll do!"* she exclaimed. From that moment on, the seal of approval from her gave way to name the house, *It'll Do*. For the Metalious family the shack was their castle.

It'll Do served them well the first few months, everyone knew they were on an adventure and barely took notice of the dull interior, the cramped spaces and the depressed like mood it could cast on cloudy days. The shack was theirs for now, and they did their best to make it a home.

That summer was another tough one, especially for George. He'd taken a summer job at the Laconia State School as a teacher. Workdays were long and, it seemed, never ending. Grace had insisted on having the car during the day, so he was forced to bike to work each day. It was a long eight miles down the country roads to the shores of the lake where the Laconia State School was located. This he didn't mind; after all it was for his Gracie, the light of his eyes and the mother of his children. He figured, since she had the kids all day, the car was essential in case of an emergency. When she was not acting like a mother, she was writing. Grace wrote incessantly, and at times it was a detriment to her family.

August was almost over. The heat was finally getting to her; it was Grace's breaking point. "Hotter than Hades," she said throughout the day, wandering around the tiny house in search of some relief. *It'll Do*, was not doing it for her. She was frustrated and angry. The summer heat caused a drought and the well to dry up. "What's next?" Grace shouted out the back window as she stood at the sink waiting for the last drizzle of liquid from the faucet to come out. It did not.

She turned around and slammed an empty glass down on the painted wooden countertop with a thud. Reaching into the cabinet next to the sink, she retrieved a pint of whiskey and poured a small amount into the glass. The Hotpoint ice box was working overtime, and the tiny freezer in the center of the interior had another secret indulgence, one aluminum ice tray.

Carefully she removed one cube from the tray and dropped it into the amber liquid. Sitting down at the kitchen table next to her typewriter, Grace sipped the now cool liquid, letting it glide down her parched throat, letting it do its magic.

She sat, reflecting on the past few months, for just a moment, daydreaming before the kids would return from playing on the river's edge. They, too, were doing their best to stay cool. Grace had looked forward to the move for so long; now all she had were misgivings about their latest adventure. Tiny Belmont was not Gilmanton with the beautiful town green and its large freshly painted homes that seemed postcard perfect. A far cry from the dilapidated house she was living in down by the river on a dirt road.

It wasn't all bad. Gilmanton was close enough to It'll Do and was easy to get to. The town proved to be an endless source of inspiration for her writing. The town that gleamed in the sunlight, could be dark and menacing at dusk and throughout the night. She loved walking the streets of the village, each named after the trees that the founding fathers had had the foresight to plant. The white picket fences she passed were a symbol of the American dream. An occasional brass pineapple so proudly displayed on the front door was a billboard to a welcoming traditional New England gesture left over from the Golden Age of sailing along the eastern seaboard. Sitting on the bench in front of the town hall in the shade of the elm, Grace's prose was unleashed. That setting was almost as comforting as her aunt's giant bathtub from so long ago.

Grace noticed the clock just as she finished her noon time refreshment. The kids would be getting hungry, and they would be coming in the back door shortly. She got up from the table and placed the glass in the sink, filled with dirty dishes. It had been days since she had washed them. Chores were still not part of her life. She secretly wished her grandmother was there to help. Like every other day, lunch would be lettuce and tomato sandwiches on white, old-style bread from Cushman's bakery with a coke. With no water and no money, coke was easier to get. Her Gee Gee's meager salary only went so far, so, *It'll Do*, was home for now but, one day, things would be different.

Since her announcement of her fourth child, her book, it had been her preoccupation, a possession that had overtaken her. Back in Durham, as George finished his studies, she would lock the children outside of their Quonset dwelling. The makeshift housing made of recycled National Guard buildings was for families on the GI bill, after the war. The University provided them, and it was shelter and a sustainable place to call home during that time. The job offered at the Laconia State School and the small shack they lived in, were a godsend for them and had come not too soon.

The slam of the screen door from the back and the thumping of bare feet on the wooden floor alerted Grace to the children's arrival. They were fresh from the water's edge, with feet blackened from the mud and small red welts along their legs. Mosquito bites during the day were the worst; the tiny pests seemed angrier during that time as the children disturbed their slumber in the stagnant water of the river.

"What's for lunch?" asked Marsha, knowing the answer before she asked. Grace placed three sandwiches of butter, lettuce, and tomato on the wooden counter. There were no clean dishes, and with a dry well, it wasn't like they could wash their hands. Mike grabbed his ice-cold coke first and took a long slug of the refreshing elixir. "Slow down, save some for your sandwich," Marsha, the oldest and the keeper of all things that related to the kids, said to him.

"Go ahead, eat on the back porch, and make sure that screen door is shut. I am sick of those damned mosquitos," Grace insisted. It was more of a dismissive command than a suggestion. "I have work to do," she said. The kids knew all too well the work she did.

"The book. The book," They whispered amongst themselves as they grabbed their sandwiches and went out to the back porch to eat their lunch.

Grace skipped lunch herself. The small pour of whiskey had gone straight to her head, and she didn't want to kill the buzz with food. She loved a slight high as she typed at the old Remington. The words would fly from deep inside her brain and miraculously land on the typed page. She was a fast typist. In her high school class, she was crowned the fastest, a skill that served her well.

The kitchen table was strewn with countless notes and pads. With a yellow number two pencil in her mouth and dressed in one of George's white shirts, she banged away at the keys. She would tell her story without any awareness of her surroundings. Discarded handwritten pages were thrown with haphazard motion onto the floor, eventually covering the cracked linoleum. It had created a patchwork quilt of thoughts, memories, and an occasional fantasy.

Pleased with her writing and the direction of her first book, she would laugh out loud and even cry as she typed away; it was her baby's gestation period. During those times the kids knew to stay away from her. Disturbing her was like waking a black bear from hibernation, and no one wanted that.

Marsha sat on the old flowered upholstered hassock and ate her sandwich. The duty of watching and entertaining her younger siblings fell on her shoulders most days and evenings during that time. She would make oatmeal in the morning, get them out of the house, and organize their play time with a watchful eye. She made sure they didn't get washed downstream in the gentle current of the river. Her greatest wish that summer was that her mother would finish the book before school started in September. The last thing she wanted to do was to be in a new school and to have to worry about her siblings.

Grace was pleased with the progress. Her novel had swelled to over 500 pages, taking on a life of **its own**. The stories she wrote were about things she knew: life, love, family, and secrets that no one spoke about but undoubtedly knew. Her words were flawless in her mind; a creation of picture-perfect New England, a place only imagined by the outsiders as they drove by on a Sunday afternoon.

The world she created in her book was an idyllic life. Her main character, blonde, beautiful, and young, was a drastic contrast to herself. Now, almost thirty and slightly overweight for her height, Grace inherited the French-Canadian genes of her mother. This, combined with a poor diet, created her less than ideal physique. Luckily, a shape her Gee Gee had adored.

George would come home after a long and grueling bike ride from the state school. He peddled in a trance-like state as he climbed the hills of state route 106. He tucked his head down as he soared down the other side and around the bends. Each day, without realizing it, he got stronger. He was a man fit for his age and enjoyed the exercise. He too hoped Grace would finish the book. It had been months since they had made love. He missed the feel of her large breasts and the soft cushion of her ass as they fucked. He pedaled slightly faster in anticipation of good news on his arrival to *It'll Do*.

Each night after work was the same. Leaning his bike against the front steps, he entered the house only to be disappointed again. The condition of the interior was as disheveled as the outside was overgrown. Dishes piled high in the sink, dirty and crusted with days old oatmeal. Clothes in a heap on the floor, dirty, and never washed; dinner never ready to be eaten. He was living a nightmare, and now he desperately wanted to awaken from it.

Friday evening, on his arrival, he opened the front screen door and watched his love. She didn't notice him standing there sweating to death in the heat and puffing like the big bad wolf after his ride. He watched her for a few moments, as she typed fast and furiously, never looking up. She was creating another world on paper, one key stroke at a time. Cautiously, he walked over to her and placed his hand on her shoulder, bending down to kiss her neck moist from perspiration and the deadly humidity.

"What's for suppa?" He gently asked. She never broke stride from the machine, never looked up; her trance never wavered.

"Marsha is making beans and warmed over potatoes." she answered him without the slightest concern to him and what his needs might be. George knew it was tinned food again, and his disappointment would go unnoticed. He was hungry, and the kids were hungry; it's best to just eat what Marsha had started. Maybe he would fry an egg or two, then it would be a real meal.

He really supported Grace during this time, never minding the lack of water, the heat or even her lack of homemaking. Even using the outhouse seemed routine. His children needed their mother that summer. Despite it all, they had gotten used to the fact that she was always preoccupied, always at the table, always writing.

George helped Marsha use a wet cloth to wipe the plates clean, with water brought up from the river in an old galvanized pail they found under the sink. It worked perfectly. The family ate together in the front room quietly staring at the Motorola television, watching the evening news from Boston. The hand-me-down T.V. was from Laurette; she had upgraded to a better model, ironically, at the same time she found a new boyfriend at the Franco-American club back in Manchester.

The reception was always questionable because of the makeshift antenna of wire coat hangers he had fashioned on the roof's eave. The slightest stir of the air would cause the screen to become fuzzy, and the figures distorted. In contrast, the sound was always clear and always audible.

"Gracie, are you sure you don't want something to eat?" George asked her from the sofa. All three kids looked up in her direction, awaiting a response. They'd never seen her this involved, this focused. "Nope," her one word answer without looking up. They looked at each other, then back at the television. The weather would soon be on and predict their activities for the weekend. They knew a trip to Silver Lake was in order. The lake served as a place where the family could secretly swim with a bar of Ivory Snow soap, bathing for the first time in a week. It was another adventure for them and a much-needed relief from the sweltering heat.

"Oh my God, George!, Oh my God!" Grace screamed from the kitchen table. She jumped away from the typewriter, bumping her head on the overhead light, a simple white milk glass globe covering a single incandescent light bulb, something you would find in a workshop but not a kitchen. Standing there rubbing her head she was electrified, beaming as bright as the light. The slightest of tears formed in her eyes.

"What Grace? What is it, are you all right?" George asked.

He jumped off the sofa and rushed to his wife. The kids barely moved as they have witnessed her reactions before when writing overtook her.

"It's done, My baby is finished." She began to cry, weeping for all the things it represented and all the things it could be.

Standing behind her and wrapping his arms around her shoulder, they looked down to the pile of neatly stacked pages, crisp, white, and oddly clear of the chaos that surrounded them.

Almost 600 pages of double-spaced typed words, piled high. "Grace, you did it. Look at it! How wonderful!" George whispered in her ear. The two of them were like proud parents standing over a newborn. The top sheet of the stack had two simple lines typed in the center.

The Tree and the Blossom, by Grace Metalious." They read it together in unison, then kissed passionately in the center of the kitchen.

"Just like the old days," he thought. The children clapped loudly and chuckled to each other. They all were so happy for her and happier that things might return to some normalcy in their lives. George had a fleeting thought, "This was the new normal, and it's only the beginning."

CHAPTER 12

In New England, locals measure distances in many ways. Some look at the length of a shadow cast by the early rising sun. Others, with a watchful eye, look to the birds and measure the time it takes for them to fly across the sky. One fail safe test to determine the speed of an approaching storm is by the sudden flash of lightning and the length of time between the flash and clap of thunder that follows. Counting the seconds softly to oneself can gain precious time before the deluge that inevitably would follow. Summertime's storms can creep up fast with little to no warning. The loud clap of thunder on a hot August night is a welcomed sign that cooling rains are approaching, and the heat of the day may finally end.

Across the way, no more than three miles as the crow flies, the townsmen had not realized that the sun had sunk behind the hills. There was no notice that dusk had crept across the sky casting a dark and foreboding feel to the hot August night. The storm clouds that had rolled in across the horizon created an eerie silhouette of the impending storm, back lit by the fading pink haze of a hot summer day.

There, deep in the cool bowels of the old Tilton farmhouse, men were trying to beat the heatwave that had gripped the town for weeks. The men could hold up for days, far out of sight, away from the watchful eyes of the prying residents. In the shadows of the stone cellar, they indulged in behavior not befitting to most. Respectable in the daylight, these men would show their true colors handed down from a generation before.

Gilmanton, like most towns in the north, had to take care of its own, either through invention or necessity. Fending for itself was what the town did. One tradition, no doubt a left over from prohibition, was the making and drinking of home brew: a concoction of corn, barley and yeast that was mixed into a mash in a makeshift still of tubing and metal pots with lids. This recipe was handed down from father to son, for years. It was never written down; like in old cultures, it became part of an oral history. When the brew was ready, it was syphoned off into empty bottles collected over the years, filled, capped, and stored deep in a cool cellar. Cellars, with dirt floors and stone walls, created the perfect temperature despite the summertime heat. There, the elixir of the past, quietly and secretly, rested in neat rows waiting patiently to be opened.

"Come on, John, give me another fucking drink," one of the men demanded.

"Hold your fucking horses," the other man yelled as he tried with all his best abilities to open the pint bottle of brew.

It was day four; this annual men's pilgrimage into the purple haze of alcohol and filth was coming to an end. They had drunk almost the entire supply of the concoction. The stench from the cellar was overwhelming and toxic. The heat of August seeped in through the cracks of the casement windows causing the urine, vomit, and other bodily fluids to rise in a giant cloud of odor, causing even the most drunk of them to take notice.

The mill where most of them worked had been closed for almost two weeks. The annual shut down was coming to an end. Soon the men would be heading back into the small woolen mill down by the river. Drought that came with the heat rendered the mills off limits and unbearable to work in. When the rains would return, this would breathe life back into the mills, making them useful and profitable once again.

Summer heat drove these men underground where drinking was the main activity, only second to more drinking. Makeshift cots with, soiled blankets, empty tins of crackers and crumbs of stale bread were the only evidence of the past few days. There, they would lay in their own remnants of their tragic tales of heroism and unachieved dreams that passed them by.

"Those fucking Nazis," Henry's words were muddled and distorted as he told his story one more time. "I was there, I helped liberate Paris from those fucking bastards," he continued, banging his empty Mason jar on the old workbench.

"Hold it still, you old ass," John demanded as the cap from the bottle was finally released, flying across the darkened space. He slowly poured the liquid into the empty jar.

Henry was by far the loudest of the assortment of men gathered. His stories would go on and on. Each time the war got longer, his deeds more gallant and more important. Everyone in the cellar had heard them over and over. By day four, all their tales had grown in comparison to Henry's. The deer they bagged last season got bigger, and the lake trout that had been caught by Joe were record breaking. Drunk men measured everything in length and girth and importance, not unlike the manhood between their legs which at that point was as useless as the tales they told.

The gathering of men, now ready to be freed from the stone encasement, was an assorted one. Henry, barely fifty, looked more like a man in his seventies. His graying hair, ruddy face and pot belly aged him. As the town janitor, he kept the school and town hall spotless, taking his duties very seriously which seemed to be a contradiction to the way he looked that night. John Tilton, the host of this event, was a mill worker and chief bottler of the brew. He was a tall man with dark black hair and piercing blue eyes. Black Irish was his claim, a product of Vikings mixed with Moors.

There was a groan from the old army cot back in the shadows, made by the light of the kerosene lantern. Joe, an out of work woodsman, dressed only in overalls, was face down. He was barely able to raise his glass jar for one last drink as John was pouring. The feeble attempt to ask for more went unnoticed; John turned and poured the last of the brew into Guy's coffee mug. Guy was the local highwayman. When he wasn't filling potholes, he was trimming the grass along the roads. A slight man, smaller than most, with sensitive, girl-like features. There was hardly a shadow from his beard, even after these past days. He was considered a momma's boy all his life, and he preferred the solitude of the highway truck.

"Thanks, is that the last of it?" Guy asked in John's direction.

"Nope, there is one more pint from the last batch; it should be ready," he replied. He sat back down on the stool next to the wood box. "Fuck it's hot."

"Yepa, hotter than hell!" Henry's words were thrown away like a line in a play as he raised his jar for a long drink.

The unmeasurable clap of thunder took this motley crew by surprise. It was loud and vengeful, shaking the old wooden farmhouse to its foundation. All the men looked startled as if they had never heard thunder before. Without missing a beat, the bright light of the lightning lit the sky above the farmhouse to near daylight, illuminating the cellar windows in bright flashes, the thunder rolled in without a second in between.

"Woo hoo," came the shouts of encouragement from the men. The rain would start, and the summer drought, with any luck, would end. Another lightning flash and louder clap of thunder immediately followed, this time louder and angrier, causing Joe to stir and sit up from his slumber on the cot.

"What the fuck was that?" he asked, slurring his words.

"Come over here, let's play another hand," answered John. Four of them made their way around the wood box and began to play cards again. After endless days of drinking and card playing the men knew it had finally run its course. Soon it would be time to exit this den of drudgery. The light of the kerosene lantern that sat in the center of the wood box, and only a single bare light bulb, hanging over the workbench, caused the cards to be in shadows, making the game just a little more difficult.

"Hit me," Henry said. "Again."

The cards were dealt for another hand as they drank, listening to the rain outside coming down in buckets. The thunder and lightning continued and showed no sign of stopping. The fierce storm would keep them buried deep in the cellar, secluded from Mother Nature's wrath and the discerning eyes of the town.

"All this rain is making me want to piss again!" Not waiting for a reply from anyone, Joe struggled to his feet and walked to the corner of the cellar. The floor was dirt, mostly sand and now damp with the encroaching rain. Dragging his foot to make a trench of sorts, he relieved himself without any care, using his right hand outstretched resting against the stone wall to steady himself.

The card game continued; with nothing left to bet, they played for fun, each one trying their best to have a higher hand. Conversation has been exhausted; no more tales to tell, trying to impress each other. Each savored the last of the brew and listened to the rain.

"You know we have a new principle starting." Henry said with some sort of clarity. "Yeah, this Greek guy from Manchester, has been working at the State School all summer," he added.

The men don't look up and only paused for a moment, each thinking, "Who the fuck cares?" Henry had been giving the office at the school a fresh coat of paint last week. He had heard all about this flatlander guy living over in Belmont at the Boudreaux shack on the river.

The school in town was small. The two-story wooden structure was right on the town green and had seen many a kid pass through those classrooms. Henry liked working at the school. The young girls were always something to look at, but after what the town had gone through with Sylvester Roberts, Henry dared never look again for fear of his own life.

The school was also a great source of gossip. It seems those in the know were either at the school or the Town Hall. Henry always swept the floors a little slower as he passed others speaking in a matter-of-fact tone in the hallways.

Like the store across the Green, the Town Hall was the place you went to conduct business. You could pay your taxes, vote, and even see a touring company perform a play or opera in the wooden bead-board paneled auditorium. It was also where the school board met, and where neighbors went to report things they observed that did not sit well with them. Since the Roberts' incident, there was an increased rash of observations and neighborly concerns.

The town librarian, Miss Rowell, told Henry all about the young family, the newest residents in the area. Seems the town could only afford a brand new teacher, one with little to no experience to be their principal. Most folks assumed, along with Henry, that Mrs. Dickerson would get the job. After all, she had taught in town for the better part of thirty years. But, in the end, the board thought she was too old. "This guy, George Metalious, will start in September.

"Did you hear me?" Henry's voice fell on deaf ears; the guys each in their own world. Henry's stories of school gossip were as uninteresting to them as what was playing in Laconia at the movie house.

"Who cares?" Joe said as he reached behind to the work bench for the last bottle of brew. He took the cap off with ease, topped off the makeshift glasses, and sat back down.

"They say the new guy's wife is writing a book," he continued. "Been all over town watching us, even been seen on the green writing in a notepad," adds Henry.

"Who?" Blurted Guy. For the first time someone in the group was interested. "His wife, her name is Grace, that's who," answered Henry.

All of them looked up to Henry, and, despite the drunken stupor they were in, they were now starting to listen to the story. They had all heard him now; "a book," they thought in unison, each secretly wondering what this woman could be writing about.

"What the fuck, Henry? Is this another one of your stories? That isn't funny." John was upset and miffed at him for ruining their time together.

"That's all I know, that's what I heard," holding up both of his hands, but not before downing the last remaining brew in his jar. "No fucking way, it can't be." John looked at the other three, shadows cast on their faces creating evil masks of demons and monsters, each with their own secrets.

The thought of being exposed was the ultimate buzz kill for the unsightly group of drunkards, the end of a glorious binge of drinking and bragging. The men glared into the glow of the kerosene lantern, recalling a time several years before, in the same cellar when Sylvester Roberts was one of the group. He was a fierce drinker and storyteller like no other, who kept up with them for years; joining the Merchant Marines was his excuse for leaving this posse of masculinity. But, not escaping before he told his own stories of manhood, accomplishments, and forbidden desires that were only known within their circle.

When the whole truth all came out, his disappearance, his murder, and what had happened up on the hill years before, the four of them swore never to talk of Sylvester's stories. They didn't want to believe them at the time, but the tales he told were true. The innocent violated, the forbidden fruit eaten, and how the outcome became so tragic.

Thunder hammered away in the dark sky, torrential rain poured down, trying desperately to wash away the sins of the past, but without much success. The men begrudgingly got up and pulled themselves together. Not speaking a word, they gathered their soiled belongings, and left the cellar. The trek to their homes would be a wet and lonely one that night, each wondering if the code of silence they had agreed on had been a wise move.

The welcomed rain continued through the night, and the entire population of northern New Hampshire spread their arms up in a collective effort to capture as much of the nourishing liquid as possible. Rain would return things to normal, to their proper order. The farmers could return to the fields, woodsman to the forest, mill hands to the mill, and the highway man to cutting the grass.

This first storm of the season had dealt a final blow against the all-time high summer heat wave and the drought that imprisoned the town. The streams started to swell and were reaching capacity, dry wells in the area filled back in, and the Tioga River, on day three of the storm, was in fear of flooding.

The entire area was preparing for the worst summertime flood in years, and Gilmanton was bracing for what was to come.

CHAPTER 13

 There is a sense of normalcy during the school year that Grace welcomed with both arms. An order of daily events that assured her that the outcome of her day could be predicted from the start. The windup alarm clock, ticking loudly throughout the night, would always seem to go off too early. The sound of its annoying ringing echoed throughout the small house and begrudgingly was heard by everyone. That had been the signal that started the day, and it was time to get moving. The groaning of her children was ignored, a breakfast of toast and tea hastily made before the screen door slammed behind the entire family as they rushed out to the old Packard.

 Sitting at the kitchen table, Grace watched the children and George as they slowly drove down the dirt road toward town for another day of teaching and learning. It had seemed like just a few weeks ago that George started as principal at the school, when it had been months. The children settled in nicely, and Marsha, for the first time, began to make friends. Grace was pleased that *It'll Do* had become their home, and for all its misgivings it didn't seem as bad as it had when they had first arrived. Alone in the house on school days, she would wait for news from a distant land called New York City.

 Every morning Grace woke with high hopes. She could not wait any longer. She walked to the end of the long dirt drive to the state road. An old, galvanized mailbox was nailed securely to an oak tree. Grace paused before opening it and thought that the mailbox looked lonely there, like a sentinel for any news from the outside world.

Mail was scarce those days, an occasional postcard from her mother or sister, each of them off on another adventure. That day there was nothing, not even a bill. Feeling a little depressed and desperate, she walked back towards the house. Her mood would lift as soon as she had a drink; that always helped.

Waiting for anything, her family, in line at the grocery store, or the news of her book, were things she had hated most. This non-flattering trait was no doubt left over from her childhood, and the entitled attitude she was raised with from her mother, Laurette. Grace was not a patient woman. As she grew older, she wanted what she wanted when she wanted it. At times, the impatient adolescence in her would rear its head in a fit of anger. This was something she was not proud of, and sometimes it got a bit out of control.

Grace reached the house and went straight to the kitchen. Opening the ice box, she took out a bottle of ginger ale and placed it on the table. The Canadian Club, which was safely out of reach of the younger children, was in the top cupboard. She retrieved it and poured about three fingers into a tall slender glass. The cold ginger ale that followed swirled into the whiskey creating her new drink of choice, a highball.

For just a moment she thought about washing the sink full of dirty dishes. Grace knew there was plenty of water in the well, but she also knew that Marsha would be home after school to do them. Chores for children were a good thing.

The car coming up the dirt drive went unnoticed by Grace as she sat at the kitchen table staring at her typewriter, sipping her drink, and wondering where her baby was. When the car door slammed shut, it startled her. She jumped up and placed her glass next to the typewriter. With some caution, she walked out onto the front porch and stopped at the railing. Standing tall, she watched a woman walk around the front of a light blue Plymouth wagon.

"Grace, Grace Metalious?" The slender, tall woman asked. She was dressed in a dark pencil skirt, white blouse, and carried a small handbag. Grace was bewildered as to who it could be; perhaps news from New York, she secretly hoped.

"Yes, you have found her." She replied, standing her ground.

"I'm Laurie Wilkens, I work at the Laconia Evening Citizen newspaper." Pausing briefly as she reached out her hand in the direction of Grace. "I hear you are writing a book. Congratulations!"

"Yes, I am." Grace was caught off guard. "I mean, I did. I wrote a book. It's in New York."

Feeling that she had just struck gold, Laurie smiled at Grace. She was relieved that the rumors she heard were true, and she had taken the chance to come meet the mysterious wife of the new principal in town, one who just happened to have written a book.

"May I?" Laurie asked, gesturing with her hand towards the porch. Grace nodded, and her feeling of caution went out with the wind. "Come up." She motioned to the front steps. "Drink?"

"A little early for me, but you go right ahead." With that answer, Grace went into the house, came back with her drink in hand, and sat down on the porch in an old wooden Adirondack chair. Laurie joined next to her. Their conversation ran the gamut, and no subject was off limits. Within a matter of an hour, the two women forged a connection that was the product of kindred spirits.

It had been like magic, Grace and Laurie laughing and tee heeing like schoolgirls, as they shared stories of their pasts and what they hoped their future would bring. Both strong women, defiant when they needed to be, and tender at the right moment. Each of them a wife, a mother and a writer. Both women had been transplanted to northern New Hampshire and dreamt of places that were more cultured and cosmopolitan.

From the get-go, nothing was held back, no topic too taboo. They spoke about their kids, their husbands, and their dreams, each professing the desire to be a famous writer. No stone was left unturned as they spent the better part of the morning sitting on the porch without leaving the grittiest details out. Grace thought she'd finally found a friend, what she longed for for many years. And she was a woman, something she feared would never happen. She didn't like many women she met, and for the first time she could relate to Laurie Wilkens; a connection was forged.

"Let me do a story about you?" Laurie asked.

"Really? I'm not sure what it would be about," Grace answered.

"It'll be about you, housewife turned author," Laurie replied. "It will be fun!"

A sudden look of puzzlement came across Grace's face. Laurie was concerned, had she gone too fast, should she have eased her into the idea? Like Grace, she was impatient and, at times, could not wait.

Grace stood up; she was more concerned with another approaching car coming down the drive than the question that Laurie just asked of her. Both women on the porch watched as the car approached the house. It was a driver with a special delivery. A letter was postmarked from New York, addressed to Grace. The car turned around and left as quickly as it arrived.

Sitting back down, Grace held the letter in her hands. What a coincidence it would be to make a new friend and perhaps get good news. Opening the letter cautiously, Grace began to read it to herself. Her eyes filled with tears and overflowed down her cheeks in full view of her new friend. It was not good news; it was another rejection letter from another publishing house. She quietly sobbed and used the sleeve of the flannel she wore to dry her eyes.

Laurie, feeling like a fish out of water, had no idea what to do. Like any friend, she got up to go fetch Grace a drink from inside of the house. It was the first time she'd been inside and was shocked with the condition of the tiny house. Laundry in piles on the floor, stacked papers, and a sink full of dishes were unsettling to her. She managed to find the bottle of whiskey, poured Grace another drink, and returned to the porch.

"Special Delivery!" She said with drink in hand and outstretched in Grace's direction. "Just for you."

Grace took the drink and stood up. "Fuck them, fuck them all." With that Grace downed the drink and went back into the house, returned in a few seconds, manuscript in hand. "Do you want to read it?" Presenting it to her new best friend, she sat back down.

"Wow." Laurie's answer was short and all telling. The 634 pages looked heavy and would need both her hands. She took if from Grace without hesitation.

For the next few days Laurie immersed herself into a world Grace had created, reading the manuscript every chance she had. It was a fascinating story. What was even more fascinating to her was how a mother of three, with no formal higher education in writing, could create this work. Laurie, a small-time reporter and armchair writer herself, was slightly jealous of Grace's accomplishment. The book had a sentimental quality, often with words that seemed too pretty for the story described from her imagination. It did tell a tale, a rather long one, she had thought.

Laurie wanted to tell Grace truthfully how she felt about the book, not wanting to offend and only wanting Grace to succeed. Laurie became nervous on how she would proceed. She decided to share some of her own stories about life she had experienced since moving to Gilmanton.

Laurie lived in a 200-year-old farmhouse on the other side of town. Like most large properties in New England, it had a name, *Shaky Acres*. It was big, warm, and full of life. A few years earlier she and her husband had relocated from Connecticut to raise their four children on the old farm she inherited from a distant aunt.

After Grace's first visit to *Shaky Acres*, she could not stop talking about the house. She loved the size, the remoteness, but more importantly, the way it made her feel. *Shaky Acres* was the exact opposite of what she had been used to and was a far cry from the modest dwelling of, *It'll Do*. The large farm kitchen, complete with a stone hearth, was her favorite room in the entire house. She and Laurie would sit for hours talking about the book. They would tell stories and would feel completely safe with a sense of solitude that only a real family homestead could offer.

As their friendship grew, so did the visits and frequency of their talks. Grace would always blow her horn as a subtle warning that she was pulling into the driveway. It was just enough time for Laurie to go into the kitchen and open the side door. Grace loved coming and going from the side door; it was just another quirk that made up her personality.

Laurie had heard the horn coming from the driveway. That day it wasn't just a honk, but the old Packard let out a steady wail with no let up. At first Laurie was concerned that something was wrong and decided to fix her a highball, just in case. She was sure Grace had something on her mind.

Opening the door, Laurie presented her with the freshly made cocktail. "Hi, Hon. Here you go," handing off the drink. "What's all the fuss today?"

The look on Grace's face had said it all. The light in Grace's face was second to none. Laurie knew she had news. Without even taking a drink, Grace appeared anxious with an uncontrollable urge to scream.

"Okay, I want you to know I did it, I did all of them." She couldn't get the words out fast enough. "**I added all** those stories you told me into the book!"

Grace was so proud. She had taken Laurie's comments to heart and without getting defensive, had pulled her book apart and, added local color to her story.

"I did research at the town library. That old bitch Rowell, librarian my ass, did not want to help me," she complained to Laurie. "So, I figured out some things, and I made up the rest as I went along." The words flew out of her mouth just fast enough to finish the sentence and take a drink.

Grace wrote about the Roberts killing that happened several years earlier. Many referred to it as the Sheep Pen Murder. The locals in town hadn't talked about it, but Laurie had. This tragedy was now the center of her revised story, the missing element to pull it all together. Under Grace's arm was a Kellogg's Corn Flake cereal box, something Laurie was very curious about. "Want to see it?" Grace asked.

Laurie was so delighted to have helped her friend get over the hump of rejection that she joined her in a mid-afternoon refreshment. Grabbing a beer from the fridge, she sat across from Grace at the farm table.

"Here you go." Grace slid the Corn Flake box in her direction. The top had been removed and inside was a stack of papers. It was the manuscript. How clever to keep it all together in an empty cereal box, New England ingenuity at its finest. Reaching inside to slide out the pages, Laurie couldn't help but notice it was lighter, with fewer pages. The cover sheet title had been changed. *Peyton Place* by Grace Metalious. She read it aloud. "I like it," That was all she said.

The book had been completely reworked to be about the story of a small New England town, located in the foothills of the mountains, along a river where everything seemed to be picture perfect. *Peyton Place* was in New Hampshire, set far away from where Grace was, along the border of Vermont. There was no reference to where she actually was living. It was truly a work of fiction, with names and places changed to protect the guilty.

"You did it, Grace." Laurie laughed, raising her half full glass of beer. Grace reached for the bottle of whisky to pour another. "What no ginger ale?" she questioned "No matter, today I'll drink it straight,"and added "I have more news."

Never breaking eye contact with Laurie, Grace took an envelope from her jacket pocket, holding it steady for her to read. The return address was New York again, but this time it was from Jacques Chambrun, Literary Agent.

Laurie grabbed the letter in a fit of eagerness, opened it, and began to read it. The letter contained good news, very good news. This literary agent presented her manuscript to Julian Messner Publishers, and they liked it. They wanted to meet next week in New York City at the Plaza Hotel to discuss the possibility of publishing her novel.

"Oh Grace, this is big, really big," were Laurie's words. "How did you find this guy?" She asked.

Grace explained that while in Gilmanton's town library, she had found a list of New York agents. The list was long, and she had picked Jacques Chambrun because it was a French name, and she was French. At one time he represented Somerset Maugham, one of her favorite authors. She thought it was another case of kismet. She wrote a five-page letter to go along with a copy of her revised manuscript with the added stories. Off to New York it went.

Chambrun apparently showed it to his contacts, but no one would touch it. The novel was too racy, too explicit and she was an unknown author. The word in publishing circles was: untouchable. Murder, incest, and scandal would never make it to the best sellers list. The novel went nowhere until it landed on the desk of Kathryn Messner, the widow of famed publisher Julian Messner.

Kathryn was one of few women in publishing in New York. A fiercely independent thinker, she ran her house with tight authority and celebrated women writers when she could. She believed this young author from New Hampshire might just be onto something.

"I'm so proud of you Grace. You did it. You are on your way." Laurie was showing true feelings of friendship and support for her new friend. Grace sat across from her at the kitchen table, sipping her drink, and thinking, "It's really happening."

CHAPTER 14

Autumn air chilled the city, not cold enough for a hat, but just enough to break out a new wool coat bought just for the occasion. New York City in October seemed magical to Grace. The air was crisp and fresh, and the hustle and bustle never ending. It had been her first time so far away from her home in New Hampshire. The city was just as she imagined it to be. Tall buildings, people dressed so fine, and everyone looking like they had someplace to be. "Why are they walking so fast? No one in Gilmanton ever walked that fast unless it was to a fire or to listen to some sordid gossip over the clothesline," she chuckled a little. She stood there, waiting patiently for the light to change, crossing Lexington Avenue could be a tricky and painful maneuver in her new shoes.

The journey to New York was seamless. First the bus went down to Concord, then the old Boston & Maine service took her down to Massachusetts, switching trains in New Haven. She traveled like a pro, never letting on to anyone that she was scared shitless.

It had taken her most of the day, but she made it in one piece, only a little worse for the wear. The adrenaline pumped through her body, keeping up with her pounding heart, acting like one of those vitamin shots she had read about in the back of the Photoplay magazine that she'd found on the train. She was on schedule to New York. Grace knew this would be the start of something big and life changing. A smile came across her face.

Grace held the hand-written note in her hand, trying to memorize the address. She repeated it over and over to herself. A yellow cab pulled up to her on the corner. She opened the back door and climbed in, "so much room," she thought to herself.

"Where to, Miss?" The driver asked, in the thickest accent she had only heard in the movies. "Well, it's says 52nd and Third," she replied, not even close to the confidence she was going for. "Here," she replied, and handed him the note now crumpled and a little moist from the sweat in her hands.

"Oh, the publisher's building, got it." He turned back and shifted the car into gear. The cab glided out into the traffic. Like a school of fish, the cars were in harmony with each other, never colliding, and never stopping, an occasional horn blast added to the excitement of the day.

Her new agent, Jacques, was to meet her at his office before the meeting at the Plaza. Sitting in the back of the cab, her heart still racing, she wondered what he was like, what would he think of her. He liked the book well enough to send for her. Would this Kathryn Messner like it as well?

She stood outside the building as her cab pulled away and looked up. It was gray, tall, and just a bit menacing in her mind. She entered through the revolving door, which glided and made a swish sound, nothing like the one at O'Shea's Department Store back in Laconia. The directory was mounted on the wall behind a granite desk. Grace felt flushed and looked for her agent's last name. During the elevator ride to the 13th floor, she adjusted herself; the girdle she decided to wear was hot and itchy. She unbuttoned her coat and straightened her ponytail. She longed to fix her lipstick, the only makeup she ever wore, but there was no time for that. The elevator door dinged and opened into an office reception area.

"Grace Metalious, Grace from *Peyton Place*." It wasn't a question, but more of an announcement to her arrival. She stood next to the desk as a gentleman reached out his hand and smiled. "Welcome." Her breath was almost taken away as she looked upon this tall, slender, man dressed in the smartest blue pinstripe suit. He smiled as wide as the Merrimack River. The slightest French accent was detected, and she knew it was her agent.

"Mr. Chambrun?" she gushed, feeling like she was meeting a movie star or something.

"Call me Jacques," he retorted, grabbing her hand and guiding her down the hall in the direction of his office. Resting his hand ever so gently on her hip, he took her small carpet bag and tossed it next to the reception desk.

"How was the train ride down?" He asked. Smiling like the Ringmaster in a circus, he never gave her time to answer. Jacques was talking like a mad man, fast, like a salesman. It was all overwhelming for Grace, giving her second thoughts.

They stopped in front of a room with a large wooden table, a conference room no doubt. Grace wondered how many other writers had sat at that table.

"Drink?" He asked. "Fuck yeah. Oops." Almost embarrassed that it hadn't been two minutes, and Grace dropped the F bomb.

"No worries. We are going to be great friends, Grace." He turned to the credenza, his back to her. "Scotch?" He asked, never looking back for a nod or a reply. Pouring three fingers into two glasses, he offered her one. That smile, captivating and scary all at the same time.

Making a gesture for her to sit at the enormous table, he pulled out a chair for her. "I got news, my dear," and away he went, talking excessively and never coming up for air. He told Grace things about her book, his plans for it, the clients he had made famous, and then more about her book. Like a machine he rattled off a pitch worthy of any investment banker who wanted to invest in a skyscraper. He made it quite clear that after numerous attempts to sell it, he had finally presented it to Kathryn Messner, the head of a small publishing house. The publisher liked it, almost loved it. There would have to be some changes. Getting it past the censors might be problematic, but not to worry, it could all be done here in New York, his carefully rehearsed words spelled out.

"New York? Changes?" Her trance broken, Grace was filled with confusion and some anxiety. He could tell what Grace was feeling and thought perhaps he went too far too fast.

"Yes, my dear." He slowed his speech and looked at her directly as she took another drink. "Your little book is going to blow the lid off life in your little town. But we don't want to start another war, do we?" He paused. "Some changes are needed."

"Mr. Chambrun, Jacques, I'm not from *Peyton Place*. It's a fictional town, it's not real. I live in New Hampshire. I have kids, a family. I can't work here." She was trying her best to lay her cards out for him.

"Details, details," he replied. "Come on, we are having drinks at The Plaza with Kathryn and her editor Leona Nevler. Do you want to change into something?" He was looking over to her, sitting there; she was wearing a simple white blouse and blue jeans.

"What do you mean? These are clean." Placing the empty glass on the table, she was a little taken aback with his question and looked down at her outfit. Her coat was new from O'Sheas, as were her shoes. It had to be her jeans. She always wore blue jeans; it was her calling card. Little did she know, blue jeans were considered for trades people, not women and especially not aspiring writers; it just wasn't done. A feeling of insecurity blanketed her emotions, and she knew instantly that she was never going to fit in, no matter what she was wearing.

Arriving at The Plaza should have been another high moment, but instead she questioned her outfit and secretly wished she had had another drink. Keeping her coat buttoned was an option. She prayed that the heat hadn't been turned on inside yet. Jacques insisted they arrive early. By sitting down first, Grace's choice of attire would be mostly hidden, and no judgements would be formed at this meeting. The man always had a plan, and Grace started to relax just a bit.

The maître d directed them to an oversized booth, large and comfortable, the leather worn and soft. The room glowed with freshly polished oak paneled walls, and the light from the giant chandeliers caused the entire place to glow in a dream-like setting. Within a second a waiter appeared out of nowhere for their drink order. This time Grace thought, CC & Ginger, a proper drink, a highball. They sat and talked in hush tones. Jacques, aware of his error, quickly back pedaled to ease her mind and reassure her of her talents.

Kathryn Messner arrived with her editor about twenty minutes late, just long enough for the whiskey to do its magic, warming Grace and calming her nerves. She was ready for anything. Kathryn didn't wait to be escorted to their booth. She spotted Jacques and walked directly towards him. Her gait was commanding and confident. Dressed in a wide lapel double breasted suit, her hair perfect and carrying a white cigarette holder, she looked more like a movie star than a publisher. She was a cross between Kathryn Hepburn and Joan Crawford, a woman in a male dominated world.

"You must be Grace," she announced, as she approached the table. "Don't get up!" A look of ease came across Jacque's face; a bullet dodged.

She slid into the booth with ease, sitting directly across from Grace in the half moon shaped booth. "This is Leona Nevler, one of my editors." Kathryn introduced her as the waiter pulled up a chair for Leona to sit in. No words were spoken between Jacques and Kathryn, just a small kiss on the cheek as he leaned over to her. Leona extended her hand to

Grace. Not wanting to shake it because she wasn't wearing gloves, Grace merely smiled and nodded to the editor.

"I simply must have this book," she demanded. The author and the agent just smiled at each other, not saying a word, holding their breath waiting for the publisher to break the silence. "I have read it, and it's a work of genius. Don't you think so, Leona?" Her announcement and question were all in the same breath.

"I found it a fun read," was Leona's only comment. Already, Grace had formed an opinion that she did not like Leona, the editor. She already knew that they were going to butt heads. Kathryn, on the other hand, was charming, smart, and beautiful.

The waiter showed up with more drinks, and food was ordered. For the first time Grace was going to try Oysters Rockefeller. A wedge was ordered and other things that suited an early dinner in New York.

Grace sat there, still a bit unsure of what was happening. They all talked so fast, and Grace was shrinking back into her shell. Her drink couldn't come quickly enough, she thought. Taking the drink from the waiter, she noticed Kathryn's eyes watching her every move. Grace did not like these feelings and was afraid to eat for fear of using the wrong fork. Her food was delivered and not touched.

The conversation turned to Jacques, and some sort of negotiating commenced. He spoke of terms, conditions, and timeframes. This was all a blur to Grace as she sipped her whiskey. She felt over her head and deferred to her new agent Jacques to sort it all out.

"How does a $1,500 advance sound?" asked Kathryn. Grace brought her focus back to the table. She looked at the publisher who was staring back at her waiting for an answer. "What? I'm sorry. Yes, $1,500 sounds great," Grace replied, a little unsure but not wanting anyone to know it.

"I will get the check, and off to my office we go." With that she was up and almost across the floor of the restaurant before Jacques caught up with her. Leona was left sorting out Grace and getting her outside. Kathryn's chauffeured black sedan was double parked in the front. When the uniformed driver opened the door for Grace, she felt she had died and gone to heaven.

Sinking silently into the back seat, soft, warm and quiet, Grace reflected on what had just happened? A bus ride, hours on the train, a taxi ride, a whirlwind meeting, and a liquid dinner had her wondering what was next?

A contract signing and $1,500 dollars, more money than she had ever seen in her life. It was all falling into place; something she had only dreamed of. She could not wait to get back to her Gee Gee and the kids. No more lettuce and tomato sandwiches, new school clothes, and a car for George. His bike would be tossed in the river down behind *It'll Do*.

The offices of the late Julian Messner Publishing, Inc., were on 5th Avenue, near the Saks Fifth Avenue department store. She had heard of the store and dreamed that one day she might go there. But she knew no matter how rich she got, it was O'Shea's in Laconia for her shopping. "No designer labels for this newly published author," she decided. Feeling just a bit of nausea, she rolled down the back seat window for some air.

"Oh dear, we have air con," Kathryn mentioned, not in a condescending manner but more as a-matter-of-fact statement. This was just another reminder for Grace of her lack of sophistication.

"Where are you staying, dear?" Kathryn asked her.

"Not sure, no hotel yet," Grace answered.

"Leona will take you home with her and get you something to eat. I will have my secretary find you a room." There, it was sorted. But not before Grace noticed the eye roll from Leona. She was not going to like this assignment one bit.

CHAPTER 15

Here we are," the driver said without looking over his shoulder.

"Thank you Arthur," Kathryn said, only slightly acknowledging her driver of 14 years. "We won't be long, please wait," she added. "After this, you can take Leona downtown to her apartment." Arthur scurried out of the car and ran around back to open the door. He was a second too late, and Kathryn opened it herself and stepped out.

"Sorry, madam." His hand reached out to hers, but she ignored it. Kathryn was gracious, but the message she sent was loud and clear. The publisher was becoming an icon to women in the literary world. Her discoveries of untested authors were becoming her trademark, a reputation she liked.

"Come along, we need to get started as soon as possible." Kathryn was across the sidewalk before she finished her sentence. Arthur stood there and tipped his hat as the entourage emerged from the back seat. Jacques led the pack, with the rest of them scurrying to catch up with the all-powerful publisher.

"Come on, Grace, looks like we are roomies, at least for tonight, anyways." Leona added and closed her statement with her distinctive eye roll. "The sooner we get the manuscript, the sooner we can get started." Grace was the last one out of the shiny black sedan. She was trying her best not to let the others see her slight limp caused by her new shoes, and she scurried into the building that held the offices of The Messner Publishing Company.

The doorman had noticed Grace's struggling stride and held the side door open for her so she did not have to maneuver the revolving door, and she could catch up to the group of fast walking city folks. The elevator attendant waited for everyone to get in before closing the giant brass doors. Not a word was spoken between the four of them. Glances from Jacques to Grace were like a reassuring uncle indicating that everything was going to be ok. The attendant never asked what floor before it started to climb. The slight feeling of wooziness that Grace felt was either from the drinks at the Plaza or the movement of the elevator, but in her mind, it was the feeling of uncertainty as to what was going to happen next.

The Messner publishing offices were more like a stately home she had only seen in the movies. Dark polished wooden panels overwhelmed the dimly lit entrance which made it feel more like a gentleman's club than an office. The slightest hint of cigarette smoke could be smelled in the reception area along with the lingering perfume from other writers turned authors. Paintings were lit from brass lamps attached to the walls, lightly illuminating them from above. The furnishings were right out of a grand hotel. Big, overstuffed, and dark, too masculine for a female publisher's office.

"Sit there." Kathryn pointed to a grouping of furniture, a small couch and armchairs. "Won't be but a minute." With that, she was gone. She walked past the reception area, down the hall and out of sight. The three sat there in silence, much like the ride from the Plaza. This was Kathryn's show, and they all knew it.

Grace was getting tired. The stress of navigating the trip down from New Hampshire was starting to wear on her. She felt tired and lonely, and she was becoming even more uncertain about this part of the book publishing process as the day grew longer. Leaning back into the overstuffed couch, she tried to relax. Really, all she wanted to do was to kick off the new shoes that had been pinching her for hours and get a highball. Yes, that is exactly what she thought she needed. She closed her eyes for a moment as her head touched the back cushion of the sofa.

"Here we are!" Kathryn's voice startled Grace from her moment of mediation. She shot back to reality like a bullet being fired. Presenting a stack of papers to her and her agent, Kathryn said, "Grace, sign here, here, and here." The documents placed in front of her on the coffee table looked legal and very organized. The pages in need of signatures were clearly marked where she would sign and where Jacques would sign as well. Reaching over for a pen, Grace could not help but notice the check for $1,500 made out to her in plain view next to the stack of documents. Despite it being a cool, autumn day, a small trickle of sweat glided down the side of her neck unnoticed. They waited for Grace to sign, an awkward moment for the aspiring author.

"I'll go first," Jacques piped in. "These look in order as they always do," he said, tipping his head in an approving manner in Kathryn's direction. Jacques retrieved the papers, pulling them closer. He leaned over the small table and signed the documents. "That was easy. Your turn, Grace." Jacques slid over on the small sofa, to give her more room to move closer to the papers. She leaned over, picked up the pen, and cautiously began to sign the first of four pages. "Here, like this?" Grace asked.

"Dear, you're so sweet," said Kathryn. "Just like at the bank when you cash your husband's paycheck," she tells her in a reassuring but condescending manner.

The entire process, from drinks to signing, took less than two hours, but to Grace it seemed like an eternity. The moment the contract was signed the check was presented to her. Leona grabbed her elbow, and with a nudge it was her signal to get going. The ride downtown seemed longer than she imagined it would be. She knew Manhattan was big, but it did not occur to her how big. Leona sat across from her in the back seat of Kathryn's limo. Arthur was driving, paying no mind to the traffic, pedestrians, honking horns. It was business as usual for these two New Yorkers. Grace was Leona's new project, but all she wanted was to slow the process down. So simple, she thought, but in reality it was not possible.

Leona's apartment was a modest building in a neighborhood called SoHo; it was like all the other apartment buildings that surrounded it. Only five stories, it was smaller than the skyscrapers of midtown. It reminded her of Boston. A sense of relaxation finally came over her, and she began to breathe normally again. Grace's bag had been placed on the sidewalk by Arthur directly in front of where she was standing. Looking up at the apartment, she wondered which one was Leona's.

"Come on, girl, I think we are going to be spending a lot of time together." Leona, trying to make the best of the situation, was still carrying the large manila envelope containing Grace's story. It was securely closed with a bright red string twisted around the grommet. She was holding it tightly in her arms, like the baby it represented to Grace. "Perhaps Leona was not all that bad after all," she thought. She bent down to pick up her overnight bag and continued to run behind Leona up the front stone steps to the apartment.

Leona held the door for Grace as she moved past her into the stairwell. "I'm on three. Sorry, no doorman or elevator. Welcome to the real New York," laughing a bit as the large door slowly closed behind them.

They climbed the stairs one ahead of the other; each tried not to let the other know how winded they were becoming as they reached Leona's floor. Both young women had spent more time at desks, exercising their minds and not their bodies.

The key was well worn, but the door opened with ease. The apartment was small with one bedroom, a tiny living space, and a small kitchen so small that Grace wondered how one could cook a meal.

"Grace, you know," Leona said as she placed the manuscript on the tiny kitchenette table, "I was the one who first read *"Peyton Place"* after Simon and Schuster passed on it. I was working there as a temp before presenting it to Kathryn."

Discovering Grace's book had been a windfall for Leona. It was her ticket from a temporary position to an almost permanent one, and with the approval of the publisher, she could ride the coattails for some time.

Leona explained that Kathryn liked her story, so much so that she canceled a dinner party to stay home and read it all night long. She called Leona the next day and insisted on getting the writer from New Hampshire down to New York as soon as possible. One call to Jacques was all it took.

"And here we are. Now I get to edit it for you." Leona finished her story; Grace was still standing there holding her bag and completely speechless. The only words she heard were edit it. "Edit it," rang in her head like the church bells at the Congregational Church back in Gilmanton. She dropped the bag at her feet.

"Drink?" Leona asked. "Highball?" Grace asked with a question. "CC and Ginger will work for you?" Grace nodded and pulled out a chair at the table and sat down. She kicked off her shoes, finally. The drink couldn't come quick enough.

Waiting patiently for her CC and Ginger to arrive, Grace's mind traveled a few hundred miles away. She was back sitting at the table in the middle of her kitchen at *It'll Do*. With her family safely tucked into bed for the night, she was doing what she thought she had done over and over: editing her book. She added stories and even changed the title which also changed the focus of the novel. The writing part always came easy to Grace. Her fingers floated over the typewriter keys, allowing her to tell her stories as fast as she could imagine them. Editing was the difficult part. These were her stories, her ideas, her babies. She loved what her new friend Laurie had helped her with. Adding the Roberts murder, the town gossips, these were all great, but she could not imagine what Leona could contribute to her book.

"Cheers." Leona's one word and a slight smile set Grace at ease as the cool liquid touched her lips and slid down her throat. Refreshing and rejuvenating, the whiskey warmed her insides while cooling her emotions. This would be the start of a love hate relationship between the author and the editor; one they both secretly despised but they knew was a necessity that could not change.

"Another?" She looked down at Grace's empty glass. Grace nodded in the affirmative.

After a few more drinks Grace was on her way to a drunken stupor. Leona was trying her best to get to know her new writer and calm her fears at the same time. This relationship was unlike Grace's friendship with Laurie, the only other writer she knew. That friendship was easy. Two mothers, two writers and two outsiders, both living in a small New England town. Leona was a New Yorker, not a mother that she knew of, and certainly not an outsider. Grace was the outsider, and Leona knew nothing about her world, so how could she edit her story?

"Here, I think it's time we take a look." Leona reached for the manuscript and took the typed pages from the envelope. Pulling out the stack, Grace saw for the first time in a long time, her original baby, her book. The two of them were rejoined. As with most reunions, it should have been a happy occasion, but, not this time, not this night. The manuscript looked a little beaten up, with dog-eared corners and marks in the margins, along with red pencil markings across the pages. Grace put her glass down and stared at it, horrified and shocked at what she saw. She was almost insulted by the way some stranger had treated it.

"Who wrote on this?" Grace demanded. "What are all those marks?" Grace wanted answers. The mixture of all the emotions she felt were now coming to a boil deep inside her.

"Well, honey, I did, I am your editor," answered Leona, trying her best not to roll her eyes.

Grace was over the top mad. She knew that her housekeeping skills were not the best, she was even a messy dresser, and everyone knew she couldn't cook, but her writing was neat and organized, her typing stellar. How dare someone deface her baby like this! She looked at her finished product as though it was ruined.

"You had no right!" Tears that were a product of the whiskey and being over tired began to flow. "How dare you?" Grace yelled at Leona. Emotions and alcohol were at an all-time high and at the point of breaking her. She told Leona, in no-uncertain-terms, she had no right to touch it, or to write on it. The editor's face went white with an expression of disbelief. Leona recognized instantly that Grace had no idea of the processes it took to publish a book.

"Grace, calm down. Listen to yourself," she demanded. "Stop and listen so I can explain." Grace picked up her drink and took a long swig from it. Leona began, "You sold your rights to the book, you signed the contract today," she said in a calm non-demeaning manner. "You wrote the story, but it's up to us to make it marketable, to get it out there to readers." This reasoning was falling on deaf ears, and Leona continued. "We have a lot to do before it goes to print; with a winter release, we don't have much time," she added. "Let us do our job."

Grace did not say a word, did not make eye contact. She grabbed the abused manuscript, shoved it back into the envelope, and got up from the table. She picked up her shoes and crossed the tiny kitchen, retrieved her small bag, opened the apartment door, and stepped out into the hall, barefoot. With tears in her eyes and a headache caused by the drinks, she slammed the door behind her. The slam of the door was her message for the night to her editor.

Grace was tired, crying, and drunk, three of the worst things she could be at that moment. She made her way down the steps to the front stoop and onto the street. Wiping the tears from her eyes, she realized that she had no idea where she was or where she was going. She only knew she would not spend another moment in that apartment with that wicked woman. She stopped long enough to slip her ill-fitting shoes back on. She began to wander, trying her best to walk without drawing attention to herself. She wanted to make her way back to the train station but she had no idea what direction that was. It was late, and there were few people on the street. Her buzz was starting to wear off, giving her a moment of clarity. "Time for a drink," she thought.

A dull neon light dimly lit the alley. She could make out "The Blue Note" directly over a door painted black. Focused on her walking, she made her way down into the alley. It had to be a bar, and a drink was in order. As she reached the neon sign, she straightened herself up, an attempt to pull herself together. As she reached for the door, it was pushed open towards her. She took a step back and stared.

A petite white woman with blonde hair was hanging on the arm of the biggest negro Grace had ever seen. She couldn't recall ever seeing a negro that tall, let alone having a white woman with him. She was a bit taken aback since this was her first encounter with an interracial couple in person. Grace realized perhaps she was over her head in the city. There were no people like that in New Hampshire that she was aware of. That had been a sobering moment for her; she definitely needed that drink.

Grace tucked the manuscript under her arm that carried her suitcase and opened the door with her free hand; the door swung open with ease. The Blue Note was filled with people, music was playing softly, and the air was saturated with smoke.

Making her way past the bar, she found an empty table near the piano player. The music was a bit melodious and downright dull. No more tears tonight. She ordered a drink and a cigarette from the short waiter with a foreign accent. Her highball showed up in record time, and the little man produced a cigarette and lit it for her.

Sitting there looking out into the bar, she could see the cast of characters that would make a book all onto its own. The whiskey was good, but the smoking was new to her; she didn't like it at all, but everyone was doing it, especially the artistic people. One drink led to another, and soon she was fast asleep, face down on the table, her baby securely in her bag between her legs on the floor.

"Come on, lady, time to go. I'll call you a cab." It was not the waiter with the foreign accent but the big bartender pulling her to her feet. The place had emptied out, the music stopped, and Grace was alone in a bar in New York City relying on the kindness of others. "Where to, lady?" The bartender asked again. She was mumbling, and he had no idea what she was saying. Trying not to lose his cool and be as nice as he could, he reached into her coat pocket and found the crumpled note with the address she had written down earlier.

Unfolding the crumpled paper, he read the address and was satisfied. "Up town, eh!" And with that he got her to the door. Using both arms, he guided her out with her bag slung over his shoulder. The cabbie was a regular for these nightly calls. The bartender knew the driver could be trusted to get her to her destination. Grace was gingerly poured into the back seat with her meager belongings safely placed in the front. She stirred and murmured a thank you to the bartender as he slammed the door shut.

The cabbie was not at all fazed by what was happening. He knew a fare would be waiting outside *The Blue Note* after the last call. He didn't expect one so young and innocent looking. The drive up and across town was quick. With no traffic it was a breeze. Pulling up to the Publisher's Building, he put the car in neutral and set the hand brake. Walking around the front to the passenger side, he grabbed the bag from the front seat and tossed it onto the sidewalk. He opened the back door to retrieve his drunken fare. He was surprised to find her half awake and helped her out. Grace's hand found a crumpled dollar bill in her pocket. The cabbie took it and slammed the door shut.

Looking up at the building she visited earlier in the day, she was startled. At night, lights from the city made it look bigger, more menacing, and evil. She started to cry. She was frightened, drunk, and felt very stupid. Mostly stupid for acting the way she did at Leona's and more stupid for not getting a hotel room. At the front door of Jacque's office building she sat down. Feeling homeless and a bit hopeless she curled up on the stoop. Using her overnight bag as a pillow she drifted off to sleep again and hoped morning would be coming soon.

Her last thoughts, as she went to sleep, was that she was thankful the October night was as warm as an Indian Summer in New England.

CHAPTER 16

Rita Rowell sat at the main desk at the Gilmanton Public Library. As a rule, she would never have stayed until it got dark, but the days were growing shorter as the calendar neared the year's end. The library had been closed for a few hours. Rita was sitting there admiring her domain. The library was a wooden building with white clapboards and a hand painted sign. It had no doubt been built with the leftover materials used to create the Georgian Town Hall next to the tiny building. It had been built a century before with fine wooden details from the caring hands of a detailed craftsman. Rita marveled at the time taken and the craftsmanship applied. She secretly hoped she would do justice for the town and the founding fathers by selecting the right books to adorn its shelves. The library might have been tiny but significant to her new town.

Books and architecture were two of her favorite things. She felt extremely lucky to have them both in her life and part of her profession. Her watch showed that it was just past five o'clock. The sun was down behind the distant hills, and the town itself was getting ready to roll up its sidewalks. She got up from the desk and walked to the front door. Earlier she heard the distinct sound of the afternoon paper as it hit the wooden front door with a thud. The Laconia Evening Citizen was the gentle reminder of the outside world creeping into their lives every afternoon.

Opening the library, she looked out into the dulled light of dusk. Searching, she spotted the rolled-up paper and walked across the front steps to retrieve it. The fall air was now chilly, the warm days of Indian summer all but a memory without the sun's rays to warm them. Quickly closing the door behind her, Rita scurried to the media table next to her wooden desk. Preparing the newspaper for the next day was just another ritual that librarians did.

Laying it flat and opening it wide on top of her desk, the newspaper was ready for the wooden split dowel to be inserted from the bottom of the newsprint. It grabbed all the pages with one gentle push. Getting the paper ready to be placed on the rack with all the other dailies that had come during the day was something she took great pride in. The newspaper rack was the most popular feature in the library, and she always made sure the papers would be ready for the next day's opening. Running her delicate fingers down the center fold, she smoothed out the creases to make it easier to read. As she slid the dowel into the spine, she froze; her actions stopped abruptly, and her left hand covered her mouth.

"Local Housewife Writes Novel of Small Town Life." The small, almost unnoticeable headline was in the center section of the right hand page. Rita noticed the by-line and knew it was from Laurie Wilkens, a local contributor from the town. Rita picked up the center page and returned to her chair to read the short article. Rita never liked Laurie Wilkins, her uppity attitude along with her pretentious farm. "A farm with a name like *Shaky Acres*, just another flatlander from away," She scoffed. Rita confided this to a friend once, convincing herself she wasn't one of those, but she was also a flatlander.

Wilken's article wasn't a journalist tour-de-force; Rita felt it was more like a teaser of things to come, written by someone who wanted to be a part of it all. The local columnist announced:

"Local housewife, Grace Metalious, wife of the new school principal, has written a book about small town life. The novel is currently in New York City being reviewed by the editorial team of Julian Messner Publishing Company, preparing it for a winter release. "

Rita folded the center page, slowly tore it from the paper, and placed it into her black handbag that was sitting next to her blotter. Returning to the rack, the dowel slid in the remaining pages with ease. The afternoon edition of the Laconia Evening Citizen was now ready, censorship at its basic level.

"No one will even notice," she thought. She dropped the edited version into the rack, grabbed her purse, and headed for the front door. Her wool sweater hung on the bentwood coatrack next to the entrance; she draped it over her shoulders and left. The single light over the front door cast a comforting glow in the now darkened Library. The sound of the key was never heard as she locked the wooden door.

The evening newspaper was never delivered down the long dirt drive to *It'll Do*. If fact, the Metalious family often forgot the papers for several days as they sat in the old, galvanized metal tube attached below the mailbox at the end of the drive. Sometimes papers would be days old before one of the children was asked to run and fetch them before they started to overflow onto the ground. Grace never read the news. She thought if you didn't hear it from someone, then how could it be true? George liked the paper, and with his new job he needed to be more on top of things outside their little hamlet.

"George, let's celebrate," Grace whined slightly. "Come on, let's go get a drink down at Christmas Island." It wasn't a question; it was a plea. Grace needed to show the world their life was changing.

"Gracie, I'll make you another drink here," George suggested.

"No. What the fuck, George! Things are going our way so let's party." She was beginning to get angry.

"Okay, sure. Grab a sweater." Her Gee Gee forced a smile.

Grace was pleased, and her mood softened a little. Her husband knew the pressure she felt in New York, and when he retrieved her from the train station a week ago, his poor Gracie was a bundle of nerves. She was depressed, tired, and insecure. Her time in New York had taken its toll on her, and she was just beginning to feel better.

Their ride down the state highway was dark. It was a brisk and cloudless night. Grace slid next to her Gee Gee and snuggled as she used to before all her publishing business started. She looked up at George as he drove in silence. Her face started to feel warm from the car heater. She was the luckiest girl in town.

Friday night at Christmas Island would be fun. The local club was positioned on a granite outcropping on the shore of Lake Winnipesaukee. Surrounded by balsam fir trees, the setting created a year-round feeling of Christmas and provided an appropriate name to the bar. It was not really an island, but it looked like one and that was good enough. The club was a special place for Grace, far away from the town green and the prying eyes of her neighbors.

Grace was in the mood to have a drink or two. Things were finally going their way; and she and George could let their hair down to celebrate. George had started his new job as the principal at the school. He'd all but forgotten the long bike rides to work each day, and Grace was happy. *It'll do* was now only temporary housing until they could move. Being the principal's wife turned author was her new lot in life. She giggled a bit to herself.

Grace took the book advance check that they had presented to her in New York and tucked it away in their checking account at the Laconia National Bank. Not one threatening letter came that week from the credit union about the personal loan they had taken on the car the year before. There were no late notices from the Public Service Company threatening to turn off their power. For the first time, the children went to school with proper, new clothes. Things were looking up for Grace and George.

Her advance check and a copy of the contract was all Grace needed to purchase a house, a real house. The Mudgett Place was a short distance from *It'll Do*. It was a modest Cape Cod style home. The house came with a torrid past on fourteen acres. It seemed a famous Chicago gangster got his humble start in Gilmanton at that same address. The back story added extra intrigue to the purchase. Grace felt she would be in good company there, in her new home, her first to call her very own.

George pulled the Packard into the lot at Christmas Island and turned to Grace with a twinkle in his eyes, "Come on Gracie, I'll let you buy the first one."

"You're on!" She laughed as she slid out of the driver's side behind George and grabbed his hand like a schoolgirl. Whiskey was going to taste really good tonight, she thought.

Rita's mouth was dry and sour caused by breathing too heavily as she made her way quickly across the town green and home to Webster Street. She was on a mission. Grace's book would be out soon. No one knew what to expect, but she was convinced that no one in town wanted it to be published.

Rita was upset, mostly upset with herself for letting that Grace woman into the library. She knew she couldn't keep people away, but she didn't have to make it pleasant. "Family ancestry, my ass," escaped her lips as the front door to her house opened. Rita felt the weight of responsibility because she helped this woman writer maneuver around the library, and she cast the deciding vote to hire her husband. She couldn't do anything about the book, but the new principal still came under her domain.

She stood in her front room looking out the large picture window onto the front lawn; everything seemed peaceful and green. The light of the day was gone, and the streetlamp lit her dooryard in a dull, incandescent glow. She was thinking about the phone call she would be making and wanted desperately to prepare herself for it. She paused before picking up the receiver. The black desk phone sat next to an old Chesterfield chair which had been with her for many years. The overstuffed arm acted like some subliminal podium for all the phone calls of concern Rita had made over the years.

Dialing the number with her extended finger, tapping her others, she was annoyed that the rotary dial was taking too long to turn around. The number completed, ringing heard, she put the receiver to her ear. When the phone was answered, she didn't wait for a greeting. "Muriel? Rita," she blurted out.

"Yes, Rita. I know what you are going to say, I saw the paper tonight!" The voice on the other end exclaimed. "What are we going to do about it?" Rita asks.

Their agitated conversation started; with a sense of panic and disgust they interrupted and talked over each other. They speculated about the book, shared doubts about the frumpy author, the disappointment in their new, handsome, and fit principal hired a few months before. "I don't want to say I told you so," Muriel started.

"Then don't," quipped Rita. Both were members of the school board that had been split on the decision to hire George. Rita had won her vote, and now wished she had not. Some of the member's objections were that he did not come from the town, and that he was almost a foreigner, a Greek. His parents were still speaking that language and living in the south of Manchester. Their case was heard, but in the end George was offered the contract.

"I feel like this whole thing is blowing up in our faces." Rita's voice now tired and spent. "We need to put a plan of action in place."

"I agree," Muriel added. With that they hung up. Rita went to her kitchen to find something to eat. She hated eating supper so late, it had been one of those nights.

The interior of the bar at Christmas Island was a mixture of traditional captain's chairs, wooden and thick with matching high-top tables. The lighting was dim and romantic with a hint of Christmas décor along the walls to give legitimacy to its name. The music that Friday night was from a brightly lit Wurlitzer box in the corner. Grace and George were nestled together in the corner next to the dance floor, each sipping their CC and Gingers. Grace was ahead of her husband by two. Her words slurred slightly, and her vision began to blur.

"Gracie, slow down. What's the rush?" George asked. "You're drinking so fast." The concerned look in his eyes was shadowed in love for his Gracie. He knew what happened in New York, and he wanted nothing but to show her support.

"Why am I drinking so fast?" Grace garbled her rebuttal. "Because I can! Because, who the fuck cares?" Grace paused and looked directly at her Gee Gee, waiting for a reply.

George knew better than to respond. On nights like this, drinking was her way of coping. The highball of earlier days was now a series of drinks, with no let up until the bottle was finished. This outing was one of those times.

"What if no one likes it? What if no one buys it?" Grace asked sadly. Her insecurities at an all-time high. Her defenses were low and unmanageable. "It's my baby," she mumbled, almost crying. "George, it's good? Right?" she asked her husband. With a reassuring hug, he stood, put his arms around her, and held her tight, wishing he had gone to New York with her.

He could only imagine how those days in the city affected her. The editing process and long nights must have been hell for her. Grace was not one to take criticism at any level. This Leona person, that he had only heard about, sounded nice enough. After all, she had found the manuscript. How bad could she be?

The nightly phone calls from Grace after hours of editing at the typewriter and drinking were rants of incoherency and vulgarity. George had only wanted his love back in New Hampshire.

"I'm coping George. This seems to help." Grace raised her glass and with a cock-eyed smile finished her drink and looked for the waiter. "I love you, George, and I want you to be proud of me," she told him. Her sense of insecurity and childlike behavior was always amplified with alcohol. He didn't answer and raised his hand to signal the waiter. Fingers extended, two more are ordered without a word spoken.

Turmoil had once again crossed paths with the new and old residents of the tiny town nestled in the foothills of New Hampshire. Some couldn't sleep for what might be between the pages of Grace's book, hoping their town's secrets would not be revealed. While others were fast asleep with no concern of the novel and its contents.

CHAPTER 17

Indian Summer was always Grace's favorite time of year. She was very particular about false signs of warming after the first frost. Mother Nature could throw a curveball, and no one could tell if warmer days would stick around. Indian Summer came late to Gilmanton that year. It lasted long enough for the town folk to take notice but was gone as fast as it arrived. The new author had noticed and wondered why it had been so hasty.

"There was a frost last night. It got those yella tomatoes. Now they will never turn red," was a typical conversation heard around the town green. The elders, too old to work and too old to care about much else, gathered on the few benches outside of the courthouse next to the town hall when warmth from the sun lingered. "Did you see the grey squirrel? His goddamn tail is so thick." Another sign of the impending blanket of winter that could arrive at any time. Such observations were all too obvious to the locals.

Grace's *Peyton Place* was being released soon, and it weighed on everyone's mind in town. After Laurie's teaser in the local paper, a series of phone calls, in hush tones to residents from reporters, flooded in. What followed was an assortment of newspaper columns in the national dailies that speculated about the novel's content. Grace had caused a rift in her world and those around her. Yet only a select few had seen the book yet.

The hard-bound novel had been strategically sent out to the right people under the PR genius Alan Brandt, because Kathryn and Jacques felt he was the right one for the job. The publicity was perfect. Word was out, and advance copies were selling like hotcakes at a country fair.

The newspapers had a time with this new tell-all book. Columnists and reviewers had a no holds bar approach to her writing. One weekly columnist billed it as "Tobacco Road with a Yankee Twist." The New York Times Book Review proclaimed her writing as a marginal success and titled their review, *Peyton Place, A Small Town Peep Show*." The last day of Indian Summer in 1956 was the final blow when The *Boston Traveller* daily featured Hal Boyle's assessment of Grace's work as it would, "no doubt be the reason for her husband's firing because of the off-color novel."

"This is outrageous, fucking out outrageous!" Grace screamed as she was folding clothes and throwing them into a cardboard box. "I cannot believe this." She told her friend and confidant who was sitting across from her at the kitchen table in *It'll Do*. Laurie picked up the clothing from the pile on the floor where a dresser had been emptied. "Grace," she paused, "they can't do that to George." Her reply did not do a good job of convincing Grace of the possibility.

Laurie had come over earlier in the day after she had read the Boston paper. She insisted on dropping the kids off at Crystal Lake for a few hours. It wasn't warm enough to swim, but the fresh air would do them good. It would also give her time alone with Grace to catch up. "I'll be right back, Grace," She told her. "Kids, come on, the day is beautiful, it's waiting for you." The screen door slammed, and Grace dumped another drawer full of kid's clothes onto the floor, adding more work as she packed up her home to get ready for the new one. She knew Laurie would be back in a flash, and that pleased her. She could always count on Laurie Wilkins, her only true friend.

"What will we do?" Grace asked Laurie. For the first time, her friend was a little perplexed about the next move. Laurie was so smart, Grace thought. She had been her inspiration, her driving force to complete the book, and her reason for finally embracing the town that was her new home.

"I'm not sure. The School Board meeting is tonight; they just called it this morning," she said. "I'll go with you if you want?" Grace dropped a pair of jeans into the box and looked up; she nodded with a look of gratitude like no other Laurie had seen.

"George isn't going," Grace told her. "He thinks it's all a bunch of nonsense and will blow over." The two continued packing in silence, each deep in thought. They never imagined that their talks around the kitchen table would escalate to this magnitude. National columnists, school board meetings, and maybe job loss for her Gee Gee, it was all so very overwhelming for Grace and a little embarrassing for Laurie.

The time passed quickly between them; folding clothes required no thought. They decided not to drink that afternoon. A clear head was needed for what was coming at the school board meeting.

"Grace, it's three o'clock, I'm going to go fetch the kids," Laurie told her. The sun would be down in a couple of hours. The moving mess was all but cleaned up. The kids would return hungry, and she hoped Marsha would be cooking. Thinking about what was for the evening meal was the last thing on her mind. Grace needed to prepare herself for those small-minded board members.

The Gilmanton School Board met once a month unless there was a special reason to do otherwise. After the aggressive lobbying by the town librarian and board member, they decided to meet. Rita was a force of nature when she needed to be. Though a junior member of the board her passion far exceeded the older less interested members. School Board meetings were always open to the public and held on the second floor of the Town Hall across the green from the library.

Grace had a habit of always arriving late to any event, from her own wedding to the birth of Marsha, three weeks overdue. That night, she was determined to get there on time. The meetings started promptly at seven o'clock with a loud and forceful bang of the gavel. She wanted to be there to hear that tone resonating throughout the hall warning the local yokels to shut the fuck up.

The drive up to town was easy, and she parked the car as close to the town green as possible. Seemed tonight's meeting had piqued the interest of more than a few townsfolk. Parking was a challenge, and there was a small crowd gathered on the front stone steps waiting to go in.

Walking up the sidewalk, Grace noticed Laurie on the steps. She picked up her pace to catch up, holding both hands securely around her purse.

"Hi, I made it." Grace told Laurie with a deep sigh and slightly out of breath. "I'm gonna show them." She opened her large purse. Laurie looked down and saw a newfangled tape recorder, small, and portable with a wired microphone. Her friend smiled and rolled her eyes. "I got it in Laconia yesterday, when I heard there might be a meeting soon. I didn't tell you because I didn't want you to talk me out of using it," she explained. Laurie smiled and placed her hand on Grace's shoulder as a sign of solidarity.

Grace had been so proud of herself. The trip to Laconia the day before proved to be a successful one. Greenlaw's Music was in the center of town, and the only store that would have what she wanted. She charmed her way with the store manager who agreed to let her borrow a new, fancy, reel-to-reel tape recorder in exchange for an autographed copy of her controversial book. She happily agreed and rushed out of the store without a complete lesson on how to operate it. Sitting there with Laurie and trying to get the thing to work would be an issue.

The gavel pounded precisely at seven o'clock, but the room was not completely seated yet. "Settle down, everyone; the meeting will start." The chairman, Seth Fowler, spoke in clear and direct words to a full house. He had served on the board for several years and could not remember the last time there were so many concerned citizens on matters of the school. The five board members sat here like puppets facing the crowd, with Rita and Muriel the only two women on each end, like the front and back book covers. Three chapters of that book were three of the oldest curmudgeons in the community; they always went with the flow.

Grace and Laurie sat in the front row. She was not going to hide in the crowd, and she would stand behind what she had written. Grace felt that the people of Gilmanton thought they were safe when they hid behind their white picket fences or stone walls that marked the land boundaries. Some residents of the town never noticed or cared what was happening or what had happened right under their noses. *Peyton Place* was a fictional town; it was not them, but perhaps some could see themselves in her words. The truth, no matter how it is disguised, can always be recognized by the guilty.

The meeting opened. At the top of the agenda was one George Metalious, Principal of Gilmanton High School. A couple of flash bulbs went off. A few reporters, from parts south, had shown up which only added more mayhem to the already sensitive meeting. A general discussion was opened about his qualifications, and then his wife's book. Whenever someone spoke Grace pointed the microphone in the direction of the speaker, trying to catch every word. It was her attempt at an intimidation tactic.

Of all the spectators in the room, only a few present had actually read the book. The famed librarian had received an advance copy from a friend in Boston. After reading it, she passed it on to Muriel, her partner in crime. Some members of the press had seen many excerpts from it and formed their own opinion. Grace's novel was going to make news, and more readers meant job security.

"Why dredge up the past?" Rita asked the crowd. "Is this any example of what we stand for?" The crowd, like sheep, all agreed in low tones and inaudible voices.

The meeting lasted less than an hour, and everyone appeared to be on their best behavior. Rita Rowell sat with a smug look on her face after dragging the novel and the school principal's reputation down. She watched Grace's every move and thought, "the tape recorder was the last straw and was as vulgar as she was."

The vote of the five board members came quickly; it was obvious to one local reporter that the members had made up their minds before entering the town hall. Laurie was taking notes and would have her take on this kangaroo court in the next day's evening edition of her paper. Grace heard the roll call as they voted to fire George as the principal; she was pissed. Feeling deflated, she switched off the recorder and sank back into her seat.

The next morning the papers were assembled neatly in the town library, and, for the first time, residents were waiting outside before Rita opened the door. There was a flurry of activity in the media room around the newspaper rack. Gilmanton was put on the map once again, and once again it was not very favorable. The gruesome murder from so long ago, that was almost forgotten, now resurfaced in a page-turning novel. No one could get enough of the news.

The next day after the School Board meeting, the columnists had a field day. The *Boston Traveller*, which always carried Hal Boyle's column from New York, was ecstatic with his Follow-up column about Grace's book. Just as he had predicted, his headline that morning, "Teacher Fired for Wife's Book" was a complete success. It was like rubbing salt into the wounds of the town and added fuel to the fire that was publicity for *Peyton Place*.

The book, still in shipment, had not even reached stores yet when reorders started to be placed. The news from the tiny town spread like wildfire throughout the country. The Messner Publishing House could not have been happier. The press strategy that Brandt had dreamed up did cost George his job, but it made great press copy and would sell books, lots of books.

Back in New York, Jacques and Kathryn met for long lunches and toasted each other over the success of Grace's work. They took the credit and the lion's share of the monetary rewards. Jacques was a wolf in sheep's clothing and Kathryn the vamp of publishing. Together, they were unstoppable. The train they were on would leave the station bound for Hollywood, leaving everyone else on the platform.

CHAPTER 18

Frigid temperatures and gray overcast sky created a sense of doom. The trees had lost their leaves. Only the mighty oaks held onto them until they dried out completely, turned brown, and crumpled from their limbs. The Town Green was no longer lush or alive; it was only a distant reminder of its healthier hay days a few weeks before. A winter chill in the air was felt by everyone, but Grace received a larger dose.

"Answer the phone," Grace yelled out to George. "No." One word, nothing more was his reply. George felt desperate and out of sorts. He had prided himself on being prepared and self-reliant, but the school-board had decided not to renew his contract, and he would soon be out of work. Sitting at the table where the trouble had started, he wondered if Grace's success would be the demise of his own self and their marriage.

The phone continued to ring off the hook. Grace buried her head under a pillow in bed. Calls started at seven when the papers hit the stands. It seemed every reporter and every fruit cake in ear shot that could find their number was calling for a statement. Grace was not talking, and surely, neither was George.

It was like nothing Gilmanton had ever seen. Big black, shiny cars, parked in random spots, appeared all over town. The visitors were all dressed alike in dark suits and with black fedora hats. Reporters arrived like a swarm of insects; all were carrying a version of the Kodak Brownie with an endless supply of flash bulbs. They took photos of townsfolk, the town green, even farms on the way out of town, anything that would stand still long enough for the camera. They were in search of the real *Peyton Place*. Try as Grace might to convince the world it was a fictional town; it was an impossible task.

Across town, not far from the original murder scene, one feisty Yankee resident, Maude Schultz, hand painted a sign on a piece of barn board, *Tobacco Road*. That image could be seen the next day in an assortment of newspapers. Grace thought Maude was a bitch, but at least her partial joke eased the reporters away long enough for her to slip over to *Shaky Acres* to hide.

"Grace, come out," Laurie demanded. Grace had been hiding in her bathroom for almost three hours; she had felt safe sitting in her bathtub, fully clothed and feeling like a kid, staying out of the prying eyes of the reporters and from the disappointing looks from her husband. She knew she had crushed George's soul and ego, and repairing the damage was not possible.

Shortly after the announcement of the dismissal of George, Grace conceded to do an interview at their home. It was the day before they moved to the new house. A reporter showed up, and Grace was nervous. She was scared of all the hoopla and tried to speak in quiet and professional tones. Everything was going well until she reached for a glass to make herself a drink, and a rat jumped out of the cupboard at her. She screamed loud enough to stop the interview. The reporter quickly made excuses as he exited the shack as fast as he could. His only regret was that the camera was not ready to help him collaborate his story.

Grace and George did their best to carry on. The move to the new house was happening so they needed to finish packing. The change of location could not come at a better time. The move took just a couple of trips with the car and attached trailer. By the end of the day *It'll Do* would be just a memory. A fond one, nonetheless, for Grace. The Metalious family made good use of the advance. Their new home was a castle to them. George was busy planning his own future and the children settled quickly into their new rooms. They were located far enough away from their parent's room; there would be no more hearing their mother and father during intimate times.

Despite it all, the past few weeks of turmoil for the family turned to gold for them. The books hit the stores and in one week sold 60,000 hard bound copies. Not all news for Grace was bad. She finally felt that her fourth baby was being accepted and that people liked it.

The honk of a station wagon was loud and somewhat annoying. Grace looked out the front window and saw a familiar sight. Laurie was giving her a lift and a boost of self-confidence as she drove her to Laconia. WLNH was the mainstay for all things radio in the Lakes region of New Hampshire. Everyone listened to it. The DJ and the announcers had made long standing careers and never seemed to leave the station. Esther Peter's show "Around Town," was a staple to the community. It would be Grace's first radio interview.

"How do I look?" Grace asked as she closed the passenger side door. Laurie gave her a smile, and with a twinkle in her eyes she reminded her friend it was a radio show. She backed the wagon around the crushed stone drive and drove to the main road as they both had a laugh. The ride to town was fast, and Laurie did not mind helping her friend and keeping a watchful eye on her. "Can I ask?" She asked softly.

"If you're asking if I had a fucking drink," Grace paused, "well, not since last night." The question was answered so now they could relax.

Esther Peters greeted the ladies and escorted them to a glass walled waiting area. It was a perfect spot to see what was happening in the radio station. Grace began to feel uncomfortable and wished a quick drink was available. Lots of booths with glass windows, others with hanging microphones and lights flashing green and red. Each, she assumed, had their own meaning.

"Sit there, dear, we are going live in ten minutes." Esther had a charming, almost motherly, manner about herself. She was like an aunt you wanted to be your mother. Grace began to feel more at ease.

Grace caught the eye of a handsome man behind the glass walls that separated them. He was a DJ named Thomas James Martin. She'd heard him many times on the radio but had never seen him. He went by TJ the DJ. A bit corny for such a fine-looking man. He had a full head of hair, clear skin, strong chin and was a bit stocky, just the way she liked them. It was a perfect distraction for her as she tried to be less nervous waiting to go on air.

A light changed to green outside one of the windows, and Esther suddenly appeared to escort her into that sound booth. TJ the DJ never broke his stare as Grace walked past him. Perhaps the ponytail, blue jeans and checkered flannel shirt were not the right choice after all. Grace felt flush. It had been a long time since she felt like that.

The radio interview went surprisingly well. Esther took great care as she interviewed the budding author and local celebrity. They both spoke softly and clearly trying not to get emotional as Grace recounted the early years in Manchester. Her desire was to be a writer while raising three children and being a great wife. The listeners ate it up, and the wheels of the PR machine kept turning. The interview lasted forty-five minutes and seemed over almost as quickly as it had started.

"And that concludes today's About Town," Esther said. "Be sure to reserve your copy of Grace Metalious's new novel, *Peyton Place;* it's already #4 on the New York Times Best Sellers List." Those were the final words from Esther.

Walking back to meet Laurie, Grace noticed TJ was not in his booth. She was slightly disappointed but shrugged it off and continued walking toward the waiting area.

"Oh, there she is now," Laurie said and gestured towards Grace. "Have you met TJ, Grace?" That was all it took for Grace to become light-headed and weak in the knees in front of this man she thought was so handsome, so strong, and so charming. He reminded her instantly of a story she wrote as a child in her aunt's bathtub about a strong prince. Grace glowed. It did not go unnoticed by her best friend.

The three exchanged niceties, and TJ went a little overboard on the success of Grace's first book, and she ate it up. Laurie suggested a stop at the Laconia Tavern for a drink before heading back to Gilmanton. They all thought it was a great idea. Off they went to discover a new kindred spirit for Grace.

Grace got back from Laconia late that night, a little drunk, but not her usual stupor. After all, she was still upright standing in the drive waving to Laurie as she pulled away. It had been a great day. The radio interview was a smashing success and meeting TJ the disc jockey would prove life altering for her. She still glowed from the kiss on the cheek he gave her as he said good-night.

The lights of the living room were on; she had figured George would be asleep by now, but he was not. He was sitting on the sofa patiently next to boxes of books.

"I thought we unpacked those, Gee Gee?" She asked him. "We did," He paused. "Gracie, sit down," he said, patting the place next to him on the sofa. Grace knew something was up.

Grace could tell George was out of sorts, not his usual supportive self. Since losing his job at the high school, he had been very preoccupied with his own future. Grace created a whirlwind wherever she went, but he barely noticed. The book was selling fast, and the royalty checks began to roll in, but he was not contributing to the financial wellbeing of the household. George did not like the way *Peyton Place* made him feel: a little jealous and a little hurt.

"Are you okay?" Grace asked from the other end of the sofa. George didn't respond right away; the wheels in his mind were turning.

"Brandt, your PR guy, called from New York. They want you to go down and talk to the press, and Mike Wallace wants you on his show; It's called Night Beat, and I think you should do it," added George. He continued to fill her in on all the day's calls; they were mostly from New York, and they were about the book. There was so much happening so quickly; both Grace and George were overwhelmed. Her feelings of happiness after the day's events and now the news of television in New York City, elated her. "How could anything be wrong?" she wondered.

"Grace, I have something else to tell you." Sliding on the sofa closer to her, he gently grabbed her hand. "I've accepted a teaching position in Stowe, Massachusetts. I start in a week, at the beginning of the month."

Grace sank into the sofa; all the feelings that had made her so happy quickly changed to those of abandonment and failure, resurfacing instantly. She knew a drink would ease her pain.

CHAPTER 19

Before Thanksgiving, the chill in the air was like no other, the beginnings of a frigid winter that would soon swoop down on the town. Grace's book was no doubt the cause for much of the chill in the air. The town's people all turned and ran from any member of the Metalious family. This was not New England hospitality at its best. Their shunning was more like downright frostbite.

" George, what are we going to do? Have you seen this?" Grace asked her husband, showing him a letter from her mother. Laurette still lived in Manchester, a few hours south, and she too was getting on the *Peyton Place* band wagon.

"Even my mother is reading the papers. Who the fuck is this Dorothy Kilgallens?" she shouted with the utmost frustration. "What the hell does she know about my book or my life?" Grace was beyond angry.

Dorothy Kilgallen, a small-time gossip columnist and regular on What's My Line, had written some disparaging words about the young author and her family life. The last thing she needed was a visit from her disgruntled mother.

"Listen, why don't we go see Bernie?" George Suggested. "He is a good lawyer and you trust him." Grace approved by nodding her head. "Yes, the Jew will know what to do. They always do."

She looked down at her watch. It was almost noon and the perfect time for a quick drink, followed by a drive to Laconia. George did his best to bite his lip when it came to Grace's drinking; after all, he would be gone in less than a week to his new job south-of-the-border in Stowe. He was looking forward to it but was extremely worried about Grace and her volatile behavior. Some relief came when his wife consented to let the kids visit him often at his apartment in Massachusetts. All three children were having troubles in school and were constantly talked about being byproducts of their mother's sordid novel and fired principal father. The apple never falls far from the tree in New England, and cold shoulders come in all sizes.

Bernie Sneirson was known to his clients and his friends as just Bernie. His law offices were in Laconia in a nondescript office building housing other independent professionals. Grace had met Bernie during some of the leaner years when she had bounced a check and needed the assistance of a lawyer's skill to get her off. He took a great liking to Grace. He admired her creativity, forward thinking, and off-the-cuff humor; Bernie was a fan.

Grace figured out, despite the age difference, that he had a crush on her, and she used it when she could. Bernie also learned that he had to drop whatever he was doing when Grace called. She was always in crisis, and Bernie was her hero; that is just how she was. It was less than forty-five minutes when Grace and George arrived at his office, anxious to get down to business.

"I've written a book, and now I have to leave town," Grace announced as they approached Bernie at his desk.

"Sit down, dear. Now, what's this all about?" The lawyer asked.

"The fucking newspapers, those leeches, are writing awful stuff about my baby, my book." Grace started to cry. "Tell him George!"

George tried to explain the tumultuous torment they had been going through for the past few weeks. Grace stopped crying long enough to look at Bernie with puppy dog eyes, as if saying, take care of me Bernie. He knew that look all too well and was a little perplexed as to what to do.

"Grace, you must have expected this attention or something like it. You are my first author client so I'm not sure what to expect." He was at a loss for words about the situation. George continued describing the flurry of late-night phone calls, ill-mannered columnists writing things about Grace, and the mistreatment of the kids was the final straw.

"They can't make me leave town, can they?" She sincerely asked her lawyer. "I love that house. Those fucking hypocrites will not drive me away from Gilmanton." Grace's tears had returned. "Can I get a drink, Bernie?" asking in the sweetest of voices.

"Grace," George started to say something.

"Don't George," she raised her hand to stop him in full sentence. "They're not after you anymore are they? It's me they are coming for," she answered.

She was partially right. George had his public moment under scrutiny when they ousted him as principal, not honoring his contract. He was lucky to get the job far away from the media circus. He also hoped the distance between them would help their faltering relationship. He wanted only the best for her and the kids.

Grace sipped on the offered scotch, thinking, "why doesn't Bernie have Canadian Club, that is what I like." Bernie and George spoke in monotone voices about how they would need his services more since he was moving a couple of hours away. George was insistent that Bernie should make himself available to help Grace if a situation arose and she needed help.

"Read this, and tell me if we can sue." Grace handed him the envelope that contained the Kilgallen article that her mother had sent.

"Okay, Grace. I will look into this. It will take a couple of days." His voice was reassuring and fatherly. It was the best way to handle her when she was in this state of mind.

Bernie knew there was not a lot he could do for her. He read the advance copy he had received a couple of weeks earlier and knew the novel was racy, almost filthy. It was the first time he had ever read anything like that before. But on the other hand, he felt all press, good or bad, would only help the sale of *Peyton Place*.

He helped Grace gain her composure as he walked them to the reception area. "Bye, Grace, I'm only a phone call away," he kissed her gently on the cheek. George smiled and opened the door for them to leave.

Bernie was torn by what he'd been told. He only wanted the best for Grace, but, unfortunately, she did not always recognize what was best for herself. With George leaving, the drinking would get worse; he was sure of it. He closed the door to his office at his desk and opened the envelope Grace had left him. He began to read the venomous words of some socialite wanna be.

CHAPTER 20

To Gilmanton's residents the events had seemed a very long time ago. The passage of time has a way of softening your memory, but no one in town had forgotten. It was that business with the Roberts girl, along with her brother. The sheep pen murder and all the gossip that surrounded it should have stayed buried in that shallow grave along with that evil monster they dug up from it. Sylvester Roberts evil was back, in the form of a young local writer.

Grace Metalious was the new monster in their midst, yielding a mighty axe in the publishing world, debunking everything most thought was untrue. Gilmanton celebrated a growth in population at that time, rising by one to 801 just 1 more resident. Small enough to know your neighbor, but large enough to turn a blind eye as most New Englanders did. "The stone walls were there for a reason," a wise old man said. Privacy was a treasured commodity.

God was said to have created the beautiful landscape surrounding their village green, and man created the miles of granite stone walls. Stone walls were first to keep livestock enclosed and secondly to mark the boundaries of one's existence. In New England this marked where one world ended and another started. It had been that way for centuries but that was about to end abruptly.

No longer would the residents turn their heads or pretend not to notice. Their small-town way of life was ripped apart. Grace had exposed their secrets to the sunlight, dug them up from the bowels of a sheep pen, and wrote about them. Like a fallen tree in the forest, rotting away with creepy crawlers hiding in its wooden flesh, you would never know they were there until it was turned over.

"*Peyton Place* is not about Gilmanton. It's fiction, Urrgh!" Grace screamed. She threw one of many newspapers in the direction of the fireplace. The open flame only inches from the stack of papers pre-ordained to their destiny. The kids were in school and unaware of the storm brewing in their world. George went to the Laconia Spa; it was the go-to spot for beer, news, and girlie magazines. His mission was to buy every newspaper he could find for his wife before heading back south to his lonely apartment and new job in Massachusetts.

The day had come; Grace's baby was about to get a crack on its ass from the press creating a screech that could be heard everywhere. It was the official date of the release of Grace's book. It seemed a moot point. Grace believed all the hype; the articles and the advance copies created a sensation catapulting it to the top of every publisher's list before it would even out. She thought it was a double edged sword with no handle.

Picking up another random paper she scanned it for news of *Peyton Place*. "Can't they find something else to write about? She yelled. Sitting all alone in her new home, the fire roaring, she was getting madder and madder. She hated being alone when she was not writing. She was thankful George was there the past few days; he made the transition to the new house easier, and the kids were extremely happy he had stuck around. Laurie was working at the paper, there was no one else for her to call.

Grace could hear the radio on in the kitchen, the familiar jingle with the call letters WLNH. Her interview with Ester Peters on About Town would be on. Grace was pleased that

Esther, unlike all the other press she had received, had never asked her if the story was about Gilmanton.

During a commercial break Grace's thoughts went back to her project at hand. Moving to the sofa next to the fire she dragged the pile of paper and magazines she was going through. The pile of papers and magazines was so heavy the brown paper sack split, spilling its contents on the braided rug her grandmother had made. "Oh, Gee Gee," Grace whispered, wondering if things would ever go back as they were.

She wanted proof that her book was out there, some tangible evidence of its existence. She planned to stay inside, keep warm, and out of the prying eyes of the press and a possible tongue lashing from a disheartened neighbor. Kneeling on the floor she surveyed the pile. There was a method to her search. She would empty the contents and toss the empty sack into the roaring fire. She made stacks of the media collection on the floor, close enough to the fire to feel the heat, but not enough to set them ablaze. There would be time later for that.

Flipping through the latest issue of *Photoplay* magazine, she spotted a decent size ad announcing her book along with her photo. Her black and white image was just right of the center, visible but not blocking the novel's cover art. Grace liked the photo well enough. It had been shot in a studio by a local Laconia guy for $15.00. She had the rights. She didn't like that the press entitled it, *Pandora in Blue Jeans*. It showed Grace with her feet on the coffee table bending over her prized Remington typewriter with a number 2 pencil in her mouth. She was dressed in blues jeans and a man's checked flannel shirt, that was her signature look.

Ripping the ad out, the magazine was then tossed onto the fire. She noticed the ice in her drink had melted, creating a lukewarm highball. Her cigarette hadn't been touched, and a long trail of ashes rested precariously on the edge of the ashtray. Grace was on a mission in her front room, and her daily highball had been neglected. The new house, charming, and secluded, which was what she wanted so badly, now smelled of smoke and booze.

Grace felt stuck, helpless, and she did not know what to do. Only a matter of weeks had passed since she signed on the dotted line, and now she was becoming a household name. Everything she hoped for was coming to fruition, the good, the bad and the unwelcome.

Time flew by. Grace never stood up until the pile of press was reduced to a pile of ashes in the fireplace. Her concentration was broken with the ring of the phone, creating a metallic almost hollow sound as the black metal phone rang and rang. Grace sat there just staring at it.

A phone ringing wasn't anything new to her, since Laurie's first article had come out. It was a constant assault; the telephone that never stopped. Changing the number to unlisted did not seem to help; somehow in the end calls found her. Some messages were short and sweet, "Get out of town bitch!" or maybe more personal like, "Go back to Frenchie town in Manchester." She was used to it; they all had the same tonality.

The phone finally stopped, but immediately it rang again. She slid over to the end of the sofa and answered it reluctantly. "Hello," Grace said.

"Grace, Grace Metalious?" The caller questioned. "Yes this___." Without waiting for her to finish her sentence she heard, "Please hold for Mike Wallace."

Grace swallowed hard and took another sip of her lukewarm drink. Mike Wallace got on the phone; his demeanor was professional and direct. "Mrs. Metalious, you have written quite a little book, and I think America needs to meet you."

Grace was shocked on many levels. "Why, thank you, Mr. Wallace. What do you mean?" Off she went down the rabbit hole into the world of television. Wallace was persuasive and charming.

He wrapped up the call, "so can you be in New York the day after tomorrow?"

"Sure." Grace answered, and Wallace followed up with, "We will reserve a room at The Plaza for you. Your PR agent will have all the details when you check in." The phone went silent.

She just sat there holding the receiver, perplexed on what had just happened. ABC had called, and once again, she was off to New York City, this time not as a bashful mother of three and housewife; this time she was a writer and a good one.

Grace wasn't going to let panic sink in. First, she needed something to wear on television. She went to O'Shea's, a family owned and run department store that was her all-time favorite place to shop. Judith O'Shea would help her; she knew exactly what she liked. Her purchase would have to go on an account; she was running out of money, and she assumed the next royalty check would come soon.

She stood up, ran her hands through her unwashed long hair, and tried to straighten the clothes she was wearing. After placing the fireplace screen securely in front of the flames, she ran upstairs to pull herself together.

The shopping excursion was easy, O'Shea's was right downtown in Laconia, a quick drive. Leaving the windows down a bit, she cleared her head from the effects of the morning highballs. She was pleased to get a parking place close to the front door. Judith met her making sure the shopping experience was painless. All she had to do was sign her name.

She had made a stop around the corner to the Laconia Evening Citizen newspaper office to see Laurie at her place of work. Grace wasn't impressed with her digs, but it didn't matter, she was on another mission.

"But you must come. It will be fun," Grace pleaded with Laurie to join her in New York. Her friend agreed and told her boss it would be a story one day. Her editor knew that Laurie's best friend would sell more papers, so he agreed to let her go and gave her a small budget for food. Laurie came out of his office, raising her hand around some cash, and exclaimed, "Road trip!" Grace clapped. She was happy.

The bus, the train, and other hassles were all too much for the ladies, so they decided to drive Laurie's wagon to the city. The family station wagon had seen better days, but it was solid, ran well, and had plenty of space to stretch out if they needed to. The faces of the valet were priceless as the old station wagon pulled up in front of The Plaza. Onlookers stared at the old New Hampshire plated car before it was quickly concealed below the hotel in their giant parking garage.

Checking into The Plaza was a thrill for them both. Laurie had been there once, and Grace tried to forget the ordeal the day of the signing. It had all turned out just fine, and now she was going to be on ABC. The elevator attendant whisked them off to the 17th floor. Their view of Central Park South was stunning.

Grace ran over to the queen size bed and plopped herself down on the satin bedspread. It was soft, cool, and very luxurious. Grabbing one of the many pillows, she tossed it in Laurie's direction with a girlish chuckle. Her friend caught it and threw it back. There was a knock on the door.

The bellman had been right behind them. He placed the two small bags on the floor next to the beauty vanity and stood there waiting. Laurie gave Grace a look of bewilderment. She reached into her handbag and found her change purse. Without a word spoken between them, neither had any idea what to tip him. Laurie gave the bellman a quarter. "Thank you, Madam." He nodded and was about to leave. "No wait, "she said and handed him another quarter. He tipped his hat and left the room.

They had arrived. The Plaza felt like home to Grace, or at least the home she always imagined. They decided to rest a bit before a car would come for them at 8:30 to take them to the studio.

The long drive down had taken a toll on Grace, but the thought of being back in New York City to appear on the local ABC program called *Night Beat*, set her adrenaline in motion. Mike Wallace desperately wanted to get her on the show. She had found out that he had spent all his boyhood summers in New Hampshire; his memories were fond and serene, nothing like what she had written about.

Everyone at Messner Publishing was happy she was doing the show. Wallace even promised not to ask if it was about her new hometown or if it was autobiographical. Brandt, the PR guru, assured Grace that those types of questions would not be asked, so she stuck to her verbal agreement with Wallace.

Laurie would watch from the green room. "Why is it called a green room?" Grace asked her friend. "There is nothing green in here." They had a chuckle and a ginger ale someone brought them.

They waited patiently in silence, each in a state of nervousness and anxiety, feeling like schoolgirls at a Junior High dance. Grace fidgeted about with her new ensemble purchased the day before. There was a knock at the door, to remind her she had ten minutes before airtime.

Grace wanted to freshen up before the show, but in doing so she ripped her girdle trying to adjust it.

"Fuck. Now what?" She muttered under her breath. Standing in the make-room she caught her image in the mirror, a bit disheveled; the girdle was going to be a huge distraction. Her nerves had finally hit her, back again in the city, live television with Mike Wallace; and it was all too much, she wanted a drink.

A young woman entered the make-up room to check her lipstick in the mirror next to Grace. Seeing her struggle, this beautiful and helpful actress offered her assistance.

"Here, let me," she told Grace. The young woman was so pretty, and her smile reassured the author that by turning the girdle around no one would notice. "There, all better."

She introduced herself; her name was Jacqueline Susann. She worked there in the studio doing the commercial spots for the show. She was so friendly to Grace and eased her sense of failure. She escorted Grace to the set, leaned over, and whispered into Grace's ear. "Break a leg," then added, "Don't let him rile you. He can be such a cad."

Grace sat down across from where Wallace would sit; he liked the element of surprise when meeting his guests for the first time. The lights were very bright. Wallace, stoic and cautious, sat down with a freshly lit cigarette. The host of the show was a bit taken back with Grace's appearance, young and innocent, but chubby and plain, like a New England farm girl. She waited a few minutes before the red lighted sign changed to "On The Air."

Wallace noticed the sign, forced a smile, and placed his lit cigarette down on the ash tray. He introduced the young author to his viewers, telling them about her new book that was causing a bit of a flurry throughout the country. Wallace had a reputation for asking hard hitting questions trying to get to the truth. Grace tried to be gracious, but was unnerved, and wanted nothing more than to get up and leave.

"So, tell me Grace, is *Peyton Place* your autobiography?" Wallace asked. The forbidden question that put her in a defensive and protective mood. Like a cornered raccoon she was going to hold her ground. Almost speechless, she tried in her mind to form an answer, and at first nothing came out.

"What gives you the right to pry and hold your neighbors up to ridicule?" He asked her. "I thought your book was basic and carnal," he continued.

"You did, huh?" was her response.

Words could not describe the mood his questions put Grace in. Her eyes got bigger and tearful; she was more nervous than she thought possible, and her constant twirling of her ponytail was a sure sign to the viewers that perhaps Wallace had hit a nerve.

The interview continued as best it could; her answers were short and not very revealing, something Wallace prided himself on with all his guests.

Grace did manage to get through the ordeal, painfully and with as much self-respect as she could find. There was a moment of clarity when she sat up straight and turned the line of questioning onto the host.

"Tell me, Mr. Wallace. How many times have you been married?" She asked, letting go of her ponytail.

The host was taken aback, and Grace fired another question. The confidence she mustered up turned the table on the show, and Grace felt she was no longer playing defense.

The hour went by quickly, and after the show, she wanted nothing more but to rush down to the car that was waiting. Standing up, she began to make a b-line for the green room.

"Grace," Wallace stood up and extended his hand. "You're a hell of a woman."

Laurie had left the waiting area and was standing offset holding Grace's coat; she knew that the interview had been a difficult one for her.

It was close to midnight when they returned to their room at the plaza. The lobby was eerily empty; the front desk clerk recognized the ladies with just a nod. Once in their room, they opened the bottle of whiskey they had brought with them. They ordered room service, lots of it. Wallace was picking up the tab.

CHAPTER 21

At the beginning of December, the first snow had started. It was time, and the fourth season began. The New England landscape was soon covered in a pure white blanket of protection. The world would seem a little less menacing once the snow storm had passed, and the bright sun made its glistening appearance, assuring everyone it would be a brighter day.

Everything in Grace's life seemed less chaotic. The move was over, and the unpacking was done. The kids settled into the new house, and the teasing at school became old news for them. The town had a bit of a breather from the earlier assault by reporters. Marsha adjusted to life in high school, something she didn't like much, and George came home on weekends. The kids adored their father and welcomed his arrival every Friday night in full fanfare like they hadn't seen him in years. This weekly display of affection caused a bit of jealousy for Grace, but she tried to hide it.

Grace continued to drink, except when working on her book and needed to be clear and concise. She was regularly on the phone with New York, either it was Jacques or Brandt and sometimes Kathryn herself when another deal was to be made. Three major studios showed great interest in her book. Rumors spread of a bidding war that was about to take place. Grace was feeling anxious again. Hollywood was at her door, and she had no idea how to open it.

After her appearance on Wallace's *Night Beat* show, the interest in the book skyrocketed. *Peyton Place* was number one, selling over 3,000 copies a week. Wallace spun Grace's story of life in a small town, and it worked perfectly. She still didn't like him any better but was forever grateful each time a royalty check arrived. She loved waiting for the postman. There was always something to read and usually something to cash.

The money was a godsend to the household. She loved to go shopping, spoiling the kids to buy their affection as best she could. They wanted for nothing, and they got it all. It was liberating for Grace. Debts were paid off for the first time in her life. The young author even went as far as to wear her new mink coat from Saks Fifth Avenue in New York to the Corner Store on the town green. Ned actually sent a note home with Mike about an unpaid tab of $23.50 to present to his mother. After receiving it, she downed her highball and stormed off to the store with a royalty check she had received to pay off the tab. Ned was taken aback with her mink coat, smelling of booze, and her check.

"Can you cash this?" was all Grace said. Ned looked at the check in the amount of $1,230. She felt vilified and left the store. "Fuck him," she said and drove back to her dream house.

Grace tried to be a good mother to the kids. Her notoriety was often bigger on paper than in real life. She still had her routines and had not settled into having hired help around. She still drove into town to the market in Laconia. She would never step into the Corner Store again.

At the grocery store, she had run into Esther Peters from the radio station. "Grace, you and Wallace were terrific together," she said. "You really told him."

Grace, quite frankly, could not remember all the details of the show, but what she did remember was the resounding unpleasant memory of how much she disliked her interviewer.

"Come back on to my show. It will be fun to do a follow up," Esther asked as she grabbed her brown paper bag full of groceries from the cart at the IGA supermarket.

"Okay," Grace agreed. Esther said she would phone her with some time slots. Grace smiled grabbed an empty cart, and made a dash for the frozen food section. All the fame hadn't helped her cooking skills.

Esther's phone call came the next day. She sounded excited to get Grace back on the program. She knew it was listeners that generated sales and ultimately paid her salary. Esther loved working, but she loved getting paid for it even better. "The young author is gold, just pure gold," the host whispered to herself after hanging up the phone with Grace.

T.J. was in the station and within ear shot of Esther's conversation, trying to convince himself he was not eavesdropping on his co-worker's call, but he had been. "Was that our friend Grace?" he asked Esther, trying to sound casual and not prying. "Yes," Esther let the answer roll off her tongue in a matter-of-fact way. T.J. turned and headed back into the sound booth. Her face said it all; she knew he was up to something.

A light snowfall had covered the roads enough to make the traffic into the next city treacherous. Grace had no problem driving in the snow. Her thirty-two years living in New Hampshire prepared her for snowy days in the North Country.

As she drove down the windy state route 106 to Laconia, she was deep in thought about the crazy times for her and her family these past few weeks. Money rolled in, and the checks came like clockwork, more money than she had ever seen in her life. *Peyton Place,* her fourth baby, was truly paying off. All that time she had sat at her typewriter seemed to have been worth it.

Grace slowed down, and pulled her car to the right when she noticed an old snowplow behind her. Sounds of metal scraping on the asphalt from the blade created an image in her mind, fingernails and a blackboard. As the plow passed, it created a clearer path for her ahead. She slowed so as not to land in the ditch or head on into a stone wall, for the roads were becoming icy. The plow was a godsend because, as usual, Grace was running late. She worried that she would miss her time slot on the radio station, and Esther would not be happy. Grace never wanted to make anyone unhappy; she was far too generous for that.

The radio station was all aflutter; Grace thought she had arrived with time enough to catch her breath. Other DJs and various other personnel walked past the glassed-in waiting room. Everyone wanted a glimpse of the famous housewife or maybe even to meet her. The staff convinced themselves if anyone wondered why they were looking in, a simple explanation of just passing by could be used. Everyone in the studio was happy that she took the time to autograph their dog-eared copy of her sassy novel, the one hidden from sight, stashed in the bottom of their desk drawer.

Grace's book was in its second printing. The entire country kept the words from an uneducated New Hampshire housewife hidden from view and out of sight from the neighbors and their spouses. When a reader read Grace's words to themselves, they acted like little electric shocks in their minds. The excitement they felt reassured them, secretly, that desire, passion, and even guilt had a place within their lives. Such feelings, for the most part, had been repressed and often unattainable. Grace gave them hope with her book and helped the masses overcome judgment from others.

"Hurry, Grace." Esther rushed her from the station's version of a green room to the sound booth. Grace was covered in snow; her scarf barely kept it off her hair and face.

"Wow, it's really coming down," Esther said.

"Yes, and could I find a fucking parking space?" was Grace's reply. Her question needed no answer.

Esther took Grace's scarf, trying not to let the snow fall on her and her stacks of notes. Grace took off her coat and hung it next to the sound booth on a chrome hook, not caring if the melted snow puddled on the linoleum floor. Her scarf rested next to the same wool coat she'd worn to New York on the first trip.

Esther explained, "We are in studio #4 today. The storm is causing a lot of cut ins," she added. The weather had taken a harsh turn from its gentle arrival that morning. Snow was sticking to the ground, and the radio station's meteorologist was doing his best to keep everyone informed. The two women sat across from each other, each with headphones on waiting for the green light.

Grace was no longer nervous. She trusted Esther and thought of her as a friend. The snow had dampened her mood slightly, and she felt wet and cold. The walk from the corner really pissed her off. She knew she wasn't looking her best and hoped no one was there to see her.

The interview lasted over an hour. The usual forty-five-minute show grew lengthy because of the cut-ins for the weather. Grace liked the way it flowed; Esther asked questions about Grace, not so much about the book. She was happy to tell the world that she had no intention of moving her family to New York, Boston, or even Concord. "Writing is what I do. I can do it anywhere, and anywhere is here," she told the hostess.

At one point though, the interview started to go not as smoothly as Esther had hoped; the host started quoting other columnists and facts about the book. This made Grace a bit uneasy, so she held tight and tried to answer as best she could. Esther quoted a book reviewer from St. Louis who questioned her lack of proper prose. Grace responded in her true classic form, "If I'm a lousy writer, then an awful lot of people have lousy taste."

The last few questions Esther asked hurt Grace a little. She felt the host was just filling in dead air. "What are your thoughts on the Rhode Island Commissioner putting *Peyton Place* on a black list?" The interviewee was dumb founded and caught off guard by the question. Without giving Grace a chance to answer or even to think, the next question was even more damaging. "We just heard Canada, the entire country, has banned your book." Esther leaned back in her chair crossing her arms. Grace paused and said, "You get angrier about the truth than you do about lies." Words well-spoken from the housewife turned writer.

When the interview had finished, Grace wanted nothing more than to get out of that station and run to the nearest bar. She hadn't seen spectators standing in the hallway watching her every move through the glass windows. Esther's questions had been so intense at the end that the gathering crowd went unnoticed by Grace. Getting up from the studio desk, Esther escorted her into the waiting area. A few employees had their books opened ready for an autograph. They were lying flat on the coffee table. Grace couldn't say no, regardless of how she felt; it only took a moment or two. Everyone was extremely grateful and thanked her profusely.

"Do you have time for one more?" A strong and masculine voice asked just as she finished the last autograph. Looking up, Grace's eyes met TJ the DJ, and some internal spark ignited. Is this what her readers had felt when they read her book with a flashlight in bed, the covers pulled over their heads?

"Ummm, sure. Love to." Grace answered, never breaking her stare. "Here, its's for TJ," was all he said and slid a brand spanking new copy of her novel across the table placed in front of her. Picking it up, she opened the book. The sound that a new book makes when it is opened for the first time is truly one of the most romantic things Grace could hear. As a child, books had been her entire life, and she was happy they continued to be her passion.

The snow did not let up. Weather report cut ins were more frequent and warnings of bad roads were announced again. The station manager decided to let his general staff off early. The lone announcer who was also a DJ had to hunker down for the night. Grace and TJ sat there making small talk on the tiny studio sofa, their world's connecting for the first time.

"Good night, Grace, drive safely back home," Esther said as she slid her coat sleeve down her arm and waved to her show's guest at the same time. Grace didn't answer her and continued to talk to TJ, with no worries about of the snow, blacklists or Canada.

"Care to join me for a drink Grace?" He asked. "Yes. Let's," she answered. Like kids' home on a snow-day they bundled themselves up in their coats and were out the door for an adventure in the pretty white stuff. Grace slipped on the fresh snow, and, in a true fairy tale fashion, her prince caught her in both arms. TJ was a tall and solid built man, no doubt a descendant from the Scots that had arrived centuries before in New England. He had no problem saving his princess in distress.

They made their way around the corner to Main Street, where all life in this tiny city happened. They headed to one of her favorite watering holes, The Laconia Tavern. Old and quiet, its best feature was no windows to see in, keeping local lurkers at bay.

"Booth or stool?" TJ asked his new friend. "Why, a booth please." Looking around, "that one!" Grace said with a girlish twinkle and pointed to the one in the corner, furthest from the bar. It was in the shadows created from the overhead lights of the pool table. "Be right back," and with that he walked to the bar to order drinks.

He returned within seconds, before Grace got her coat and scarf hung up at the end of the booth.

"CC and Ginger, right?" the sly fox asked his young rabbit. Blushing a tiny bit, she nodded and took the highball in a grateful gesture and smiled. One drink led to another and another; no one could drink Grace under the table. Many tried, and most failed. Her new DJ called TJ kept up pretty well.

Snow was coming down like a nor'easter. The streets were deserted, and the lonely bartender was waiting patiently for the two in the corner to head home. He was anxious to close the place up and make his way up to his tiny apartment three floors up. One of those new frozen Birdseye dinners waited for him. The warmth of the oven would take the chill out of his cold dwelling.

"Grace, I am so happy our paths crossed." The Scotsman was practically gushing over her. He knew the encounter was not all entirely by accident. His was a well thought out plan, including the brand-new book he had bought a few minutes before her arrival to the station, along with all the reading he had done about her since their last encounter. He had done his homework and figured she would be a feisty one and with lots of new money. He grinned from deep inside his soul and thanked the heavens for the snowstorm. He hadn't counted on such an early display of winter's fury, but it did help his cause.

"Let's get out of here, sweetie." Grace slurred her words as she looked into the bottom of her empty glass. "I have to get home to feed the kids," she said, pausing for a moment and then burst out laughing, a deep guttural laugh caused by too many cigarettes and drinks. Her new friend had no idea what was so funny, but he laughed anyway.

The two helped each other walk along the uncleared sidewalk; the snow was barely six inches deep, but the real danger lay below the fluffy white stuff. Black ice was not something to mess around with. Fearing it like a black cat on Halloween would be an understatement.

They made it to Grace's car parked down the street. It was now entombed with snow and a fresh bank caused by the plow. Neither of them was in any condition to dig the car out or to drive. They headed back to the bar; the bar man was just locking the door when the two drunks caught up to him.

"Not fit for man or beast," he tells them. "Try the hotel next door."

The Laconia Tavern Hotel was not part of the bar but shared a name and history with the long running watering hole. Grace and TJ walked the few steps to the front door, kicked off the snow, and approached the desk. "We are snowed in!" TJ told the elderly man behind the desk. "You and everyone else around the lake. This storm really snuck up on us," he added. "Got one room left, the honeymoon suite." A sly smile between them as only men can share.

It was a short climb to the third floor. Their room faced the street. A bit chilly for Grace's liking, but the whiskey and her hormones created their own hot flash deep inside her groin. Without a word, or even a thought of drawing the curtains, they embraced like two star struck lovers ready to do battle between the sheets.

"Fuck me, TJ, fuck me." Grace fell back on the bed, her coat still on. Snow melted from her dripping boots and formed small puddles on the floor.

CHAPTER 22

Grace was in the shower trying her best to clear her head. It was Friday morning, and she wanted to be her best when George arrived home that evening. Her late nights with TJ the DJ had taken on a life of their own. She didn't want her husband to know about them. She hoped her concealment of his existence worked. She tried to keep it from the kids as well, but had failed miserably.

The hot water felt great as she rinsed off the previous night's stench of drinking, smoking, and sex at Laconia Tavern. The *LT,* as they called it, was code for their place to meet in secret. Her fondness for the rugged Scotsman was growing stronger each day as they grew closer. Grace feared the outcome. He was everything her George wasn't: tall, broad, bold, and the best lover she ever had. Their lovemaking was epic, and his perdurable performance never disappointed. Just thinking about him caused her hands to linger in her private areas a little too long. The water caressing her like his touch had. She did not hear the phone ring again.

"Fuck! Stop calling," she screamed from the shower as she ripped open the flowered pattern curtain. Carefully she stepped onto the white chenille rug, grabbed a towel off the hook, and headed into the bedroom. She was pleased how the new house was turning out. Renovations seemed endless, but her master suite was the first to be finished. She had a bathroom all to herself and a phone extension in her bedroom. She would never have to leave. She felt quite accomplished at that moment.

"What!" She answered the phone.

"Grace, are you okay?" the voice questioned. Her caller was the one and only Kitty Messner. Grace had sunk to a new low, yelling at her publisher. At a loss for words, Grace just listened.

"I'm sorry to be calling so early. I want you to be the first to know," Kitty told her, "and of course I wanted to call you myself."

Twentieth Century Fox had won the bidding war. It seemed *Peyton Place* was destined for the big screen. The powerhouse publisher who prized herself with perfection for her authors was overjoyed, but her excitement was contained and professional. Kitty never showed emotion unless it was disappointment. Catholic guilt at its best. "Grace, isn't this great news?"

The novel continued to sell fast, faster than anyone expected, breaking records. Another printing was in the works, and the interest growing internationally was unstoppable. They began translating it into a number of different languages. Grace was speechless; she knew there was interest, but her book had only been out a short time. Her head was spinning. Everything was happening so fast for her.

"Grace, my dear, there is no stopping where this could go."

"Ms. Messner," she started.

"Grace, call me Kitty. I'm on your side," she reminded her.

"Kitty, what does this mean?" she asked, standing next to her bed, dripping wet, wrapped in a towel. "It means you are coming to New York again, maybe going to Hollywood." There was a hint of excitement in Kitty's voice, no doubt fueled by dollar signs.

Grace sat down on the edge of the bed and scrambled for a pencil or pen and something to write on. "Hold on," she said tossing the receiver onto the bed. George's nightstand always had pencils, paper and the occasional True Crime magazine from the Laconia Spa tucked in the back. Grace didn't mind about the black and white rag; she had her own hand's full with her new man.

Grabbing the pad, she rolled back to her side of the bed and picked up the receiver. "Okay, say again." Kitty explained that a group was coming in from the west coast next week. Grace was needed at their meeting at The Algonquin Hotel in Manhattan. She scribbled notes as fast as a New York minute as Kitty filled her in on the details.

"Got it. I'll be there," Grace told her. "Will the hotel room be in my name or yours?" she asked. The two exchanged the details; both are ecstatic with the news. She slams the phone down and laid back across the bed, the towel at her feet. She was stark naked. Her fleshy skin pale from the winter sky and slightly curvier than before. Success seemed to be landing on her hips, but she didn't mind, and neither did TJ.

Grace's day was a long one for her. She wanted to prepare dinner or at least have it ready for the kids and George; he would be hungry after the drive north to Gilmanton. Grace had set the table in the dining room. It would be the first time they ate at the table as a family. From the front room the children were suspiciously curious as they watched her flutter about the kitchen.

Their mother plopped the family size tray of frozen Salisbury Steaks into the oven and reached for a box of Potato Buds. "What's gotten into her?" Mike asked his older sister. "Not sure, but I guess we will know soon enough," Marsha answered. "Why don't you and Cindy watch TV in here, I'll go see if I can help Ma." With that the kids curled up on the sofa in the front room, as their older sister made her way to the kitchen.

"Can I help?" she asked.

"Sure, make me a drink, will you, sweetie?" Grace, never looking up from the side panel of the instant potatoes, reading the cooking instructions. "Who knew potatoes were this easy to make," she chuckled. "No peeling, no boiling," she added.

Her older daughter wanted her mother to stop drinking. It was really out of control. There was a bottle of Canadian Club open in every room, placed in plain sight and easy to reach. She hated seeing them. Marsha knew the drinking was getting the best of her mom, but she was a kid, what could she do? Her father used the excuse of his job to flee the clutches of her mother's addiction. She knew the truth about the drinking, but there always seemed to be enough money to distract the family.

Darkness fell on the house on Meadows Pond Road. The entire family waited for the sign of head lights coming up the drive. Finally, around six o'clock the lights of the old Packard were spotted, and the kids ran to the front door to greet their father. Little Cindy, the youngest, switched on the lantern light next to the drive from the center hallway. Each of the children breathed a sigh of relief as their savior for the weekend, arrived. Grace stepped back to allow the children the glory of greeting George. It also gave her time to refresh her highball.

"What's all this?" George asked as he was greeted at the front door, as usual on a Friday, but that night there was more than a little anticipation.

"Mom's made dinner. She wants us all to eat together," Mike gleefully exclaimed. "Wow, that's great!" Marsha helped him with his coat, and Mike grabbed his briefcase. It was old and worn, no doubt filled with papers to grade. Cindy ran ahead down the hall to the kitchen. "Ma, Dad's here," the youngest gleefully exclaimed.

The scene in the kitchen was not as they imagined it would be. Grace sat at the breakfast table next to the bay window with a bottle of Canadian Club next to her and a half full glass. She stared out the back window into the darkness, deep in thoughts of her own. She had wanted it to be perfect, to be a family night, but the drink took over, and the night was ruined.

"I can't even make instant potatoes," she said when her husband entered the kitchen. The stove was covered with milk that had boiled over; the scorched liquid seeped onto the floor. The flame was washed out, and a hint of propane gas lingered in the air. George rushed over to turn the knob of the gas to the off position. He looked to Marsha for help. Not a word was spoken between them as his daughter picked up a dish cloth, and he his wife.

Dinner wasn't a total loss; the frozen Salisbury Steak dinner was warmed perfectly, and it tasted good on toasted white bread. The kids could always make something out of nothing. It seemed adversity ran deep in their veins. Very little shocked Grace's kids. Their mother's fondness for whiskey actually toughened them a bit, while making them grow up too quickly.

Grace hadn't eaten after the incident. She was embarrassed and withdrawn. She instead retired to the front room to sit and nursed her drink. George had made the drink with extra ginger ale which clearly out-proportioned the whiskey.

Everyone still wondered why their mother went to all this trouble for a Friday night supper. Agreeing to wait until the dishes were done, they would all go together down the hall and ask her. "Everyone have enough ice cream?" their father asked as he shoved the carton of Hood Neapolitan into the freezer of their new Hotpoint refrigerator.

"Yes," replied in unison. Grabbing their bowls, they turned towards the front room, each hoping that their mother's mood was better and just a little more coherent.

"I'm sorry, I wanted it to be perfect," Grace said. The watered-down drink did its trick. She seemed more sober, but still rambled on a bit. "You are all perfect babies, my Gee Gee."

"It's alright, Ma. We have ice cream," Mike told her, and she smiled.

George snuggled in next to Grace, took the empty glass, and put it on the side table. The kids sat on the floor in front of the overstuffed sofa and began to eat their tri-colored frozen dessert.

"Tell us your news, Grace," her husband asked in the kindest of tones.

The four of them remained motionless and speechless as she began to tell them about the phone call, the movie news. She once again apologized for making a mess of dinner. The words Hollywood, movie, New York, created images that bounced around their heads like a silver ball in a pinball machine up at the Weirs Beach Boardwalk. The kids looked at each other in disbelief and couldn't wait for bragging rights at school.

After the dessert dishes were washed and put away, George insisted that he and Grace go to their room. He was tired, and he knew his wife must be exhausted. Sleep can cure most anything, and a fresh start on a crisp winter Saturday morning was in order.

"You kids don't stay up too late. We'll go look for a Christmas tree tomorrow," he told them. Their first Christmas together in the new Spring Meadows Road house would be a good one.

Lying in bed next to his wife, the moonlight shone through the small windowpanes, past the Cape Cod curtains, and hit George squarely in the face. He couldn't sleep. It was too bright in the room, and he also had something on his mind. He wanted to talk to Grace, but her condition and her news always trumped his.

The TJ the DJ conversation had to happen. Enough was enough. "Screw the movie," he thought as he rolled over and tried to sleep.

CHAPTER 23

And here is a little tune for Grace," the radio announcer said. They hadn't been on the road ten minutes when George heard TJ the DJ dedicate some melodramatic song of love and loss by Patsy Cline to someone named Grace. He knew exactly who it was intended for. A bit annoyed, he reached across the dashboard and aggressively turned the round knob to the off position.

"Hey, why did you do that?" Grace asked. "Esther is on next, and I want to hear how she will muck up another interview." Looking over to her handsome driver, she wondered if he knew. She hoped he didn't.

"We are almost to the interstate where we will lose the signal. Find another channel if you want." George was short and almost rude as he answered his wife.

She folded into the front seat like a wilted flower, as far away from the driver as she could without opening the door. Thinking at that moment, if she did fall out, all her troubles would be over. Fantasizing, as only a writer could. Her body would hit the pavement, rolling over and over, covered in blood. Then an innocent car passing by would have finished her off once and for all.

The drive south through New Hampshire was a quiet one. They didn't speak and barely looked at each other. Tension was building, and it was ready to erupt at any moment. Grace had thought the news of the movie deal would have been good news, great news, in fact. Her husband liked the idea of the movie; the excitement and the notoriety his wife's book would get. He did not like the fact that the same notoriety had created a chasm between the two of them with no way to bridge it.

Turning onto the newly completed Mass Pike, George rolled down the window and paid the toll. The attendant took the coins using the tips of his fingers, the knitted tips of his gloves cut off, making the transaction fast and easy. The air outside was brisk and very cold. The last storm came and went leaving the roads clear. Their drive to New York would be an easy one.

"Are you hungry, Gee Gee? Grace asked from her side of the car, trying not to get too close for fear of a fight. "A little," he answered.

They continued to drive in silence heading for New York. Next stop, The Algonquin Hotel in midtown. It was a Sunday so the turnpike was nearly empty. George was making great time, and he agreed with her about food. A bite to eat would lighten his mood and give them a change of scenery. The familiar orange tile roof was up ahead at the next exit; a Howard Johnson's would be their unofficial halfway point.

Howard Johnson's, in New England, was always a welcome reprise from a long drive on the interstate. The bright orange leather interiors matched their signature roof. You couldn't miss them. Grace and George entered the restaurant and were escorted to a booth against the faux stone wall. The booth sat directly under gleaming lights, custom made from hand blown colored glass in, none other than, orange.

"I should have brought in my fucking sunglasses," Grace told him as she slid into the booth and leaned back so the light wasn't blinding her. She reached for her handbag and opened it. A Chesterfield cigarette was produced, and George reached over and lit it for her. She offered him one and against better judgment he took one and lit it. He then placed the chrome lighter next to the half empty pack on the table.

Coffee and pancakes were ordered with a couple of sunny side eggs on the side. When Grace wasn't cooking, she did enjoy her food. The coffee tasted so good with her cigarette. A long exhale escaped her lungs as she lifted her mug and sipped the steamy liquid. "George," she said. "This will be great. The movie deal is unbelievable; our kids will be taken care of for life." They both looked across the brightly lit booth, nowhere to hide or conceal their true feelings.

"Yes, I agree," was his answer. He believed that in his mind and his being. He had taken a few days off from his new job to accompany Grace to the city while she met the studio executives. He worried that all this pressure had taken its toll on her. Drinking was clouding her thoughts, and now the distraction from this TJ guy; it was all too much. Her husband was protecting her as he had always done and at the same time protecting his own interests.

The remainder of the drive was a breeze. Grace slid closer to George and rested her hand on his leg. Things might work out after all. His Gracie was his one and only. He wanted nothing more than to be back at *It'll Do*, biking his way to work at the State School. But better judgment knew that would never happen.

The valet in front of the hotel on 44th street was dressed like a guard from the film, *The Wizard of Oz*. Grace thought the long coat, the big brass buttons, and the silly hat was too much. "What the hell," was her attitude. She wasn't footing the bill, and by this time tomorrow they would be even richer.

The Algonquin Hotel was a legend in the minds of most. Famed round table discussions held each week between such literary figures from Dorothy Parker to George Kaufman. This thrilled Grace to no end. She was now a part of this world, this secret society of making money by telling stories.

She grabbed her husband's hand and looked through the large wood and glass doors into the grand foyer. In her opinion, it was nicer than the Plaza: smaller, less glitzy, more humbling. The front desk was straight ahead. It was an imposing piece of wooden furniture, deeply carved and highly polished, truly magnificent. The tall, plastered ceilings were richly ornate. Tall palm trees potted in giant urns from China transported every guest into a world of privacy and luxury.

"Madam," the doorman tipped his hat and smiled at the two of them. He pulled the door open and the young couple from the north stepped in. Grace tried not to look, not to leave her mouth open at the handsomest doorman in New York. George walked to the front desk to see about their arrangements. Grace sheepishly trailed behind.

"We have been expecting you. How was your journey down?" The man behind the front desk asked. "New Hampshire, right?" George was amazed with the carefully handled transaction and the fact that the staff knew their itinerary and gave them the VIP treatment. There was something to be said for notoriety in any form which you received it. He thought, he could get used to this, and at the same time thought, it was exactly what he didn't want. Always in a quandary, never an easy way out.

"Mr. Wald from California would like you to join him and his associates for dinner in the Oak Room," the second most handsome front desk attendant in all the city told the couple as he handed George the keys. "Would seven PM work for you and Mrs. Metalious?" George nodded and took the big brass key. "You are up on the eighth floor." He ended their conversation.

"The Oak Room Supper Club! George, can you believe it?" Grace said as she unpacked her suitcase trying to shake the wrinkles out of a pale green suit she had bought at O'Shea's a few days before. Putting her things into the massive set of drawers, she thought the room was nice, but decided the Plaza was her favorite. They had a couple of hours before the dinner. At first Grace thought they should relax and have a drink, then her practical side took over, so they laid down on the oversized bed and tried to sleep awhile.

The nervous couple entered the elevator, and the attendant closed the doors on their way to the main floor. The concierge was expecting them and casually escorted them to the dining room. Grace dressed the best she could, her hair back in her signature ponytail and her only makeup, bright red lips. George was smart in a new suit from the local department store he had bought with the help of Judith O'Shea. The fabric was shiny and tailored to fit his trim body. He did his best not to let fame and fortune end up on his hips as it had for his wife.

Approaching the dining room, she was pleased to see her friend Jacques, the agent that had gotten her to this place, and the wonderful Kathryn; her publisher looked like she had just stepped out of a Hollywood backdrop, channeling her best Mildred Pierce suit for their guest of honor. Grace realized that she would be sharing the evening's limelight with Jerry Wald, the famous screenwriter and producer.

The three of them stood up to greet the couple. George shook hands, and Grace received a soft kiss on the check from Kathryn in true New York style. Greetings are friendly and civil, something Grace admired when doing business in New York.

"Jerry, this is Grace___" Kathryn began the introduction, only to have her words cut off in mid-sentence.

"I would know that face anywhere. You are quite a sight. Welcome to New York." He acknowledged George only slightly and gestured for her to slide into the booth next to him. The others followed suit, anxiously hanging on every word from the larger-than-life Hollywood icon. This was Jerry's show, and they knew to sit tight.

"We have big plans for *Peyton Place;* this is going to be huge my dear," Wald started right in. They all watched the expression on his face, captivating, and almost comical at times. His hand gestures were as big as the Empire State Building, when he says how high is high. He lured them in with his vision of her novel and continually told her what a great writer she was. Glowing from the inside, Grace was now scared shitless. "Big, big I tell you," Wald went on, never giving any one else a chance to talk. "Grace, my dear, you created a Hollywood masterpiece. I bet you didn't even know that?" Was it a question? Did he want an answer? Grace sat speechless.

When drinks were ordered, George, gesturing towards Grace, told the waiter she would have a Bloody Mary. A bit confused, she looked at him, but went with his judgment. A lot was riding on this meeting, and whiskey might get in the way. Everyone agreed *Peyton Place* at Twentieth Century Fox was the best fit. Laughter throughout dinner could be heard in the dining room. More drinks were ordered, and the table filled with smoke from all the cigarettes they were burning.

Dinner seemed to last for hours. The oysters were sublime, and the prime rib was so rare, George even made an attempt at a joke. "I thought I heard the cow mooing earlier," the punch line landed like a lead balloon. His attempt to be a part of the conversation was unsuccessful. Everyone smiled for a brief second and continued with their meal. That had been another nail in the coffin for him and this new life she was embarking on. All he wanted was for the meeting to end. His thoughts turned to, "When is the dessert coming?"

"Now, don't be late tomorrow. Jerry has a five o'clock flight back to the coast," Kathryn's departing words as the doorman held the door for her and Jacques. Grace and the handsome doorman made eye contact for a second; no one noticed, not even George.

Grace's meeting had turned into a celebration, and it lacked the usual confusion and mild mayhem of the past. Grace felt good, and maybe tonight she and her husband would rekindle what they had lost.

Grace was surprised to find a fifth of whiskey on a silver tray in the center of the bed. A note leaned against the bottle of Canadian Club. She recognized the stationary as her literary agent, Jacques. It simply read 'Be careful what you wish for; you may just get it. Your friend, Jacques." She tossed the note to the side and grabbed the bottle. She reached into the silver ice bucket for a handful of cubes and filled the cut crystal glass. The drink tasted so good to her and gave her the feeling of confidence she had lacked throughout the dinner meeting.

George, disgusted, turned, left the bedroom, and went into the bathroom. All he wanted at that moment was to be in the car heading back to his tiny apartment in the Berkshires, to his school, away from New York and Hollywood. But, more importantly, away from Grace.

The next morning Grace woke up with only a sense of fuzziness; the light from the windows and the sounds of the city made sleeping late almost impossible. Sitting up in bed, she surveyed the room and quickly determined George was nowhere in sight. She jumped out of bed and checked the bathroom and still no George. Had he left? Had they had another fight? She couldn't remember.

She returned to the bedroom and sat down in the overstuffed armchair next to the vanity and noticed the empty bottle of whisky on the floor within inches of the note from Jacques. The stress of the drive, the meeting and all the Hollywood hype had gotten to Grace more than she let on. George knew this and decided a long walk through Central Park could help him. For a moment Grace thought he had left her.

She started to feel sorry for herself needing to figure out what her next move would be, when a knock came to the door. Grace rushed to open it. "Did you forget your key?" she asked, expecting George. It was room service with two pots of black coffee and toast.

"Ma'am, your husband asked me to tell you that he went for a walk," the attendant said.

"Well, I guess he will be back," she said with a hint of fear and disappointment. "Put it there," she gestured and turned to look for her purse to tip the guy. She didn't have the slightest sense of feeling embarrassed about the condition of the room. Dishevelment came to mind.

The drive back to Gilmanton was supposed to be a joyful one, but it was cold and quiet, each of them sticking to their own side of the car. Any conversation was strictly all business during that long ride home.

Earlier after checking out of the hotel, they went to Kitty's office to sign the deal and gather the check for the movie rights for her novel, *Peyton Place*.

Grace's attorney, Bernie, came down from Boston that morning as well and met them at the publisher's office. Kitty, Jacques, and the studio lawyer presented the contract, and they all reviewed it. For Grace it was an emotional time. Her baby was on the auction block to the highest bidder, and all the clauses in the contract confused her to no end.

With George's help they got through the paperwork. Grace was happy Bernie had come; he had been a godsend. She had little use for contracts; they intimidated her. The offer was clear: $250,000 dollars for the movie and television rights, $75,000 that day, the rest to follow. Grace's head was spinning. George pushed for a percentage of the profits, which would have lowered the cash sale. "What if the film flops?" Jacques argued, pushing the confused author into the direction of a clean sale. Grace knew Jacques was on her side, and she was too close to the book to think clearly. She wanted to be done with it, "Well, Jacques, are you sure?" She asked, never acknowledging her husband or her lawyer's advice. Her agent turned friend, nodded. "Where do I sign? "she asked.

CHAPTER 24

"Come on, Grace, just one?" TJ asked with an impish grin as he turned and pushed on the door. She tried not to look at his face because she knew she could never say no to him. He was truly her Prince Charming. The young author could not have created a better likeness to a prince than what she found in TJ the DJ. A true man full of virility and strength, something that her husband George lacked. She looked out of the revolving door of O'Shea's Department store to where her new lover stood. A frowning face with a gleam in his eyes, like that of a child not getting his way, staring back at her through the glass. Grace pushed on the brass handle, and it moved with ease. It glided in a circling motion like a figure skater. The fresh December air was a welcomed relief from the overheated store that seemed to have taken all the energy from her.

It was almost Christmas; Grace and TJ had spent the better part of the day doing errands, mostly shopping for the kids, her mother, and even her estranged husband who was still living in Massachusetts. Grace had taken on the holidays with passion and generosity. The book was doing well; the money was flowing. She loved the idea of credit, something that she never had the pleasure of having before *Peyton Place*. She could now walk in, find something, and all she had to do was to sign her name. Like magic it would be waiting at home for her. It would be neatly wrapped in brown kraft paper and tied with an unassuming green ribbon, a trademark of O'Shea's. It represented a liberation for her in her mind, a payoff for all the hours spent at the typewriter.

    She reached TJ on the sidewalk. She stopped abruptly to button her wool coat and tilted her head back ready for a kiss. The height difference between the two was almost comical, but they managed a sincere kiss in front of the store for the world to see. TJ leaned in and bent down. She opened her mouth wide in a vulgar attempt to show her true affection. "Grace," TJ pulled back a little. "Fuck them!" she said. With that, her head went back in a laugh. Laughing felt good. Something she wanted to do more of, and now she felt she had a reason to. "Okay, why not? Let's have that drink," she told him.

    The Laconia Tavern was now their place. After the fruitful night when the deal was sealed in the honeymoon suite during the snowstorm, they knew they were two peas in a pod. They were joined at the hip in some awkward display of physicality and affection. The Tavern was right around the corner from the main shopping street. In fact, everything in Laconia was just around the corner. Carrying the few purchases that were not being delivered, they made their way to the bar.

    Stopping just short of the door, TJ placed the bundle onto the sidewalk. Her Prince Charming stood at attention as he reached the well tarnished door handle and pulled it open wide, making a gesture as if royalty had arrived at the palace. "Fool," she whispered as she made her entrance into the dark bar. The smell of stale cigarettes wafted by them like an unwanted breeze. Picking up the packages, he managed to slip in before the big door closed. "If I am a fool,?" he told her, "Then I am the court Jester, and you are my queen."

    The place was rather empty for a weekday afternoon. "Perfect," they thought but did not share the sentiment out loud looking at each other. Their usual booth was available, and they headed for it. The lonely bartender was hunched over reading the afternoon paper with a burning cigarette in the corner of his mouth. He looked up for a second. He'd seen those two before, and they kept him way past closing during the storm awhile back. Not tonight.

An old Yankee of both body and mind, his judgment of some smutty writer and a cad of a DJ wasn't going to disrupt his shift or his business. The papers had been full of this book business. "*Peyton Place*, my ass," he thought. The book had Gilmanton written all over it. She can claim otherwise, but that murder was too much like the Roberts' case from years back. Frank had been the bartender at the tavern since he was a young man. Nothing happened in that area without his hearing about it. He was of the mind to let sleeping dogs lie, especially when it was as tragic as the Barbara Roberts' story was. The book Grace wrote opened a can of worms, and no one liked worms.

Closing the paper, he turned to his wall of liquor. The Canadian Club was in reach, and he knew without even asking: a couple of highballs for those two. Creatures of habit. Everyone from Christmas Island to the Weir's boardwalk knew what she drank. Her ability to hold her drink was as infamous as her portrayal of a New England town.

The freshly wiped glasses glistened in the dim light as amber liquid was poured into them. A lonely ice cube cracked under the pressure of the warm whiskey. Frank always felt that ginger ale in anything was a sacrilege to the booze. The soda should only be drunk warm for an upset stomach. Picking up the drinks, he crossed the floor to the happy couple that were tee-heeing like teenagers secluded in the privacy of the old leather booth.

"There's the man. Thank you, Frank," TJ acknowledged the drinks and took them from the bartender. Frank turned, did his best not to show them his disgust for these two day drinkers, and headed back to his safe place behind the bar. "Cheers, Darling." Grace smiled at her new man and drank the highball; it tasted good, refreshing and rejuvenating to her, not unlike a boxer, after a round, quenching his thirst with a cool ladle of water. The two sat and drank for a couple of hours. They hadn't noticed the bar filling with patrons at the end of a workday.

No one would admit it, but some patrons thought a snooping photographer might appear and get a picture of the scandalous writer and catch them in the background at the same time. Most locals would cringe at the thought of appearing in a tabloid magazine. Grace put them on the map, good, bad, or indifferent. Hollywood was knocking, and everyone wondered who would be the lucky one to answer the door.

Darkness fell, and it being a weeknight, even Grace thought it was time to go home. "Let's go, love." She didn't ask, but suggested it. It was her time to charm him, something she did so effortlessly. It didn't take TJ a second to agree, and with a twinkle in his eye, he picked up his drink and downed what was left in his glass. "Ready." They stood up in a sloppy, yet carefully thought-out way, trying not to be too obvious to the prying eyes that watched their every move. Whiskey gave them both a glow inside and out. Grace wanted, almost needed, the affection of her Scotsman between her legs.

Neither of them had any business driving that night. The walk to the car was brief, as they had parked on the street a block from the bar. TJ retrieved the keys from his front pants pocket and opened the trunk. Bundles were placed into the back with care. There was nothing breakable, and if there had been, it didn't matter. Credit and alcohol were a retailer's dream come true especially at Christmas time.

The drive up the state route to Gilmanton was fast; the roads clear and dry. TJ managed to drive as if he were sober, but he was not. Grace slid over to the middle of the seat and rested her left hand on his thigh. Heat from his crotch was doing things to the writer's mind that could be considered inspirational to her work. Moving her hand up his leg, her only thought was that she was thankful for his choice to wear boxers. The stiffness of his cock was all she felt. She exhaled slowly letting the buzz of the drink and the heat of his manhood overtake her mood, creating another torrid scene in her mind.

"Grace, come on, darling," he pleaded, "We're almost there, just a few miles." She withdrew her hand and rested her head on his shoulder. He drove with all the concentration he could muster up. The whiskey, his erection, and the moonless night were all he could handle. He thought about Grace and how fast things were moving. He really loved her, her creative mind, her sassy demeanor, and the way she made him feel when he fucked her. No woman had done it for him until he met this housewife turned writer. There was no question in his mind that *Peyton Place* was anything but a book written from the experiences of the writer, nor further from the truth.

The house ahead of them was dark as they drove down the driveway. With no moon out to light their way, the meager headlights illuminated the snow, making it look gray and menacing. He could tell the front steps to the porch were frozen and in need of a layer of rock salt. He pulled the car up next to the walk and jumped out. He ran around the back of the vehicle using his left hand to keep his balance. He opened the car door for Grace.

"Here let me," offering his hand. The slippery condition of the driveway took control of his balance, and he slid down to the ground. He had landed squarely on his knees like a comical routine of the leading man and his damsel in distress. He was not amused. Grace chuckled, giggled, and then she laughed. It was all too funny, and the whiskey the enabler.

They helped each other up the steps and onto the porch. She opened the door with ease. Locking the front door was something she had never done and never even thought about. In New England rarely did anyone lock their doors. The Yankee wisdom was that any unwanted guest would get in if they wanted to. This way the intruder would not damage the door. A light switch was flipped on; the house interior was bathed in the warmth of incandescent lights. It cast out the cold and filled her dream house with the feeling of life. Closing the door behind them, the young couple did not notice the car parked up the road in the shadows.

A burning cigarette glow can light the darkest of spaces, so he covered the tip to conceal the light. He did not want to be seen. The smell of the smoke could travel for many yards on a cold, dark and still night. He had to be careful with that as well. The smoker kept the windows up in the car, not allowing it to escape into the night. Smoke filled the interior space creating a mist of mystery as he watched the antics of Grace and her current lover put on their little show of drunkenness that he could see from the glow of the dome light in her car. He was disgusted, but he waited, taking a drag and holding it in, savoring the way it calmed him.

Inside the house the furnace spewed hot air as fast as it could to warm the farmhouse. Grace dropped her coat, her purse, and her clothes in the middle of the front room floor, not caring where they landed. She headed to the sofa where she dropped in a big plop. TJ managed to hang his coat on the hook next to the front door and headed directly to the fireplace. He was happy he'd arranged the kindling and logs in the fireplace before heading out. He knew Grace loved to fuck on the floor in front of a roaring fire, and he never wanted to disappoint her.

It was the start of the school holiday break; the kids were spending the night at *Shakey Acres* with Laurie. Since TJ was in the picture and George was out of town, the Metalious children looked for any excuse to be away from the house on Meadows Pond Road.

"Baby, how about a drink?" she asked. He knew he had to get it. He waited long enough for the first burst of new flames inside the fireplace to start. His skills as a fire starter improved with every visit to Grace's new home. She leaned back onto the sofa and closed her eyes, the reassuring sound of the crackling of the fire and the closing of the cupboard door. She knew he had done his duties. TJ was a good man, she thought, as he sat down next to her nakedness on the sofa, a bottle of Canadian Club and two glasses in hand. Her eyes opened, and she smiled.

He poured, she purred. They drank the warm whiskey and watched the fire in silence. No word was spoken between them, but like conjoined twins they knew each other's thoughts. His large hands found their way to her groin and began to open her with his fingers, ever so gently, ever so cautiously. She gasped slightly, trying not to let him hear the sound escaping her mouth. Her gentle giant pleased her body in ways she'd never felt before with her husband. For the first time she was calling the shots. She would decide when and where she would make love and with whom. TJ the DJ was her man, and no one could change her mind.

Call it art imitating life, she didn't care. Grace lived in the moment. She became a character of her own imagination and wrote a story in her mind, one scene after another recording what was happening in her memory bank for future use. The caresses became kisses, the kisses became deeper, the total engulfing of each other was like a cannibalistic ritual of flesh and lust. They moved onto the wool braided rug that acted as an island on the cold hardwood floor between the couch and the fireplace. Grace was spread eagle with TJ on top of her, his eyes glazed in a fit of passion, hers closed tightly, and her moans so loud they startled the smoker as he softly stepped onto the front porch.

It was George. He traded the cigarette for a Kodak Brownie and stepped quietly onto the porch mimicking a hunter stalking his prey. Through the window he could see the entangled mess crudely displayed on the floor in front of the fireplace. They were so involved with the pleasure of their own bodies, that the sound of the door opening and closing went unnoticed. Her estranged husband shook violently, not because of the cold, but because of the fear he felt. He could not believe that he was sneaking into his own house, armed with a camera. He feared the truth about what his oldest daughter told him.

Marsha had not lied. What he was watching was not the person he thought he had married. The woman, directly in front of him, was grunting and groaning like an animal. Disgust overwhelmed him in a blanket of nausea.

The flashbulb made a loud "pop" as George pushed down the lever on the side of the camera. Pop again and the second flash was seen. George acted quickly, removing the red hot bulbs and discarding them on to the floor, while at the same time winding the film forward. His adrenaline was so high that he never noticed the burnt fingertips on his right hand caused by the hot flash bulbs as he changed them. By the third round of flashing bulbs the startled couple opened their eyes and broke their embrace, pushing each other away with shock and embarrassment.

"What the fuck?" Grace screamed. "You fucking bastard," she retorted grabbing a crocheted afghan from the sofa in an attempt to cover her naked body. "George, what the hell?" Grace exclaimed and scrambled like a schoolgirl caught in the act.

"Is this your husband?" the DJ asked.

"Yes, the asshole, George," she answered as the fourth flash of light rendered them blinded for a second. "Stop it!" she screamed, her voice clear and authoritative. She showed no sign of a drunken stupor but only that of a mad hen caught in a rainstorm.

George looked around the room and retrieved TJ's shirt from a heap of clothes on the floor. Grace sat up on the sofa, holding the colorful knitted blanket tight around her exposed body and looked at her husband. Anger overwhelmed her. All she could think about was hurting him and hoped her lover would do just that. TJ buttoned his shirt and pulled on his boxers that were next to him on the floor. The two lovers sat there on the sofa straining to make sense of what had just happened.

George tersely controlled his breathing and his thinking as he sat down on the overstuffed armchair across from the sofa. He reached over and turned the lamp on next to him and placed the Kodak camera on the end table. He waited patiently for them to compose themselves. Controlling his anger and his resentment was difficult. He knew he had to stick to his plan.

"What was that little stunt?" Grace screamed. "How dare you?" she continued.

"How dare I?" George asked with a sense of irony and sarcasm. "Need I remind you this is still half my house, and that is my mother's braided rug you were all over like a whore." He still did not raise his voice. "Is this your current research?" he asked pointing to TJ who was trying to conceal his manhood with both hands.

TJ knew he'd been caught, literally, with his pants down. Slipping out into the cold night was not an option. He waited for the emotions of the situation to diminish as he wondered what the outcome would be.

"TJ, my dear, meet my husband George," Grace stated it as a sarcastic fact. Her anger hidden only by the knitted blanket that was wrapped around her. "Where the fuck is that bottle?" she added. Grace looked for the whiskey and found the half empty bottle on the floor next to the sofa. She picked it up and took a long drink straight from the bottle. She put it back onto the floor and wiped her mouth with her forearm while trying not to expose anymore of herself. The gesture she made was defiant and bold. A line was drawn in the snow.

"What do you want?" was all she asked.

CHAPTER 25

Come on, pick up the fucking phone!" Grace was frantic. Her frustration with the situation peaked, and cheap whiskey couldn't help her. "Bernie, get your ass to the phone." Her voice was a mixture of desperation fueled by sexual disappointment and alcohol. "I pay him a lot of money; the least he could do is pick up the fucking phone." She retorted.

"It's late, call him in the morning," TJ piped in his two cents' worth, while scrambling to find his pants and his dignity, both of which had been misplaced earlier in the night.

The entire scene that night was something out of the latest Photoplay magazine. The writer in her went into plotting, something she hated to do. "Young married author beds younger lover as estranged husband breaks in and takes sordid photos."

Grace slams down the phone and throws it across the room, barely missing her lover's feet. TJ bent down, checked for a dial tone, and placed the receiver back on the base. His head nodded, and then he placed it back on the floral hassock next to the sofa.

"What will we do? If that fucking George thinks he can barge in here and blackmail me, he better think twice about it." Grace spewed out angrier words. She searched and found her almost empty drink; the lukewarm whiskey was not enough to cool her mood. "TJ, where's the bottle?" she demanded.

"Here," TJ extended his right hand to his lover who was now sitting on the edge of the sofa ready to burst into tears. He sat down next to her and raised the bottle to check the contents. It was near empty. He managed to pour a small amount into her glass. "Drink this, then let's go upstairs. Nothing will be solved if we are both hungover tomorrow."

"Okay baby." She sheepishly agreed with her prince charming. She stood, still clutching the multicolored afghan, her security blanket during the ordeal. TJ wrapped his arms around her and steered her to the center hall stairs that led to the master bedroom. The roaring fire that had been so dramatic, so romantic and inspired so much passion, was now a glowing pile of embers, not worthy of notice.

Morning came sooner than either of them anticipated. The dark green fabric shades, pulled down tightly the night before to guard against anymore prying eyes, did not block the morning rays. The crisp December air only magnified the sun's brightness as it rose over the nearby mountains. Grace's bedroom window faced east. It was planned that way because on most mornings she loved to write in her bed. That morning was not most.

"I'll make coffee while you jump in the shower." TJ was the voice of reason. He knew a lot was riding on how the situation would be handled. Grace moaned slightly and rolled over to her side of the bed, burying her face in her pillow.

"Baby, we have to do this," he continued. "This Bernie guy will fix it for you. He seems to have fixed other things for you before."

Bernie Sneirson was her go to for everything lately. The book had caused such a stir. When the contracts and meetings became a distraction to her, he handled them. Bernie settled a lawsuit about one of the book characters, Thomas Markis. He was tall, dark, and handsome in both the book and in reality, an acquaintance that Grace did remember meeting. He had claimed her writings caused him pain and suffering. She just wanted it to go away, and with Bernie's help it did.

Grace knew Bernie could sort this out. Rolling out of bed, Grace stumbled into the master bath she had designed. It was not Auntie Georgie's back in Manchester, and it wasn't the outhouse from *It'll Do* either. It was her bathroom in her dream house. She knew a long soak in the cast tub was what she wanted, but that morning a shower would have to do.

Grace and TJ drove back into town in silence. There was no flirtation, no groping, no conversation. An air of pensiveness hovered in the car. As they turned down the road to the state highway, someone had posted a crude sign in the snowbank. Painted on a cedar shake shingle, the message was offensive and clear. "Get out slut."

To say Gilmanton was not pleased with *Peyton Place* was an understatement. Not with the sordid story, not with the notoriety, and surely not with the author. It had come full circle for the town and for Grace. The cold shoulders and the random messages still occurred. Grace's resolve was better and had improved with each incident. But what happened with her husband the evening before was icing on her cake.

"Hello, Mrs. Metalious, you can go right in. Mr. Sneirson is expecting you," the receptionist said and motioned for Grace to proceed through the closed door. "What the hell?" Grace asked. "How did Bernie know I was coming? He never picked up the phone last night?" She knew her lawyer was good, but not that good. "Mr. Metalious is already in there," the receptionist added. Grace looked over her shoulder in the direction of TJ and glared at her lover. "This is going to be good," she said with her eyes.

TJ knew this was her battle, and he would stay put. Grace turned the doorknob to Bernie's office with a feeling of apprehensiveness, but her self-defiant attitude took over, and she started to overcompensate, channeling her publisher, Kitty

Messner. "How would Kitty handle this situation?" went through her mind. The door swung open, Bernie stood there with his hand out ready to greet her or catch her, whatever came first.

"Before you say anything, Grace," her lawyer with both hands upright tried to hold her back. "George was waiting on the front stoop before I even arrived this morning." Bernie had to set things straight with her, otherwise it would turn ugly.

Grace did not respond. She moved to the side table where he'd already poured her a drink. As gracefully as Grace could, she picked up the drink and sat across from her husband on the small settee. Sipping it she noticed the Kodak Brownie in the center of the desk. Leaning back with her drink, she was all ears.

Bernie and George seemed to have discussed the situation for a couple of hours, at least that's what Grace thought. George told him everything that was happening in their world. They discussed the best-selling book, and that he was aware of the lucrative movie deal. They spoke about Grace's lifestyle and his untimely departure from Gilmanton to Massachusetts to live during the week. He painted quite a behind the scenes picture of Grace and their family. Her lawyer tried not to choose sides, but Grace still felt it was the old boys club. Her husband beat her to the punch with Bernie. TJ was a recent part of this story. Grace sat and relived all the moments of the past few months, maybe years, that brought her and George to this moment.

George critically listened to the lawyer to be sure that nothing was missed. Not the drinking, not the spending, not the neglect of the children, and surely not the cheating. He had known TJ was not the first; others had been overlooked. They were in the public's eye, and he could not go through another personal scandal like the previous fiasco that had cost him his job.

"Well, Bernie, it seems you and George have had quite the little talk this morning," she calmly alleged to her lawyer. "Tell me this, what the fuck does he want?"

" Come on, Gracie, let's try to be civil. I only want the best for you." Bernie told her. "Well, you could have fooled me," quipped Grace.

"Divorce," George spoke. "Divorce and enough money to get a Master's degree. That's all I want." George had thought the situation through the night before. After sneaking into the house and catching his wife with that man in those photos, he knew he'd lost her forever. A side of Grace that was dirty, sexual and crass was evident in her writing. He knew that deep within his wife lurked the heart of a woman, but what she was emerging into was unrecognizable to him.

"Fine," Grace spoke, albeit one word. She agreed and leaned back to finish her drink. She waited for someone to say something; someone needed to say something. Biting her lip, like in a poker game, she did her best not to wear her cards on her sleeve.

Bernie had drawn up the papers before Grace had arrived. He was sure that after a night like that she would be in his office first thing. Predictability and Grace were synonymous at times. The agreement was quite simple, and, being uncontested, it was an easy document to draw up. "George already signed it, Grace. All you have to do is sign here," Bernie told her. "I will file it at the Lakes Region Courthouse tomorrow," he continued.

Taking the papers from Bernie, Grace had no interest in reading them and wanted nothing more than for the meeting to be over. "These are in order?" She asked her lawyer, deep down knowing he had her best interest at heart.

"It is quite fair on George's part," Bernie told her. *Peyton Place* was doing very well; lots of money kept rolling in. It was all too overwhelming for her. She knew George had no interest in the money affairs. It was clear now that he could have asked for lots more. Any judge would give him half of *Peyton Place*, she knew that. Fifty percent of the money would not make her happy, so signing the document was the easiest thing for her.

"Where, Bernie? On this line?" Grace spoke in the sweetest of voices. "There," he pointed with a pen. "I will let you both know as soon as it's filed." She took the pen and scribbled her signature in one fast motion, never letting the pen off the surface of the document.

Grace walked over to the desk where the camera was there waiting for her. She picked it up and examined it like a piece of evidence in a trial. Determining quickly how it opened, she removed the back of the camera and pulled out the roll of exposed film, re-exposing it to the daylight. She yanked on it with one pull, and it unraveled from the spool and landed in a heap in the center of Bernie's desk. Ever so gently, she replaced the back of the camera and handed it to her soon-to-be ex-husband.

"I believe this is yours?" she questioned with sarcasm. "I think I will stop at O'Shea's to buy myself a new one. Christmas will be here before you know it."

Without another word, she turned and nodded to Bernie, this was her seal of approval for fixing what could have been more of a mess. She was not going to look back. She and George were through, "Merry Fucking Christmas" she said to herself and left.

Opening the door of the office for her, Bernie leaned in for a kiss on the cheek. He wanted her to stay and sort out other affairs that were pending, but he knew her marriage had just ended. Grace might have acted like a New York businesswoman, but deep down she was as vulnerable as a schoolgirl from New Hampshire.

"Happy Chanukah, Mr. Sneirson, enjoy your family. I know I will be enjoying mine," Grace added as a dig to her newly divorced husband who was in ear shot. Grace knew he would be spending it in a studio apartment, south-of-the-border, all alone.

"Darling, sorry to take so long." Grace took TJ's hand. "Come, let's stop at O'Shea's. I am in the market for a new camera." TJ was a little puzzled but knew she would tell him everything in due course.

"And if you are a good boy, I will let you finish what you started last night," Grace chuckled.

CHAPTER 26

The sky above Gilmanton grew dark. It was barely noon and already it looked as if the street-lamps around the town green would suddenly pop on. The New England winter sky could be an unforgiving force of nature. A true New Englander could look to the sky and predict if another nor'easter was fast approaching. In a few hours it would descend upon the tiny village as a reminder that Mother Nature was still in control.

The screen door of The Corner Store slammed open with a crash, pushed by the mighty north wind and the force of the town Librarian as she scurried into the store. "Ned, can't you do something about that door?" Rita barked at the proprietor of the establishment. Rita Rowell was wrapped head to toe in the local mill's wool. She had purchased remnants from the factory store to make various layers of clothing. Anything to ward off the cold of a New Hampshire winter. "What are you reading?" She asked as she moved closer to the counter and unwrapped the JP Stevens wool scarf she made from around her neck.

"Oh, howdy, Ms. Rowell. Didn't hear the door." Ned never looked up and never paid too much attention to the front door. It slammed in all four seasons. It was his reminder that things never changed in Gilmanton. It slammed when his father ran the place, and it would slam when he was long gone. "The Boston paper came very early today. The driver wanted to get south before all this shit began falling." Ned looked up and like a smart ass, he smiled at her.

"Anything in the paper that I should be aware of?" Rita looked down to the newsprint laid out on the counter. The Boston Evening Traveller was a daily paper that printed stories based on facts, not a real tabloid but written with as much desire to entertain, as well as to inform. She knew That Book, as it was referred to, was in the paper daily, touting stories of the author's mayhem and success of smut in the written form. The town librarian, never recognizing the book, tried her best to rise above it all. She continued to remove articles from the dailies so residents would not have to look at it under her roof. Rita took her job very seriously as the town's literary over-seer and member of the school board.

"Well, well, well," Ned whispered as his head shook back and forth like a newfangled fuzzy dashboard animal. "She's done it this time." Ned turned the paper around so that Rita could read it. "Oh my!" Rita showed the slightest of emotion as she read the headline.

GILMANTON HOUSEWIFE TURNED AUTHOR FILES FOR DIVORCE. The headline was on the front page tucked under the fold and on the inside corner. Not the best place, after all it was newsworthy, just not world news. The tag below the short article also read, "More news on *Peyton Place*. Page 23." Rita flipped through the paper to see what else would be arriving as if the approaching storm wasn't enough.

Ned turned from his customer and placed food items on the shelf behind the counter. Canned goods would be in high demand, thanks to Old Man Winter. Nothing like a storm to boost sales. He paid Rita no mind as she stood and read the articles to herself, never saying a word to the shopkeeper. The book was only out a few months, and it had brought in a whirlwind of prying eyes, nosey reporters, and Sunday drivers in search of the sheep pen where the now infamous murder had taken place. *Peyton Place* had come full circle for that tiny village, and most residents had wished it had never happened.

Rita looked up to Ned. Her eyes now were dull and lacked the life they had before. "I could cry, Ned. That woman, that," she paused to gain control. "That woman should have left town when we fired her husband. Who was she to dredge it all up, who was she to tell the world our secrets?"

Ned personally agreed with her, but would never say anything, because business was business. The number of new customers he received to his store had been growing since the first article was released about her novel. Ned explained, "Just this past Sunday some flatlander was in the store looking to buy a postcard." "A postcard?" It was January, folks from the south only came in the summer to enjoy the lakes and mountains. When the customer asked, "Is this *Peyton Place*?" Ned wanted to throw him out of the store. In retrospect he was glad he didn't because the Bostonian purchased nearly $5.00 worth of stuff, including several old postcards Ned had dug out from under the counter. After that sale, he decided to leave the box in reach for the following weekend.

"Rita, I am not one to make a fuss. That woman wrote a book and told a story that most of us turned a blind eye to." "It will all blow over like this storm today." Ned took the paper from Rita as if it were a deadly weapon. He was trying to save the librarian from her own dark thoughts. Folding the paper and placing it back on the pile next to the counter, he paused and looked directly at her with a smile, "What can I get you?"

The look on her face was pure frustration. It was clear Ned was not going to agree with her in regard to the Metalious woman's book. He was a true opportunist. Everyone in town knew it, just like they knew everything else that happened in this town. "Maybe Gilmanton was *Peyton Place* after all," she thought to herself for the first time.

Rita turned from the counter and walked to the back of the store. Her mind preoccupied with the story from the paper, she opened the beer cooler and grabbed a pint of Kruger Ale. When she realized what she was doing, she quickly placed it back and opened the lower door. A quart of milk was what she needed. Feeling slightly out of sorts, she hurried back in the direction of the counter, grabbing a loaf of Cushman's Home-style bread as she passed the rack. Tea and toast would fix everything just as soon as she flipped the closed sign on the library's front door.

"Anything else, Rita?" Ned asked. Rita looked up and gave him a little smile. As curt and unpleasant as it was, she would never let him get to her. "That'll do, thank you." She stood there looking into her change purse. Not wanting to break a dollar bill," Put it on my tab, would you Ned?" she politely asked him.

As Ned retrieved a brown paper sack from under the counter, he started in again. "You know just last month, Grace, you know who." That was not a question, Ned's humor was dry and tasteless at times. "She marched in here dressed in a mink coat she bought from one of those fancy stores in New York. Well, I just wanted to laugh out loud. A mink coat in Gilmanton." Rita was all ears. "What did she want?"

"It seemed that she wanted to settle her tab. She was miffed that I had sent a message home with her son a couple of days before. The coat was one thing, but she asked if I would cash a personal check made out to her." Ned continued, "I said sure, and she pulled out a check from New York for $1,230."

Rita knew Ned's stories could be a bit over-the-top, she stood there and listened as he rattled on. She only felt better knowing she would soon be out of his presence.

"Well you couldn't cash it, could you?" she asked.

"Hell no, her tab was only $23.10," Ned says.

"Then the strangest thing happened," he told Rita. "I handed her the check back and said, "I don't accept out-of-state checks," smiling, Ned paused before he finished his story, Rita waited with bated breath. "She took the check, stuffed it into her coat pocket, and then let the fur coat fall open. She was stark naked under that thing. I almost fell down on the floor. Sweet Jesus." Ned was now roaring with laughter. Rita turned three shades of red and grabbed her parcels to leave.

"Rita, one more thing," he looked her straight in the eyes. "When will the library have a copy of the book? My wife is fixing to read it soon. She wants to know if she is in it." Ned continued to laugh. Rita, without taking time to rewrap her layers of wool, pushed open the door.

"Over my dead body. There will never be a copy of that trash in my library," she shouted back. The door slammed loud, deafening as a crack of thunder during a winter storm; it could be heard across the town green.

The sound went unnoticed as a new white Cadillac convertible made its way across Spruce Street on its way to the state highway. It was headed south to warmer and more exciting destinations, no doubt.

CHAPTER 27

"Come on, Grace, put the paper down," TJ insisted from the kitchen. "The kids are in the car already." TJ walked into the living room where Grace was sitting on the couch reading the Boston paper. She was visibly upset. "Why did Bernie tell the papers? He said he would wait until we left Gilmanton before releasing the news." Grace asked her man, her prince charming.

"Sweetie, it doesn't matter. Once he filed the papers, they became public. The news would have been out sooner or later," he tells her. "Let's just go. Snow is coming, and I would like to make it to the interstate before it starts." Grace knew he was right, but she wanted to be as far away from Gilmanton as she could before the news broke. She and George were divorcing. It was over, and she was moving on with TJ the DJ. Grace could not have been happier.

The past few weeks, after her meeting with Bernie and George, were like a dream come true. TJ gave up his apartment in Lakeport and moved into the house. The kids started to warm up to him, and they might actually have liked him. His stature was the polar opposite of George. Tall, strong, big boned and a full head of hair. He was Grace's dream boat, and the kids knew it. TJ was excellent with the children as well. He communicated with them at their level. Marsha thought he was dandy, and the younger ones just liked having him around.

Christmas was nearly perfect for them. Gifts hidden in the barn were brought into the living room on Christmas Eve. There were so many that they were stacked in three piles. Each had its own wrapping paper to identify which child got what. It had been Grace's idea to wrap them that way; it saved creating name tags for each gift. There were other presents, one for her mother and a couple for her sister Bunny, in case they decided to make the trek north from Manchester to see her and the kids.

TJ got up early Christmas morning and made a roaring fire in the hearth. He plugged in the multi-colored lights on the tree. Each time he hoped one hadn't blown out to render the string bad. He wanted the kids to wake up to a brightly lit tree and a warm toasty living room.

That special day he watched Grace from across the room. Her energy and generosity were infectious. She'd never been good at hiding her emotions, good or bad. That morning they were only good.

Her idea of money was to spend it when you had it, because it might be lost at any time. Cindy and Mike, the younger of the clan, were thrilled with all the gifts and toys. The room looked as if a bomb had gone off with multi-colored wrapping paper in shreds throughout the room. Grace just laughed and enjoyed the moment.

TJ was happy, Grace was happy, and the kids were happy. Their morning couldn't be spoiled by the press, the neighbors, or even George. The outside world was far away from her dream house, nestled on the tree lined road, deep in the woods of New Hampshire.

"Oh, Ma, thank you," Marsha gushed, "I love it." She wrapped her arms around her mother and kissed her on the right cheek. Her oldest had unwrapped a beautiful cashmere sweater set that had been beautifully wrapped in an O'Shea's gift box. "You can wear that in Hollywood," Grace added.

It was the dead of winter and already plans were set in motion for a departure to places warmer and more glamorous.

Grace and her family would be far away from the icy frostbite of New England. TJ was looking forward to the trip, in the new Cadillac.

"Grace, don't forget your notes," TJ stood in the doorway of the kitchen. He jingled the house keys ready to lock up; she would get the message. After that fiasco with George, TJ had the locks changed and now using them was the norm.

"Okay, darling," and with that Grace was up off the sofa and out the front door in sixty seconds. "Did you grab my notes dear?" She asked passing through the front door, leaving it wide open. Not bothering to put on her coat, she jumped into the front seat of the warmed convertible.

TJ gathered her notes, a small stack of steno pads filled with scribbles that were on the coffee table next to her leather satchel. He slipped the notes into the satchel with one motion. He double checked the fireplace to see if it was truly extinguished. Satisfied, he was out the door and the sound of the tumbler turned in the latch. That was the last sound heard that morning at the Metalious house.

The new convertible handled beautifully, he thought, as he drove it south along State Route 106 in the direction of the interstate. A canvas top in the dead of winter might not have been practical, but come summer, he and Grace would be the envy of the town. The heater inside the car was on full blast trying to ward off the cold that seeped in from around the windows and through the seams of the frozen fabric.

Everyone was excited for this trip, a real adventure. As they would say, "When Hollywood comes calling, you better head west." Jerry Wald, the producer of the film *Peyton Place*, was a master of publicity and stunts. He had rung Kitty and Jacques in New York just before Christmas. If anyone could convince Grace to come to the west coast, they could. Her publisher was her idol, and Jacques played the role of the long lost friend she never had. Wald wanted Grace for photoshoots and to help with the actual script. She hadn't needed much of a push. She agreed once TJ told her it was the best thing to do for the book. "Okay, let's go then," was what she actually said. Looking to the kids, she asked, "Wanna go too?"

The storm, brewing since early morning, became a full-fledged nor'easter. The snow was light and airy. It swirled over the front hood of the car and did not stick. The temperature dropped. Roads, dry and clear, would soon accumulate the white stuff making driving more dangerous.

"Turn the radio on, Grace. Get that station from Nashua, that does the weather all the time."

Grace slid over to the center of the seat and turned the knob trying to pick up a station, any station. Static was loud, and picking up a signal was not going to happen until they got further south, nearer to Boston.

They were not concerned. The new convertible cruised south along an almost deserted highway. It grew darker now but still enough daylight to see. They wanted to get to Connecticut before nightfall. Their halfway point to New York was the Howard Johnson's they had stayed at many times. The bright orange roof would be a welcome sight.

Quietly, together, the little family watched the snow as it fell and the darkness approached . They decided this trip would be a ball. No eating sandwiches made in the back seat, no stuffing everyone in one room, and surely no school until they returned. TJ was finally getting to see California, and Marsha might even get to meet Elvis Presley. Grace, on the other hand, was more than a little intimidated but would not show it to anyone, let alone admit it to herself. Hollywood, movie making, fancy hotels, and palm trees, all seemed too much for her. She took assurance in knowing that a pint of CC was carefully concealed in her handbag.

Howard Johnson was a welcome sight, as were all the various motels along the way. TJ mapped the route west, trying to stay south away from the winter storms in the Midwest. January was not the best time to cross the United States by car, but Grace hated to fly in the winter months, and this way the kids could go.

The trip to the west coast seemed to take forever. Driving through the daylight hours and arriving long enough in one city to check in to a roadside motel and have some food at the diner that usually was attached to the property. Their routine was the same: the giant neon light would beckon them off the interstate with intriguing images of food, cabins, and swimming pools. Each stopping place along the way was different, yet the same.

In most places the kids stayed in one room, and Grace and her Prince in another, never an adjoining door. After checking in, they would make their way to the restaurant for supper. The kids loved ordering anything they wanted to and as much as they wanted. The only rule was they had to finish everything on their plate. Grace's rules were many, but the most important was not to disturb her once she and TJ retired for the night. Marsha was in control of her younger siblings, a job she took very seriously. Besides, she knew what was going on.

TJ and Grace tried their best not to drink in front of the kids. They always kept a stash of whiskey somewhere in the car or in their luggage. Drinking was a way of relaxing, breaking the monotony after a long day of driving. Grace was working constantly, always making notes about her story. She hoped Jerry Wald would use them in the movie. She filled two more steno pads in a week but never brought them into the room at night. After dinner was their time, and once the whiskey did its magic, she was ready for some adult fun.

"I'm tired Grace. Can't we just go to sleep," TJ pleaded from his side of the bed. "We have a big day tomorrow if we are going to make New Mexico." Grace alerted the studio they would be there in three days. The call from the diner earlier to her agent was quick because she had very little change.

"Jacques and Mr. Wald are expecting us Monday. We need to check into the hotel in Beverly Hills on Sunday." Grace knew he was right, but she was horny. It had been almost twenty-four hours. She poured herself another drink and picked up a magazine from the nightstand. Her lover turned off the light above his head and rolled over in the opposite direction. Grace was miffed.

The next day was a long one, almost thirteen hours in the car with only a stop for lunch. Everyone was getting anxious and annoyed at the same time. Mike and Cindy had to be separated with Marsha in the middle. The youngest were the most irritated with the drive and each other. Grace felt tired and was upset with her prince. They were at each other whenever the kids weren't around. The road trip was wearing them down, and she didn't like that feeling.

"Look, we are going around El Paso, so we'll figure out a place to stop," TJ announced. Everyone's attention was suddenly on the views from their respective windows. The desert at dusk was a constant display of colors as the sun sank over the horizon.

"Look, Ma," Mike pointed to the billboard out the passenger side window. "It's called The Wagon Wheel Motel. It has a western shop and a pool." Mike was excited, and it was his turn to pick the stop.

"That's another forty-five minutes to Las Cruces," TJ said. "Can you all hold on? He asked. The rest of the car was delighted that there was a light at the end of the tunnel for that day of driving; the end was in sight.

The Wagon Wheel was a destination hotel. Perched on the edge of the Chihuahuan Desert, it was a tongue-in-cheek attempt to combine adobe style buildings with a cheesy western store front. There were wagon wheels, cactus, and a fake teepee that served as the front office. TJ had driven enough for one day, and Grace just wanted to get away from him. The stop could not have come soon enough.

TJ parked in front of the makeshift teepee and walked in the direction of the neon sign flashing, "Rooms available with hot showers." The kids jumped out of the car as soon as Grace gave them the look and a nod. Their pent-up energy was ready to explode. Steam needed to be released, and Grace knew that. She also knew that tomorrow, if all went well, they would be arriving in Hollywood. She had no idea what to expect.

"Ma, can we go into the gift shop?" Cindy asked. "Sure, I'll come with you." She never looked in TJ's direction. Her mood had not softened, and she felt a little distance between her and her lover was needed at that moment. TJ knew the check-in routine, and he was fine with that.

The gift shop resembled a western town general store, complete with wooden sidewalks, oil lamps, and a variety of barrels outside. The children ran past Grace and pushed their way into the store. The shopkeeper was dressed in a prairie style gingham dress. Mike ran right over to a mannequin dressed like Wild Bill Hickok, six-shooter and all. "So cool, isn't it Marsha? "Yeah. It's okay," she answered and headed towards the jewelry display. It was filled with western style turquoise necklaces. Everyone scattered in the shop to different corners. Western fashions and accessories were never seen in Gilmanton, let alone New Hampshire.

In less than thirty minutes, the Metalious children had picked out an assortment of items they wanted: Cindy a white cowboy hat; Mike a six-shooter and a leather fringed coat; and Marsha chose a high collared white blouse with a bola style necklace to finish it off. Grace never said no to them. After all, the money was hers. Her writing had paid off, why not spend it?

Dinner was in the restaurant next to the teepee, appropriately called "Chuck Wagon." Everyone ordered a T-bone steak, mashed potatoes, and their famous biscuits. The weary travelers ate in silence. The road trip was getting to them, and they could not wait to see California. Both TJ and Grace broke a major rule and decided to have a drink with dinner.

One round after another, they sat in silence, still upset with the other: Grace with him for denying her the pleasures she enjoyed and he with her because rest seemed the sensible thing to do at the time. Dessert was strawberry shortcake. The kids got up from the table and took it to their room; television programs on Saturday night were always the best. "Night, Ma," Cindy kissed Grace on the cheek. Mike ran out the door holding his bowl with both hands. After all, the first one to the room got to pick the show.

Alone at the table, the restaurant nearly deserted, Grace looked to TJ. "What the fuck is wrong with you?" With that and another round of Canadian Club Whiskey, they duked it out, one jab after the other. They had fights before, but they were becoming more frequent, more volatile. They tried their best to keep a civil tone to their voices; they were used to that. The waitress retreated behind the counter around the corner from their table. She hoped it would act like a circle of covered wagons to protect her from this battle.

TJ knew that Grace was feeling the pressure of her notoriety for her work. The disapproval of some people and the expectations of the studio added pressure. It was all coming together, but she was felt cornered.

"Grace, are you sure you want another drink?" he asked in the kindest of ways.

"Fuck yeh, and so do you," She told him. She shot a look over her shoulder to the waitress. Without a word spoken, two doubles with a side of ice arrived in seconds.

After another round of drinks, they came to a resolution. A peace treaty was reached when TJ placed his hand on hers and smiled, "Shall we go back to the room?" His lover answered with her eyes. His sexy invitation was needed reassurance to Grace for another day.

He paid the bill and left a generous five-dollar tip for the waitress. She would be pleased, and so would Grace. Spreading the wealth was something they both liked to do. They held hands and made their way across the gravel parking lot to their adobe style bungalow.

It was fortunate for the kids that Grace and TJ's room was not near them that night. Sounds of adults making love would be too much for their adolescent ears to hear. Once inside the room, they locked in a passionate kiss, hands groping each other's private parts. Buttons popped, and zippers made their way down. Their night of lovemaking was epic, in a true dime store novel fashion. The nakedness of their bodies glowed in the darkness with only the glow from the neon light shining through the window from the motel's sign.

The next morning everyone had a new sense of urgency and energy. It would be their last day on the road. Only eleven hours to Hollywood and the famous Beverly Hilton. Grace had picked that property because she read it was owned by The Plaza in New York, her all-time favorite hotel, so it just had to be the best.

CHAPTER 28

There it is! "exclaimed Grace, pointing across the now dull, almost beige, hood of the once stark white convertible through the dirty windshield. Majestically rising from a perfectly manicured lawn sat the Beverly Hilton Hotel. A true icon among the rich and the nearly famous. Staying here was like staying in The Plaza on Fifth Avenue, with much less city. "Isn't it beautiful?" Grace asked her man. "We are so lucky to stay here, We have a three-bedroom suite complete with our very own maid." She turned around to look towards the back seat where all three of the children were sound asleep. Shaking her head, she turned back, grabbed TJ's right hand and sat up straight as he turned into the circle drive of the hotel.

The Beverly Hilton was brand new, opened just two years before by the famous hotelier, Conrad Hilton. This property was a testament to all things possible in tinsel town. With multi stories of accommodations and with all types to offer, it was the best of the best. They spared no expense when it came to pleasing guests. Grace had done her research on her last visit to New York. Her friend at the concierge desk told her she must stay at the Beverly." It was run by the same company. She loved the Plaza, so the Beverly would be a shoo-in she thought.

"Oh TJ, I'm so nervous," Grace whispered.

"It will be great, baby," he assured her. "You just wait and see." Leaning over, he kissed the top of her head. "Hey kids, we're here," he raised his voice as he opened his door and moved his seat forward to let them out.

Grace's brand-new Cadillac, serviced and cleaned a little over eight days before, was now dirty and worn. The road trip west combined with a lack of responsibility rendered the inside of the vehicle an embarrassment. Empty coke bottles, candy bar wrappers, and leftover crust from a peanut butter sandwich now littered the back seat. The outside was no better. Desert dust, and a spotty rain shower they drove through in Riverside, just added to the unfaltering appearance. TJ went to the back and scraped dirt from the trunk's lock in order to insert the key to open it.

In less than a minute a bellman was at the back sorting out the contents of the trunk. Their assortment of luggage, shopping bags and other items were arranged carefully on the cart to swiftly get this rag-a-muffin lot to their room. Always a professional, the bellman tried his best not to pass judgment on arriving guests. After all, they had the look of Texas oil money, the worst sort of guests, but the best type of tippers. He had learned to bite his tongue and put on a poker face.

"Let me out," Mike said as he raised his toy pistol in the direction of his sister. "Come on, Marsha, I need to find me some Injuns." The kids were overjoyed. The trip had been a long one and they needed to run and let out some pent-up steam.

"Come, Cindy, bring your hat." Grace rolled her eyes and grabbed her handbag. She stopped briefly to say hello to the door man who was extremely tall, so tall she remarked about it to him. He smiled and gently opened the door and directed her to the front desk lobby.

The interior was more magnificent than she thought possible. Bright colors, marble, and modern lighting were so fresh; she knew instantly she was not in New England anymore.

As she walked to the desk, giant mirrored walls caught her reflection in every direction. Grace slowed her pace, aghast at the image. After another long day in the car: her ponytail was a mess, the jeans she wore were soiled with a mustard stain from lunch, and her best shirt wrinkled. She was a mess. In a burst of insecurity, she quickly returned to the tall man and asked for the powder room. He discretely pointed to it, and Grace casually walked in that direction.

Grace pulled out a new head band, brushed her hair, and threw some water on her face. Her only lipstick was in the bottom of her bag. It was bright red, not appropriate, but had to do. Tucking in her shirt was the only thing she could do to save her appearance. She hadn't thought about her arrival; now it was too late.

Sticking her head out of the ladies' salon, she noticed that TJ and the kids were outside, Mike and Cindy chasing after each other. The tall doorman nodded to Grace and his seal of approval gave her enough strength to approach the front desk.

Carefully choosing the younger of the attendees, she approached. Without her having the opportunity to speak, he said. "We are sold out." There it was; the judgement that the bellman or even the doorman did not allow the guests to experience. Four little words that turned an insecure country woman into a little rooster.

"Well, I guess I'm in luck. I have a reservation," she said biting her lower lip trying not to be the bitch she could be. "Metalious, Grace" she snipped. "Or try Twentieth Century Fox."

The front desk clerk was scrambling to find it. He searched the handwritten log book of the day until he found the entry. VIP was boldly printed next to the Governor's Suite. "Yes, Ma'am, here it is," he smiled, trying not to upset her. "Your suite is ready. Let me call the bellman."

Grace's suite was located on the top floor of the hotel. The double door entry was opened wide to make room for the clan of New Englanders to enter as gracefully as possible. The kids ran to the large picture windows and looked down onto the pool directly below. The view of the city was straight ahead. They were impressed and quickly ran to the bedrooms to check them out.

An assortment of flowers and fruit baskets, each with a card, were placed throughout the center room. "It's like a funeral parlor." She'd never seen such exotic floral arrangements. Suddenly she felt giddy, almost special. The nervousness from before was subsiding. "Ma, don't these look beautiful?" Marsha asked, picking up a vase filled with Bird of Paradise. This plant was something none of them had seen the likes of before.

TJ instructed the bellman where to put the bags, the girls in one room with twin beds and Mike in the other. The master suite was for the lucky author and her lover turned manager. The fight at the Wagon Wheel Motel that night proved successful for TJ. His role had been elevated from lover to manager on about the fifth round of CC and Gingers.

Grace walked around the suite and gathered up the note cards. Plopping herself on one of the opposing sofas, she read the sentiments written. They were from Kitty, Jacques, Bernie, and even her mother, which she felt uneasy about. "What does she want now?" flashed through her mind. Well wishes and luck were the overall messages. She was very happy until she realized there was nothing from Jerry Wald, the man-about-town and producer of the film. He was so kind and enthusiastically eager with Grace in New York; was it like him to overlook such a detail?

The bellman was eager to leave once TJ tipped him, and he had finished showing him the details of the suite. TJ closed the door behind the young man and took a deep breath of relief. Finally, he was in California, a dream come true. He strode across the giant suite and turned towards Grace; he felt on top-of-the-world. "We did it, baby," he told her, as he sat down across from her.

"We're in Hollywood," Grace said. "Now it's time to see what all the hullabaloo is all about." In unison they leaned back into the sofa and felt the comfort of down and floral damask against their weary bodies. Only a moment had passed when the chime of the door could be heard. Neither were expecting anyone, and neither wanted to move. The chime went off again. Mike ran to the double doors to swing them open. Grace was too tired to protest, and TJ was a million miles away in his exhaustion and thoughts.

A handsome man dressed in a dark shark's skin suit entered the room. "Please, Miss Metalious, don't get up," he told her. Jerry Wald had not forgotten her. He had arranged the manager of the Hilton to bring dinner to them in their suite, along with champagne and a special bottle of Canadian Club. "Mr. Wald hopes you like Oysters Rockefeller and steak," he told her. "There is even spaghetti for the little ones." With that there were two attendants who wheeled in carts of food and booze and set them up in one corner of the room where a small dining table was.

"This is for you," the suited man handed Grace a note card, a beautiful ecru embossed envelope with the initials JW in the upper left hand corner. Before she could say a word, he exited using both hands to close the double doors, not unlike the closing of the Loretta Young Show.

Grace and TJ looked at each other. The kids ran to the food. Each thought, I could get use to all this Hollywood stuff." Grace read the card and handed it to TJ without a spoken word. "Big things, my dear, big things. Fondly, Jerry"

When morning came, they woke to find a dreary day in Hollywood. Rain came in the night before. In the words of a true New Englander, "Looks like we are socked in." TJ pushed the drapes far to one side to let in more light in. Morning light was Grace's favorite. He knew without it, her creativity would be at a low. "Come, Baby, breakfast is served," TJ announced to his half-awake lover and partner.

That morning the five of them sat at the same in-suite table as the night before. Room service at the Beverly never did disappoint. Fresh orange juice was perhaps the best thing the kids had ever tasted. So fresh, so sweet, and so colorful. Fresh oranges were a poor substitute for California sunshine, but it would have to do that morning.

The driver from Twentieth Century Fox waited patiently in the lobby of the hotel for Grace and TJ to come down. He'd been a driver for years and knew patience with these artist types was the main thing he needed, along with a good sense of direction. They were a few minutes late, and Grace looked to her favorite doorman for a clue as to whom they were to meet. The tall man discretely pointed to the third chauffeur from the left.

The ride was short, about a five-minute ride, less than two miles. In fact, Grace thought, they could have walked to the back lot. She chuckled to herself that the press would have a field day if they got wind that the famed author of *Peyton Place* walked to the studio

"Mr. Wald will be waiting for you in his office," the driver told them. Once they got through the gates, he instructed them on where to go. He boasted to them, that behind that door was movie magic.

"Thank you," Grace said as she offered her hand to him for assistance getting out of the car. This was a far cry from how she was first treated on her arrival to New York. Still a little nervous, TJ came around the back of the black sedan and took her hand.

The lot was alive with people everywhere. Some in costumes and others dressed in beautiful suits carrying stacks of papers. Everyone seemed to be in a hurry, almost too much of a hurry.

"They all look frightened," remarked Grace. "Here's your hat. What's your hurry?" Laughing out loud was a normal sign that she didn't feel herself, out of her element, and a bit mystified with all that was happening.

Jerry Wald's office was not what she had imagined. The furnishings were not that special, almost temporary looking. TJ closed the door behind them, and a young woman greeted them. "Mrs. Metalious," she said, "Oh, I'm so sorry, Ms. Metalious," the receptionist apologized for her mistake.

"Don't you worry about a thing. I'm still Mrs. at least for a few more months," replied Grace.

"There you are! Welcome." Jerry Wald, larger than life and louder than she remembered, came from the open door behind the desk to greet the couple. He was dressed in his signature Hawaiian print shirt and khakis, and his voice boomed in the tiny reception area, startling Grace. He leaned in for a Hollywood kiss and shook TJ's hand with as much strength as a professional arm wrestler. "Hold it," he instructed.

"Pop, Pop," the sound of flash bulbs went off, and they were all blinded for a brief second. Grace was instantly taken back to that awful night at the house when George intruded on them, taking pictures. Every time she heard a flash bulb now, that was what she remembered. "Just a few shots for the glossies," Wald said. "We have to give the readers what they want."

That onslaught of photographs was the first of many. Hundreds of flash bulbs followed her throughout her first day. Jerry and TJ were at her side the entire time. Grace was awestruck with the size of the operation, the lot, and everything around her. The driver was right; this was movie magic.

The day seemed to fly by for Grace. Constant moving from one building to another, avoiding moving sets, hearing the buzzer of the sound man during filming to quiet the set, was exhausting. Not to mention the constant lookout for stars. Grace kept a keen eye open for Hollywood royalty.

"Jerry, when will I see my office? I have a ton of thoughts and notes about the script," Grace said from the back seat of a golf cart that Jerry had insisted on driving himself. She used both hands to hold on as he swerved and darted down the alleys and in between sound stages. It was only the first day, and Grace had feelings of confusion and frustration. Grace had agreed with Kitty and Jacques that she would come out to help with the script for the film; after all she was the author, and who knew the story better than she.

"Here we are!" he announced, feeling proud that he made it in one piece. The studio commissary was where everyone went to eat: big stars, script girls, makeup artists, and set designers alike. As TJ helped Grace out of the back of the cart, she shot him a look of confusion. Wald did not even acknowledge her question about the office.

A late lunch was a welcomed thought; the stop at the commissary had come at the right moment. Jerry had been so gracious to them and had talked nonstop the entire day, that a drink would taste good right about now.

No big stars came in as they waited in line for their lunch. Lunch was a glorified cafeteria; the food was not great, but she had been so hungry a hotdog from the pushcart would have tasted good. They sat in the center of the room. Any opportunity Jerry had to be seen, or his stars to be seen, he made it happen. A true master of the PR machine.

"I'll be right back," he told them, and off he went in the direction of a table of beautiful girls.

"Honey, he's a cad, isn't he?" She questioned her statement. TJ, who knew her best, just looked at her and drank his coffee. Not a word was spoken, but the look in his eyes spoke volumes.

Moments later Jerry returned to the table and announced that he had lined up those girls for a casting on Friday.

"Those girls?" questioned Grace. "There is no one that pretty in all of New Hampshire, let alone that thin." Her words were a general misrepresentation of the entire population of the state, but nevertheless there was some truth to the statement.

Jerry just smiled. Again, no comment, no commitment on his part.

"Hey, is that Orson Welles?" TJ asked. It was, in fact, the famed writer, author, and larger-than-life actor.

"I adore him, so handsome, so talented," Grace gushed.

"Want to meet him?" Her producer asked. Her eyes widened, and like a deer in the head lights she was momentarily stunned. "Here, write him a note, and I will have someone bring it to him," Jerry suggested.

Thinking as fast as she could, Grace scribbled down a couple of lines on the back of her business card. On Jacques' recommendation, she had had them made for this trip. She handed it to Jerry. A studio intern from his office was always nearby and in ear shot. He quickly came over to retrieve the note. They all sat and watched Citizen Kane take the card and read it. Without looking up in any direction to find the sender, he crumbled it, set it aside his plate, and continued to eat. No acknowledgement was given, nor did he feel it was needed.

Grace felt like someone had slapped her in the face. She often felt like that back in Gilmanton when local residents shunned her like a pregnant Amish girl. In Hollywood, amongst her peers, how dare he? Grace remarked. "I never really liked him," she told the table. "Besides, he is losing his looks and getting fat."

The rest of the day was more of the same: meeting studio executives, shaking hands as a photographer followed them wherever they went. The constant flash bulbs annoyed her. She was in such need of a drink. When Jerry suggested they call it a day, there was no push back on Grace's or TJ's part.

The driver was right outside the office where they had been dropped earlier that morning. Grace thanked Jerry for a lovely day. She told him she couldn't wait to get started on the script. After all, she was the consultant, and she wanted to consult.

"Now don't forget, dear," he told her, "Tomorrow night is the Screen Writers Guild Dinner. Jack will pick you up at six o'clock sharp. Spend the day by the pool, a little color goes a long way, in this town."

Well, if Grace hadn't been miffed before, from that comment, she certainly was now.

CHAPTER 29

Grace retreated into their bedroom the moment she arrived back at the hotel and locked the door. It had been a week since their arrival to Tinsel Town, and each day her mood worsened. Her daily routine was to seclude herself off in the suite; there she could reflect on the day and start her decompression. She could start the evening's activities with a stiff drink.

"Grace, come on," TJ yelled through the door in their suite. "We really should get going," he continued. There was no answer and no sign that the occupant behind the door had heard him.

Mike and Cindy had been out and about in the hotel for hours. Marsha was still at the studio where she watched Elvis Presley shoot his latest movie.

TJ wanted nothing more than to get Grace out of her mood. "Gracie, are you okay?" he asked. "I'm making a drink. Can I get you one?" He knew what to say at the right moment, and it did the trick.

The master bedroom door slowly opened, and Grace emerged looking like she'd lost her best friend. She had showered and was dressed in the hotel's robe. Without her lipstick, her signature ponytail, and real clothes, Grace was rather plain and somewhat frumpy. At that moment, TJ realized, all this Hollywood hype was taking its toll on Grace. He was aware of her failing appearance.

"Hey there," TJ gave Grace a reassuring hug and gave her a soft kiss on the mouth. He could taste whiskey on her lips. She was not even trying to conceal her afternoon's libations.

TJ sat on the overstuffed floral sofa with two highballs in hand. He looked directly into his lover's eyes and shook one of the glasses, making that distinctive sound, to entice her to sit down with him. It worked. She curled up next to him, sipped the ice-cold drink, and lay her head on his broad shoulders.

"Can you tell me about your day?" he asked cautiously. The silence was deafening. It lasted a few moments, long enough to have a million scenarios go through his mind.

"Oh, sweetie," she began, "why did we come here?" Grace had let the genie out of the bottle, and there was no putting it back.

She was so disappointed with the entire experience so far. She was unclear if it would ever get better. "Hollywood is not for me," she confessed to TJ. "I felt like a fish out of water the moment I entered the hotel lobby." TJ was confused. He knew she had been extremely nervous at first but thought it would pass. She got very nervous when she was not in control.

Jerry Wald, the fast talking, Hawaiian shirt wearing, loud movie producer, lured Grace across the country with the promise of her actually contributing to the movie script. But it had been over a week, and she had not seen her office or been asked to consult. She explained how her days were filled with watching stars from afar, moving from one set to another, and always in the wings talking in hushed voices. It was no doubt an attempt to keep her entertained under the muse of movie making.

Having lunch in the commissary was becoming boring and ordinary. At best it was cafeteria food and average. She did agree with TJ, that some stars were thrilling, but after the snub by Orson Wells, her ego was fragile. Some of her observations were straight to the point: Jayne Mansfield was beautiful, but chewed gum nonstop like a dock worker. Grace had found it repulsive. Elizabeth Taylor's beauty was so magnificent it would take your breath away. Taylor smiled at Grace causing her to blush. The writer went on and on about her day. It had been mostly disappointing. TJ got up to make another round of drinks.

"Why am I here?" Grace raised her voice slightly as TJ poured the whiskey over the cubes. "Today," she continued, "if you can believe it, I was finally asked to attend the story meeting." Wald arranged for Grace to sit in on a creative meeting with some other team members to talk about casting the film. The meeting was held in one of the many board rooms. There were a handful of executive type men and a few secretaries taking notes. She was the only woman at the table, and that was very intimidating for her.

"Can you believe it?" she paused. "Someone suggested Red Skelton to play Kenny Stearns" This was obviously another tipping point for her mood. "Kenny Stearns is the town drunk in the book." The meeting had lasted a couple of hours.

"No one takes my book, my baby, seriously," she told TJ. "Pat Boone's name was thrown out to play Michael Rossi," she went on. "The idiot executive also suggested they could work up a song for him to sing. The entire table laughed like fucking hyenas," she paused to catch her breath. "But what pissed me off the most, someone had the suggestion that he could sing The *Peyton Place* Blues, "Grace told TJ. "I got up and went to the ladies' room for a good cry."

Grace's facial expression said it all. She went on to another level of frustration he had not seen since that fateful night with George a few weeks earlier.

"I'm sorry, Gracie. Do you want to leave?" he asked her. Before she could answer that question, a loud rap was heard on the door. TJ got up and opened one of the double doors of the suite. He was surprised that Cindy and Mike were there looking guilty, held by their shirt collar. The hotel security guard didn't look amused. "Sir, please refrain your children from entering employee only areas of the property." He was not asking but telling him. The kids ran into the room and jumped on the sofa where their mother sat sipping her cocktail. TJ gave a look of disinterest to the guard; he had bigger fish to fry. He closed the door securely and returned to Grace's recollection of the day.

"See, that is what I mean," Grace said. "Kids will be kids. This Beverly Hilton is nothing more than a glorified motel."

Grace's day had been a bad one, but not everything was bleak. She told everyone how after her lunch in the commissary, Jerry introduced her to Cary Grant. "He was so charming, and so handsome. I think he really knew who I was. Said he'd seen my book but not read it," she added. "Then, right on cue, flash bulbs went off making the most annoying sound and blinding us. At least I might get a signed photo out of another one of Wald's PR stunts."

The sound of a key was heard in the door. Marsha came running in, thrilled beyond words. She was glowing. "Ma, Ma," she couldn't get words out fast enough. "I met Elvis, Elvis, can you believe it?" Grace welcomed her thirteen-year-old over for a big hug. Her mother, smiling with no trace of her previous ranting, could pour her charm on with a moment's notice. Grace was quite the actress herself. "Oh, Marsha, isn't that so exciting? Was he as handsome as you thought?" her mother asked.

Some in the clan from northern New Hampshire were happier than others. Hollywood was a learning curve for them. They knew it and would ride the wave as long as they could. Jerry arranged for Grace to attend another one of the studio's events. Wald had asked Grace what movie she would like to see as a private screening. She picked, "On the Waterfront."

"Are we going?" TJ asked. Grace nodded and placed her empty glass on the coffee table. Forcing a Hollywood smile, she leaned over, kissed him on the cheek, and scurried back off to the bedroom. There wasn't a lot of time before the studio driver would be waiting in the lobby for them to descend from the top floor. She knew she needed to hurry.

Marsha was in charge of the kids, and the three of them had learned they could order anything they wanted from the room service menu for dinner. Room service had been their best friend for nearly two weeks. They favored the burgers and shakes. Marsha discovered the assortment of salads they offered. It was winter back in New Hampshire, and fresh salads were rare that time of year.

TJ went into the bedroom to see how Grace was getting on. Being late for events was something he hated. On entering the bedroom, he saw Grace standing in front of the vanity brushing her hair. It was longer than usual, and TJ loved it down. In one fluid motion, she grabbed it, twisted, and placed a rubber band around it, creating her signature ponytail. "What do you think?" she asked, turning to face him. Grace was dressed in blue jeans, a man's long sleeve shirt, and flats. "This is what this writer wears," was all she said.

TJ grabbed his sports coat off the bed and put it on. He was going to change into something nicer but did not want to start something with Grace. He would go with-the-flow and take his lead from Grace.

In the living room the youngest children were fighting over the television and what to watch. Marsha was curled up in one of the easy chairs away from the television reading the Photoplay Magazine that Elvis had signed earlier in the day.

"You kids lock this door, this ain't Gilmanton" Grace demanded. Marsha nodded. "Order anything you want for dinner. It's not like we were paying for it!" She smiled at her man as he opened the door. Grace was ready for whatever Hollywood would throw at her. TJ knew it had all the makings for an interesting evening.

CHAPTER 30

Southern California sunshine can be a welcome sight, nurturing and healing to the body after a long night out in tinseltown. The morning skies in Hollywood can often be dull, overcast, and foggy, like a massive hangover the morning after. This would cause most to roll over and sleep late. The Marina Layer, as it is known, eventually burns off, and, like the hangover, it disappears with the bright beautiful sun that everyone has come to expect.

Grace and TJ were napping poolside one morning, having only a Bloody Mary for breakfast at the pool bar. They decided a little rest would do them good. In reality, the previous night's party was long. Champagne had flowed, and they figured a little hair-of-the-dog could not hurt.

Their visit to Hollywood was now in its fourth week. The small band of New England characters came to know the Beverly Hilton as their home away from home. The 20th Century Fox movie studio served as a means to an end. Lavish dinners, celebrity sightings, and power lunches were all a front to continually keep the young writer from the movie script. Grace was aware of their ploy. So, she found comfort and support as she always had with TJ the DJ and in a bottle, but not necessarily in that order.

One of the more eventful lunches the studio arranged was with Frank Sinatra. A few days earlier Grace and TJ had met Mr. Sinatra with Jerry for a private lunch at the studio. Grace found him to be charming, talkative, and very engaging. He asked her about New England and how she came to be a writer. She was flattered. Writing was her passion and story telling her trade; as the two of them chatted like old friends, Jerry and TJ watched from across the table.

Sinatra had ignored her companion, perhaps not intentionally, he was a women's man, and Grace was the only game in town for that lunch. Jerry was a little put off as well, waiting for the right moment to get into the conversation.

"Writers are the necessary evil," he interjected. Both Grace and Frank looked at each other and thought that was an insensitive remark that didn't need to be shared. The luncheon dissolved into a PR photo shoot, and they dispersed after coffee and dessert.

The kids loved their time in Hollywood: no school, no agenda, and really no supervision. They spent most of their time in the room when they were not at the pool. They refrained from riding the service elevator after the security guard had presented them to their mother the week before. They all agreed in unison, the best thing was the room service menu and the endless supply of treats whenever they wanted it.

The sun peeked out, and like magic the grey dull sky turned blue. Suddenly everything seemed better. Grace stirred from her slumber state long enough to nudge TJ who was next to her on the chaise lounge. The pool was quiet that morning. It was March and still considered winter, no doubt. But for New Englanders it was quite balmy and a perfect morning to sleep off a hangover pool side. "Sweetie, can you get me another Bloody?" Grace asked her guy without really moving.

TJ had to get up anyway. He was desperate for a cigarette and needed to use the toilet. This would kill three birds with one stone. On the way past the pool bar, he held up his right hand with two fingers extended. The bartender knew exactly what he wanted. Grace and TJ were now infamous at the Beverly Hilton.

Grace wished she hadn't drunk so much the night before, but drinking was her coping mechanism when she felt uneasy or insecure. The cocktail party the previous evening was at Jerry's house in the hills, not far from the hotel, but a world away. A beautiful modern home with lots of glass and a big pool, something she would have never seen in New Hampshire. The party seemed to start out great, lots of pretty people, waiters and waitresses in their tidy uniforms, passing drinks and canapés throughout the house.

Grace and TJ arrived by the studio VIP car that Jerry had sent. The driver drove over the crushed stone drive. The tires crunching the rocks made a soothing sound and announced their arrival. Grace wore the mink she had bought in New York. TJ was smart in a white dinner jacket and bow tie. "You are my knight in shining armor," she whispered. "Keep me safe with these people." Her emphasis on the word "people" made it sound derogatory.

"Grace, Grace Darling" a voice beckoned, "Over here." It was Jerry, raising a glass of champagne and waving them to join him across the vast grand foyer. His foyer was about the size of the first floor of her dream house back in Gilmanton.

"Hello, Mr. Wald," Grace leaned in for a peck on the cheek. She could play Hollywood with the best of them. "Fake it till you make it." Words of advice from long ago when she was an aspiring playwright. TJ extended his hand to shake it. The producer, ignored TJ, turned without shaking his hand, and signaled to a waiter, raising his glass to get more champagne. TJ was miffed; Grace was disgusted.

The party took off full speed. Her mink was whisked away, and a beautiful cut glass of champagne landed in her hand. The trays of bubbly were passed, one after the other, reminding her of a parade from her youth: the glasses all straight and perfectly aligned, marching side by side, soldiers showing off in a military parade in her hometown.

Guests were talking non-stop. The few that she did speak to had nothing to say in return. They rattled on about how Jerry was the most brilliant producer in Hollywood, and 20th Century Fox was lucky to have him. One old studio executive even commented on his style of business, "He is so smart, he finds the story, pays nothing for it, and we all make millions." The comment was unnerving to Grace, and she looked up at TJ. "We need to get the fuck out of here."

Making her way back through the house to the giant foyer, she grabbed two more glasses of champagne; they were not to be shared. When Grace was in this state, it was every drinker for himself. TJ recognized the mood. She was mad. She was also sad and disappointed with how this trip was going. She drank down both glasses of champagne without caring what those moronic guests thought. She placed the empty glasses on a table with a huge floral arrangement, and like magic a waitress was there with her mink. "At least the staff," she said aloud, "are nice."

Grace left without even saying good bye to her host. It wasn't like she was going to see him the next day. Jerry arranged a late luncheon at Romanoff's Restaurant, some famous eatery he insisted they try. She knew that tomorrow's meeting was the one she dreaded the most. Jerry had finally arranged for her to meet the official screenwriter who would take her baby from book form to the silver screen. "That transformation would be interesting," was her last thought before slipping into the back seat of the town car and letting the buzz from the booze take over.

Grace's hangover was all but a memory. She and TJ left their empty Bloody Mary glasses on the table next to the pool. They returned to the suite for a long and soapy shower, which had turned into a hot and erotic encounter between the two of them. Sex was always her best cure for a hangover and a bad mood. TJ performed like a blue movie star, and when she had her orgasm, she screamed a little too loud, hoping the kids were still down by the pool, but she really didn't care.

Romanoff's, a Beverly Hills legend, had recently opened its new location on South Rodeo Drive. According to the driver, the owner claimed to be a descendant of the actual royal family for Russia. "Mrs. Metalious," he said from the front seat, "You must try the frog legs, out-of-this-world, I have been told." Grace was mildly impressed, "Frog legs," she smirked. If the driver only knew that the river behind her shack, It'll Do, provided a bounty of those slimy morsels.

It was a real swanky place, TJ thought, standing at the Maître'd station waiting to be seated. He couldn't help but stare at all the movie star photos on the wall. It seemed anyone, who was anyone, had eaten there. From Kirk Douglas to Marlon Brandon, black and white glossies were framed and hung in perfect order. He secretly hoped his and Grace's picture would end up on the wall one day; after all, she was the bestselling author of all time.

Jerry sat in a large corner booth on the other side of the room with the screenwriter, John Michael Hayes. The introduction was about to happen. A sense of dread overcame Grace. The men stood up to greet the couple, and Grace leaned over for a typical brush on her cheek from Jerry. She nodded in the screenwriter's direction and shook his hand. "Mr. Hayes," she said. Jerry gave TJ a big slap on the back to welcome him and gestured to sit next to him. That was so uncharacteristic of the producer's greeting towards TJ. Maybe he was slightly apprehensive of the meeting as well.

The foursome ordered a round of Bloody Mary's and started small talk, like every luncheon she had for nearly four weeks. She just sat back and let Jerry do his thing; after all, it was his nickel.

"Now, Grace, did you know Michael was also from New England?" he told her. "Worcester, Massachusetts, right?" He looked to the accomplished screenwriter. "Yes, I was born there, my folks are still there." he answered. "But I have no idea why; it's not a pretty place." There it was. "A Massachusetts flatlander," Grace thought.

They ordered lunch; Grace passed on the frog legs and ordered a Waldorf Salad and Noodles Romanoff, another highly recommended dish. It seems Hayes had just finished another script for Alfred Hitchcock, *The Man Who Knew Too Much*. "It will be released in a few months," he interjected.

"Grace, we are so lucky to have him on our little film," Jerry beamed.

Their food arrived, and there was still no talk about working with Grace. Neither the producer nor the screenwriter showed the slightest interest in what she could contribute to the project. Another round of drinks arrived, and things began to loosen up a little. When Hayes did finally ask a probing question, like most writers do, it was: "Is *Peyton Place* your autobiography?" The table went dead silent. The men in her life knew that was a question not to be asked.

A few seconds went by, but it seemed like minutes to TJ. He looked at Grace for her reaction. Feeling the effects of the morning Bloodies, she calmly answered, "I beg your pardon?" With that she stood, threw her drink in the screenwriter's face, and stormed off to the bar.

Hollywood had done it. The new-found author, trying to fit in, found out the hard way that she didn't. Grace went to the bar, sat down, ordered a highball, and waited for her Prince Charming to rescue her.

The ride back to the hotel was quiet; even the driver knew something was wrong. Grace never said a word, stewing in her own madness mixed with a dose of embarrassment until they reached the front door. Looking at TJ, she sternly announced, "We are leaving. I want to be on the road after breakfast tomorrow. Fuck Hollywood and fuck all those wanna-bee's that are dead in the head."

CHAPTER 31

April is the cruelest month, breeding lilacs out of the dead, mixing memory and desire." Grace was reciting from memory one of her favorite passages from T.S. Eliot's *The Wasteland*. "That poem is what started it all for me," she continued as she sat cross legged on the sofa next to the roaring fire. "I read that in junior high school, and I knew at that very moment I wanted to be a writer," she added.

Grace was again in her element. No more Hollywood parties and no fancy dinners. She was in her house, in her town, in the little world she created. *Peyton Place* was soaring off the bookshelves in every bookstore that dared to sell it. Everyone in her circle and beyond wanted a piece of the action; after all, money fuels friendship, and Grace suddenly had more friends than she knew what to do with.

TJ was in the kitchen retrieving another bottle of Canadian Club for the bar in the front room. People from the radio station, the newspaper, and some he had no idea who they were, filled the house on Meadows Pond Road.

"Grace, tell them about, *It'll Do*," Jacques insisted. Her agent had even come up from the city. He obviously wanted to protect his investment, so he was a regular visitor to Gilmanton most weekends after their return from Hollywood.

"Eliot's poem," Grace explained, "stirred something in me that no other had." The opening paragraph in her book was also about a season, not April as locals referred to it, but Mud Season. It had been Indian Summer, and in direct contrast to Eliot, her prose talked about love, women, and possibilities. "I just love autumn in New Hampshire," she said.

Grace told her group of new friends all about the shack down the road where she wrote her torrid novel. "One summer the well went dry," she said almost pleasingly. "We all had to wash up down at Silver Lake," laughing. "And before you ask," pausing, "we used soap. Ivory Soap, that won't kill the fish, will it?" The room roared. Grace extended her almost empty glass for a refill. TJ felt obligated, so he scurried back into the kitchen for more ice.

Once the parties started, they never seemed to end. Grace was riding the wave to the best of her ability, hosting weekend gatherings and shopping whenever she could. The house was still under construction and coming along. "I don't care what it costs," she would say. Due to her fear of bathing in the lake again, an artesian well was dug. Her dream house was becoming exactly what she wanted it to be.

"Grace," Bernie her lawyer would say, trying to reason with her, "You paid only $5,000 dollars for it. I think you now have over $100,000 into it." She didn't care, Her attitude about money was to spend it when you had it, because you would never knew when it would be gone.

"Bernie, it's Okay. TJ will now look after everything." Grace unofficially made her lover her manager, keeper of the pocketbook, and personal confidant. "Talk to him; he has it under control," she would tell him. Bernie knew Grace, and he also knew TJ, but resigned himself to the fact that a watchful eye is better than no eye.

The house on Meadows Pond Road was Grace's sanctuary, where she could pull up the drawbridge and keep the prying eyes of the press out. She asked her lawyer to purchase all the land around the house. She didn't like neighbors, especially nosey ones. Controlling her world was what she needed to do at that moment, and she stopped at nothing to get it done.

"Grace, it's not a good deal," TJ told her. Bernie explained that the land was grossly overpriced; no doubt the farmer who owned it read the papers.

"Look, it's my money. I want it, just do it," she screamed at TJ.

He did not like it, but knew never to disagree with her when she was in this state. Her mood was that of a queen holding court, during one of these gatherings. "Do not presume I'm one of your groupies," he'd screamed at her. In hindsight, he should have known better.

They did not always see eye to eye; in fact the closer they grew together, the further they seemed to drift apart. The drinking was taking a toll on them, physically and emotionally. Grace put on weight, a lot of it. She carried most of her weight in her ass and her breasts, but now her face seemed fuller, and her skin had lost its glow. Her moods were more extreme, and her drinking legendary. TJ was a big man, handsome and strong, but signs of a double chin and belly were starting to appear. After fights, after the spilled liquor was cleaned up, after the broken glass made its way into the trash bin, they would make up.

Making up was what they did best. The sex they had after one of their fights could be heard throughout the house. Thankfully, the kids all had their own bedrooms on the other side of the house, but no doubt heard their mother screaming in ecstasy from time to time. They were used to the screaming during fights and the screaming that came shortly after. The excesses were taking a toll on them as well.

"Let's go, everyone, breakfast is ready," he would say, rapping on the kid's doors. Mike was always the first to the kitchen table. Remorse was often served at breakfast the following day. TJ would make pancakes and announce to the house to get up; bacon could be smelled frying throughout the entire house. "Wait for the others," TJ would tell him after he snuck a slice to gobble up. Mike and TJ formed an alliance of sorts, the only two males in a house of Metalious women. It became worse when Grace's mother and sister, Bunny, would visit. "Us men need to stick together," he would tell Mike, handing him another slice of the crispy goodness.

Months passed rather uneventfully. The kids were in school, and Marsha was going to graduate from Junior High School, a milestone they all took very seriously. Despite their long trip to the west coast and numerous snow days, she managed to complete her required courses. A celebration was in order.

"How about right after graduation we take a trip?" Grace asked one morning over a plate of pancakes. "Yeah," exclaimed Cindy, "Are we going back to Hollywood?" She asked. The answer was clear to everyone at the breakfast table except the youngest; one day she would understand.

"How about New York City," was not formed as a question but a statement. School would be out soon, TJ could get some time off from the radio station, and Grace was feeling better than she had in weeks.

After the last big fight, both she and TJ decided to drink only on the weekends, go on diets, and she started to write again. She dug out an old novel she had started during George's university days. It was a simple story of man's inhumanity towards man. Going to New York would be a perfect time to talk to Jacques and Kitty about her next book. She had not forgotten she signed a four-book deal with her publisher.

So, it was settled. TJ would drive her into Laconia, and they would go to the travel agency to set things in motion. The drive to town was as fresh as a spring day could be. Bright green leaves were popping out of their buds, lilacs were in full bloom, and the smell of the air reminded her of love. "After all the fifth season was love," she always said.

She insisted on putting the top down on the convertible. "Gracie, it's not that warm," TJ told her. She reached into her pocket, withdrew her favorite silk scarf, and wrapped it over her head, tying it securely under her chin. She smiled and opened the door. "Okay, you win," he said. There was no need to start a fight over such a small thing.

A week after Marsha's graduation they all headed to New York. Grace had made the drive so many times that it was old hat for her. She played navigator, and TJ drove. The entire drive south was pleasant and very family-like. Grace surprised them all by renting the largest suite they had at The Plaza. Each of the kids had their own bedroom, and she and her lover the grandest of all the master bedrooms in the entire hotel. Pulling up to the front entrance this time was a little less offensive on the valet. He didn't rush them out in order to hide the car in the garage.

On the top floor of the hotel, you could see all of Central Park. The view was breathtaking, and Grace stood there holding TJ's hand, gazing out onto their new front lawn, of sorts. The Plaza was Grace's all-time favorite place to lay her head, with no worry about what it cost.

"Where should we go first?" she asked. "Let's go for a walk in the park; I'm in the mood for a pretzel," he answered. The kids hadn't finished exploring the suite or even started to unpack when they were easily persuaded to do something as simple as go for a walk. They cheerfully agreed and off to the elevator they ran to take them to the ground floor.

The entire trip would be like that, doing exactly what they wanted to do when they wanted to do it. New York in June was the perfect time to visit. Not the summer heat everyone wanted to escape from and surely not the freezing temperatures of winter.

The suite was huge; it felt like the entire floor of the building. There was plenty of room to entertain her new friends and spacious enough to feel wealthy. Entertaining in the suite was something she loved to do. Cocktails overlooking Central

Park South made such an impression. She wanted to be like Kitty in the worst way. Kitty had had money from the start, so when Grace invited her, everything had to be perfect.

"Grace, have you heard from Jerry?" Kitty asked. "How is the filming going?" Grace tried with all she had to remain civil about the movie, Hollywood, and especially Jerry. She realized she spoke an entirely different language than those she met on the west coast. So, she felt all that was in the past.

"Well, they did cast Lana Turner as Constance," she answered. That was all she said on the subject, hoping Kitty would get the message and move on.

Grace stewed about the whole experience, while Fox sent a crew to scout out locations for the shoot. Grace opened her home to them, hosted a little dinner, and even drove them around the area to get a feel of it.

"Grace, we don't think Gilmanton is New England enough for the shoot; it's just not that pretty," is what one scout told her. Grace was madder than a wet hen, but with her new attitude she refrained from her usual responses. She bit her tongue and instructed TJ that from that time forward he would do all the talking to the movie makers.

"Mom, can we go watch television?" Mike asked. Her gatherings were boring to her children. A Motorola larger than what they had at home waited in their room away from the adults. "Sure, sweetie, you kids go run along," and with a kiss on her youngest head they hurried into the bedroom.

"Kitty, did Grace tell you her good news?" Grace did not have to turn around because that accent was distinctive; Jacques had slipped in, without notice, to the party. "Jacques, how the hell are you? So nice of you to arrive on time," Grace added. She'd been much better about not speaking her mind, but with some, like her agent, she ran the show.

"News? Do tell." Kitty was all ears.

Jacques spilled the beans about Grace writing again. "It's called, "The Tight White Collar," he told her. Kitty listened intently and hoped for the best. *Peyton Place* had them both running to the accountant and banks weekly. Never in her wildest dreams did Kitty think that the success of a writer could be so successful.

"Oh, Grace, it sounds fascinating," Kitty said as she leaned over and gave her a sincere embrace of encouragement and support. The author blushed slightly, turned, and headed to the liquor cart for a drink from her favorite butler at The Plaza.

The entire family trip went without any complications to speak about. They dined when and where they wanted to. The weather was near perfect the entire trip, and everyone seemed to have a great time. Grace saw Sammy Davis Jr. perform. He even sent a drink to her table after his set. She was star struck with his style. There would be no repeat of the Hollywood trip in New York; this was a totally different animal.

On the day before they were to leave, the entire clan went to Rockefeller Center to go ice skating. This might have been the highlight of the trip, but little Cindy tripped and broke her leg on the ice. After a visit to a midtown hospital on the east side, she was almost as good as new. Grace never lost her cool when the next day she and TJ went to check out. The hotel bill was over $5,000. Grace simply smiled and said, "TJ, you have the check book. Can you take care of this please?" There was no scrutinizing the tab or checking the math. Grace had her manager pay it. After all, it was The Plaza.

CHAPTER 32

Summer has a way of fading gently into the next season with little to no notice. Only the keen observer with an eye on the distant sunset could tell that the days, once long with the sun high in the sky, had shortened. Hot muggy nights along the New Hampshire coastline that normally kept holiday makers awake at night were slightly cooler and more calming. Ocean breezes were a welcomed relief after the dog days of summer.

"Baby, hand me a cigarette." Grace nudged her prince who was lying naked beside her in the antique brass bed. TJ rolled on to his side and reached for the pack, never acknowledging her request with a verbal sound. He lit the cigarette with one flick of the wrist. The chrome Zippo lighter that he had received as a gift from a studio executive did the trick. He looked at the lighter and reminisced about the trip to Hollywood.

"Here you are, Gracie," handing her the lighted cigarette, "You okay?" he asked. Grace just smiled, took a long drag, and held her breath, letting the nicotine do its work. "Are you sad?" Still trying to get a response.

Summer was coming to an end. Their time on the coast would be ending in a few days. The kids would return to Stowe to live with George, while she and TJ returned to Gilmanton. The house was nearly completed. The summer weeks had flown by. Only a few months had passed since the couple snuck off in a chartered plane to Haiti, their first of many jaunts financed by the success of her book.

"It had been the right thing to do," Grace thought at the time. TJ was her man, the man of her dreams. Strong and handsome, he was always in control, made all the right decisions and looked after her when everyone else seemed to turn their heads. Grace loved TJ. He was everything George was not. She had the freedom to travel, the freedom to live.

With the divorce papers filed, there was nothing more to do than wait. Making it finally legal would take some time, unless they went to another state where there was no waiting period, something they both thought about.

Until then, Grace and TJ needed to tread lightly in public. Adultery was never a pretty side of divorce. "Grace, let's wait," TJ told her. "Bernie thinks it's not a good idea to rush things." A few weeks before they had sat on the front porch of Meadows Pond Road, drinking most of the afternoon, neither of them thinking very clearly.

"George took the kids to Massachusetts," she told him. "We are alone. My writing is going well for the first time in a long time," she added. "Let's do it. I am tired of the looks I get, Let's make it legal." Grace was determined to not let society dictate her actions, she thought but marrying TJ could only help the current situation.

Getting out of town was the only answer for a quick reprieve from all the scandal and gossip. The hotel they chose was a distant reminder of the days of yesteryear, when people of status escaped to the coastline for the cooling breezes and fresh air. The Ocean Wave Hotel was an old wooden grand hotel that had seen better days. It was a perfect place for the couple to escape the press, forget the prying eyes of Gilmanton, and spend some time with the kids during the summer.

"Thank you, baby," Grace exhaled the smoke which mingled in the salt air from the gentle breeze off the water. The room overlooked a rock outcropping of granite and dunes.

Hypnotic sounds of the surf gently caressed them to sleep each night. "I'm not sad," she said, "well, maybe."

Both were lying in bed, sipping their drinks, and catching up on all the news of the movie. The Boston Globe, the Portland Press Herald and the latest edition of Photoplay magazine were strewn about the hotel room. *Peyton Place* the movie was taking downeast Maine for a ride. 20th Century Fox movie studio had set up camp out in Camden. For weeks they were making movie magic only a few hours away.

"They didn't even invite me to the set," she exclaimed. "Fucking Hollywood," Grace sat up straighter in bed. "Now my baby has no place to go." She held the cigarette in her left hand and tossed the magazine to TJ; he caught it. He briefly looked at the article. There were many black and white photos of the town and stars working on set while filming. He knew she was upset, but what could he do. Grace was no match for Hollywood. From the signing of the contract to the studio visit, she was out of her element, and she knew it.

"Can you believe it?" she said gesturing to the magazine. "That bitch, Lana Turner, won't even go to Maine to shoot her scenes." Grace seemed angrier than sad. Turner was cast as one of Grace's major characters, Constance Mackenzie, and she refused to travel to Maine. This detail enraged the author. "Who does she think she is?" Grace asked her lover. *Peyton Place* had been her fourth child, and she longed to mother it to maturity but realized she could not.

"Grace," TJ said. "It's ok; the movie will sell even more books." Grace knew he was right; the movie could only help the book. Sales were out of this world; no one had predicted such success of her book, least of all for a first-time author.

Grace finished her cigarette and snuffed it out in the ashtray on her nightstand. TJ tossed the magazine onto the floor in a gesture of "fuck it." No words were spoken as he turned off the light and rolled over to kiss her.

Their relationship was like the winding country roads of New England with its twists and turns and uphill climbs. They, too, had their challenges, but things during that summer's end were more calm. Even though Hollywood was right up the road from them, as the crow flies, it was still far enough away from them.

TJ reached for Grace's breasts. They were fuller and more sensitive these days. The weight gains and evidence of her topless sunbathing created an irresistible urge for him. "Easy," she whispered. With that gentle cautionary command, he lowered his head and used his tongue to soothe the heat from the sun on her nipples. Grace groaned with a guttural noise only recognizable to him. Once again, he had found the magic spot to please her, securing their relationship for another day.

It was the end of August, and their time at the beach came to an end. It was back to reality. The kids would go to George's new apartment and she back to her writing studio. *The Tight White Collar* was almost complete. Like the renovations of her home, both projects had seemed to take way too long. TJ would return to WLNH radio and spin records nightly, dedicating his favorite songs to his lover, and, hopefully, soon-to-be wife.

The breakfast room at the beach hotel was somewhat dated. Dulled white curtains with faded cabbage roses caught the breeze which caused them to float gently in the morning sunlight. The oak tables, with embroidered tablecloths, were just as faded, and the china a little old and worn. She thought it was perfect for her, it provided a sense of grounding. There was enough anonymity there for her to blend in and go unnoticed.

The other guests came down to eat their first meal of the day and paid no mention to Grace. TJ and the children chatted away as they exuberantly ate their breakfast. "What shall we do today?" TJ asked the table. "The beach," Mike answered. "A picnic," exclaimed Cindy. "Yes, a picnic sounds exactly like what we should do," Grace had settled their plans.

The drive from the hotel to the state park was a short one by car, but it had taken a lifetime for them to get there on that day. Odiorne State Park had been where she and George picnicked on cucumber sandwiches and lemonade. It was there that she had announced to herself that her next baby would be born.

This picnic was less basic and more befitting for a bestselling author. A quick stop along the beach road at The Clam Shack, where TJ secured "lobsta" rolls and potato salad for everyone. The kids enjoyed ice teas, and the adults the perfect highball from a thermos. It would be their last day at the beach before heading inland, to the foothills of the White Mountains to resume their lives.

CHAPTER 33

For December in New Hampshire, the weather that week was a great improvement compared to the previous week. In the early morning the sun was shining on the frosty ground which warmed slightly as the sun's rays rose in the sky. Snow had not arrived, but most knew the weather could change on a dime. Being prepared was the key to everyday life in Gilmanton.

"Where is Bud?" Ned asked the folks waiting patiently for the taxi to arrive outside The Corner Store. The village green was faded and dull. Winter's arrival would cover what remained of life. "There he is," a voice exclaimed.

A honk was heard as the old black taxi rounded the green, pulling up in front of the small group of residents waiting for their ride to Laconia.

"Okay everyone, it's *gonna* be tight, but we can make it," Bud told them through the rolled down window. Each of them with a small suitcase, managed to close the doors. The taxi was full with five eager passengers. The cramped and somewhat grouchy group slowly pulled away from the green.

20th Century Fox movie studio offered twenty-five Gilmanton residents the chance to go to New York City and see the premier of *Peyton Place*. It had been a real hard sell to most residents of Gilmanton. Most never responded to the invitation, but, Ned persuaded a few of his loyal clients to accept their offer. He organized the ride to the Laconia Tavern to meet up with the Concord Trailways bus for the trip south.

The ride to downtown Laconia was a quick one. Energy generated by the passengers fueled the journey, and it seemed to take no time at all. Bud dropped them in front of the tavern directly behind the idling bus. The heater was running full tilt inside the bus creating a cozy and warm interior.

There was a total of sixteen passengers making their way to New York for the previewing Grace's scandalous novel on the silver screen. The film studio pulled out all stops to create a memorable trip for these townsfolk. It was December 13th, the day after the world premiere in Camden, Maine. One very important guest decided not to attend that event the night before.

"Grace," TJ whispered, holding his hand over the receiver. "It's Bette Davis." He urged her to move and answer the phone. Grace sat in the corner of her floral sofa next to the roaring fire. She was most comfortable, and there she would remain. TJ knew that look; there would be no moving her.

"I'm sorry, ummm, Grace is resting," he said into the phone. After a brief conversation with Davis, TJ placed the receiver back in its cradle. He headed to the bar at the other end of the living room and poured two drinks with lots of Canadian Club and very little ginger ale.

Grace casually looked up from the magazine in her lap, "Thank you, sweetie, you were reading my mind," she said, forcing a smile. Grace was hurt and continued to be dismayed with Hollywood, the movie business, and especially with Jerry Wald.

"I will not attend that premiere in Maine, let alone New York City," she said. "Fuck them all," holding her glass up in a mock toast. She knew all too well what was going to happen in Down East Maine on December 12th. The local theatre would have two showings of the film as a benefit to the local hospital. Bette Davis and her husband Gary Merrill were residents of

Camden, and they would represent the Hollywood brass that night.

"Look TJ, if Lana Turner can't go to Maine to film," she told him, "then this writer is not going there either. Besides, they waited too long to invite me." Grace had been in a mood for a few weeks. Her hard drinking had started again and she felt vulnerable. TJ recognized this destructive pattern and tried to keep her occupied.

It was a hard time for the household that fall. The movie dominated the press, the articles, and the advance movie stills. It created such a stir that Grace hid in the house, refusing to answer the phone. The other side of the story is that all the publicity only helped the book continue to sell faster. It was breaking records, and royalties continued to be mailed to Grace.

A couple of weeks had passed since Ms. Davis phoned Grace. As a personal favor to Jerry Wald, Davis had been persuaded to attend the premier with her husband. Wald was a money maker for Fox, and most stars knew it. People did what they could to make the executives happy and, Davis was no different.

NBC radio, in New York, had a live feed from the Theatre on Mechanic Street in the small coastal town of Camden. Most of their affiliates picked up the broadcast. Grace had asked TJ not to turn the radio on that evening. She would read about it the next morning.

By all accounts, news and gossip columns stated that the event was a resounding smash in Maine. The Hollywood couple acted as master of ceremonies and charmed the crowd of over 1200 moviegoers with two shows. There was a party in the local high school gym for all the extras that had helped film that past summer. A fifty-piece marching band entertained the guests. Gary Merrill officiated a charity auction like a pro.

"That's it," Grace told TJ the next morning. "There is no place for *Peyton Place* to go. It's all over." She was totally devastated.

"Baby," he pleaded with her, "it is just the beginning." Grace is not sure about that but accepted a sincere hug from her Prince Charming.

That day a few locals had packed their bags for an overnight jaunt to the Big Apple on someone else's nickel. The premiere in New York would be another sold out affair, but only a handful of local residents took up the invitation from the studio to represent the state of New Hampshire.

The bus ride was smooth and seamless. The chatter amongst the passengers all seemed to be centered around what stars would attend, and what they were going to be wearing. The consensus was that the lucky attendees from New Hampshire would dress as locals. They would don their best hunting jackets and caps, along with their locally sourced jackets handmade from the finest wool fabric made in New England. Ironically it had been a wise decision on that frigid night because the subway workers had decided to strike, and so the attendees did what New Englanders do, they walked to the premiere from their hotel.

The morning after the New York showing was much like the day before; Grace sent TJ down to The Laconia Spa to get a New York paper and the Boston dailies *Peyton Place*, the movie, was big news.

Grace was still nervous and somewhat befuddled with all the hype around the film and how that translated to her book. She mixed herself a stiff Bloody Mary and dropped some sliced bread into the toaster. The drink was exactly what she needed, and the toast went untouched. Food was not to her liking these days.

TJ arrived back with a stack of papers, some from the previous day from Portland. The Press Herald covered the opening extensively. Assorted other papers were mostly from Boston.

"Put them there, sweetie," she told TJ, motioning to the overstuffed hassock next to the fireplace.

Grace flipped erratically through the papers searching for any mention of last night's movie affair. Reviews were all over the place. Grace continued to be more confused and distant. The *Boston Traveller* positioned one of their reviews prominently on page three, above the fold. No reader would be able to miss it. The article stated: "20th Century Fox transformed a worthless dirty book into a good movie."

Grace screamed, and a tear ran down her cheek. It was happening all over again. Just like after her book was released, all the unkind things people said were repeated. TJ knew that the movie was out of their hands; Grace had no control over the movie and its future.

It was a very cold Christmas at the house on Meadows Pond Road. Grace withdrew even more. Her drinking was becoming epic at times, and as much as TJ tried to curtail it, she continued in spite of it all.

The children were looking forward to Christmas and would go back to Gilmanton for their school break. When she withdrew from society, in an attempt to satisfy the need to be liked and be loved, she overcompensated with her family.

"Sweetie." She often started sentences like that when she felt vulnerable. "Let's go down to O'Sheas and spoil the kids," A shopping spree, anything to get her out of the house.

The movie continued to open in more and more theaters across the country. Like the novel, it was a huge success making more money than anyone projected. But, unlike the success of the book where the New Hampshire author reaped some of the benefits, Grace had sold all her rights to the film which meant no royalties would come her way.

This loss did not bother her during that shopping excursion for all she had to do was sign for it. "I can write a book. I can sign my name," she chuckled at the Laconia Tavern where she waited for all the purchases to be gift wrapped. The children would enjoy the holiday even if Grace would not.

CHAPTER 34

1958 began with a bang. Grace's party had started around six o'clock with everyone arriving on time. The author's parties were the best in town. If you were lucky enough to be invited, it was very difficult to say no to Grace. "It will be a smashing good time, sweetie," she would tell them. The crowd was smaller than she would have liked, but it was the dead of winter. The snow had arrived to make a picture-perfect white Christmas for the village to enjoy.

TJ poured the drinks for the guests, and food had been laid out in a party buffet style on the dining table, in the room that was only used for special occasions. The kids had helped set it up and promised to go to bed at eight o'clock once everyone said hello to them. With the kids out of sight, the booze flowed. Guests enjoyed the sounds of Judy Garland as she was Grace's all-time favorite. The singer belted out tunes of lost love and non-acceptance which always put the author in a melancholy mood. Grace identified with the tormented entertainer; her own troubles never too far away.

"Well, fuck you!" Grace screamed at TJ, seconds before throwing the empty bottle of whiskey in his direction. Her lover ducked in time to avoid the glass from doing any damage to his head. "Happy Fucking New Year," she continued to yell at him. Her party had ended about an hour ago. The usual Gilmanton suspects were in attendance. Everyone had had too much to drink, notwithstanding Grace's consumption.

"Grace," pleaded TJ as he bent over to pick up the bottle that did not break. "Please, calm down. You have had way too much. It's late. We should go to bed."

Grace was not having any of it. In her mind her Prince was trying to control her, steal her money, and seduce whomever he could. "I saw you in the kitchen with Jarvi's wife," she slurred and stumbled off the couch in the direction of the bar. To most, TJ's actions were innocent, but to a very drunk Grace these were contemptuous, and she was having no part of.

"You do what you want," he told her. "I'm going to bed." TJ placed the empty bottle on the bar and headed off to the master suite without looking back. Grace walked in the direction of the bar, trying her best not to stagger, composing herself as best she could. She sat down at the bar and stared at the empty bottle. The whiskey was all gone except a slight drop on the bottom. She reached for it, to put it to her mouth. She stared at the last drop searching for some sign of her existence, some sign of her purpose. Feeling totally lost, with no emotion, she returned it to the bar. If she wanted another drink, she knew what had to be done and picked up the phone.

The drive from the house down the state route to the Tavern took longer than usual. Her eyes were blurred from tears, her thinking foggy from the whiskey, and her ability to drive was impaired. The roads were dry and free of any of Mother Nature's hazards, and the moon reflected the light off the snow as if to guide her journey.

Arriving at the Tavern just before the 2 am closing time was something most people did not do. Being New Year's Eve, the bar was still open, and a few remaining patrons still celebrated. She found her favorite booth back in the corner, the place where it had all started for her and the DJ. The bartender knew that a CC and Ginger would be ordered, so he didn't wait for her to summon him. Grace's nod of approval was all he needed to ensure a sizable tip when she had her fill, which he hoped would not take her not too long.

She sat there trying to feel invisible, not letting the casual looks from others bother her. "Fuck you all as well," she muttered. The bartender delivered another drink, and she did her best to sip it as slowly as possible; the effects of the whiskey were taking its toll on her, and she needed to be alert.

"Grace, Grace," trying to break her out of her trance. "I'm here now," the voice told her. She looked up, and there was George. He appeared worn out and disheveled. He had received her frantic call almost two hours before. The ranting and raving about TJ alarmed him. He sensed that his soon-to-be ex-wife had finally hit rock bottom, something he always feared and dreaded. "I'll meet you at the tavern," he told her, "Yes, right now," he assured her.

Grace didn't want another incident at her house like the winter before. She insisted on meeting him at the Tavern. She would wait for him in the bar. "Oh, thank you, my Gee-Gee," she said with a gravelly voice that came from too much booze and cigarettes.

George was prepared to drive north anyway. They had a meeting scheduled with Bernie about an upcoming Look Magazine photoshoot. It would be an article about the author at home with her husband and children. They wanted Bernie to look over the details of the arrangement before letting *Look Magazine* into her dream home. George thought it was a good idea since the general public still thought they were together. Her lover had never been widely admitted.

"Oh, George, how could I have been so wrong about him?" she questioned. Grace was feeling so vulnerable and distraught that her husband no longer knew how to console her. He motioned to the bartender to come to the booth. "Can we get some black coffee?" Moments later two steaming mugs of hot coffee was place in front of them. Grace's expression was a combination of distain and comfort. Her Gee-Gee had come to her rescue.

It took George almost an hour to convince Grace it was time to sleep. A room upstairs in the inn was available, and it had two single beds. "Perfect, we will take it," George told the bartender who had closed and locked the doors of the bar.

He helped Grace out of the booth and to a connecting door that led to the Inn's back stairway. She sobered up enough to know exactly what was happening. She also knew that sleep would be her best friend, second only to her estranged husband.

Morning came much too quickly for her. The light was bright, shining through the window, causing her to roll over in the tiny bed. Pulling the blanket over her head, she fell back asleep. She was trying to ward off the new year, which was not starting well for her.

George was up for a few minutes and dressed. He knew more coffee was needed to get her upright and coherent. The bar downstairs would have coffee; if not, the Laconia Spa would. They boasted to be open 365 days a year. There was no life at the bar so he buttoned up his coat and walked around the corner to find a sweet roll and coffee. The mission was successful, and back to his ailing wife he headed.

Coffee did the trick, and Grace was thinking more rationally and much clearer.

"George, I'm really through with him." Last night had been the worst fight ever for them. George could not tell because he had not been there to witness the lovers in action. All he knew was his Gracie needed him, and he needed her to need him. They drank their coffee sitting across from each other in the single beds. The room was a far cry from The Plaza in New York that she'd grown accustomed to. They decided they should see Bernie sooner than later. Look magazine would be there in a few days, and it was important to show the world the happy housewife and mother turned author.

George called the lawyer from the Inn's front desk. Bernie decided to meet them at his home on the lake since his office was closed, and he had plans that afternoon. George and Grace drove to Lakeport to their lawyer's home to review the magazine arrangement and discuss other business.

Bernie's home was not as large as Grace's redesigned country estate, but it was a beautiful wooden clapboard home, complete with a view of the frozen lake.

Bernie opened the door and did not mention the condition of Grace, or even question George's presence in Laconia on New Year's Day. They sat in the parlor. Bernie's wife made coffee for their meeting, anything to speed it up. Bernie and his wife were aware of Grace's erratic behavior, and all they had wanted was a quiet and peaceful holiday.

"The agreement looks straight forward," Bernie told them. "I think it will be good to show the world that your home and family are not affected by the fame you gained." That had been a mouthful even for a small-town lawyer. He knew all too well the current situation with her and that DJ. But she was a good client, and the bills were being paid.

"Thank you, Bernie," George said, "Before we go, what about the trusts for the children and the will?" Bernie sat back into his chair very cautiously and looked to Grace for a response. "Not now," Grace said. "But Grace," Bernie said like a very concerned parent, "We need to address this."

Grace regained her focus; the previous night's intake of whiskey had worn off, and she was back. "Why are you both ganging up on me?" It was both a question and a statement. She felt like a mouse cornered in the pantry. It was time to find an escape route. She got up from the couch, placing her cup on the wooden coffee table and leaned over to kiss Bernie on the cheek. Nothing was said as she retrieved her coat from the hallway bentwood rack. The men looked at each other and knew it was time to go.

"Thank you, Bernie," George said, shaking his hand. "Happy New Year to you and your family."

George hurried down the front walk to catch up with Grace to open the car door. They headed back to the house. She would pick up her car at another time.

A couple of days later, as scheduled, Look Magazine arrived at Meadows Pond Road. The doorbell chimed, and Grace, with a huge Cheshire cat smile accompanied by all the charm a New Englander would have when welcoming flatlands into her home, opened the polished front door. All their kids were in the front room, dressed in their everyday, but nice, clothes, and playing monopoly. The collapsible card table was set up between the sofa and the hassock. George was in the kitchen making a pot of coffee and placing some doughnuts on a plate. The house was in order with no signs of the usual chaos or dysfunction.

The journalist was charming and insightful. He'd actually read her book, or at least that is what he claimed. The photographer, who shadowed them the entire time, only spoke when he needed to direct them in a pose or expression. The children enjoyed it tremendously and were on their best behavior. The entire shoot at the house finished within a few hours. The final interior shot was of Grace at the kitchen table in front of the old Remington typewriter with George leaning over her shoulder. It all appeared to go well, and Grace was relieved when she heard the car doors shut and the engine start.

She went directly to the bar in the front room for a bottle of whiskey. A drink was what she felt she needed. Her mood changed as fast as the weather. Pouring it into a glass, she didn't even wait for the ginger ale before she drank it. The kids all went to their rooms, and George was cleaning up in the kitchen. Grace sat down at the bar and dialed the phone.

George finished in the kitchen and walked to the front room. Grace was nowhere in sight. He thought she must have gone upstairs to lie down. The day had been exhausting for everyone. The whiskey bottle and empty glass went unnoticed until he heard her car door shut. He rushed over to the window in time to see her speed out of the drive and turn in the direction of town.

George was baffled and furious all at the same time. Had he been duped by his wife yet again? Where could she be going, and why didn't she say something? He wondered. He went upstairs to see the kids; maybe Grace had said something to them. He never noticed the two-word note on the entry table next to the front door.

" I'm sorry," was scratched on the notepad.

CHAPTER 35

    Grace could not wait for the end of the school year that summer. The days had been perfect, the gentle breezes blew through the town green, the grass green like Ireland, and soon the strawberries would be ready to pick. Grace was happy. It had been a long six months, but now the children would be coming home for a few months, leaving their father back in Massachusetts. "Where he belonged," she thought more often than not.

    TJ had gone back to the radio station, working most afternoons and some nights. This gave her time to write, time to let her own thoughts appear on paper. It was not an easy process for her, TJ knew it, but if giving her space and isolation was what she needed, he could live with that.

    In just a few days the house would be full again with laughter. The noises that the children made pleased her. It did not please her one bit on how it all came to pass. She had run out on George on that cold winter afternoon to TJ's apartment, and there they had made up. It was also the same time that George had packed up the kids and took them back to his three-room cottage in Massachusetts where he insisted they enroll in school. In retrospect the distance he had created was good for Grace and TJ.

That day she was feeling overly confident; her second book was coming along, maybe not as fast as she would like, but she was writing again. She had been elated and dismayed, all at the same time, by an article in a Boston paper she had read that morning.

It had stated that by that summer, one in every 29 Americans would have read the scandalous novel, and the sales had now surpassed Margaret Mitchell's, *Gone with the Wind*. Truly an accomplishment neither she nor Kitty could have imagined, but then the writer went on to state that not everyone in Gilmanton has read her book. It seemed the novel was yet to be in the collection at the town library on the village green. Grace thought she could fix that.

The drive to The Corner Store on the green was easy, Grace had done it so many times she could do it blind folded. She parked the car directly across from the town library. She had prepared herself for a talk with that old librarian and would present an autographed copy of her novel. Stopping momentarily on the sidewalk, she composed herself, as if she were going into battle with Rita Rowell, the same school board member that had fired George so long ago.

Grace pushed open the wooden door and stepped into the library foyer. At that moment and unexpectedly she had found herself face to face with the very librarian she dreaded. Both women looked startled.

"Ms Rowell," Grace greeted her.

"Yes, Mrs. Metalious, or is it Mrs. Martin now?" she replied. Grace knew instantly that this meeting was not going to go well. That old bitch still hated her for the book she wrote. Like a western duel, neither of them would make the first move, each keeping their hand ready to draw if the other made a move first.

"Well, I'm glad you have done your homework and have been keeping up with my life," like butter the words came out of Grace's mouth. "Please just call me Grace; after all, we go back a long way," she retorted.

Rowell was mystified as to why on that day this less than credible writer chose to darken her door of her library.

"Well, Rita, can I call you Rita?" she sarcastically asked. "You are not the only one to have done their homework." Grace informed the librarian she was aware that her book was still not in her own library where she paid taxes that supported it.

Rita looked alarmed. She was being confronted by a town resident and the very author of a piece of trash that she despised.

"If you don't mind, I will call you Mrs. Metalious," she continued. "The good people of Gilmanton have entrusted in me the duty to uphold a standard for its residents, both in this library and with the school curriculum," she continued. "That book, that piece of trash that you have been promoting across the country, has done more damage than good. You took a dark chapter of the town's history and extorted it for your own good," she stopped and waited for a reply.

Grace stood there, feeling like a schoolgirl that had just been scolded for smoking in the girl's restroom. This spinster and shell of a woman made Grace feel small and unworthy. The author had underestimated her as a librarian and overestimated her own self's back bone. It was not going as she had hoped.

"Well, Rita, that was a mouthful," She replied. "I guess you have been waiting a very long time to say that." Grace was lost again within her own words, and all she wanted to do was to get the hell out of there. What had started as a goodwill gesture had turned down a dark and ugly road very quickly. Revenge is best served on the printed page, and the author had a moment of clarity and knew exactly what to do. Rita Rowell would, somehow, be a part of her new story.

"Now, Mrs. Metalious, I have work to do. Is there anything else you wanted to say?" Rowell asked her.

"Yes, as a matter of fact there is," She paused. "Fuck yourself, no one else will!" A defining statement from the author who clearly was fed up with the situation. The autographed book never even came out of her handbag. The drive back to Meadows Pond Road was as fast as possible.

TJ had gotten home about eight o'clock and found Grace in the corner of the living room, cross legged on the sofa, a drink in hand, and a glazed look over her eyes.

"Hi, Baby, how was your day?" He asked Grace. He could tell she had been crying and was feeling quite blue. Noticing the fresh new book on the hassock, he knew it had not gone well at the town library, and the last thing he wanted to do was to bring up a sore subject.

Before either of them spoke a word, the phone rang "Saved by the bell." TJ thought. He got up, crossed to the bar, and picked up the receiver. It was Jerry Wald calling from Los Angeles.

"Hey TJ, it's not too late there is it?" he asked. Without giving TJ an opportunity to answer, the studio executive asked, "How is my baby, is Grace there?" Wald could be quite excitable when he wanted to be.

TJ knew that Grace was in no mood to talk to Jerry Wald of all people. She had been shot down by the town librarian, and by the look of the bottle sitting on the bar, she was well on her way to a drunken stupor. "Grace can't talk right now," he tried to explain to the producer.

Jerry wasn't buying it and went on to tell TJ the reason for the call. He had a brain epiphany to create a sequel to *Peyton Place*; his movie magic had paid off, and the film had garnered nine academy award nominations and made millions for the studio. He had struck gold with her talent. Grace, of course, was not seeing a red cent of it since she had left the contract negotiations before they could be revised.

"Please give Grace the message: I only need 10 pages, tell me what the characters did after the book ended," he was almost pleading. "I will pay $1,000 a page for her time." TJ wanted out of this conversation. As much as he knew the money was great and quite frankly they needed it, he had to hang up.

"I'm sorry, Jerry, I have to go. I will tell Grace," Wald did not like being dismissed at all.

"TJ, thanks, I will call back soon." The phone was placed back on the receiver, and he poured himself his own drink.

"Well, what did that cad want?" Grace asked. TJ tried to explain that he too thought it was a good idea to write a sequel to her book. "You are so talented; it would take you no time to write," he told her. She wasn't buying it; the last thing she wanted to do was to stir the pot in Gilmanton anymore. She had been somewhat naive to think that the town had finally accepted her, and all the hoop-la that was in the past. If anything, that day's altercation only reaffirmed her need to distance herself from Gilmanton.

But money, as always, was TJ's main reasoning to push the idea. "Baby, it would come in very handy," he told her. The last six months had been a whirlwind: the house renovations completed, the adjacent property around the house purchased and both of them bought new cars, again. They had spent much more than they should have the past few months; the royalties were still coming in as the book sales sold into the millions.

"TJ, no!" Grace blurted. She was knee deep writing her next book, *The Tight White Collar;* what *had* started as a revisit to an old manuscript had been much harder than she anticipated. She found rewriting it was not the same creative process as *Peyton Place* had been. Her days in her studio always started with the vim and vigor of an athlete but ended like that of a depressed barfly. She was worried her inspiration was waning, her thinking was that the highballs would help her confidence. TJ knew they would not.

They both sat in silence, sipping their drinks. They knew they had reached an impasse, and without saying a word they decided to table the conversation, thinking that they should have some supper, but neither was hungry. The whiskey would be their substance for the night, not the best idea, all things considered.

The phone rang again; this time it had only slightly startled them. Grace gave him a look; he knew exactly his role. Answer the phone, get rid of the caller, leave the phone off the hook.

A neat order of tasks that he knew all too well from the past year, after all he was her manager.

"TJ, it's Jerry again," Wald was calling. "Now, don't hang up, I have sweetened the deal," Grace watched intently as TJ listened and nodded his head, both in agreeing and disagreeing with the caller. The conversation lasted for only a few minutes, just enough time to perk up Grace's interest; she knew deep down that the money would run out if they did not curtail their habits. She had signed a three-book deal with Kitty and had been receiving advances on her second book. That had made her nervous because the writing was not happening as fast as either of them wanted.

He hung up the phone, grabbed the bottle of whiskey, and returned to the sofa. Topping off each of their drinks, he picked up his glass to drink. "Well, tell me," Grace said

Wald had upped his offer to $25,000 for 25 pages; she would need to start right away because it would go straight into movie production. Wald knew a sequel would be a money maker. Her manager turned husband had done a great job stating the producer's case while adding his own spin, but Grace was the one to deliver the goods.

Once again, they returned to silence, each staring into their drinks. Neither of them said a word. Ultimately, it had to be Grace's decision; whatever it was, TJ would support it. He also knew life would have to change drastically until the next book was completed.

It was getting late, and the effects of the booze had finally relaxed Grace to a point of submission. She needed to go to bed. Sleep would be her friend, and the next day she would start again, thinking about writing and thinking about not drinking; both would challenge her to her core.

TJ helped her up the stairs and out of her clothes. It was only moments before she was fast asleep. He hoped she was dreaming of better days. He sat on the opposite side of the bed, and removed his shoes, he also was ready to sleep. The phone rang again; this time the sound was softer and less starling. Grace had turned down the ringer on the extension in the bedroom; TJ reached across the nearly passed out Grace to answer the phone. It was Jerry calling again from Hollywood. Before TJ was able to say hello, "Tell him ok, I'll do it, I'll write the fucking book," was all she said without turning over.

A sense of elation came over TJ as did Jerry; both the men in Grace's life were happy. They agreed to talk in the morning. TJ hung up the phone and kissed her on the cheek; she was almost asleep.

"Heaven help me," Grace whispered, then drifted off into a haze of whiskey and regret.

CHAPTER 36

The Edwardian Room at the plaza in New York was buzzing with anticipation. There had been a call to the press from Jacques; Grace's agent had asked for a full room of reporters to hear what she had to say. He himself was still in the dark about her sudden need to talk to the press, but like every good ringmaster, press is press and cash is king.

It was a grey day in February, but in New York every day during winter seemed grey to Grace. The sunshine never made it onto her face. "Too many tall buildings," she told Kitty. "I prefer New Hampshire." Taking the girl out of the country did not mean the country in the girl was removed. Grace was a simple, meaningful writer that wore her emotions on her sleeve like a badge of honor.

Grace and TJ rode the elevator down to the Edwardian Room, a richly paneled event room with large chandeliers and windows overlooking Central Park and the Pulitzer Fountain. Grace would never admit it, but she fantasized about accepting the award on behalf of her baby, *Peyton Place*. The Pulitzer for fiction was awarded to literature that dealt with American life. She thought her novel had done that and more.

Neither of them spoke; Grace had made a few notes on the hotel stationary the night before. She was nervous, but with TJ at her side, she knew it would be okay. The doors opened, and

Grace took a deep breath and grabbed TJ's hand as they strolled to the press conference.

"Grace, Darling," Jacques leaned into his prized cash cow to give her a peck on the cheek. "Right this way. Most everyone is here," he told her. TJ admitted, even though he and Jacques never seem to agree on things, Jacques could be the rainmaker when he wanted to. TJ caught Jacques's eye and nodded slightly in an approving manner.

The room was set up with rows of chairs and a small riser with a table for the couple to sit at. Before the couple had a chance to sit down, flash bulbs started going off creating that distinct sound and smell that sent Grace back again to a time when George had exposed her and her lover. She thought, "Fuck George and his black mail."

"Thank you, everyone," said Jacques, trying to settle the room down. "Mrs. Metalious has a brief statement to read before answering questions." Grace took out a folded piece of hotel stationary with her notes. After taking a deep breath, she waited for the flash bulbs to stop before reading.

Grace was nervous but had not had a drink that morning. TJ advised against it, and she had agreed. She decided to dress professionally, omitting the blue jeans and flannel for another time. The grey suit with a simple white blouse created an older and more weathered look for her. She had, after all, gained some weight and was now thirty-three; the innocence of the young housewife had faded into the harshness of a novelist turned reclusive drinker. TJ was in his best double-breasted suit with wide lapel and wing tips, all courtesy of O'Sheas department store and his lover's signature.

"I would like you all to know, based on the popularity of *Peyton Place*, I have decided to write another book. It's called, "The Tight White Collar, man's inhumanity against man." Taking another deep breath, she continued; she read like a great orator and did not miss a word as she described the premise of the new novel. The reporters ate it up. They wrote mostly in shorthand on steno pads, and the flash bulbs continued as photographers knew those shots were pure gold to them.

"Thank you," Grace paused. "There is more." And with that the flood gates were open, reminding her of the mighty Merrimack River back in Manchester. No holding back the spring thaw, as now, no holding back Grace. "I have decided to divorce my husband George and marry my Prince Charming, Thomas J. Martin, if he will have me." The words were not out of her mouth before a couple of the reporters ran out of the room back to their desks to scoop the others. The small group of journalists that remained all in unison raised their hands in an attempt to be called upon. There were lots of questions.

Now that the cat was out-of-the bag, there was no turning back. Adultery was a crime, and gossip was the sentence to all those that dared cross that line. "Tomorrow I will fly down to Mexico City to finalize my divorce from George," she tried to explain in between the over talking and photos being snapped.

The reality was that Grace had upstaged herself, something she had never thought about. By announcing her next novel, she paved the way to also announce her next chapter in life. Art was imitating life; Grace was creating her very own *Peyton Place* where she resided with the rest of her characters. Her larger-than-life presence, with all its turmoil, deceitfulness and drama, seemed to have been ripped from the pages of her own book.

Every reporter and photographer who had the least bit of interest in the author's life knew she had been shacking up for a year with this guy, this DJ from a small-town radio station. Some even thought the story couldn't get any better. Copy would fly on the typewriters later in the newsroom.

Grace didn't know how to handle the questions that came at her fast and furious, like an angry baseball pitcher. She didn't even have time to swing the bat. The last thing she wanted to do was get angry and short with the reporters. Jacques came to her rescue, sort of, to calm the reporters and organize the questions. They ran the gamut from the origins of the first book, to where she got her inspiration. But one question was never asked: if it was her autobiography. Each reporter knew all too well what would happen if they proposed such a sensitive question.

When asked why she wrote *Peyton Place*, "I thought about it for a very long time. Frankly I needed the money," she answered. Another question, "Why TJ?" That question she felt was none of their business. Secretly she wanted to tell them all that he fucked like a racehorse and was hung like one, too. Just the thought made her a little moist and blush. "TJ has been my manager, and he can do things I can't. It's a perfect relationship," was her answer, and she quickly moved on.

"What about the new book?" was a popular question, "What is your inspiration for *The Tight White Collar*?" asked a reporter. "This time I am neither frightened or angry; it will not be another *Peyton Place*," she told the room in the most definitive manner.

It was time to wrap up the conference. Grace was getting edgy, and Jacques knew it. He spoke to the room and explained the need to finish with their questions; he would take two more. He looked out for just the right reporter. He pointed to the only one not jumping out of his seat. A tastefully dressed and somewhat unassuming writer stood up and asked, "Can you tell our readers, what are the downsides of being so famous?"

Grace felt like she had been punched in the gut. The pain was so deep that even her trusty heating pad could not help her at that moment. Without missing a beat, she replied. "It has to be the misquotes, the misconceptions, and downright lies printed about me, my book, and my family." The room went quiet as if a giant hand had suddenly appeared floating above them with a straightened index finger, shushing the reporters.

With that, Grace and TJ stood up and were about to leave when the same reporter said, "You said two questions, didn't you?" looking directly at Jacques. They both paused and looked at each other; they were done with the conference and did not want it to go further. He blurted the question, "Will there be sequel to *Peyton Place*?" Grace turned to the reporter and simply said, "Heaven help us."

The press conference was over. They hurried to the elevator, and in seconds they were in their suite pouring a stiff glass of Canadian Club over lots of ice. They folded into each other's arms in an embrace that was nurturing and erotic. Their mouths intertwined, and the taste of whiskey on both tongues stirred their groins. For the first time they truly were free of the ridicule and gossip that surrounded their relationship.

Telling the press corps, they were going to Mexico was Grace's idea. No one needed to know their real plans. After speaking with Bernie and Kitty, who knew everything, Mexico was not needed to finalize the divorce. Alabama was the answer. Phenix City, Alabama had no resident requirements to finalize a divorce. It's no wonder it was called, "Sin City, USA." What a befitting place for the couple to be on the lam.

The flights to Alabama were bumpy in more ways than one. Grace eluded the press long enough to get out of New York, but the winter storm that they flew into was not as easy to circumvent. The small plane had no business being cleared for take-off. The twelve-seater was almost empty and was jostled in the air like a child's toy. The entire flight felt like they were riding in a box car along the Boston and Maine Railroad.

After landing, Grace realized how much she liked being on the ground and how much she hated flying. The relief came when the documents were signed, and she had them in hand. She was free of George, and marrying TJ was the next adventure.

Grace was learning so much that winter, how to quicken a divorce and now how to quicken a marriage. Elkton, Maryland, called the Gretna Green of the United States, was the answer. It was notorious for the ease of marrying with no age or resident requirements, just like its counterpart in Scotland had been for centuries. Elkton was right outside of Baltimore, close to New

York. A few of her friends could attend. It would be easy breezy, she had thought.

"TJ, I will not get on another plane," she insisted. "My love, let me take care of it," he told her. After a few calls, arrangements were made. A driver would take them to Atlanta where they would board a train to Baltimore. Elkton was about forty miles from the station.

Jacques was alerted, and he and a photographer would be at the Hotel in Baltimore right after the ceremony. Kitty and even Leona showed up to support the newlyweds. It was the 25th of February, two days' shy of her 15th wedding anniversary with George.

CHAPTER 37

Fourth of July fireworks were just the reason needed for the family to get away from the house and have a change of scenery. TJ insisted on taking Grace and the kids to Lake Winnipesaukee for a couple of days. They checked into the Old Cape Codder Motor Court overlooking the lake. The motel and cottages had seen better days, but finding accommodations was difficult because he waited too long to call. That evening, they sat on the front porch of a miniature cottage watching fireworks burst over the water. Having a bird's eye view was so much better than watching from the boardwalk with hordes of tourists along Weirs Beach.

A dark cloud lifted from over them, and they felt they had dodged another bullet. A month before, Jerry Wald had called. So much had changed, yet so much had remained the same. Grace accepted the challenge and the financial offer to write a sequel to *Peyton Place*. This deal made TJ happy and fattened the checkbook, but at the same time it increased Grace's insecurities and self-doubt, giving her more reasons to drink.

The press continued to print whatever they wanted, whether it be the truth or their version of it. It did sell books, but it also gave them no end to trouble. *Variety Magazine* got the story all wrong by inadvertently announcing the next book as *The Tight White Collar* and a third as *Return to Peyton Place*. Both books were nowhere near completed: one not even started and the other only a couple of chapters. This only increased the pressure on the author.

But it was the Fourth of July. Everyone was in a good mood, and there were so many things to be grateful for. The children were home, and the $165,000 check from Dell Pocket Books as an advance for the sequel fueled the celebration. "Here's to Jacques," Grace raised her glass high in the air. She threw her head back in a giggly manner as the fireworks exploded high over the lake directly in front of her. Jerry Wald could make movie magic and money, but Jacques had secured the cash upfront to keep the ball rolling, all reasons to party that holiday. TJ smiled at Grace and lifted his glass. The toast was a symbolic gesture to bid good bye to their current money concerns. "Hear, hear," was all he said. Reality would soon catch up with them. The weekend was a mere respite from the task at hand.

"Today, TJ, today," Grace insisted, sipping the last bit of coffee from her mug. The breakfast table on Meadows Pond Road had been cluttered with crumbs of toast, the dirty dishes piled in the sink, the smell of cooked bacon still lingered in the air. Her dream house was not in the condition she hoped for. TJ was doing his best to pick up after the kids who had rushed out to go to Silver Lake to go swimming. His wife nursed a rather large hangover from a night on the town. "Okay, Grace," he paused, "I get it, but you have to start the outline at least. Everyone is waiting," he told her.

July passed, and now the end of summer was in sight. It was August 1st, and time was running out for the author. She knew the commitments she had made to her agent, to her publisher, and to the studio. Jerry Wald called every other day asking for updates. Her excuses were as creative as her story lines, if she had ,in fact, written some. "I'm sorry, sweetie. The entire house came down with summer colds," was a popular excuse. Wald wasn't buying any of it. He already started film production, from casting to seeking out locations, all without a story or a script.

Grace stood up from the breakfast table and placed her empty mug on the pile of dirty dishes in the sink. The kitchen was a mess, but she could've cared less. "Where is my grandmother when I need a good housekeeper?" she thought. "I will be in my studio. Please take the phone off the hook," she told her husband. Dressed in her signature attire of old blue jeans and one of TJ's white dress shirts, she left the kitchen and headed to her office clutching a pack of Parliament cigarettes. She knew she had to lock herself away from the world. She and her typewriter had to be one in order to complete this task, one which she dreaded as much as she feared.

Her original book, *The Tree and the Blossom* took her years to actually write. She began her storytelling and note-taking back in high school, long before George. The final version of *Peyton Place* had taken a few months to edit and rewrite before Kitty would publish it. The feeling of dread was evident as she sat down at her desk in front of her new electric typewriter; the old Remington was neatly displayed on the shelf, right next to the very first copy she received of *Peyton Place*. She lit a cigarette and took a long drag as she stared at the blank piece of paper.

She had not lost her talent as a typist. She was faster than any other in her class in school or any of her co-workers back in Manchester during the war. She worked so many jobs in offices during that time, but typing was her saving grace. She hoped the electric typewriter would now only speed the process.

She pulled out a large manila folder stuffed with handwritten notes, some more legible than others, which she had made over the past weeks. The legal-size sheets of yellow paper were torn from the pad, each page identifying the returning characters for the sequel. The plain white pages were descriptions of new residents of Peyton Place, some more realistic than others. Grace had decided that her favorite librarian needed to be depicted as a shrew and a spinster, this is where her art had imitated life.

Unlike in her kitchen, these notes were arranged and neatly identified in an orderly fashion.

She placed the half-smoked cigarette into the ashtray next to her on the desk. She then flipped on the switch to her magic machine. A quiet hum emitted from it. It was familiar to her. The relaxing sound stimulated her creative senses. She began to write.

Downstairs in the kitchen TJ had decided to clean up a bit. Waiting for Marsha to return to do it was not fair to the young girl. She realized her friend of many years had now become her boyfriend. A teen-age love interest was always more exciting than cleaning up the breakfast dishes. He also wanted to hang around the house to keep an eye on his wife. She needed support as much as she needed coaxing in order to get her to write. Writing would keep the checkbook filled.

Feeling satisfied with the condition of the kitchen, he wanted to check on Grace but did not want to disturb her. The house was very large and somewhat soundproof. He had to be a little sneaky. As he climbed the center stairs to the second landing, he noticed her writing studio door was closed. "Perfect," he thought. He reached the door and pressed his right ear against it. He heard the reassuring rattling sound of her new typewriter; Grace was writing; he was pleased.

Labor Day, which came the first weekend of September, was the unspoken deadline on which to have the sequel off on its way to New York. This date was an aggressive goal, one which Grace gave to herself. The kids would be leaving that weekend to return to live with George. Her other book, *The Tight White Collar*, would need to be finished as well.

Every day, after a few mugs of coffee and some toast, she climbed those stairs to her studio and closed the door. She grabbed a fresh pack of Parliaments from the carton kept in the cupboard next to the ice box. Routine was the answer for her to be productive. Breaking her routine was not an option.

It was like clockwork. As the sun and the bright light of day turned to a glow in the sky, sometimes amber and sometimes grey, her studio door would open, and Grace would emerge in need of a drink and lots of moral support.

It was a good time for TJ and Grace. They were closer than they had ever been. Her writing prevented them from fighting, and the kids added an element to complete the family. Like Grace, the children really did adore TJ. His bigger than life personality and his physical being just gave them more to love and hug. The fighting was something everyone learned to live without. It was almost nonexistent. It was a win-win for everyone in Meadows Pond house.

After the evening meal, the children disappeared: Marsha on a date and the other two glued to the television in the family den. TJ would make a round of drinks and wait for Grace to appear with pages from her day. There, in the comfort of the front room, sipping CC and Ginger, she handed over her pages for TJ to read aloud to her. TJ the DJ had not lost his silky smooth and sensual voice, which made her words roll off the pages as easily as they rolled off his tongue.

The story was coming together. The descriptions of New England and all the characters, waiting to be awakened, came alive again after a long slumber. Grace's voice could be heard in their dialogue, as each character dealt with the triumphs and tragedy of small-town life. "Baby, you are nearly there," TJ told her. "Do you like it?" he asked.

"I never had the slightest intention of writing a sequel," she abruptly told him. "I feel I'm not writing a novel, but some sludge for Mr. Jerry Wald." Grace stood up and went to the bar; another drink was in order. She was glad the project was nearly completed. She had done her duty. The book, *Return to Peyton Place*, had been sold weeks before, and the film studio offered over $200,000 for the film rights.

Thirty days, to the day, Grace came down from her writer's studio with a stack of typed sheets. *Return to Peyton Place* was finished, at least for her, as far as she was concerned. She was exhausted, drained, and happy at the same time.

Kitty would get her hard bound book that she desperately waited for. Dell Publishers would get their paperback. The studio would have something to write a script with, but mostly TJ would stop nagging her with his concerns about the money.

"Let me call Jacques," TJ insisted. "He's still coming up for Labor Day weekend, right?" he asked. The holiday was only a few days away; the manuscript could go back with Jacques to New York. He could hand deliver it to Kitty.

"Yes, but I want to remind him, before I sign with Fox I have a few stipulations." Grace had learned from her past mistakes, and lightning would not strike twice in the same board room.

Labor Day was a relaxing time in Gilmanton. Jacques and Grace talked at length about her requirements for the deal with 20th Century Fox.

The kids packed up their worldly possessions to head south as they resumed their life with their father. Grace and TJ celebrated. It was the beginning of September, and they were empty nesters again.

Return to Peyton Place had only been 256 pages of what Grace called, "all dribble." *Peyton Place* was almost 400 pages of what she felt was her, "fourth child." There was irony in Gilmanton that summer. It reminded her of the time she was at the film studio, and someone had told her, "Hollywood takes good writers and makes them bad screenwriters." This frightened her.

CHAPTER 38

The flowering Crab trees that Grace insisted on planting in the front yard in Gilmanton finally reached maturity and was in full bloom. The blossoms were rich in color, a mixture of pink and white. The branches themselves were almost hidden by the amount of flowers on them. They seemed to float in the breeze while dancing in the fresh air. Grace had almost forgotten the simplest pleasures in life. It was her dream to sit on the front porch and watch the clouds float across the sky, and just simply sit and smell the fresh air that a New Hampshire Spring would bring.

She absolutely loved how her home had turned out. It was worth every penny. What had started as a modest Cape Cod home, she had turned into a renovated country estate worthy of a name. She just hadn't found the right name for it yet.

Years before, *It'll Do* was their first place they lived in in the area. That tiny shack, with all its faults, was a distant memory for her. She worked very hard to get to where she was, but, she also remembered her roots, the poverty, and discrimination, both as a woman and as a French Canadian. Those wounds never healed and were always a basis for her writing. Sitting in an old Adirondack chair she had rescued from the barn, she felt comfort in knowing that not everything needed not be new and shiny, no matter what TJ said.

Return to Peyton Place was released in January, and, like her first book, the reviews were all over the place. Messner and Dell, the two publishing houses, struck a deal to release the paperback and hardbound at the same time, another brilliant tactic Brandt and his world of PR did to create the buzz. The reviews were not favorable; in fact, most critics did not like her new book at all. *The New York Times* did not even bother to read it or review it, leaving the sole review to a reader's lengthy opinion, which was not a positive one.

Grace felt humiliated on so many levels. She returned from Washington DC where Dell had set up press conferences centered on the pocket paperback. She felt like she was being played a fool after seeing a printed copy.

"This is not how I wrote it," throwing the book across the hotel suite in the direction of her agent.

"Grace, they had to edit some of it." Jacques was trying to calm her down. She demanded he call room service; a drink was needed.

Within seconds, the room service attendant arrived with a bottle of whiskey, ice, and 7-Up. "7-Up, where is the ginger ale?" she asked the staff member. He explained that they had none on property, and this was the closest thing. She did not care; she needed the drink and, with a slight hand gesture, motioned Jacques to tip the guy. Sometimes Grace could be downright disrespectful.

Jacques knew her original manuscript that he had carried to Kitty was pure crap. He had read it on the train back from Boston and knew the publisher would have a fit. Grace was in no condition to do a rewrite, or even get through the edits. Since the rights were owned jointly between Messner and Dell publishing house, a ghost writer was called in to clean up the story. "No one need be the wiser," Kitty said to the small group in her office last fall.

"Grace, here you are," handing her a drink. "You know you reacted almost the same way when Leona started edits of *Peyton Place*," he continued.

"Your fucking right, Jacques," she said with the emphasis on his name with a French Canadian accent. "I did not like it then, and I do not like it now." She felt used, again. "I've been played a sucker all round." With that she downed her drink and extended her empty glass for another.

Sitting on her front porch that afternoon and reflecting on that awful trip, she was glad her head was now clear. Her mind was releasing endorphins, small bursts of creativity and ideas that drifted in and out. She got exactly what she wanted from the movie studio in regard to the new book. After the creative and release snubs of the first film, Wald agreed to hold the world premiere of the sequel there in Laconia, at the Colonial Theater. He had paid dearly for the movie rights, along with a small percent of the proceeds back to Grace. He shelled out even more cash for the rights to, *The Tight White Collar*; it was only a third written. Who ever said "April was the cruelest month," Grace thought and smiled.

A car honked as it turned into the door yard. She had been expecting it for at least an hour as she sat on the front porch. Grace jumped to her feet and went down the front steps to greet Laurette. Her mother had decided to pay her a visit. It had been over a year since they last spoke and ages since they'd actually seen each other. Laurette stepped out of her brand new 1959 Chevy, dressed in her Sunday finest, looking as fresh as when she left Manchester hours before.

Grace knew all the money she sent to her mother and her sister had financed the car, the clothes, and even the new lipstick in her purse. She would say nothing and try her best to enjoy their visit.

"Grace, my dear" her mother said. "Let me look at you." It had been a long time. Her daughter had obviously put on a few pounds, in fact a lot of weight. Her skin was no longer peaches and cream, but there had a slight yellow tint to it. "How are you feeling?" Laurette questioned. "Fine, just fine!" Grace was miffed at the judgement on her mother's face. "Let's go in," Grace needed a drink to deal with this visit.

TJ still worked some at the radio station and decided to work late in order to give his wife some alone time with her mother. He knew how estranged they'd become. The last thing he wanted was to get in the middle of some French-Canadian female shouting match.

"The house looks wonderful," her mother told her. Grace beamed with pride. Her mother had actually given her a compliment, and it had baffled her. The tour of the house was the highlight of the afternoon. The children were still with their father so there would be no visit with them this trip.

The house was in exceptional condition; Grace had hired a couple of local girls to scrub and clean the entire house just in case her mother had worn white gloves. She was relieved she had not.

Sitting in the kitchen at the breakfast table, Grace made drinks. Her mother professed to be a teetotaler, but her daughter knew she liked a good whiskey just as she did. The conversation was just a bit guarded; neither one of them feeling totally comfortable to be themselves. It had been way too long between visits, and too much water had spilled over the dam. "We missed you at Meme's funeral," Laurette confided. "You know you were her favorite." Grace stood up, reached for the bottle, and topped off both their glasses.

"Let's go into the front room; it's my favorite in the entire house," she told her mother. She sat cross legged in her favorite spot on the sofa. It was only then that she felt more comfortable.

"Grace, a lady doesn't sit like that," her mother said in a condescending manner. With only a couple of drinks in them the mother and daughter act started to clash over various topics;

nothing was left off the table. Laurette had her own ideas on George, the children, and her new husband.

"After all, TJ is handsome, but is he really husband material?" Her mother pushed all her daughter's buttons. The comment was once again made about, *Peyton Place,* being Laurette's original idea.

"Oh, look at the time," Grace said. "I have booked a table at the Winnisquam House for an early dinner. My husband will be joining us after his work, you know, TJ, the handsome one," Grace snapped.

"Sarcasm will get you nowhere, my dear," was all Laurette said. The two ladies went off to their respective corners of the house to freshen up.

Alone in her room, Grace reached under her nightstand and retrieved a bottle of whiskey; it was her hiding spot in the house, perfect for a day like that. A cut crystal mouthwash glass from her vanity served perfectly as a vessel for the whiskey, anything to help blur that afternoon conversation. Grace thought for a moment to change her clothes, but the thought evaporated as fast as it was formed. Her mother would not have approved of anything she chose anyway.

Grace decided to take the red Buick Station wagon. It was her country car, she figured, and they were in the country. Secretly, she knew it would piss her mother off that they did not take the new Cadillac that was parked next to it.

"A station wagon?" Laurette asked. "Yes, mother, I need to pick up a load of manure for the garden on the way home." Grace was feeling no pain.

The drive down the state road towards the town of Winnisquam was about equal distance to Laconia which was in the opposite direction. The small town was a mere village on the lake it was named after. The Winnisquam House was a stately old wooden structure that was the center of gentile life for folks that summered on the lake. It was a perfect spot for dinner and drinks; her mother would love. It was the polar opposite of The Laconia Tavern which Grace preferred hands down.

There wasn't much talk during the drive. Laurette felt the effect of the whiskey; it made her calmer and less judgmental, Grace thought. The old station wagon handled the drive well. The three on the column was distracting to Grace, but after a few miles on the main Route 3 road she was sailing along smoothly.

"Dear, are you going just a tad fast?" it sounded like a question, but it was truly a statement. Grace was drunk, but not blindly drunk, just drunk enough to look down to the speedometer to see she was doing nearly fifty. "Oops," she said with a chuckle.

It was only a split second, the time it took for her to read the speed and look up, when she heard her mother scream. It happened so fast. The station wagon had veered out of the lane they were in and into oncoming traffic. At 50 mph it was a deadly situation. Grace's adrenaline momentarily counteracted the alcohol in her system. Her first thought was to slam hard on the brakes and turn to the right out of the oncoming lane. But she forgot to step on the clutch as the car jerked and stalled. The red Buick station wagon went over the embankment and slid almost 75 feet coming to rest just a couple of yards from the railroad tracks. With the engine off, no sounds came from the interior.

TJ arrived on time at the Winnisquam House. He sat in the bar drinking a Manhattan. The Spanish peanuts were exceptional that night. The sun was setting over the lake. It was a befitting spot for Laurette to dine. He was sure she would approve. Looking at his watch, which had been a gift from his wife the previous Christmas, he wondered where they could be? They were nearly forty-five minutes late.

Sirens off in the distance were barely heard in the dining room, let alone in the bar. The loud piano player drowned out the outside world. He was doing his job.

CHAPTER 39

"I think this is it," TJ told Grace as he pulled the convertible into the rental house driveway, the crushed stones under the tires making that distinct sound. The couple arrived at their vacation rental on Hampton Beach.

"I thought it would be bigger," he apologized. "Oh, sweetie, it will be fine; not everything has to be grand and perfect, after all, I'm just an uneducated writer from the backwoods."

TJ saw Grace had hit rock bottom after the accident. No charges were filed, and it was kept hush-hush locally. But a small story appeared in a trade journal called *Spotlight*. TJ was sure that only a select few in the business ever read that rag.

The New Hampshire coastline was Grace's go-to place when her life was on its way to falling apart or had fallen apart. She was lucky to have only been knocked unconscious in the accident, and her station wagon was repairable. Laurette, unfortunately, did not fare as well. She received a slight concussion and a broken arm. After being released from the hospital, Laurette insisted Grace pay for a driver to take her car back to Manchester that very day. They had not spoken since.

"TJ, this was a perfect idea," she told him as they stepped out of the new car he had bought her. He'd decided not to repair the station wagon but trade it in. Their latest model of another new Cadillac convertible had more bells and whistles than TJ'S. Grace's new car was powder blue, his wife's favorite color.

"This house is adorable, TJ, shall we buy it?" TJ never knew when it came to money, if she was serious or not. One day Grace could be a fanatic and the next a spendthrift. He liked only the finest of things, and he was pleased with himself that he'd elevated most of Grace's taste from that simple New Englander to an international bestselling author.

Peyton Place was fast approaching eight million in sales, and there seemed to be no stopping it. The movie was doing unbelievably well. In Italy alone it had grossed over 1.2 million dollars, but the author had not seen one cent of it. Grace was banking on the success of the sequel. She was going to get a piece of that action. Despite bad reviews, *Return to Peyton Place* had made the New York Times best seller list, something she thought would have never happened.

The vacation house overlooked a rocky outcropping, and a small beach that was inaccessible at high tide; it was perfect to keep out prying eyes and private enough for them to sunbathe in the nude if they chose to. It had three bedrooms and a large living room that overlooked the sea. The view was spectacular. The best part was the huge wrap around porch where Grace went to sit and write.

The Tight White Collar was nearly complete. It was a chore for her to write. Grace knew finishing it had to be her priority. After the car accident, Grace and TJ had decided to stop drinking, eat better, and lose some weight. She still remembered her mother's disapproving look of her belly and ever-growing ass. Genetics were not kind to her, but she could have cared less as long as TJ loved her body.

Grace brought along an extra suitcase she called her office. It was quite heavy when packed up with her electric typewriter, pads of paper filled with notes, various other unfinished stories, and a box of pencils; everything a writer would need to create the next best seller. She still questioned her talent and her skills.

"I can't do it," she told TJ. Her frustration level was obvious. "How will I top *Peyton Place*?" He walked over and placed his hands on her shoulders. It was early morning; the tide was out and the sand pristine. "Let's go for a walk." His suggestion was spot on, and the two strolled slowly along the frigid water's edge. Without drinking, they both realized they had to change their environment, and also their habits. Walking was one of them, giving her an opportunity to run story ideas past him.

It seemed to work. Words came to her quickly, making her fingers fly across the keys of the typewriter; page after page, filled with the antics of another small New England town called Cooper Station.

"No, it's not like the others," she tried to explain to her husband. "Think about all the things society does, the mistreatments, the discrimination, and the judgments." TJ was not getting any of it. He was just happy that she was writing again, and the third book commitment to her publisher would be fulfilled. "Excellent, Grace," he would tell her after a successful day at the typewriter. Time was flying by; they had only a few more weeks left on the house rental.

Iced tea had been their new refreshment of choice. When Grace was not writing or going for her walks, the Monopoly board was permanently set up on the small dining room table. The second bedroom was only used for Jacques, who came from New York to keep an eye on his investment. TJ would drive to the train station in Portsmouth to retrieve him on Friday afternoons. Jacques was good company for him and also a great sounding board for Grace. Her agent understood how to spin anything into a profit. Grace adored him even though her husband had second thoughts about his business style.

"Grace," Jacques commented on her writing, "I like this music teacher. The fact that he is a fag, and no one knows it is powerful, really good stuff." Then he would go on, "Grace, this Pappas family is Greek?" he questioned, "What's the big deal?"

Discussions about her work went on for hours. Jacques with his questionable French accent and Grace stone sober was an unusual combination. At times it was all too much for TJ, so he would sneak out for a walk and a couple of cigarettes.

With the novel finally finished and no time to spare, Grace and TJ packed up the car and headed north to Gilmanton. It was time to put the finishing touches on the manuscript and get it to Kitty in New York. The drive was less than two hours. The new convertible sped along the back roads as if it had a homing device under the hood.

They had almost finished unloading the car when the phone began to ring. TJ was in the middle of the hallway carrying Grace's mobile office up to her studio, so Grace went into the kitchen to answer it.

Picking up the handset, she recognized the voice instantly. Listening intently, she sat down at the breakfast table and rested her forehead in her free hand, visibly troubled by what the caller was saying.

"Okay, I get it. Let me look in the mail."

Grace hung up as TJ appeared in the kitchen doorway. "Who was that?" he asked. All Grace could do was shake her head in disgust. "It was Bernie. Can you bring me the mail, sweetie?" was all she said.

The pile of mail was smaller than usual after a time away. It had taken no time to go through it. TJ separated out the letters that contained royalty checks, while Grace searched the others for a certain return address in Manchester. "Ah, here it is," she exclaimed. "Can you tell me what is happening?" her husband asked. "Well, it seems my fucking mother and her new husband are suing me for $60,000 dollars." That did it, she needed a drink.

It was almost six months since the crash. Grace and Laurette had not spoken to each other. Her mother had blamed her for being drunk and causing the accident. That altercation was the last conversation between them, outside of the Laconia Hospital the day they were released.

Her mother filed suit, and so did her new husband, one for permanent damage and the other for loss of services. "Whatever that means," Grace said after explaining the situation to TJ.

Grace felt the first drink was something she needed, the second was something she wanted, and by the third there was no stopping her. "Fuck it," said TJ, as he jumped off the wagon as well. Keeping up with her was a challenge he took seriously. He knew a lawsuit would hurt the checkbook, and the publicity would fuel more turmoil for them.

It hadn't taken Grace long before she began to wallow in self-pity, negating all the positive things that happened at the beach house. She knew her mother was a mercenary and would do anything for the almighty dollar. Poverty and a life of falsehoods can create the strangest of ideals and morals. Laurette was no stranger to both of those traits. Grace regretted ever inviting her mother to Gilmanton to bury the proverbial hatchet.

"Oh, TJ, I'm such a disgrace to her," she cried out nearly in tears, "That woman never approved of anything I did." TJ sat there with a drink in hand and let her carry on about her mother and the rest of the family she had left back in Manchester. She was so angry with her mother. TJ tolerated Laurette, but he always thought to himself, "Don't kid a kidder."

"You know my dear Aunt Georgie," she asked TJ. "I don't think she has read any of my books." Her aunt had been so supportive so long ago, buying Grace her first ball point pen, something she kept all these years in her desk drawer. Grace began to cry. Her husband was at a loss as to what to say to console her.

"Grace, I'm sure that is not true." The words were not even out of his mouth. "What do you know about family?" she blurted. "You have none!" He thought that was low even for his wife to say. He could tell she was withdrawing again in a defensive manner, ready to strike like a cobra.

He thought perhaps another drink would calm her; it was too early to go to bed, and he hadn't finished unpacking. His stuff was still in the trunk. Grace took the drink and looked at him with contempt in her eyes. She was beyond her limit, and there was no reasoning with her at that point.

TJ was worried about money, the bottom line, they would need to protect themselves from a lawsuit. Most everything was in Grace's name and perhaps talking to Bernie would be the next thing to do. "We will go see Bernie on Monday," he told her. All Grace could do was a nod of approval in a drunken manner. The more she thought about it the angrier she became.

Being played the fool by so many gave her great embarrassment. The wheels in her head were spinning fast, turning back the clock to the first meetings with Kitty in New York, to Jerry Wald in Hollywood. Each of them was smooth and stylish in their own ways telling her something they thought she wanted to hear. "Am I that naive?" she thought sipping her whiskey, "and now my own mother is trying to take what she can."

The Canadian Club was doing its trick; Grace seemed a little calmer, not as agitated. Little did TJ know Grace was reliving every fight in her mind including every argument with her husband.

"Could he also be part of the problem?" She questioned. George claimed for years before that TJ had been taking her for a ride, but she never believed it.

"Darling," TJ said as he sat down across from her at the breakfast table. He was trying to get her to focus on the moment. "We should be prepared for our meeting with Bernie, maybe list our assets." TJ figured, if there was one lawsuit, and it was successful, perhaps others would follow. Protecting themselves would be the key.

"Assets?" Grace snapped back. "What do you mean?" That was a concept way over her head.

"Like the car, the house, they are all in your name," He told her. "Maybe we should put some things in my name. After all, your mother is suing you, not me," Then it hit her like the bell in a carnival strong man game; the mallet came down hard and rang clear in her head, "He wants the house," she knew it, "that must have been his game all along."

Alcohol and deceit make great lovers. You can't have one without the other. They went hand in hand to make an unhappy relationship.

"How dare you!" She got up from the table and walked to the front of the room; distance between them is what she wanted. "Who do you think you are?" Grace screamed, furious with him. It became all too clear to her. He was just another one of her groupies, only this one she ended up marrying.

She threw her near empty glass at him with all her might. He had managed to duck, and the glass smashed somewhere on the floor of the kitchen. TJ stood up and started in Grace's direction to be met with her lunging at him in the middle of the floor. Her size next to his, he well over six feet and she just over five, made an unfair match. He grabbed both her shoulders to prevent her from getting any closer. "Stop it, Grace!" he yelled at his enraged wife. She seemed to be suddenly possessed.

"Fuck you. You were a fucking DJ when we met," she screamed. "Was that chance meeting all your plan as well?" Their meeting at the radio station flashed through her mind like a rocket on a launching pad, where he just happens to have a new copy of her book to sign. Grace was having no part of it any longer. She managed to break away from his grip and swung her right fist with all her muster in the direction of his head. Drunks fighting can be almost comical to watch, but nothing funny happened in the front room that afternoon.

TJ also became more defensive and angrier. He, too, like his wife, had a snapping point. He caught the right hook she sent him in mid-air and retaliated with a back hand to her face with his left hand. "Enough," that one word could have been heard all the way to the town green if anyone were listening.

Grace was shocked. The pain against her cheek was like nothing she had ever felt before. Her instinct was to hold her face with one hand and point to the front door with the other.

"Get out," If ever she meant it, it was then. "Out!" she repeated her message so there was no misunderstanding.

Her man, her Prince Charming that she had created on paper and in life, was leaving. He was not looking back. He too had enough of the drinking, the fighting, the press, and most of all, his wife.

Grace sat back down on the sofa and wept. She cried for all the things that should have been, and for all things that could have been. As it turned out, TJ had been nothing more than one of those weekend friends from the town that drank too much, ate too much of her food, and spent way too much of her money.

The powder blue Caddy sped out of the driveway, kicking up gravel as it turned onto the main road in the direction of town. Grace had second thoughts about being wrong, but she went to the bar to find another glass and the bottle of whiskey.

CHAPTER 40

Summer had not looked at the calendar, and it lingered. The heat was almost unbearable for Grace. Her morning coffee turned to afternoon coffee, and it was best served iced. Her drink of the morning soon turned to her standard CC & Ginger. The author was becoming a recluse, spending her days at the typewriter in her studio. Writing would start after the drinking had taken its dulling effects on the reality surrounding her. Grace created a world on paper, and she was living it herself. Her art was not imitating life but dictating it.

That had become a pivotal time in the author's life. The meetings with Bernie were continuous, "Bernie," she would say with the most authoritative voice she could muster. "Just file the papers, sweetie." Her love affair with TJ had been over that drunken afternoon when he had suggested transferring the house into his name. She was really through with him this time. Convincing her lawyer should have been easy; after all, Bernie saw right through the DJ. His motives at times were so transparent.

"Well, the good news in all of this is," her lawyer told her, "since you are not incorporated, everything he signed for became his problem, not yours." There was a slight inflection in his voice of satisfaction. The only way out for TJ was to file bankruptcy. Grace never said a word. She signed the papers and headed to the Laconia Tavern for a liquid lunch.

The final version of *The Tight White Collar* was in the hands of Kitty; Grace was more relieved than thrilled. Jacques had informed her that editing the new book was the next step. Just the word edit would cause Grace to be upset, but this time around she rolled with the punches Unlike her previous book, Kitty was pleased. "Overall," she told her agent, "it was a good solid story with just a little cleaning up." When Jacques relayed the message to Grace, she was happy. Happy for the first time in weeks, but now she feared the reviews on its release.

Grace sat there on the front porch desperately trying to catch a cooling breeze. She sipped ice coffee and waited for the mailman. It brought her back to the days sitting on the porch at *It'll Do,* when she had been waiting for a word from any publisher in New York. This time it was a royalty check that was needed, from any one of her many arrangements. What arrived was a special envelope with a copy of the latest *Glamour Magazine.* She had all but forgotten the story she wrote would appear in the glossy. Edna Brown and the Charming Prince was a story she penned months before, and was now in print. "A day late and a dollar short."

George had brought the kids back home to Meadows Pond Road for what remained of the summer. He had thought the dust had settled in more ways than one, and they could spend their time at the house, and Marsha could be back with her friends that she missed dearly.

The house was theirs once again and that pleased Grace. Her ex-husband turned friend gave up his job in Stowe and that fall had accepted a position as a high school guidance counselor on Martha's Vineyard. Without TJ in the picture, George was less angry and more attentive to Grace. He watched out for her when he was in Gilmanton, making sure there was food in the fridge, and the children were eating and not getting too distracted by their mother's drinking and sleeping until noon each day. Surprisingly, the kids took it all in stride most of the time. They were just happy to be back at Meadows Ponds Road.

Grace got up from the porch with the mail and went to the kitchen. The kids were having an early lunch or was it a late breakfast? Grace never knew the coming and goings of her kids those days. George was due to arrive that afternoon. He would come on weekends to see the kids, but he wanted to ask his ex-wife a favor that day. She joined them for lunch and waited for him to arrive. Cucumber sandwiches on white bread with King Cole potato chips sounded perfect. The kids were pleased their mother was having lunch with them.

"Grace, can I ask you something?," George wanted to talk the moment he got through the kitchen door. All summer he was taking the last of his classes at UNH, preparing for the finals of his master's degree that she had paid for, a sore reminder, in her mind, of the blackmail scheme. In retrospect she thought it was almost comical. "Can I stay for a few days during the exams?" he asked. The drive back and forth to his cottage south of the border exhausted him, so staying at the house would give him more time to study. Grace never gave it a second thought, "Sure, sweetie, you can take the den," she answered.

He was pleased for a second, then after thinking about her answer, his reply was a bit short, "I'm not one of your chic friends from New York. Do not call me sweetie." Words were never clearer to Grace, and from that moment on she would try never to use that general term of endearment on him. She left the kitchen and walked to the bar to retrieve a fresh bottle of Canadian Club.

She was off to her studio to return to her fantasy world of millworkers, smokestacks, French speaking immigrants, and feisty women. She would write for hours until the effects of her drinking made her crawl into bed alone, not even bothering to undress.

She felt her new project was going to be her best yet and told Jacques and Kitty this on several occasions. They would reserve judgement until they could actually read it. *No Adam in Eden* was a novel set in a mill town, centered around four generations of women, each with their own demons to battle. Grace had much to draw upon from her childhood and her ancestors. Unlike *Peyton Place*, this novel would be as close to an autobiography as possible.

The remaining days of summer passed quickly. The kids had developed healthy summer tans. Marsha was growing up fast. George passed his exams, and Grace continued to be sequestered in her studio most every day drinking and writing. George planned to move to the island the week before school had started. He rented a modest house with plenty of room for the kids. They would be starting school, and life would begin anew for all of them once more.

One night after a family dinner, one of the few Grace made it to, she and George sat alone at the dining room table sipping a drink. It was a pleasant evening, the summer was over and change was in the air. Advance copies of *The Tight White Collar* were sent to be reviewed. It was a good night all around.

"Gracie, why don't you come to Martha's Vineyard with us?" He asked. A little dumbstruck, she did not know how to reply. "Gilmanton is my home, why would I want to leave it?" turning his question into her own question. "Because I love you. I have always loved you." His ex-wife had tears forming in her eyes and looked through them towards him, "Oh, Gee-Gee."

The ferry out of Woods Hole was much smoother than any plane ride Grace had taken over the past few years. On the top deck facing the bow, the salt air blew the cobwebs out of her mind. She felt excited for the first time in many months. Her favorite silk scarf was tied tight under her chin. The sun was beating on her face, and the wooden bench, where she sat holding George's hand, was hard on her ass. She did not care. Her Gee Gee made her feel safe and secure once again.

"Grace, did you see this?" George, letting go of her hand to securely grip the folded *The New York Times* so the wind did not catch it. "They liked your new book; this reviewer wrote something positive." She smiled and leaned into him, discretely rubbing the inside of his thigh. She couldn't wait to share a bed with him again. They had decided to wait to make love until they arrived at George's new rental house on the island.

Martha's Vineyard seemed to agree with all of them; George's new job was going well at the high school, and the kids liked their new digs. Grace loved living in Edgartown for a few reasons: one being the proximity to the ocean for her long walks, and another the fact that it was one of the few towns on the island where she could get a drink.

The Harborview Hotel, a local icon to hospitality, was just a hop, skip, and a jump from their rental home. Grace could stop there before or after her daily walks for a discrete drink. But, like in her books she created, nothing went unnoticed in any small New England town. The tourist season had unofficially ended at Labor Day, when the summer folks returned to the mainland and only the hard core locals remained. Fewer people meant Grace's alcohol consumption was more conspicuous, like being the only one in the hotel bar at 11 am. Bloody Mary's and toast were her standing order.

She sat quietly in the corner of the bar, looking out onto the water letting the hypnotic view of the surf relax her as she enjoyed the Tabasco and vodka enriched tomato juice. Always with a notepad in her handbag, she made detailed entries of her memories and other random thoughts that were worked into her new book.

She got to know the regular bartenders, who were well-seasoned from having worked in the hotel for years. They knew most of the residents as well as the mainlanders who came regularly for the season over the years. Martha's Vineyard was no stranger to old money, writers, artists, and the occasional journalist. Nothing went unnoticed on the tiny island.

The press had died down slightly, in regard to Grace's antics. The island was like hiding in plain sight. News of the day centered around her first novel, which was surpassing 9 million copies. The movie was still popular, having already grossed over one and a half million dollars in the United States. "Jerry was right," she thought. "He would always be a rain maker for the studio."

Reading the daily papers in the bar was something she enjoyed doing. They were usually a day old before they reached the foyer table to the front desk. That morning, the day before Halloween, Grace stopped in for her daily libation and picked up a copy of the previous day's *Boston Record*. It wasn't as sensational as the *Boston Traveller* where Hal Boyle's column appeared, but it was known for good writing. She had almost finished the paper when suddenly an article's headline had grabbed her attention.

"*Batten Down the Hatches Martha's Vineyard; Hurricane Season is Not Over Yet;*" the article's headline was designed not to be missed. "Bestselling author Grace Metalious has set her sights on the comings and goings of our very own island." The writer seemed to know more about her time in Edgartown than her own family. Her daily walks and daily routines were all there. Grace felt exposed and concerned. She did not want another repeat like in Gilmanton. George did not deserve the fallout from her endeavors, even though she had no intention of writing about the island.

"George, it's fine," Grace told him that afternoon as soon as he had gotten to the house. My early departure has nothing to do with the article," she continued. In reality, her decision was not done hastily; the article only helped speed her decision. She had spoken to Bernie on several occasions; he needed her back in Laconia. The truth be told, the divorce to TJ was being finalized that next week, and she needed to be present.

The family all went to the ferry landing with her the next morning. It was Saturday so the entire household had no plans except for an evening of trick or treating around town. George opened her door, and Grace stepped out, feeling sad to say good bye to them. But, for the first time, she was doing the right thing for her family.

" Ma," Marsha gently grabbed her Mother's elbow, gaining her attention. "What is it?" her mother asked? "Eddy and I want to get married. We are in love." Grace had been dreading that statement since the first time she witnessed her daughter going from tomboy to young lady. Marsha was barely 17, and Grace wanted so much for her. Marriage could wait.

"Sweetie, that is something we will talk about over Thanksgiving," was her short answer. Grace walked to the attendant and presented her return ticket. Slowly walking up the steps to the ferry, she waved back to her family, her pride, and joy and her reason for doing everything. Unlike her mother, Grace always wanted to provide for them. It was just the drinking that always seemed to get in the way.

CHAPTER 41

At the end of one year and on the eve of the next, most people reminisce on what has happened and look to what might be in the coming new year. The very cold and dark January did not start so well for Grace. Alone in Gilmanton, she did her best to keep the home fires burning. Keeping the house warm was the easy part. The new oil furnace was worth every penny she had spent for it. It did well during those record-breaking cold temperatures.

Grace fell ill; she thought it was the flu, a nasty cold turned ugly. She tried to weather the storm alone, on her favorite sofa. She wrapped herself in an afghan next to the fire that she would never let go out for fear she would have to call someone to start it again.

She had been sick a few days, or maybe a week; she was losing track of the time. Her illness did not curtail her drinking. Climbing to the stairs to her bedroom was all too painful. The sofa became her domain, and the electric heating pad that never left her abdomen was her security blanket to help ease the pain. She wondered if this was the change of life. That thought discouraged her more; the fear of growing older and wondering what else would happen to her body.

She tried to ring the kids and George every few days. Since it was the dead of winter and she was mostly alone, she would check in with her family. Now that TJ was finally out of the picture and the divorce final, Laurie, her long-lost friend from *Shaky Acres*, resurfaced. Laurie had no use for TJ and also thought him to be a supreme opportunist. Grace always thought that with the bad, some good things could come out of it. Her friend was one of the good; she was back.

"Grace, Grace," a voice called out. The author was sound asleep in the fetal position, laying on the sofa in the front room. "Grace, what is wrong?" her dear friend asked. Laurie rushed over to her, instinctively using the back of her hand, checking to see if she had a fever. "Why didn't you call me?" Laurie asked. Grace tried to sit up and be in the moment, but the cramps from her belly were still painful. Laurie decided that a doctor should be called right after calling George on Martha's Vineyard first.

Laurie thought it was too late to rally her, so she stayed the night to help her old friend with whatever she might need. Grace managed to sit up and eat some soup Laurie found in the cupboard. Campbell's chicken noodle soup can do wonders on a cold January night.

George arrived the next afternoon and thanked Laurie over and over for calling him. "I would have been here sooner, but the ferries have limited service during the winter months," George explained. She did not mind and would stay as long as she was needed. Grace was awake and actually sounded better. Perhaps the soup the night before had done the trick. George helped Grace upstairs to her bathroom to shower. She needed to clean herself up before going to the doctor. Laurie remained downstairs to clean up the house. Empty bottles, papers, and magazines in stacks everywhere. Dirty glasses and a collection of crusty plates in the sink appeared to be weeks old.

Upstairs, the shower, that George insisted on including in the remodel, helped. Grace was feeling better. He dressed her in her chenille robe, sat her at the vanity, and began to dry her hair. Grace began to sob, really sob. "Gracie, I'm here now,

What is it?" Grace motioned to the pile of mail on her nightstand.

"All I have left is $500, and I am going to drink myself to death." Her sobs bordered on hysterical.

George appeared at the doorway of the kitchen, startling Laurie. Feverishly scrubbing dishes, she was on a mission to return the house to some sense of order. "You scared me," she blurted. "Is Grace ok?"

George apologized and told her he had tucked Grace into bed after a long hot shower. "Can you help me?" he asked. "Anything, George, you know that," she replied.

He produced a pile of statements and invoices that had been gathering dust for a few weeks, many of which had never been opened. They sat at the breakfast table and tried to organize the documents. Without TJ, the keeper of all things financial, Grace had no clue what was happening. It had taken George and Laurie some time to sort it out. With the help of an adding machine he had found on the desk in the den, they determined over $100,000 dollars was missing. It was only 3:00 pm; Laurie had been there over 24 hrs. George hesitated, but he asked if she could help with one more thing?

Laurie agreed and waited patiently in the kitchen next to the wall phone; George sat at the bar in the front room with his notes and a New York phone number. He dialed, and the phone began to ring on the other end. He signaled Laurie to pick up the extension just in time to hear the receptionist say, "Jacques Chambrun's office, how may I help you?"

Unlike Grace, George could maintain a level head about these matters, calling her agent on this matter was something he looked forward to. Jacques had always been a slimy character in his mind. Now George had the opportunity to question his motives and to hear his explanations.

Jacques had worked for a percentage of what a writer received from the publisher. After taking his cut, he was contract bound to send the remaining funds to the author, a standard practice in the world of publishing.

"Oh, George," feeling like he had gotten caught with his hand in the cookie jar. "You are completely correct," he told him. "I must have forgotten." The agent was trying to back pedal, using the abrupt departure of TJ as an excuse. He assured George that he would direct his accountant to send a check for the missing royalties by the end of the business day. George felt satisfied and hung up.

George thanked Laurie for listening in and bearing witness to what could have been a sticky situation. "I don't think that is the last of old Jacques," George told her. The opening of the movie, *Return to Peyton Place,* was only a few weeks off, and he would surely be at the world premiere in Laconia.

George stayed in New Hampshire a few days. He took Grace to a doctor who advised her to eat better and to slow her drinking down. A combination of the flu and an infection was thought to cause the pain. Some medication was prescribed, and he brought her back to her house.

George needed to return to work and the kids. Spring break would be the next time they were all together celebrating the movie. Grace stood on the porch for a moment to wave to her ex-husband. It had seemed she was always saying good bye to someone.

Grace started to feel better; the antibiotics were working, and the cold snap finally ended. Her life returned to her routine of sleeping late and writing. The stories she put down on paper were troubling to her. Most of the things she remembered caused her great anxiety. A highball was all she needed to move past it. George found most of her bottles during his brief visit and dumped the whiskey out. He did not want a repeat performance of an ailing ex-wife.

Her health improved just in time to take a call from 20th Century Fox. The marketing and event team was heading to

Laconia soon to start to review the details of the movie premiere.

After that call, Grace became more and more involved with the movie release and what details the studio would handle. She never imagined that she would have to be this aware of how much went into it. Most things she deferred to Bernie. His wife, Muriel, offered to host a private cocktail party for a select few which would include the film stars that were attending from Hollywood. Carol Lynley, Jeff Chandler, and Mary Astor were on the shortlist to be at the Colonial Theater in April. This caused the author's blood pressure to rise slightly.

Alone in her big house, Grace managed to keep it together. She was feeling better, and the writing was going just fine. Her drinking was curtailed some. She drank mostly beer because she could get it at the The Gilmanton Corner store. She ran out of the bottles of whiskey that George missed. Beer seemed to agree with her stomach better anyways.

"Look, Peter, its Grace Metalious, you know me," she sounded desperate on the phone. "I'm sorry, I won't make a home delivery, it is 1 AM," The store owner was standing his ground despite her being a great tipper. "I can't be driving out to Gilmanton at this hour." The Laconia Spa was the only store open that late, and she needed more to drink. She was writing and fielding questions all day about the movie opening, which would be happening in only a few days. "I need a case of beer now!" her demand fell on deaf ears, and Peter Karagianis hung up the phone. Being open 24 hours a day had its drawbacks.

Less than forty-five minutes later the store owner saw her car pull up in front. With the headlights on and the engine idling, Grace popped out of the driver's side. She was slightly intoxicated and had a mean look on her face. Dressed as she always was, a flannel shirt and jeans, she grabbed a case of beer, paid for it never saying a word, and, like a dock worker, threw it in the backseat with the slightest of effort. When she pulled out of the spot, she reversed and hit a parking meter, causing it to bend over. Without even noticing her infraction, she drove away back to the security of Meadows Pond Road.

Practically all the citizens of Laconia were coming out to witness Hollywood magic in their very own downtown. Lines in front of the box office started forming early around 5:30 pm that unforgettable night in April. The Colonial Theater had opened in 1914 and could hold upwards of 1400 paying guests. It was as elegant as any playhouse in the state. It was the only choice in the city to hold such a historic event. By 7:00 pm the tickets sold out for the one and only show at 8:30 pm.

Grace was a nervous wreck. She spent most of the day getting ready. Laurie joined Grace and the kids at the Meadows Pond Road. All the girls spent most of the day together; it was an exciting time. Marsha was thrilled to be back in the spotlight again, this time it was for all the right reasons: the movie and her unofficial fiancé, Eddy. Cindy was so excited to go to a movie premiere; she never stopped with the questions.

All the Metalious women wanted to be their best. Grace wanted the premiere to be perfect for her family, but more so for the city. This was her opportunity for a do-over after all the bad publicity of past years. She wanted everyone to shine bright like the stars of the film that would be arriving later.

Her dress was from O'Shea's right around the corner from the Colonial on Main Street. June O'Shea helped Grace find the perfect outfit. It had an empire waist; not only was it stylish it was very forgiving of her swelling belly and breasts, the weight being her second challenge after her drinking. Marsha helped her with her hair, a French Twist had been all the rage. For her reward, she allowed her oldest daughter to wear her mink. "Oh, Ma, thank you," squeezing her neck. "Eddy will love it."

When they arrived at the Sneirson home, in Lakeport, for the cocktail party, George ran over to open the passenger side door. "My Queen," he said, gesturing. Grace blushed and wanted nothing more than to get a drink. The house was full of her friends. Esther Peters complimented her on her dress and gushed over the anticipation that floated in the air. Opening night for *Return to Peyton Place*, "In our very own town."

Laurie and her husband had already arrived at the party. She was there as Grace's supportive friend and also as the only reporter. Everyone came that had received the special invitation, even the studio executives that had planned the main event happening right after dinner at the Tavern.

"Grace, how beautiful you look," Bernie told her. "Can I see you and George for just a moment?" he asked. Her lawyer guided them down the hallway to his home office. The pain in Grace's stomach now seemed to move up her throat. "What could possibly be happening?" she thought. Was TJ in the other room? Had the $23,000 accident settlement check to her mother bounced? Bernie closed the door and pulled out a telegram from the studio.

"Oh, for heaven's sake Bernie, just tell us," Grace said. The telegram apologized and stated in no uncertain terms, there would be no film stars appearing that night for the premiere. George looked at Bernie and waited for the shoe to fall. Grace was in no mood for drama; there would be enough of that later on the screen. "Fuck them, who needs Hollywood," she said. "Sweetie," looking at Bernie, "All my stars are right here." With that she headed back to the party desperately seeking a highball.

She was determined not to let Jerry Wald ruin another opening; too much was riding on it. The book had already sold over one and half million copies, Kitty was sending the royalty directly to her now, bypassing her agent who by the end of the month would be let go, as his services were no longer required. Jacques had fucked with the wrong writer.

The rest of the night was movie magic in Grace's eyes. Muriel had done a wonderful job with the private cocktail party. Everyone departed promptly at 7:00 for the next event. The dinner at the Tavern looked wonderful, though Grace was too nervous to eat. She tried her best not to drink too much, as it would be a long night. When she arrived at the Colonial,

George had pinned a beautiful orchid corsage on her left shoulder. It made her feel more like a queen than ever before.

From the curb to the entrance, the red velvet stanchions held back the non-ticket holders and had allowed time for the various members of the press to snap their photos. Their children were eating it up, loving the attention. George beamed with pride for his ex-wife; he truly loved her despite all her faults. Just before entering the lobby Grace blew Laurie a kiss, who was never far from the author. That was a thank you, for their very first encounter shared one day during a summer drought so long ago.

Looking around the lobby, she took satisfaction in knowing the wounds of the past were healed. She was finally accepted into the community of Laconia. Gilmanton was an entirely different animal. That would have to wait; the movie was about to start.

CHAPTER 42

With every success comes a failure; for every good deed there are at least two that could go south. Grace was elated after the release of the movie sequel. "Finally," she said. "People are not crossing the street to avoid me. I actually got a smile out of Ned at The Corner Store," Grace rattled on to Laurie, who popped in to check on her friend.

The premiere made all the right papers for all the right reasons. Hollywood magazines purchased some photos from the local photographers and ran with them. The missing stars were never even mentioned. That night Laconia shined like a bright new penny, and, as the author had hoped, the attitude of the locals towards her continued to change.

The aftermath of that night gave her the confidence to continue work on her next book. Screw the demons in her head. The story poured out of her. Sounds of her electric typewriter could be heard in the upstairs hall all summer long. Grace was happier than she had been in years. The kids returned home, and George came right along with them.

"Third time's a charm," referring to her reconciliation with George. She smiled at Laurie. It seemed like no time had passed between them. Things were just as they seemed. This time they sat in Grace's home reading from her new work, sipping afternoon drinks, sometimes to excess. Friendships can be challenging. With Grace it was no different. Laurie didn't want to upset her, but she knew Grace was over her limit of highballs for the day. "I think I'm done," she would tell her, placing her glass in the sink. "Suit yourself," Grace replied, and then would proceed to the bar to refresh her own drink. Once the author was over the edge, there would be no stopping her. Laurie would graciously bow out.

The Tight White Collar had gotten its wide release both in paperback and in hard bound. Unfortunately, despite decent reviews, sales had been measured. Within 6 months, both of the *Peyton Place* novels had sold at least a million copies. Grace's latest creation barely 400,000 had gone out the door. The new book was her favorite. Because it was not doing well, it depressed Grace, causing her to drink even more when no one was looking.

Calls from Kitty were encouraging, but bottom line she wanted the final manuscript of *No Adam in Eden,* her work in progress. Grace had loved the title as much as she loved the story: a house full of multi generation immigrant women coping with their inner demons without the support of the men that always seem to leave.

"Oh, Kitty, you don't love me anymore. You used to be so patient with me." Grace would do her best to play the guilt card, right after the victim card. Her excuses remained very creative, but her publisher knew Grace was drinking again. Kitty confided in Grace's new agent, Ollie Swan, who had hoped the author, like other writers, didn't have an expiration date on her work.

Ollie Swan met Grace back in 1955 when he passed on the original version of her first book, *The Tree and the Blossom*. Grace liked him so after the written dismissal of Jacques, she called Ollie on a whim in New York. A lawyer by education and agent by success, she felt he was the man for the job. They spoke on the phone daily; nothing on her mind was held back. They discovered Jacques made many mistakes, some intentional they were convinced. His side deals concerning her works ran the gamut. Grace had no idea how much money he stole from her with his bogus dealing. "Let's move on. Jacques can go to hell, fuck him," she told Ollie. Her new agent got her message loud and clear.

"Grace, I received the first few chapters of *No Adam in Eden*. It read pretty good" he told her. "When do you think it will be done?" The question was on everyone's mind, Kitty's, Bernie's, George's, and now her new agent's.

"Sweetie, I'm writing every day. I feel it will end up at 400 pages," she told him. That was encouraging news for the new man on the job, barely aware of Grace's ability to spin the story. She wasn't sure a new book release would pull her out of her financial hole.

"I knew it," George told her. Saying, "I told you so," was not his style, no matter how much he had wanted to say it. First Jacques, then Jerry, and finally TJ, these men all had a hand in the cookie jar.

"Oh, Gee Gee, we need that money." In hindsight they should have been more on top of the situation from the beginning, but too much trust was given to the those in her inner circle. The only thing to do was to regroup and restructure how she would move forward. She had to finish the next book. She had thought briefly about locking the door of her studio and never coming out until the manuscript was completed.

Her attitude towards money had always been a flippant one. "You have it one day, you better spend it, for the next day it might not be there." Words spoken so many times now bit her in the ass.

A car was heard coming down the gravel drive. She had thought it was George and the kids, but it was not. It was her lawyer; Bernie would never drive out to the house unannounced unless something was wrong. Grace thought she mustn't overreact. "What could it be?" Worried, she walked to the kitchen door to let him in.

"Hello, Grace, we need to talk." He apologized for not calling first; he felt the situation was grave and didn't want to speak about it over the phone. They stood into the kitchen while Grace made him some fresh coffee, and she poured herself a tall glass of iced coffee. The whiskey would come later. The kitchen table had always been the spot for any news of the day, good or bad. Sun shining on the table added to the warmth the kitchen emitted, making any news easier to take. Besides, how bad could it be?

The conversation was a quick one, but nevertheless it had to be face to face. Bernie was one of her closest friends and her lawyer,; the last thing he wanted to do was to upset her. "I'm afraid, Grace, that the news is not good."

The year the first book was released, the taxes were estimated and paid to the IRS in good faith. But a severe mistake had been made and what happened after had compounded the situation. The audit from the IRS had been returned, and based on the success of her writings, it was shocking. Not even Bernie thought it would have come to that number.

The Tax Man, as Grace always referred to the IRS, was seeking retribution for the error. Her new tax bill was $66,000 dollars plus a penalty of 6% payable immediately. Grace sank into the chair, staring at the ice coffee, and wishing it were whiskey.

CHAPTER 43

Grace was not angry but stating a fact. "George, we are driving. Northeast Airlines sucks." She did not like flying after the last few bumpy flights she had taken with her Gee Gee. "Besides, if we leave at dawn, we will have the check by noon," she said with a hint of desperation.

The morning light at daybreak can be so refreshing in New Hampshire, a calming force with a sense of renewal for another day. The sun hadn't yet risen over the mountains that surrounded Gilmanton, but the light met the darkness and chased it westward to the edge of the previous night.

The drive was quiet. George could almost put the car on autopilot as it made its way south along the turnpike in the direction of New York. Grace was sound asleep with her head on George's shoulder. She had a hangover after her nightly routine of drinking. There was little traffic that April morning so the drive would be smooth and their trip hopefully successful.

They headed back to The Plaza, their home away from home. It was still Grace's favorite despite the challenges of payment. Money was being drained from the checkbook, and the embarrassment of a couple of bad checks only clouded George's mind. He had the foresight to withdraw some cash from her account back in Laconia. His only hope was that it would be enough for the short stay they were planning in the Big Apple.

Grace committed to do three appearances, a couple of radio interviews and a press conference to promote *The Tight White Collar*. She was dreading all of them. How fast things changed. What was exciting and glamorous once was now frightening and routine.

"Let's just get it over with," she told George. "The sooner I get my money, the sooner we can go home to New Hampshire."

She forced a smile as she gave him a peck on the cheek. George shifted the car into neutral and applied the hand brake. A valet and bellman appeared curbside like a choreographed dance. The passenger door opened, and Grace stepped out. She was all smiles, hiding the fear and dread like a professional. "Welcome back to the Plaza, Mrs. Metalious," Jack the Bellman said, greeting the still infamous author. "Thank you, sweetie," she said and headed to the foyer, never looking back as George scampered along to catch up.

This trip had been planned for a few months; her latest creation that she furiously had finished was now ready to be delivered to Kitty and Ollie. *No Adam in Eden* had swelled to 429 pages. The manuscript she carried in a large manila envelope was secure in her handbag. The plan was to get a royalty check, promote her last book, and announce the new one. With George at her side and Ollie her agent having her back, she believed nothing could go wrong.

" Oh, I almost forgot," The front desk manager told George as he signed the registration log, "There is a telegram for your wife." George took the envelope and walked to the elevator where Grace was waiting. She wanted to get upstairs to her room before she was noticed. "Here Grace, a telegram came this morning." George delivered it to her in the elevator as they rose to their usual suite. Apprehensively she took the telegram, not wanting to open it until they were alone in the room. She worried about the contents. Elevator operators were notorious for listening to guests so they could become an anonymous source for the latest gossip column; something she had learned the hard way.

"Fuck, Fuck," Grace, securely in their suite alone, said as she sat on the edge of the giant king size bed. George was in the bathroom, and her distressed voice was not heard. "George," she yelled in the direction of the bathroom. "He fucking doesn't want it." Throwing the telegram on the floor, she headed to the welcome basket on the coffee table. The gift from the hotel included a fifth of her favorite whiskey; if ever she needed a drink, it was then. George ran out of the bathroom and retrieved the discarded telegram to read it while Grace poured her a hefty glass of Canadian Club.

Jerry Wald from 20th Century Fox decided to pass on making *The Tight White Collar* into a film version. "Sorry, Grace. Maybe the next one. Jerry," was the closing sentiment after a brief explanation that he couldn't find a way to make a decent film from her latest novel.

Grace was devastated. She was so disappointed and mad she could not cry. Grace rarely cried. She concealed her emotions by drinking and withdrawing into her cocoon of safety on Meadows Pond Road. Since New York was far from her sofa and the warmth of her fireplace, drinking would have to do.

"It's okay, Grace," George tried to reassure her. "We will see Kitty tomorrow morning; Wald is a fool." The new book had finally reached a million and a half in sales; Ollie. the genius released both the hard bound and the paperback at the same time. Kitty would also be pleased with Grace's finished novel. Tomorrow there would be a check to pick up as she dropped off her latest baby. "Tomorrow will be a good day. Let's go down for an early dinner." She thought the Palm Court for dinner sounded like an excellent idea.

Morning came with spring sunshine illuminating the suite to a warm and comforting glow. Grace was determined not to let the movie pass bother her. Wald had already bought the rights before seeing the final product. "There was nothing I could do," she confessed to George in the taxi to the publisher's building. Kitty and Ollie would be expecting her, and she would not disappoint them. She hoped neither of them would disappoint her.

It was like old times, Grace and George back in the infamous publisher's office. Only this time no crooked Jacques and with a very smart Ollie. They spoke about the past successes of Grace's work, movies, and the future. No word of TJ was mentioned, no word of Jacques was uttered; it was all good. Grace relaxed in the moment without any hint of despair.

"Grace, dear," Kitty said, "Here is your check for last month's sales." Feeling relieved, Grace handed the check to George for safe keeping. "Now you have something for me?" Kitty asked. Everyone was all smiles. The anticipation of *No Adam in Eden* was overwhelming for the author and the publisher, each having their own different reasons.

Handing the bulging envelope to Kitty, Grace relaxed back into her chair and took a deep breath. The four of them had been the only ones in the conference room around the giant mahogany table that gleamed in the sunlight. Kitty looked at the envelope and smiled. She paused for a moment before opening it.

"Grace, there is something I have to tell you," Kitty said as she opened it and pulled out the massive manuscript. "I won't be publishing this." The sunlight instantly disappeared as the sun went behind a cloud; it darkened the room to a dull gray. A feeling of foreboding was cast over the meeting. What had started with such promise was fast going down the drain.

"I don't understand; we have a contract." Grace tried not to get angry.

Ollie was aware of the news and wanted to make the best of the situation. "Grace, it's okay, there is a plan in place," he told them. Kitty decided to pass on *No Adam in Eden* because she felt that the material she had read to that point had lacked something. As she compared it to Grace's previous works, this might not live up to expectations. After all, the outcome is only money.

The discussion was not an easy one. Kitty knew that later that day Grace would be on the radio for an interview about her books. The last thing anyone wanted was for her to be nervous and bluntly lash out; her reputation, preceded her. Grace was deeply disillusioned but happier when Kitty explained the contract had been sold to Trident Simon Schuster, another publishing house. "And more good news," Ollie added. He had successfully negotiated the sale of the movie rights to 20th Century Fox, to be paid in three installments. "Here is your first check," he said. "From your new publisher, and here is your second," he smiled and handed her another check, "from Fox."

Grace was thrilled and saddened at the same time. The thought of her latest book becoming a bestseller and a movie would be just the ticket to get her back in the swing of things, both creatively and financially.

It was time for lunch; they decided to have it together. Grace had been a bundle of nerves and only wanted a highball; in fact, she wanted more than one. Lunch was strained, but they managed to muddle through it. Kitty apologized once again for her decision, never letting on the real reason behind it. Grace sensed that it might be her publisher's health but didn't want to pry. She hoped that that was the reason and not that she didn't actually like her latest book.

The short taxi ride across town was very quiet. Ollie accompanied Grace and George to the radio studio on the 56th floor of the Empire State Building.

The interviewer was a seasoned reporter. It was like most other interviews, just the two of them in a sound booth with a giant microphone. The questions were all safe to start. Grace was feeling the effects of the cocktails with no lunch, but still had all her faculties. She looked up at the clock on the wall in the booth. She made it through half the interview before it went sideways.

"Mrs. Metalious," the announcer asked. "May I call you Grace?" She smiled and wondered to herself where this was going. "Sure," she answered. He looked her squarely in the eye, trying his best to rattle her. "Your books tell a story of what life is like in New England. Is it truly that way or are you making it all up?" Dumbfounded by the question, she paused and returned his gaze.

"To a tourist, they look as peaceful as a picture postcard, but if you go beneath them, it's like turning over a rock with your foot, all kinds of things crawl out." Not waiting for a reply, she continued, "Everybody in town knows what goes on, there are no secrets, but they don't want outsiders to know."

It was the announcer's turn to be dumbfounded. Her answer was directly on point to the question. He knew his time was running out. Grace felt beads of sweat trickle down behind her ponytail. She needed to get out of there. "Fuck this guy," was going through her mind.

"One last question," he said. "Based on some of the comments from learned reviewers, they claim your writing is in bad taste, what say you to that?" Grace knew this guy was trying to turn the interview to her lack of education and skill. "Bad taste you say?" answering with a question. "Well, if I'm a lousy writer, then an awful lot of people have lousy taste." With that she stood up and exited the sound booth. Her husband and agent had listened from the outer room. Both stood to meet her. "Fuck this, George," she said. Looking at Ollie, "We are out of here."

They hastily left the studio and made their way to the ground floor. Not a word was spoken between them. George hailed a taxi, and Ollie stood on the sidewalk, waiting for a sign from Grace as to her next move. The taxi pulled up, and George opened the door. Grace turned to Ollie, "Cancel the other interviews. Fuck them." There was no questioning her. "Come on, George, I need a drink."

The taxi pulled away from the bottom of the Empire State Building, leaving Ollie alone to sort through another mess Grace managed to get herself into. Canceling the next day's radio interview would create just another controversial issue in his new client's life. "Taxi," he yelled, raising his outstretched arm.

The next morning Grace laid in bed, and George was still sleeping. This gave her some time to decide what she was going to do. She was worried. Her life was just like the metaphor she used about the rock being overturned from the previous day's interview. She had many things that were about to be exposed. The first was her continued excruciating pain from her abdomen; it came and went and often overpowered her thinking. The impending income tax bill from the IRS that was coming due now was over $100,000 dollars. That alone had her wanting to crawl under that rock.

"Oh, Gee Gee," she asked, nudging her husband's shoulder. "Can you find me a heating pad? These cramps are all too much." The pain was distracting and overwhelming. It would cloud her judgment. George got dressed and went down to find a drug store. He left his ex-wife in bed with toast and coffee that room service delivered as he was leaving. He was not aware that in the side table a small bottle of whiskey was stashed by Grace on arrival, *just in case*. That was what she called her stash; in fact, there were many more hidden throughout the house in Gilmanton, *just in case*.

Back in New Hampshire the summer passed without incident; Grace's tax bill had been paid, and things seemed to be fine. Grace fielded calls from Ollie and the new publishing house about *No Adam in Eden*. A few calls with her agent ended not too kindly, but overall, the process of editing was done over the summer.

Trident fast tracked the publishing of her latest book. They wanted to capitalize on her notoriety and not her prose, something no one dared admit to the author. *No Adam in Eden* would be released with a limited advance printing in hard bound in just a few weeks. That had pleased Grace, and she was convinced the reviews would make the sales jump.

Once again, expenses far exceeded income. Grace had to curtail her habits. George had taken over as her manager, lover, and confidant, grew weary of the continued stress from her spending and her drinking, both of which he could not do anything to stop.

"Grace, can we talk?" George cautiously asked her one night as she sat on the sofa looking through magazines for evidence of her existence. "Sure, George," she said without looking up. "It's about the phone bill," he told her. "Fuck the phone bill!" Then she looked up. "What is the problem?"

George tried to maintain the balances of her accounts and constantly looked for ways to cut corners. When the phone bill broke the $300 mark, he thought it was a good example to use. He was wrong.

"What the hell, George?" She flew off the handle and let him know in no uncertain terms that if she wanted to call fucking Africa, she would. "What's $300 dollars anyways? Stop trying to control me," she blurted out. The fight escalated way beyond what George had thought it would. He knew she was unaware of the situation with her finances and the sales of her books. The last royalty checks barely got them back in the black. Her drinking and her inability to compromise were the main causes of the problems. There would be no reasoning with her as long as she continued to drink.

It had been seven years since *Peyton Place* had been published. George personally could not go on; the volatility of their relationship had returned with her drinking. Each day the relationship became more uncomfortable, more strained. He decided he would go back to work. The Master's degree would be useful. He accepted a job in Vermont at another high school. He had tried to tell her that night that it was not working out between the two of them. Her drinking was affecting everything, even the kids that were left at home.

Marsha had escaped at 18 by marriage and was living in Laconia with her new husband, Eddy. She was like her mother at that age, blissfully happy and pregnant. George was convinced that leaving with Mike and Cindy was best for everyone. It hurt George to have to leave Grace, but any love that had been left had dissolved between them.

Grace passed out on the sofa after finishing the remainder of her *just in case* bottle which had been stuck in between the cushions, hidden from view.

George and the two children packed as quickly as they could. There were no tears, just a sense of urgency that they needed to go and go quickly without waking the bear. This exit was a long time coming for the Metalious family. Everyone but Grace had tried their best. Leaving was the only option left.

George loaded the station wagon and managed to get a couple of his own suitcases tied to the top. He was not going to let this affect his outlook on the future. His new job and another start were something he and the kids were used to.

Before heading back out to the car to join the children waiting patiently for him, he stopped and sat at the kitchen table and contemplated how they had gotten to this point. How could something so good cause so much turmoil? Life had a funny way of imitating art.

He wrote a simple message to Grace on the back side of an empty royalty check envelope. "I'm sorry. I love you. I will always love you. George"

CHAPTER 44

"George, bring the kids home!" Grace screamed into the phone and slammed the receiver down. Grace was not only hung over, but exhausted. Feeling exasperated, she crossed her arms and buried her head into them on the kitchen table. Tears started and feelings of hopelessness overcame her. Alone in the kitchen in her dream home, the one that was to bring her so much joy, she wept like a schoolgirl.

It had been over a week since that fight over money and being controlled by George. "Fuck him, those kids need to be home in Gilmanton with me, their mother." Everyday George called to check on her. Every day it ended up the same: a screaming match and someone slamming the receiver down, either on her end or his. The outcome was the same. The impasse was great, and the resolution unsolvable. "Grace, you need help," George would say. "Drinking is destroying you and the children." Then the phone would go dead, and George would go back to creating lesson plans for his new job in Vermont.

Grace was unaware that someone had entered the house and was watching her sob at the kitchen table. Laurie paused a few moments before making her presence known. She secretly had hoped that perhaps this would be the breaking point that her friend needed to pull herself together and get sober.

"Grace," Laurie said softly. "Grace, are you okay?" An inaudible grunt escaped Grace's lips as she raised her head. "Sweetie, I'm fine," Grace lied. Laurie went to the kitchen sink, grabbed a dishtowel, and sat down next to her. She slowly dried Graces' face, trying to get her to calm down. "What happened?" Laurie asked.

"I'm giving up writing; I have nothing more to say." That was a statement Grace thought she would never hear herself say aloud. "I've created a *Peyton Place* of my own," she continued. "Now, I have to live in it."

Without knowing what happened to get her to this point, Laurie stood up and went to make some coffee. The local reporter knew they both needed it. Listening to Grace's story would be a long morning.

Grace got off the sofa and waddled to the kitchen wrapped in an afghan. She explained to her friend the situation with George, the kids, her money problems, and all that happened in New York. "Laurie," she said, "I looked into the empty bottle, and I saw myself." On the verge of tears again, they comforted each other like old school pals.

"Grace, I almost forgot why I stopped by," Laurie told her. "When were you going to let me know about this? I would love to go." Retrieving a folded newspaper clipping from her jeans pocket, Laurie unfolded it and placed it in front of Grace in the kitchen. "Fuck, I forgot about that," was all the author said.

Her friend cut out an advertisement from the Concord Monitor announcing a book signing along with reading from New Hampshire's favorite author, Grace Metalious. The ad boasted that her new bestselling novel, *No Adam in Eden,* was a tribute to her New England heritage.

Grace was upset and felt hopeless on so many levels; she did not know where to begin. Without a manager how was she expected to remember these things? "Oh Laurie," she started. "I'm alone now, no Jacques, no TJ, no Jerry, no Kitty, no George and now, no kids," Grace started to cry again. Laurie reached out and gave a reassuring hug that things would get better.

Returning to Manchester was something Grace never planned to do. It was less than an hour away, but a lifetime separated her from the origins of her youth. The triple decker walk-up, the smell of garlic wafting through the air, the color of the foam on the Merrimack River depicting the color of wool being dyed that day and the city were part of her past. Yet, they contributed to her success by giving her countless images of injustices and prejudices throughout her childhood. Writing *No Adam in Eden*, resurrected those memories and feelings that had been dulled by her drinking.

Grace was so happy to have Laurie at her side. When she offered to drive, it pleased her greatly. The Chevy station wagon pulled up to the curb in front of The Apple Tree Book Shop. "You go in; I will find a parking spot," she told Grace. The author's eyes widened like she was being fed to the lions. Grace believed if she could put Mike Wallace in his place, this would be a piece of cake. It also allowed her enough time to take a drink from the small bottle in her purse before entering the shop. "Okay, sweetie," she said. "I'll see you in a minute. I'll be the one signing autographs."

The book signing was a true success. Grace was in the spotlight, and she managed it like a pro. When push came to shove, she was the ultimate actress. She could think on her feet, not letting anyone get the best of her, well, at least not in the public's eye.

Over fifty people attended, all wanting to get a glimpse of the infamous local and perhaps an autographed copy of her newest work. Grace chose a section from her novel about the migration of French Canadians to the fictional town of Livingstone, NH, a thinly veiled reiteration of Manchester. The crowd was pleased, and book sales were encouraging.

"Grace," the owner of the book shop said. "May I introduce you to Mr. John H. Rees? John is a reporter from

London and dying to meet you." Grace looked in the direction of this foreign reporter and was slightly taken back. "Hello," was all she managed as she offered her hand. John Rees was, by all accounts, an English gentleman: taller than most with dark wavy hair, a trimmed beard and dressed in a traditional tweed jacket. Instantly she envisioned him with a pipe and a Red English Setter walking the moors of Merri Olde England. Grace was awestruck.

The drive back to Gilmanton had a completely different tone than it had on the way down. "Laurie, it was a divine evening," Grace said. "I think they really liked the book." Laurie drove while Grace rattled on about the event. Laurie was pleased that she had been able to rally Grace to this point from the previous day's misery. "And that John," she continued, "so handsome and a reporter from London, London, England." Laughing, she reached into her bag and finished the small bottle of whiskey.

"Let's have a late dinner," Grace insisted. She noticed a sign off the turnpike and exclaimed, "Take this exit." The Highway Hotel was an icon in Concord, and it happened to be directly off the turnpike. Without hesitation, the Chevy station wagon glided down the ramp and into the parking lot. Laurie shifted into park looked at Grace, and smiled. "Thank you," Grace said to her best friend in the world. "Anything you want, my treat," she insisted. "The Lobster Newberg is divine."

The Highway Hotel was the best restaurant in town with the best service. Grace considered it to be New Hampshire's version of The Plaza. It wasn't even close, but it pleased her to think of it that way. Grace was still on cloud nine, glowing with energy and sparkling creative thoughts chasing her doom and gloom away. John Rees was the main topic of discussion. Laurie did not mind; she was just happy that Grace was happy.

The highballs continued during and after dinner for Grace. Laurie stopped at two drinks, knowing they still had forty minutes left to drive back. A repeat of the Winnisquam accident was not going to happen. She would make sure of it.

"Grace dear," a voice was heard. "I thought that was you." Esther Peters from Laconia crossed the dining room to greet her prized interviewee. "Grace, so good to see you again. It's been ages," the radio commentator told her. "Esther, sit down and have a drink." Grace said. "Just for a moment; my husband is in the bar," she said. Reluctantly, Esther pulled out a chair and slid in next to Grace. She thought there might be a moment of discomfort because the last time they were together, Grace had gotten drunk and passed out in her bed. Not a word of that night came up. The three ladies, two hometown journalists and a homespun author, chewed the fat as only women can.

"Grace, how about a follow up interview about your new book?" Esther asked. "Everyone wants to know more about it, and I hear you could use the plug." And there, Grace thought, was the rub. Her motive wasn't malicious; it was just straight to the point as any reporter would be. "How about next Wednesday? We can do lunch after at the Tavern." Grace thought for a split second; she was feeling too good to get into a discussion on the air again. New York had been a nightmare. WLNH in Laconia was no WNBC, but the outcome could result in the same. "Oh, next week is not good," she said. "I have a writer from London coming to the house to do a feature on me for the *London Daily Express*," she said as she left.

Back in the car, Laurie quietly wondered what would come of this John Rees and Grace. The remainder of the drive was pleasant, the entire evening fun and successful, despite running into Esther Peters. She was not a favorite of Laurie's, but she would never tell Grace that. "So, which day is John coming to interview you?" she asked. Grace wasn't sure, and didn't care. She just knew he would come and that pleased her to no end.

Back in Gilmanton, Grace rallied a bit. That night out with Laurie had worked its magic. The next day's conversation with George was a good one. He had noticed a sense of clarity in her voice, something he not heard for a while. She also neglected to tell him of her new friend and prospects of a London feature. The creditors were still calling, and a boost in sales abroad could hold them at bay a little longer. "I'll bring the kids for a visit on Friday," he told her. Monday would be Labor Day, and the first day of school would be the following Tuesday. "Thank you, Gee Gee," Grace said and hung up the phone.

Feeling a sense of accomplishment, Grace was about to make a drink. It was already 11:00 am; it was time. The phone rang. She thought it was George forgetting something. "Yes, George?" picking up the phone. It was a man, just not her ex-husband. "Grace, it's John Rees," the caller informed her. Feeling a bit foolish and flushed, she apologized to her new friend. Their conversation was sweet and unexpected. "Okay, are you sure you can find the house?" she asked, listened for the answer, and hung up the phone.

The London reporter just happened to be in Gilmanton and wanted to pop by to see her and to talk about the feature he mentioned at the book signing. John had called using the payphone that was attached to The Corner Store on the town green, the same phone where so many calls had been made, some innocent and others with motives of evilness. His presence had not gone unnoticed by some of the townsfolk. Even Ned, as he took the afternoon bundle of the afternoon newspapers out of the wooden box on the front stoop, noticed the tall stranger.

"Afternoon, sir," Ned said to the overdressed gentleman as he placed the receiver back on to the cradle. "Good afternoon," John replied. "Might I ask you to point me in the direction of Meadows Pond Road?" he questioned the store owner. "Oh, you looking for Grace?" Nothing gets past Ned. The English chap had no idea how small the town really was.

Standing on the front porch of Grace's dream house, John gently knocked on the door. Grace was still upstairs trying to pull herself together and did not hear him open the front door to make his presence known.

"Grace!" He called out with a raised voice. She heard him and rushed down the main hallway upstairs. "John, is that you? Come in, come on in." she told him.

He stepped into the foyer off the front room and was amazed at the size of the country house, something his English origins did not provide. Houses were neat and tidy across the pond. That was what he had known. His first impressions of grandeur and New England charm were guarded as he moved further into the front room's chaos.

Grace, after hanging up from his call, took time to mix herself a drink, change out of her flannel shirt, and pull her hair back into her ponytail. Somehow she had forgotten the condition of her home. It was no secret amongst her family and friends that Grace did not keep a tidy house. In fact, house cleaning was something she rarely did.

John stood and assessed what he saw. There were literally hundreds of magazines stacked on every piece of furniture in the room, ashtrays full of cigarette butts on the bar, the coffee table, and the mantle. The fireplace looked as if the ashes hadn't been emptied since winter and some spilled onto the flagstone floor. There were plates with remnants of food on them, days old he thought. But the number of bottles throughout the space was shocking. No question that whiskey was her drink of choice. "What had he gotten himself into?"

CHAPTER 45

The town green in Gilmanton was prepared for another long winter in New England. It was not even Thanksgiving yet, but predictions of a bad winter were all about. The *Farmer's Almanac* and the thickness of the squirrel's tail were both true indicators. Local men, who on warmer days sat on the bench to watch life pass by, were but a memory. The trimmed hedges lining the walkway to a granite rock that immortalized fallen service men from the town, were now wrapped in canvas and securely tied up to help save them from what was in store.

Winter snow was the blanket that Mother Nature covered her soil with to comfort and protect it and at the same time hide the ugliest parts after Indian Summer. It was the time when lawns and fallen leaves turned brown and began to decay; the rot of autumn seemed to go unnoticed.

Grace was looking forward to winter. Her elusive Indian summer came and went without notice. The cold snap, that took everyone but the squirrels by surprise, arrived and it would be months before the crocus would blossom again.

"John," she asked. "Would you get me a drink?" Grace was in her zone since the arrival of the British reporter on her front porch weeks before; she felt a sense of creativity that she had not felt in years. The English gentleman turned her upside down and spun her around. Grace was happy, that on that cold

November weekend, he moved into the house on Meadows Pond Road.

"Coming right up, my dear." John eagerly answered his new sweetheart. With drink in hand, he returned to the front room. Grace patted the cushion next to her on the sofa. "Here sweetie," suggesting that he sit next to her. "I'm freezing today; come keep me warm." The two snuggled like kids. The roaring fire barely warmed the large room. Two in the afternoon was just late enough to be on their second cocktail, but early enough to still be alone before Cindy and Mike returned home soon from school. Someone had to think about feeding them. Everyday Grace thanked Mr. Swanson for his clever invention of frozen dinners.

The kids had come back home to live; the demands of George's new job and the sudden turn about in Grace's behavior were factors in the decision. Whatever the reason, Grace was pleased to have them home, and even more pleased to have John there as well.

"I've been thinking," she said to John. "Yes, please do tell!" The genuineness in his voice was masked by the effects of their alcohol consumption. "I am going to write *Peyton Place Three*," she announced. "And the best part, you are going to help me." Without a chance of rebuttal, she shouted, "cheers!" She lifted her glass in the direction of her new lover. She had no idea of the origins of clinking glasses, but she always felt good doing it.

Their whirlwind romance started with a chance meeting at a book reading, then blossomed into an orgy of kindred spirits, something like she felt when she met Laurie for the first time. Their meeting also had been by chance. Now with John it was like a rebirth of her confidence and creativity. Within a few weeks Grace and John did the deed and secured their relationship with some fantastic sex, something she'd not had since TJ. George might be the love of her life, but their sex was not inspirational. "Never confuse sex with love; it gets too complicated," she confided to Laurie.

Grace was still concerned with money, after a series of bad reviews about the last book, and sales had leveled off. One review in the *Boston Traveller* claimed, "You better hurry; it seems Mrs. Metalious is running out of talent." That cruel reviewer had put her over the edge. In a drunken stupor she asked John to be her manager. When he accepted, she invited him to spend the night. After that fateful night the responsibility for her money was now in her new manager's hands.

Grace could not wait to call Laurie the next morning after the deal was sealed. "Yes, how many times can I say it, Laurie, truly, he is a gentleman." Grace wanted to convince her friend of his intentions. "Where is he now?" Laurie asked. John had decided to go to The Corner Store to get eggs. His fondness for cooking breakfast reminded her of TJ in the early days. Being alone in the house was the perfect time to call her best friend. Laurie was happy, but she could tell Grace was still drinking. She could hear it in her voice, but, what more could she do?"

Before John entered Ned's store, he used the pay phone. It wasn't the first time he was seen using the public phone. Many locals thought it was sinister. This overdressed foreigner with an uppity accent, was making calls at a payphone instead of on his home phone. Ned, too, found this strange and wondered if he was a spy or a member of some mafia. Rumors about his behavior spread past the store's front door.

John placed the carton of eggs on the counter and waited for Ned to check him out. "That will be 52 cents," the store owner told him. John reached into his front pocket and retrieved a leather coin purse. He pulled out some coins and laid them on the counter. "I'm sorry, I can never get used to your money," he said. "Do you mind?" Ned didn't mind at all and reached down to pick up the required change.

"How are things up at Grace's?" He had to ask. "Is her phone out again? It's mighty cold out there to be using that damned pay phone all the time." John did not respond; he felt exposed and smiled like a criminal. He carefully picked up his eggs and left the store. Ned knew something was up, and it was killing him to not know. After all, he was the unofficial sleuth of Gilmanton.

The new couple made notes about *Peyton Place Three*. The idea came up a few times, and they hoped it could be a lifeline to bail Grace out of her troubles. The days were gloomier and colder than normal for December. The predicted snow had not arrived, and the dreariness of winter lingered in the air like the stench of death.

"Honestly, sweetie, how can I write about spring in *Peyton Place* when all I see are grey clouds and barren hills?" It wasn't a real question, but a statement made to her lover turned manager. The trouble with being a writer is that you have to write. At times that is the last thing they wanted to do. John knew it; Grace knew it. So, weekends when the kids were at George's, drinking was once again the main event.

They grew closer. The whiskey flowed, as did their creative efforts with the typewriter and in the bedroom. Nothing was off limits as they found a rhythm of their own, pleasing each other like professionals that you could read about in dime store paperbacks. They were all the rage. Grace took a sense of satisfaction that writing about women and sexual freedom was a small result of the success of *Peyton Place*.

Not all was peaches and cream for their new partnership. Grace was severely in debt, and prospect of relief was not coming anytime soon. She and John went to see Bernie at his office in Laconia. Perhaps some advice from her trusted friend and her paid employee could help. They reviewed the debt situation and thought a new book would be the solution. "But, Grace," her lawyer said. "We need to complete your will." Grace knew he was right. He wasn't ganging up on her; he was doing what she paid him to do. For the next couple of hours, they drafted, in a note form, her will. This was purely her thoughts and desires. "I will have the official documents ready for you right after the holidays." Bernie got up from his desk and escorted her and John out of the office.

Back in Gilmanton, when she was sober enough to think, yellow pads of note paper would appear, and she'd outline her thoughts. John contributed where he could. They both knew that the story was in her mind, but writing commercially this way was something repulsive to her. "Writing for money required less craft and less commitment," she told him, but she muddled through with enough ideas to send to New York.

"Grace, I like the notes you sent on PP3," his name for her latest project. Ollie told her, "It could be even bigger than the original, maybe television." She listened but the reason for her call was that she desperately needed him to push her work as her agent. She thought it being Christmas Eve, maybe he would be more willing to help her. "Thank you, Ollie, but I'm calling for a favor," she said. "Anything, Grace, what is it?"

The sound in Grace's voice was a mixture of groveling with a hint of an apology. They both knew her last series of events in New York was not good for her reputation, his business, and, ultimately, books sales. "I need you to make your magic happen," she confessed to him. Money was running out. The royalty checks were slowly getting smaller, and the residuals from *Return to Peyton Place* were almost nonexistent. Like her last book, the movie sequel was to be a dud.

"Get me an outline after New Year's;" PP3 could be a winner, but I need paper, lots of paper." Paper was another word he used for something tangible, something Ollie could pitch to the Trident or 20th Century Fox. Words can be cheap, but paper sells. She hung up and looked over to John who was slowly preparing drinks at the bar. He waited patiently to see how her mood would be after hanging up.

Her mood was somewhat better. She smiled slightly and reached for her highball. "Merry Christmas, darling. Here's to a New Year." With that, she curled up on the sofa, wrapped her afghan around her and stared into the flames, letting the hypnotic colors of the fire transcend her to a better place.

Sipping her drink, she tried to hide the pain she was feeling; the emotional stress of not knowing what the outcome of the call to Ollie would be, and the physical pain deep in her abdomen. The cramps had returned a few days ago, and the thought of going to the doctor again frightened her as much as it frustrated her.

She pulled the afghan closer to her body; it gave her little comfort. She needed the heating pad that was hidden under her bed. She did not want her new lover to know she was not feeling well; that would be the last thing they needed on Christmas Eve.

CHAPTER 46

    The overcast sky of a February winter in New England can block out any evidence that there is even a sun that shines in the sky above. Dark grey clouds, looming low across the horizon, create an opaque layer of winter that is waiting to be blown away by warming winds of spring. It was a cold morning; the frozen ground was covered in snow. The lilac bushes were barren of any life and the smell of the burning wood wafted through the still air. There was snow in the forecast, and in anticipation everyone was battening down the hatches and moving just a little faster to reach their destination.

    The bitter cold morning that awaited Grace made her long for warmer days at the coast with the sun beating down on her face. It seemed like a lifetime ago that she actually felt warm. The fireplace barely heated the front room, and the boiler in the basement worked overtime keeping the chill out. She was thankful for John and how she felt in his arms on cold winter nights. He held her tight, sleeping like a gentle giant next to her in her bed. While scanning the newspaper for reviews of her new book released in paperback, she longed to feel his embrace and the warmth it provided.

No Adam in Eden, Grace's latest, was now officially out a couple of months, and she rarely saw any sign of its existence in the press. There was no mention in the February issue of *Photoplay m*agazine, nothing in last night's *Laconia Evening Citizen* and not a word in the *Manchester Union Leader*. Feelings of despair never seemed to leave her. Her fingers moved in an uncontrolled manner as she flipped through the stack of papers from the past week. They had piled up on the coffee table in front of her. She surveyed the pages quickly, discarded like old lovers, and then moved on to the next.

"There has to be something." Grace knew that the press was her ticket to success. Whoever said, "No press is bad press," was absolutely right. She knew deep in her being, and all the past stories of her, true or not, sold books, lots of books. She was worried. Money was running out. Her novel, *No Adam in Eden,* might have been her favorite, but it was not doing well at the bookstores. She drank out of desperation. Orange juice nicely layered with a couple of shots of vodka was her morning pick me up, carefully concealed from John's concerned eyes. He hated her drinking before noon.

It had been weeks since Grace or John had left the house. She hadn't had a visit from anyone. New Year's Eve had been the last time Grace had seen Laurie and wondered why Laurie had been so distant these past few weeks.

Grace had thrown a New Year's Eve party for her closest friends to celebrate the new book and to introduce them to her Jonathan. His name sounded so proper, and she loved to say it with a British accent.

The party was a marginal success with too much to drink and too many regrets. Tears, booze, and friends don't make a happy outcome. "Fuck them all," she told Jonathan the next morning, just before wishing him a "Happy New Year." That was weeks ago now. Stewing about it never helped her.

She did not hear the car coming up the drive or even the kitchen door close, but she felt the cold air of a draft enter the room and drift past her. She was startled for just a second and looked up. Her morning cocktail, an attempt to jump start her, usually rendered her a bit sluggish and her vision cloudy. By the third drink she was back to her normal fierce self, ready to take on the world. Straining her morning eyesight, she focused, and a smile came across her face; the warmth she was seeking had finally arrived.

"Marsha." she exclaimed. "Ma, it's been so long, I'm sorry," her daughter said, tossing her coat on the armchair next to the sofa. She leaned down to hug her mother. It had been almost a year since the two had seen each other. Marsha had her own life in Massachusetts, with Eddy. Grace completely understood. Mike had moved in with her, and Cindy had stayed back with George after the holiday break. It had been John's idea, and Grace had gone along with it; something she regretted but did not let on.

"Sit, let me look at you." Grace patted the space on the sofa next to her, after pushing discarded periodicals onto the floor. The fireplace was the final resting place for any printed matter that dare not write about her work, her life, or her lovers. Grace's despair and exhaustion did not go unnoticed by her oldest child.

"Ma," Marsha paused, "are you okay? No one has heard from you for weeks. Cindy and Mike are worried," she continued. Looking at her mother she could see their concern was justified. Marsha had inherited her mother's strong will and determination. "So, I jumped in the car, and here I am." Marsha did not let the impending winter storm scare her from the two-hour drive to Gilmanton. Sitting beside her mother, she felt similar despair overcome her.

Grace looked like she hadn't bathed for days. Her chenille robe was tattered, with worn fraying cuffs, and she wore men's slippers. The sight was not a pleasant one. Her daughter knew instinctively that the bottle was winning the war in New

Hampshire. Hopelessness filled her, and she wondered what she could do.

"Darling, I'm fine. It's February; everyone looks like shit in this town." A chuckle was detected, but neither of them thought it was that funny.

Marsha leaned in and kissed her mother on the cheek. "Coffee," she asked. "I am dying for some after that drive." She stood up and grabbed the closest empty glass next to her mother. Picking it up, she cautiously smelled it and grimaced. "You still take your coffee black, right?"

Grace stood up and tightened the belt around her waist, securing her robe as she followed her daughter into the kitchen. "She turned out okay; the bad times were in the past," Grace thought. Marsha had married at 18 just like she had. With her husband, Eddy, they worked together at the same school. The distractions of *Peyton Place* were a thing of the past.

Grace caught her image in the hallway mirror. She looked at herself, looking back. The hair once kept neatly in a ponytail now a tangled mess in need of a shampoo and brush. The house coat, once her favorite, was now destined to the box of rags under the kitchen sink. Her skin was ashen with a yellow hue and her cheeks puffy, making her face bloated like some unrecognizable character from one of her books. It saddened her.

"Marsha, coffee is in the canister, there," Pointing to the stainless steel cylinder filled with Maxwell House. Grace sat at the kitchen table and watched Marsha as she filled the Procter Silex percolator with water, before inserting the basket that holds the coffee.

Not looking up from her task, Marsha questioned, "Mom, can I ask you something?" "Don't start with me, Marsha. Let's just enjoy this moment." Grace was firm, yet loving. Their last encounter had ended on very bad terms. A tear formed in her daughter's eye, but Grace never noticed because her vision was blurred. "Did I tell you the book was picked up in paperback?" Grace attempted to change the subject.

They continued small talk about things that did not matter to a mother and daughter who were estranged, things that were a mere avoidance to the real issues. Issues like Marsha's disapproval of her mother's current lover, the way she lived, and the concern for her health that was deteriorating, and of course, her drinking were not discussed.

The drive she took to see her mother would be fruitless, and nothing would be resolved, she thought. But an attempt was made on her part which made them both secretly feel better. They sat and sipped their coffee, lost for words. The ones they did choose were like the careful footsteps of a tight rope walker strung between two aging trees ready to topple in the wind.

"Grace, are you dressed?" A voice shouted from the top of the stairs. "We should hit the road before the snow. I hate that damned drive down 93." It was John, and he was ready to roll. "Marsha, did I mention we were heading to Boston for a few days? We just have to get out of this town every few months, just to get those tongues wagging. Give them something to talk about." Her daughter was not amused or even surprised that her visit was going to be cut short. Nothing stood in the way of her mother, her lover, or her drinking. After nineteen years as her daughter, she was used to it.

Through the back kitchen door Marsha could slip out undetected as she had slipped in. The love between a daughter and a mother is not one that grows with acceptance, but merely tolerance. They were not even there yet. Grace retrieved her coat and helped Marsha dress." Here, take this. It's my favorite; it will look beautiful with your eyes." Her mother tied the silk scarf she had received as a gift around her daughter's head and knotted it under her chin. A kiss on the cheek and a hug were all Marsha could offer, trying her best to make a clean getaway, from a life she once had and one she hoped never to see again.

Grace stood in the doorway of the kitchen and watched the car that held her first born maneuver out of the snowy drive and make its way up to the main road before disappearing out of sight. She pressed her hand against the cold glass holding it there in an attempt to tell her daughter she was sorry. Sorry for it all. She wanted to cry, but she could not. Tears were never helpful in any situation, but a drink might be. From the cabinet over the sink, a flask of Canadian Club was retrieved, and she slipped it into the pocket of her robe as she headed up the stairs to get dressed.

Grace was not feeling right. Her head was clogged with memories and mucus. She had the beginnings of a cold, something she despised and would not let on to John. Reaching the top of the stairs, she turned to the master bathroom. A hot shower would knock out the cold; colds hated hot showers. The cramps of menopause were another thing. Nothing had seemed to help those lately, so she had just learned to live with them.

CHAPTER 47

Grace and John's drive south was uneventful for a Thursday. The traffic was light, and as they approached the skyline of Boston, the clouds grew darker and menacing.

Boston's tall gray buildings were nothing like her beloved Manhattan. Bean Town, as it was referred to, held many memories: trips to Gilbert and Sullivan shows in high school and eating in the North End. When Park Avenue couldn't do, Beacon Hill would have to.

They had never stayed at the Parker House on Tremont Street before. John booked them into a suite on the top floor. The hotel was Boston's version of the Algonquin, stately, woody, and not overdone like that of the Copley Plaza in Back Bay. Built in the 1850's this institution was hailed as Boston's literary hotel. It attracted writers and artists from across the country. The much-heralded Saturday Night Club met weekly and was by invitation only. This group of authors had yet to acknowledge Grace's contribution to the world of the written word.

The hotel was private enough for them and close to their favorite shopping at Filenes & Sons, a couple of blocks away. The Italian section was nearby and their favorite area for dinner after a stroll along Atlantic Avenue. Any hoop-la that was centered on her had weaned a good bit, so Boston would be a great diversion for a few days. Now only two things bothered her: the cold and the snowstorm on its way.

John pulled the car up to the curb as close as possible. The snow had been cleared, a never ending task this time of year. It was past four o'clock, and darkness began to fall on the city. A doorman dressed like a remnant of some royal order, leaned over and opened the door. Grace clumsily got out. "Thank you," she said, trying her best not to be out-of-place. She always felt out of sorts when arriving at a strange place. She never knew what to expect. The temperature dropped, and it was snowing lightly. Without an acknowledgement to her lover, she scurried up the carpeted sidewalk and through the giant wooden revolving doors to seek the warmth of the dark wood panel lobby.

Their suite was not as big as The Plaza, but it was equally as nice. The bellman carried the bags into the bedroom and came out. He paused for a moment catching Jonathan's eye. A dollar bill was produced from his front pocket. Grace rolled her eyes and touched his arm. "Here, dear," handing the young man a five-dollar bill. "It will be a slow night with this storm," she added. The bellman's eyes showed deep gratitude as he handed the keys to her and left the room.

"Why did you do that?" John asked.

"Darling, we are not poor yet!" Grace answered in a shrill voice. "Besides, he practically had his hand out." She always felt a good tip went a long way when staff didn't know who she was. This time anonymity would be her friend. They had registered as Mr. and Mrs. John Metalious Rees just to confuse the hotel in case some lonely reporter lurked about, looking for a story. Grace would pay in cash, and everyone would be happy.

A typical February snowstorm continued throughout the night. Grace had no desire to go out. Jonathan called down to room service, and a couple of steaks and baked potatoes were delivered to the suite along with a full bottle of Canadian Club. After eating, they decided to turn in early, bringing the last of the CC to bed. The empty bottle was placed on the nightstand. Grace passed out first, and Jonathan, still wide awake, watched her sleep.

Wind whipped around the windows of the suite on the eight floor and accumulated on the wooded panes. By morning the city would be a ghost town, and their plans would have to be altered to enjoy their time together. John listened to the rhythmic sound of the howling wind, almost matching the labored breathing of Grace. It amused him. Looking at her, he knew she wasn't well. She'd put on a lot of weight during the short time since they first met, her skin looked unhealthy with a yellow tinge, and her demeanor was more annoyed than usual. Try as he might, she would not see a doctor. She detested them as much as she did the press, even though both were needed. It was a double-edged sword.

When morning arrived, the snow had not stopped. John looked out of the window and knew instantly they would not be going out. Grace had slept through the night, and he hoped it would help her feel better. Dressing in the soft robe he found in the ornate wardrobe, he went into the living room of the suite to order breakfast. When she did wake, she would be as hungry as a bear.

Grace stirred in bed, rolled over in her lover's direction, and stretched out her arm. She felt nothing and panicked for a second, wondering, "Where was he?" Slowly focusing her eyes, she sat up and felt a massive headache in her temples along with a pain in her stomach. Whispering some obscene comment to herself, she knew she was sick. The flu continued to rear its ugly head. But there was a bright side of things; she could smell the coffee from the other room.

They drank their coffee in silence and ate the food that was delivered. She only wanted toast with butter. The fried eggs and beans turned her already upset stomach. "Dear, can you order me a Screwdriver?" she asked. "Better yet, maybe a bottle of vodka. That sweet young boy will go run out and get it." Grace was on her best behavior because more than anything she needed a drink. Whiskey with breakfast was something John would just not tolerate.

The storm passed. They dressed and rallied for an afternoon stroll. Grace was slightly high from the drink and feeling better. They decided to go to the shops down on Washington Street. By now they should be cleared of snow. Her youngest, Cindy, wanted a Beatle wig, and she couldn't disappoint her. After a few hours of roaming in the streets, the sidewalks blocked with uncleared snow, they returned to their suite after a stop in the bar next to the restaurant. Grace had a few highballs. She tried to eat a lettuce wedge, it was all the rage, but she was not impressed.

Back in the suite, Grace laid down. John sent a note to Cindy on stationary from the desk, telling her about the storm and that, "they were both full of colds and aches. Their time shopping was not fruitful." He folded up a ten-dollar bill, put it inside, and sealed the envelope. On the outside he wrote, "See you Monday" trying to mimic Grace's handwriting with her signature smiley face. He went down to the front desk to mail it. Grace was finally asleep, and he wanted to spend some time away so she could rest and get better.

The next day, Grace was no better; her desire to eat was gone, and her need for a drink had vanished. She remained in bed all day, telling John that, "It is all in my head; tomorrow will be better." On Sunday she wanted to attend mass and light a candle for her grandmother. There was a chapel around the corner on Arch Street. She always had a desire to return to church after being away for so long. She slept most of the day, and keeping the bedroom door open so he could keep a close eye on her, he read in the living room. Her refusal to see a doctor was as annoying to him as staying in all day and reading, knowing the streets were clear and life carried on downstairs.

Room service came and went. Grace did not stir, and her food remained untouched. He decided to sleep on the couch that night after finishing a dime store paperback he was reading. Last he looked in on her, she was sleeping silently and appeared peaceful. Maybe she had turned the corner, he thought. Returning to the silk sofa, he laid down, and sleep soon overtook him.

"John! John!" A bellow from Grace woke him from his deep sleep. He sat up on the sofa and sprang to his feet. "Help me!" There it was again, panic in her voice. He ran into the bedroom, dressed only in white boxer shorts. The bed was empty. "Grace!" he yelled and ran into the giant bathroom. There in the fetal position, naked, was his lover curled up in a ball and moaning. "What is it?" he asked. "I'm bleeding, I can't sit up," trying to explain what she felt was worse for her than the pain. He noticed blood on the floor. He looked into the toilet, it was crimson red. Grace was having some sort of seizure and was bleeding.

"I'm calling downstairs for a doctor. You need one!" Not waiting for a curt comeback, he ran to the nightstand. The empty bottle of whiskey tumbled to the floor as he grabbed the phone. The front desk answered and assured him someone would be up shortly. Running back into the bathroom, he saw that Grace had managed to sit up. The pain was less severe, but she was still bleeding from between her legs. He thought briefly, "Could it be a period?" Grabbing a plush white towel off the warmer, he wrapped it around her and lifted her up. They slowly walked back to her bed to await the doctor. The bleeding had not stopped, and the snow-white towel that held her, had absorbed as much as it could and was soaking through. The situation was going from concern to serious in a matter of seconds.

"Where is that fucking doctor?" John let a cry out. "Gracie, hold on. It will be okay," he assured her as he pushed a pillow under her head and held her tight. Grace moaned slightly; the cramps were subsiding, but the bleeding continued. They looked at each other and spoke only with their eyes. They communicated fear in unison.

It seemed like an hour, but it was just a few minutes when a loud bang on the door was heard. "Doctor, here" The voice was so loud it could be heard across the entire floor. Still dressed in white boxers, with Grace's blood smeared all over him, John ran to the door and flung it open. The doctor looked at John; he had no clue what was happening. "Not me, in there!" John pointed and grabbed the doctor's wrist frantically dragging him into the bedroom.

They had not even reached Grace in the bed, when the doctor turned and said, "Call downstairs; we need an ambulance. Get dressed." Now John was even more frightened. The front desk was extremely helpful and instructed him to leave the door open. The manager would come up and wait for the medics with him. John opened the door of the suite and went to find his pants and shirt. Luckily, they were on the floor next to the tray from room service. Quickly dressing, he sat down long enough to tie his shoes. Going into the bedroom, he saw that the doctor was giving Grace an injection into her arm. He placed a small glass bottle of clear liquid on the side table with an empty syringe. Before he could say anything, the doctor told him, "Don't worry; this will help her with the pain and help her to relax. Now, help me wrap her in this blanket. It's very cold out there, and we need to keep her warm."

The hotel manager's arrival to the suite went unnoticed. John and the doctor carefully secured Grace in blankets like a swaddled baby. Curious eyes watched them. She was barely conscious and moaned when touched. The blood had not soaked through the blankets, and both thought it had momentarily stopped. Two male policemen showed up carrying what looked like a canvas stretcher, something a fireman would use in a burning building. "In here," the manager directed. He was concerned about reporters and newspapers. He knew from the get-go that this guest was that writer from New Hampshire, the one who had caused all the fuss a few years back. He would not have a scandal, not on his watch.

"Doc, no ambulance is available. One is out, the other cross town." The uniformed man said. "We can get her to the hospital, don't worry," looking at John assuredly. The two policemen unrolled the canvas gurney and set it next to the bed. Carefully, with the help from the doctor, they slid her onto it and were out the door in a flash. John grabbed his coat and trailed after them into the corridor in pursuit of his lover and three strangers.

"I'll lock up the suite, ring us later with any news," said the over protective manager. Standing in the center of the suite, he thought of Marilyn Monroe's death a few months before. Even though this nearly famous writer was not dead, the trouble it could stir up might be detrimental to business. Quickly surveying the area, he went into the bathroom, saw all the blood in the toilet, and flushed it instantly. Back in the bedroom, the blood-smeared sheet was quickly rolled up into a ball. The empty liquor bottles made their way into his bundle. He disposed of his collection as quickly as he found it. Locking the door behind him, he headed to the service stairwell.

CHAPTER 48

"Sir, Mr. Rees," with a light touch the nurse made contact with John's shoulder. "You can go in now," she tells him. "Oh, okay, thank you, miss," He stood and walked across the hall to the room where Grace had been for hours. He lost all sense of time, from the ride down the service elevator to the back door of the hotel into a waiting Police Paddy Wagon. With no ambulance to be found, the Paddy Wagon was the only thing available to get her to Beth Israel Hospital. The ride was four miles but seemed like forty. The doctor decided not to turn the siren on so Grace could remain peaceful. This had made the trip take forever; the traffic was not cooperating. He sat up front and watched Grace through the grate, trying to remain calm as a uniformed race car driver maneuvered the streets of Back Bay in the Fens on the way to Brookline.

Grace was semi-awake for most of the ride, not really coherent but enough to know what was happening. The doctor held her wrist, constantly checking her blood pressure and pulse. The other cop held the stretcher tightly to keep it from sliding along the smooth metal bed of the wagon. "Hold on, fellas, I don't want to slide out into a snowbank," Grace murmured, half awake. That attempt from Grace put John's mind to rest for that moment. He turned to watch the brownstones of Beacon Street fly past him. It was hard for him to believe that all this happened almost six hours before.

Grace was put into a private room, before the nurse downstairs knew her name. She probably had a dog-eared copy of Peyton Place in a drawer at her station. Lonely nights in a hospital were filled with Grace's steamy words that occupied her mind, like millions of others that had bought her first book. The hospital room was simple; the white cast iron bed was from another time. The hospital was undergoing a renovation, but clearly not on that floor. The attending doctor, a resident of the hospital, was on duty that early Sunday morning when the police Paddy Wagon arrived with Grace.

He explained that she would sleep most of the day. Her condition was critical. She had lost a lot of blood during the hemorrhaging, her liver had started to harden, and her vitals were low. He went on to explain, when the liver fails, there is no coming back. Grace had liver damage, cirrhosis. She was gravely ill.

John's face was the color of the sheet that covered her. Her entire body was motionless. John leaned over and kissed her on the forehead. He looked at her, almost seeing her for the first time. A deep sigh rose from the depths of his soul. He knew his friend was failing. Sitting down on the cold metal chair next to the bed, he waited for a sign. Anything would do. His patience was tested. He fell asleep again wondering how he ended up in this place, with this writer in less than six months.

Sunday turned into Monday, and daylight came up over the horizon, casting rays of bright sun onto the streets of Boston. The light hit Grace's face as the rays shined between two of the other buildings of the hospital.

"Jonathan, darling, wake up," Grace said from her bed. "Oh, how sweet you slept there all night," she said. He woke up and stood next to her. Placing his hand on her shoulder, he asked, "How do you feel?" She responded as only she could, "Like shit, how do I look?" He just shrugged his shoulders and said nothing.

The nurse came in to check on Grace, and John excused himself to the men's room down the hall. There was no change in Grace. She was awake, still groggy from the pain medication and the loss of blood. Keeping her comfortable at that point was all they could do. The doctor entered the room , and the nurse handed him the clipboard that showed Grace's current vitals. The silence between the medical team was deafening; they both knew it was only a matter of time. Grace sensed it and accepted it.

John went back into the room just as the nurse was leaving. The look on her face told the story of his lover's condition. No words were necessary between them. He approached her bed. Grace stared at the ceiling deep in thought, her eyes open with a look of despair and with a sense of determination.

Turning towards him, "Darling, call Bernie," almost as a whisper, her voice dry and horse. "He will know what to do." Her lawyer in Laconia was both friend and confidant. "I need him, John," she said, then turned back to stare at the ceiling once again.

Finding Bernie was not as easy as he had hoped. The lawyer was not available, and out of sheer frustration John slammed down the phone at the nurse's station. "Damn it," he muttered. "Mr. Rees, can I help?" questioned the nurse on duty. He explained he needed a lawyer, that Grace had requested one. She said she could help and called downstairs to the administrator's office.

Setting down the phone, "We are in luck; a lawyer from Beacon Hill is in the building." Feeling relieved, he thanked her and headed back to Grace's room. John Clemens, a lawyer from Boston, had delivered some papers to the administrator's office that morning and had just left. The secretary who took the call ran out into the lobby to find him. She spotted him crossing the street walking to a newsstand. With no coat on, she braved the cold winter morning air and ran to tell him a patient needed him. He finished buying his paper and returned to the hospital.

"Where is Bernie?" Grace asked when she awakened. "Grace dear, Bernie is in New Hampshire. This is Mr. Clemens; he is a lawyer here. He can help you." John said, doing his best to sound confident. He finished the introduction while holding her hand. Grace focused on the young man at the foot of her bed; it was a bit difficult, but she managed. He was dressed like a lawyer so he must be a lawyer. A Chesterfield wool coat, the fedora he was holding, and the oversized weathered leather briefcase resting at the end of her bed were the clues. "I need a new will," she stated. "Can you do one now?" Grace tried to sit up but could not. John helped her by pushing a pillow behind her shoulders. At that moment, she realized she was dying. The strength in her body was gone; she felt weak and useless. The young man looked at the patient and nodded his head. That was all she needed.

It took an hour or so before the young lawyer came out to the waiting room to get John. He needed a signature from a witness for what he had just written on Grace's behalf. Her lover did not want any part of signing as a witness, or even knowing what was in the document. He excused himself from her bedside for that reason when they first started their discussion. Scandal followed Grace like a plague, and he didn't want to be the next topic for the press to have a field day with. Clemens had to get at least another signature, and the nurse was nowhere to be found. He went out into the hallway.

"Sir," walking over to the only other person in the waiting room. "Could I bother you to witness a signature of one of my clients? She is just down the hall," he asked ever so guardedly. An older man dressed in a simple grey suit, holding his jacket in his lap, looked up, and shrugged his shoulders. The rumpled tie and open top button of his shirt were good indicators that he'd been there a while, doing what most do in a waiting room. Clemens took the physical gesture as a "yes" and headed back to Grace's room. The old man laid his jacket on the empty chair and followed.

John wanted to go back to the hotel and change. He needed a proper meal, a bath and a drink, not necessarily in that order. But it was not the time to abandon Grace. The stress of the situation was too much for him, and he thought about his exit strategy. It was as if she had written the scene in one of her notebooks, and he was the reluctant leading man being cast aside for the heroine's bigger role, death.

Hearing footsteps in the hall, he looked up. The two men were coming in his direction. The old man returned to his seat, picked up his jacket, and returned it to his lap. With a hint of empathy, he caught John's eyes. "You can go in; she is still awake." The lawyer told him. "I will get this copy up to Bernie Sneirson in New Hampshire by tomorrow." John stood and shook the lawyer's hand and started for her room. His feet were heavy; his walk sluggish like a slow-motion movie. Like a cold chill invading his body, it created a sense of foreboding that he did not realize he was capable of feeling.

"John, come here." Grace said in a rasping, dry voice. "Tell me you will look after the children, take care of them," her words labored. "I did it, I did it for you," she added.

"Shhhh," he whispered. "It's time to rest, my love." Walking closer to her side, he couldn't think of a time when Grace had looked so poorly, not even after a weekend binge. The whites of her eyes were now yellowed as decayed autumn leaves. Her body swollen and sunken at the same time with limbs listless and painful to the touch.

"I'm dying," she said. "Grace, you will get better. I'll go find the doctor." John told her. "Where is that fucking nurse?" Unforgiving words, so uncharacteristic of him, flew from his mouth. No one heard him. He reached for the cord next to Grace and pulled it hard. A light flashed down the hall at the nurse's station but went unnoticed. He was panicked and at a loss for what to do or what to say.

Looking up, Grace wanted to say something to him. With all her strength, she moved her hand and touched his to assure him it's ok, she was good with it. Grace's mind wandered, through the streets of Frenchtown and along the rolling hills of her beloved New Hampshire. There were Images of autumn hillsides bathed in light and crystal-clear lakes refracting the sun to almost blinding, only blurred with the interruptions of the nastiness of Hollywood and the coldness of New York.

Tears formed in her eyes, tears of regret and tears of joy equally connected. Grace was slipping away, and John knew it. Feeling a slight squeeze on his hand, he knelt down next to her and listened to the words she was trying to form.

"Darling, be careful of what you want. You may just get it," words from her grandmother so long ago, from a different time and place, but which rang true that cold February morning. "Run for your life, sweetie, there's trouble coming." Turning her head and closing her eyes, Grace drifted into unconsciousness never to wake.

Laying his head onto Grace's hand that held his own, he closed his eyes and tried to think of the place where they first met, before he had fallen in love with her, before all the trouble started.

A flurry of activity was fast approaching down the corridor, sounding like a herd of wild animals in a stampede. Someone finally saw the lit call light. John stood up and stepped back, letting the nurses and the doctor attend to Grace.

He walked to the window and stood staring out into the courtyard towards the horizon. The sun again dissolved into the gray skies, with no sign of life. Pressing his hand to the windowpane, he felt the coldness travel up through his arm, to his heart. He looked to her bedside where she laid.

He knew it was too late, Grace had passed. He began to sob.

CHAPTER 49

T.S. Eliot wrote that April was the cruelest month. He had never experienced a cold, bleak, and gray day in New England. In contrast, for Grace, in 1964, it had been February.

Against her wishes, for fear of a side show, a gathering was held for the famed author. Grace's funeral was a direct contradiction to her life; it was private, small, and subdued. The setting was simple. Only a few invited mourners attended the service in Laconia at the Wilkinson-Beane Funeral home, not far from her favorite watering hole, The Tavern.

Reverend John Morrison, a stout and virile man with a kind face, came in from the Gilmanton Federated Church to console those left and offer his services for the controversial author. Attendees were a few of Grace's family, closest friends, and supporters. Aunt Georgie had come up from Manchester, making the drive alone and representing her mother and sister who did not arrive from Florida. Her once closest friend, Marc, made the trek from Manhattan despite the threat of snow, and Laurie attended with her husband.

"George, my deepest condolences for you and your family," he told the father of Grace's children while gently resting his soft and empathetic hand on his shoulder.

"Shall we begin?" The Reverend asked. Her ex-husband just nodded and reached for his daughter's hand. Cindy and Mike were on either side of him sitting in the front row; the closed dark oak casket rested only a few feet away. Against her mother's wishes, Cindy insisted on flowers. Pink, white and red carnations were tastefully arranged on top of the coffin, each color representing one of the children.

The Reverend performed a quick and meaningful service; closure at this time is what he had thought was best for the family and perhaps the community. He was well-aware of the voices from locals on the town green. "I don't want that bitch buried in my home town," was a sentiment heard at the town library the day after her death. Grace's death did not pass unnoticed by the press and the courts.

The will that was hastily drawn up on her deathbed left her current lover, Jonathan H. Rees, her entire estate. Also, adding salt to the wound of Grace's memory, an injunction to keep her body from resting in Gilmanton was filed. Rees, for fear of scandal that his wife and five children back in England would find out, did not object to the will's invalidation. The New Hampshire Supreme Court tossed the injunction against her burial location out as fast as it was filed.

It had been Grace's wish to be buried at the Smith Hill Meeting House cemetery close to where she had felt the safest and most secure, her dream home on Meadows Pond Road. After the ruling, the subject was not open for discussion, and the town elders had not blocked the efforts of the Reverend to secure a final and thoughtful resting place for the young mother who had passed way too soon.

The few in attendance took their cue from the Reverend, took their seats, and waited in a respectful quietness for him to begin. There were no tears that morning for Grace. Her departure from earth was as dramatic as her life. She, without knowing it, had created her own reality where she resided. Like her writing and her characters, each had their own set of challenges; she had become the girl from *Peyton Place*.

Reverend Morrison stood in front of the mourners and read a selection of Psalms that he had chosen the night before. He hoped his selection would resonate with Grace's family. He purposely did not mention the author's name and referred to her only once in a prayer, "May Grace rest in peace," his final words before standing aside to allow those who wanted to pay their last respects.

George stood up slowly and encouraged the two youngest to stand as well. He reached down, took both their hands, and walked to the front of the coffin. Both Cindy and Mike had some apprehension that their feelings of sadness would be noticed by others.

George's caring eyes filled with tears as he looked to the children, assuring them it was okay. The three approached Grace's casket. George fell to his knees and wept. His wails were uncontrolled and his guttural gasps for air were heard throughout the funeral parlor. His sadness was felt like a wave of despair that floated throughout the room, touching each mourner until they felt his pain.

Cindy burst into tears, and soon Mike was crying as well. They were sad for the loss of their mother. It was the first time in their lives they had seen their father cry, and that had made them even sadder. The emotional outcry that they were feeling had been building up over years of trying to help Grace, only to realize the final outcome. She was gone, never to return.

The attendees in the room started to disperse, not wanting to interrupt the family. They retreated to another sitting room, giving the family some time alone with Grace. Marsha, who had been very emotional those last few days, had tried her best not to cry, but witnessing such pure love and devotion from her father was uncontrollable. She stood up, leaving her husband, and joined her family with her outstretched arms kneeling behind them, embracing them like the security Grace felt with that crocheted afghan, hiding away from the world on her sofa.

As the family they had always wanted to be on that gray February morning, they said farewell to their beloved Grace Metalious.

"There's not more or less here because of Grace Metalious, the wind still blows."

>Sybil Bryant, Gilmanton
>New Hampshire Times
>1982

ACKNOWLEDGMENTS

My fascination with Grace Metalious's *Peyton Place* started with the second film by 20th Century Fox's, *Return to Peyton Place*. That movie had been a frequent rerun on afternoon television in the 1970's where I grew up.

The world I witnessed that Hollywood had produced was not that unfamiliar to my own. The attitudes and lifestyle in a New Hampshire town rang true to me. It wasn't until I found *The Girl from Peyton Place,* a biography written by George Metalious and June O'Shea, at a church rummage sale, that I became interested in the life of the author.

Everyone had a story, and Grace's was one I thought should be told with as much colorful grit as she lived and wrote about in her novels. There have been many articles, papers, books, and blogs written about Grace Metalious. Her writings had changed millions of people's attitude on what life in a small New England town was like. But more importantly, it liberated the mind for all of us that actually lived in one.

Writing historical fiction has its roots in truth; my research for *The Seasons of Grace* took me on a wild ride through the backwoods of her adoptive home to her final resting place in Gilmanton, NH. Articles over the past 60 years are countless and far too many to mention. They have appeared in newspapers and magazines around the world. *The New York*

Times, Yankee Magazine, The Boston Globe and *Vanity Fair,* all spun their version of her turbulent life during these past decades.

One biography, written in the early 1980's by Emily Toth, was another treasure trove of insight into her life. *Inside Peyton Place: The Life of Grace Metalious*, is a finely crafted work that celebrated her life and her contributions to both storytelling and the feminist movement, a by-product that Grace had never known in her lifetime.

Story telling is always at its best when you have sincere and supportive listeners that actually become readers. A special thank you to Christine, Linda, Arna and Dawn for their time and attention to detail.

Writing can be a very lonely endeavor and at times a daunting task, one that is easily stoppable. It does take determination and craft to be a storyteller, but like Grace, the force behind her was her husband George. My force was my husband, Patrick, in so many ways that will go unmentioned.

Made in the USA
Monee, IL
13 May 2023